# SAVAGE MAYHEM

## *Mayhem Series #9*

Amidst the wild and u̲̅ giving landscapes of Yellowstone Park, join Mayhem, a fearless Apache warrior and champion of the Natural World, and his partner and protégé, Shawnee, as they race against the clock to protect an American Buffalo herd from the ruthless Killzme Corporation.

With a massive bounty on their heads and an army of killers on their trail, Mayhem and Shawnee must use all their cunning and survival skills to outsmart their enemies. They will risk it all to preserve the sacred lineage of the Innocent Ones.

There is no line Shawnee and Mayhem won't cross.

Even murder.

As the danger intensifies and the clock winds down, will they be able to save the herd? Or will this be the mission that finally breaks them?

# SAVAGE MAYHEM

Mayhem Series #9

This book may not be used to train artificial intelligence (AI technology) without the express permission of the author.

This story is a work of fiction. The names, characters, places, and incidents are products of the author's imagination. Any resemblance to actual events, locales, or persons, living or dead, is entirely coincidental.

# Contents

# Dedication

As you drift off to sleep, may your burdens be lifted... may you dance across the heavens... and may you awaken refreshed, inspired, and connected with the beauty of your soul.

# Acknowledgments

The heartfelt message in the dedication is a Native American blessing.

A special thank you to all the consultants and sites that helped add realism to Savage Mayhem:

InterTribal Buffalo Council

Shane & Wally at Navaho Traditional Teachings

Alaska.org

WebMD

The Spiritual Naturalist

GreaterGood.berkeley.edu

Silver Gate Lodging

Exo Mountain Gear

Unalaska.org

Science of People

National Park Trust

WWF

NativeHope.org

Heather Woolery Photography
D.U. Clarion
Jim Crow Museum
Bison Central
Universe Today
USGS.org
Native American Totems
FieldArchery.org
Yellowstone National Park
WikiHow
adl.org
FacingHistory.org
us.archive.org
National Geographic
Daily Montanan
Yellowstone Country Montana

Hugs and kisses to my family, Bob, Bobby, Kathy, Berlyn, Scarlet, Joey, Frank, and Dad Coletta. Thank you for remaining my loudest cheerleaders. Love you all!

Last but not least, thank you, Creator, for blessing my life in unimaginable ways.

# Chapter 1

*Saturday, 11:11 p.m.*

"You did what?" Mr. Mayhem's husky voice boomed through the screen door of the sliders.

Out on the deck, I cringed. Whatever my grandfather confessed didn't go over well, but I stayed out of it—safer that way—an ear cocked toward the kitchen of the log cabin, our home base while battling the largest animal trafficking ring in the country.

The Alaskan wilderness silenced around me, the sweetness of pine and cedar sickened by the discord between the two most important men in my life. Even the bazillion stars above me cowered in the night sky. Ebony and white wings slashed the darkness when Odin and Spirit Crow neared, talons smacking the tabletop in front of me to land.

"Cheveyo," *Shicheii* said, his whole body pleading for forgiveness, "I was only trying to help. Carolyne agreed it was the right thing to do."

I winced. Not good.

"You brought Carolyne into this? That woman almost lost her child." Mr. Mayhem paced around the butcher block island like a caged cougar. In a leather blazer and pressed jeans, he always dressed to impress, except for when he went shirtless—my personal favorite time, his chest and abs chiseled in light chestnut.

"How on earth will I explain your actions to Running Bear?"

"Cheveyo, please. We don't have to inform him."

"His entire family is in danger now. How can we not?" More pacing, more mumbling under his breath. "Jot down the address for me."

"Please don't go there."

"What choice do I have? We need to know who they called after you left. The address, please. Now, Jacy Lee."

*Shicheii*—grandfather in Diné, aka Navajo—scribbled on his sketchpad, shoulders hunched in defeat so his long gray braids dragged on the island.

Mr. Mayhem scrubbed a hand over his face. "Thank you."

The sliders glided across the tracks, but he stayed in the kitchen.

I snapped my attention to the yard. Even Spirit Crow and Odin pretended they hadn't overhead the conversation. None of us dared to look in his direction, fearing misdirected wrath or painful recrimination.

"Cat, pack your bags. We leave tonight."

Those words cut me deep. "Tonight? But I thought we were gonna chill for a few days."

*Shicheii* laid a gentle hand on his shoulder. "Cheveyo, please. Poe shouldn't travel yet."

As if touched by a stranger, he whirled around. "And whose fault is that?" After a never-ending scowl at his closest friend, his piercing gray eyes shifted to me. "Say your goodbyes to Odin, Cat. Someone needs to safeguard the Sacred Land."

A ghostly hand tore the heart from my chest, my gaze straying to the sweetest raven in Alaska. "But he's family. We can't leave him behind."

"You can thank your grandfather for that, as well." He snatched his fedora off the counter then soldiered out to the deck. "I need to warn Running Bear." Storming down the stairs, one long braid dangled down his back. "We'll be lucky if he ever speaks to us again."

"Mourning Dove," *Shicheii* called through the screen, using my traditional Diné name, "please accompany Cheveyo. He's much too heated to go alone."

And so, I careened down the stairs. Caught up to the Caddy as it reversed out the driveway, my arms waving for him to stop.

Idling with the tail end in the road, the driver's window zipped down. "Cat, please pack. If I don't warn Running Bear before Killzme moves in, he could lose Carolyne and the kids."

"I know. I'm coming with you." I scuttled around the back bumper to prevent the Caddy from moving. When I slid into the passenger seat, I reached for the door handle, but he gunned it before I grabbed hold. "Gimme a second, will ya?"

He stomped the brake. The Caddy lurched forward, and my face slammed off the dashboard, my fingers feeling for missing teeth. Not that he noticed, hawkeyed on the road ahead. The passenger door snapped shut on its own. Again, he accelerated. And "accelerated" didn't mean a slow, steady increase. Hell, no. The force pinned me to the passenger seat, my fingers clawed into the armrest.

"Though I enjoy a good death ride as much as the next girl"—I added plenty of snark—"I'd rather not crash. How 'bout you?"

No response, but the blue lit dashboard illuminated a slight smirk. The Caddy slowed somewhat. Not a lot, but enough to loosen my grip.

Minutes dragged on for days. Trees' silhouettes whizzed past my window, the headlights tunneling through the darkness. Palpable anger radiated off him, lessened only by the deep lines of concern etched in his forehead.

In a soft voice, I said, "What'd *Shicheii* do?"

His icy stare landed on me, piercing gray, almost translucent, the intensity strangling my voice box. All I could do was point to the road ahead. *Let's not forget who's driving.*

"Please call Running Bear. Remind him it's an open line and ask for his location."

"Why, ya think Killzme's listening?"

He huffed out a hard breath.

"Okay, alright." I thumbed Kuruk's number on my cell. "Want him on speakerphone?"

"I do."

He answered on the second ring. "You all right, Ghost Dog?"

Running Bear always used our Apache names. "Yep. Fine." My gaze sidled to my mentor, best friend, and parttime fake husband. "Over this open line, I gotta ask you somethin'."

"Is Shadow Wolf with you?"

"Yep. Where are you right now?"

"Next to Barb."

Carolyne's mother. Running Bear built their home next door to his in-laws on gifted land. "Don't leave. We're on our way."

"Copy that."

Five minutes later, we drove through a tunnel of trees to a cedar-sided ranch at the end of a dirt road, conifers exhaling sweetness through the vents. Kuruk waited on the lopsided porch he insisted on building without the help of the pissed off individual beside me in the driver's seat, the rest of the house arrow straight.

In khakis and a tight tee, Running Bear's long dark hair blew in the warm evening breeze.

A somberness thickened the air inside the Caddy as he shifted into Park. "If Carolyne and the kids are home, I may need you to divert their attention, Cat."

Only he called me Cat—long story—and no one ever used my given name, Shawnee. "Aren't they staying at his parent's house?"

"Running Bear believes the danger has passed. Thus, he may have brought his family home."

I stayed clueless about the details, but judging by the look on his face, the news couldn't be good. So, when he hopped out of the Caddy, I followed.

After scanning the wood line around the property, Mr. Mayhem approached the house. Silent, he slid onto the edge of the porch beside Kuruk. "Are you here alone?"

I sat on the other side, sandwiching Running Bear between friends who loved him like family.

"For now. Carolyne wanted to stay another night with my folks. Why're you here, Shadow Wolf?"

*Based on his tone, he must suspect something's up.*

"Do you recall the couple from the recording?"

My eyeballs almost exploded from the sockets. *That's what this is about?*

When Mr. Mayhem and I went undercover at Killzme's gala for conservation—a scam event to con empathetic souls into funding their animal trafficking activities—we met a couple we palled around with named Cynthia and Elliot. Didn't know it at the time, but the husband cooked the books for Killzme's shell company.

We managed to plant a listening device while there. Through it, we discovered Killzme's plan to murder the couple once Elliot completed his assignment. At the time, I wanted to warn them. Begged for permission. In the end, we agreed it'd be safer to text the recording after we left Alaska. That way, if the couple double crossed us, the animal traffickers couldn't retaliate.

Running Bear said, "Are they dead?"

"Not that I'm aware of." He fingered his shirt collar. "Jacy Lee took it upon himself to pay them a visit."

*He, what?* Now the uncharacteristic rage made sense.

"How? Jacy Lee doesn't drive."

"Correct. However, your wife does."

A loud gasp coiled through the treetops. "How would Carolyne even know where they live?"

"Did you know she used to work at the Eagle Bay Lounge?"

"What does that have to do with—"

"Evidently, she still has friends there who were all too willing to phone her when the couple stopped in for brunch."

"I still don't see how Carolyne—"

"She followed them home."

*Whoa. No wonder she caught Running Bear cheating. Carolyne's got some serious sleuthing skills.*

They both turned toward me, and my shoulders sprang to my ears. *Did I say that out loud?*

"Not appropriate, Cat."

*I wasn't talkin' to you. Stay outta my head!*

"My wife," Kuruk echoed in disbelief, "followed home a Kilzme employee?" Long fingers clawed through his hair. "After they abducted our son?"

"I'm afraid so."

He paced in circles. "What the fuck was she thinking?"

"Running Bear, listen to me, please. Stop." Mr. Mayhem slapped a flat hand on his chest. "Jacy Lee asked for her help. You know how close they are. Carolyne refuses no one, especially family. The fault does not lie at her feet."

"He's right." The truth illuminated only one name—mine. "Don't blame *Shicheii*, either. If I hadn't pushed to warn Cynthia, he never woulda gotten involved. If I knew he even had the balls to do somethin' like this..."

"Oh, he does, Cat. There's nothing your grandfather won't do—no mountain he won't climb, no river he won't cross—for the ones he loves."

Running Bear's forearms weighed down my shoulders, his dark gaze connecting with mine, hard lines melting off his chestnut complexion. "This isn't on you, Ghost Dog." The beautiful moment ended when he spun to Mr. Mayhem, who also mentored him back in the day, though with sketchier details. "What's the play here, Shadow Wolf?"

"I instructed Jacy Lee to pack. We leave tonight. Is it possible for Carolyne and the kids to stay with your folks till things blow over?"

"'Course. They'll be thrilled to spend more time with their grandkids."

"How can I help?"

Head rocking, Kuruk searched the night sky. "This is a lot to absorb."

"May I offer a suggestion?" He withdrew a wad of cash. "Take this. On second thought, no." He passed him a credit card instead. "Update all your iPhones for better security and buy whatever else you need."

"Why're you leaving? You never run from a fight."

*Good point. Why are we?*

"Run from a fight." He scoffed. "You know better than that. If we get embroiled in another battle here, we'll miss our window to stop their next hunt. Our immediate departure removes any temptation to delay us." When neither of us responded, he said, "Now, if you'll excuse me, I need to place a call."

"House is open. We'll wait out here."

"Thank you, Running Bear." After a reassuring pat of his shoulder, Mr. Mayhem strode through the front door.

Kuruk and I sat in silence for a long while before I tried to lighten the mood. "Poe's wearing a dead crow's feathers on his ass."

A loud guffaw echoed in the stillness. "No shit?"

"Swear to God. *Shicheii* did the transplant while me and Shadow Wolf were in the Arctic."

"Aw, man. How'd that go over?"

"Not great, if we're being honest." Understatement of the year. Mr. Mayhem wanted to strangle him. Not that he would, but still. "*Shicheii* dropped that bomb minutes before this one."

"Sounds like it'll be a fun trip."

"*Aack.* Tell me about it."

How many hours would I be stuck in the car with tension thick enough to choke on?

# Chapter 2

> *"What is life? It is the flash of a firefly in the night. It is the breath of a Buffalo in the wintertime. It is the little shadow which runs across the grass and loses itself in the sunset."*
> —Chief Crowfoot

*Sunday, 12:03 a.m.*

Moonlight cascaded through the windows, the fieldstone hearth and wood stove casting long shadows on the wall. Mayhem lowered to the sofa in the living room. Little Tamak's teddy bear nestled in the corner. If Cat hadn't boarded Killzme's ship to save him, the stuffed animal would morph into a constant reminder of a sweet child taken far too soon. She sacrificed everything to help Running Bear—a magnanimous gift no one could ever repay.

Calling family at this hour wasn't ideal, but the time change should help. Klee and Ferron rose before dawn to pray and give thanks for another day, a spiritual time enjoyed by many.

He dialed.

The phone rang thrice before connecting. "What's wrong, Cheveyo?"

"We've hit a snafu, I'm afraid. Need to leave immediately. Does your offer still stand?"

"Of course. Do you still have the coordinates I gave you?"

"I do. However, I need to run an errand first."

"If you're delayed, let me know. Otherwise, I'll meet you there."

"Thank you, Klee. Give my love to Ferron. See you soon."

Mayhem strode out to the porch. "Under no circumstances should Carolyne and the kids return until you hear from me."

"Copy that."

"Please stand." When Running Bear rose, Mayhem locked him in a bear hug. "We'll get through this together like we always do. In the meantime, rest. You'll need full strength to stay alert."

"I can't sleep. Do you know where the couple lives?"

"I do. In fact, we're headed there now."

Shawnee's jaw slacked. "We are?"

In hindsight, perhaps he should have shared the plan—Cat had a right to know—but Jacy Lee's confession rocked him to the core. He needed time to process the initial shock and formulate the best course of action to move forward.

"I'll follow you, Shadow Wolf. If they contacted Killzme after my wife left, I need to know."

"Understandable. Ride with us." At the Caddy, he opened the passenger door for Shawnee, but Running Bear hopped in instead.

"Hey—" She pursed her lips. "That's my seat."

"Does it matter? Jump in back."

Mayhem winced. *Not smart, Running Bear.*

With fists planted on both hips, she refused to concede. "You jump in back."

Before this got out of hand, Mayhem stepped in to mediate. "If the lady wants the front..."

With a breathy exhale, Kuruk rose. "Sorry, Ghost Dog. Lost my head for a second." While Mayhem circled the front bumper, Running Bear waited for Cat to get in before closing her door like a gentleman should.

Now behind the wheel, Mayhem thanked him through the rearview mirror. With one escalation diffused, he drove to the address on the paper.

No lights brightened the humble seaside cottage. An older model BMW sat in the driveway. Across the street, he parked curbside.

"What's the play here, Shadow Wolf?"

"Watch for movement inside while I knock."

"Copy that." He hopped out to open Shawnee's door. "C'mon, Ghost Dog."

"Where? Nobody ever tells me nothing."

Did she not overhear his and Running Bear's conversation? The objective should be obvious. Regardless, Mayhem stayed quiet to let things play out.

"We need to watch his six," Kuruk said. "Got a weapon on you?"

She patted the side of her moccasin boot. "Always."

*Adorable.*

"A baby knife?" Kuruk reached between her shins, and she stiffened, her widened emerald gaze locked on his head as he rummaged beneath her seat. When he withdrew his hand, he held Mayhem's backup piece, which he passed to Shawnee.

Oh, boy. "She can barely shoot an arrow, Running Bear. Let's not tempt fate with a firearm." Mayhem reached for the weapon, but she angled it out of his reach.

"I got it."

"I admire your confidence, Cat. I really do. However, ideally, we should all survive this encounter, and you with a pistol decreases those odds." He slid the weapon from her shaky hands. "Thank you."

Once his team got into position at each end of the cottage, Mayhem rapped his knuckles on the front door. No lights blazed on. He knocked again. Jabbed a chin at Running Bear, who returned a no. When he gestured to Cat, she also shook a no.

He knocked harder.

Still no movement, nor lights.

"Cat"—he hustled closer, his voice in a low whisper—"have you spotted any entry points?"

"Plenty of 'em." Confidence oozed from her and shot a tingle up his spine. "Duffel still in the trunk?"

"It is."

"I'm on it."

"Thank you."

Moments later, as she prowled toward the cottage with her tools, Mayhem sidled up to Running Bear. "What Cat lacks in weaponry skills, she more than makes up for in other areas. Watch and learn."

"Copy that."

When he spun to follow her, Mayhem gripped his arm. "Do not get in her way. That woman can get downright feral if she feels crowded." He'd learned that lesson the hard way. "And whatever you do, don't question her methods. She knows where to funnel her rage."

Without a word, Kuruk shielded his crotch.

"Precisely."

"Copy that."

If Cynthia and Elliot woke, they better not lay hands on her. Or blood will spill.

# Chapter 3



Behind the cottage, waves lapped against the shoreline, the night air sprayed with salt water. I cracked my knuckles, rolled the bones in my neck, shook out my arms and legs. Gotta stay loose and flexible for this job.

With the penlight clenched in my teeth, I rummaged through the duffel for the flathead screwdriver. Running Bear stood at the edge of the patio while I snapped on black latex gloves.

Most cottages had double-hung windows. Child's play for a pro like *moi*.

First, I wedged the flathead into the beading channel—a plastic or metal strip around the window frame—then pried it out a little at a time, working my way to the opposite corner. Once I loosened the strip, I pulled it free. Because the vertical beading didn't overlap the horizontal, it made my job much easier.

Next, I inserted the screwdriver between the glass and frame. Pried with light pressure to lever out one pane enough for me to reach the inside lock.

After which, I pressed the pane back into its mount. And the window glided up the tracks with ease.

"Impressive work, Ghost Dog."

"Thanks." I swept my hair off my shoulders. "Tell Shadow Wolf I'm in. Gotta go unlock the front door."

"You want me to leave? What if they wake?"

Had to chuckled at that one. If he only knew how many homes I'd broken into through the years. "Appreciate your concern, but this is hardly my first rodeo. Go. I'll be fine."

Before he left, he boosted me through the opening. Not that I needed the help, but it made him feel better.

The cottage had high-end furniture, hardwood floors, and sand-colored area rugs, all of which cost some serious dough. On my way to the door, I kept my head on a swivel. The home was quiet. Too quiet.

A floor-to-ceiling bookcase towered behind a long, stiff couch. Light beige, with lime green toss pillows. Rose, bourbon vanilla, and a musky citrus lingered in the air.

Cynthia's perfume.

A matching loveseat lounged across from a tan-and-white upholstered chair. A hard-shelled briefcase stood beside it. Probably Elliot's favorite spot. I could almost picture his wife serving him, King Shit's feet propped up on the ottoman.

The whole prim and proper living room screamed Cynthia's name. Hard to believe this couple got involved with Killzme Corp, but money and status were important in their world. The upper echelon put material needs above everything else. Even to the detriment of the Natural World.

Shame on them.

By the time I swung open the front door, Mr. Mayhem stood alone on the stoop. No fedora, shirtsleeves rolled to mid-forearm, black-leather gloves, and the pistol strapped into a shoulder holster.

*Man, he's sexy.* "Where's Running Bear?"

"Perimeter check." He stepped inside. "Problems?"

"Nope. Either they're wicked sound sleepers or no one's home."

"Let's solve that mystery first."

"Right behind ya." Safer that way.

Through the living room we trekked, then banged a left down the hall. He hand-signaled for me to check the rooms on one side while he cleared the others. Behind the first door, my penlight encircled a vanity and sink with overhead bulbous lights.

Bathroom.

I moved on. Daybed, more lime green toss pillows, empty dresser, and no personal belongings on top. Probably a guest room.

"Cat—" His deep, raspy voice carried across the hall. "Join me, please."

Rather than call back, I hustled into the master suite, where he stood beside an unmade bed, the sheets and duvet halfway off the mattress. Lime green shams littered the tan carpet.

When I raised the bed pillow, a bullet hole tunneled straight through it.

Breath tangled in my chest. Blood splattered the sheets, more crimson speckles across the upholstered headboard.

Speechless, my heartbeat sputtered to a stop. "We're too late."

As usual, Mr. Mayhem showed no reaction. "Evidently, yes."

"It's our fault they're dead. If *Shicheii* never came here—"

"Cat"—muscular forearms weighed down my shoulders, his safety and reassurance reminding me to breathe—"your grandfather mustn't know what transpired here. It's too much for him." Even after I agreed, he held my gaze, and I fell deeper and deeper into his pupils, our souls waltzing on an alternate plane. "How are you, darlin'?"

"Better." I really was.

He kissed the bridge of my nose. "Good."

Only then did he step back.

"Where're the bodies?"

"Hmm." Gloved fingers swept through the blood. "Still wet." He leaned back to peek through the window blinds. "We need to search for intel."

"Like what?"

"Elliot worked as an accountant, so ledgers, receipts, notes, tax documents, and the like."

"I'm on it."

"Quickly, please." His balanced tone didn't match those words. No urgency, no fear. The man never flinched, even with rifles aimed at his face. "We have little time to waste."

Why wasn't he freaking out? If the cops came, they'd catch us in the middle of a crime scene.

Arms pumping, I booked it down the hall.

Running Bear barreled around the corner and almost rocketed the heart from my chest. "Time to go, Ghost Dog."

Mr. Mayhem's voice rolled over my shoulder. "Distance?"

"Two streets over."

I swiveled between them. "Who? The cops? Cynthia and Elliot?"

For a hot second, my mentor's head shook as if he didn't know how to respond. "The frightened kitten replaced the warrior again. Okie doke." His gaze lifted to Kuruk. "Escort her to the Caddy, please."

"I'm not losing it, if that's what you're thinking." I stomped the floor. "Dammit. I'm the one who got us in here. Tell me what's happening."

"Cat, Cynthia and Elliot are dead. I thought we'd already established that."

"Then who's—?" A ghostly tongue licked up my spine. "Killzme..."

"We're out of time, Ghost Dog." After grabbing my hand, Running Bear bolted, damn near dislocating my shoulder from the socket.

At the end of the hall, I ground in my heels. "Gimme a friggin' second, will ya?" From the living room, I snatched the briefcase before racing out the door behind him.

Across the street from the cottage, we dove into the Caddy. But Mr. Mayhem never emerged. With my gaze bouncing from window to window, I couldn't find him anywhere.

Headlights cascaded through the trees. A vehicle turned on to the street.

"Where the hell is he?" My leg hammered the passenger seat. "He was right behind us."

"Don't worry." Running Bear scrolled through his phone like we were perfectly safe, and I'd overreacted over a minor point. "Shadow Wolf knows what's what."

*Glad someone does.* Not trusting the side mirror, I poked my head out the window to gauge the distance of the approaching vehicle. "He's never gonna make it in time. Shit. Whattawe do?"

Head reclined, he slung his arms over the top of the backseat. "Lean into it, Ghost Dog."

"Into what?"

"The thrill of the chase. Feel that anticipation build. Let it tingle up the spine." He grinned. "You can't tell me this shit doesn't turn you on."

"Alright, maybe a little. Still, I'd rather not die tonight." In the back windshield, headlights brightened more and more. "For fuck's sake, what's he doing in there?"

Again, his head reclined. "Lean into it, Ghost Dog."

When I spun to check the cottage again, Mr. Mayhem slipped behind the wheel. His sudden appearance nearly catapulted me out the window like a squirrel who hit a live wire by mistake.

Like this was just another ordinary night, he veered into the road. High beams tunneled through the Caddy, and I slumped down in my seat.

"Oh, my God. You took too long. Where were you? Why didn't you follow us?" I raked back my bangs. "We coulda been outta here before Killzme knew the difference. But now? Now, we're fucked."

His gaze flicked between the road and the rearview mirror, the blue lights of the dash cascading down the bridge of his nose to the soft V of his upper lip. "The colorful language is not helpful, Cat."

I didn't dare chance a peek. The cops I'd worked with told me they looked for suspicious activity. If a motorist kept adjusting their mirror or the passenger couldn't hold it together, that alone triggered alarm bells. Many of Killzme's henchmen were also military trained, so they probably looked for the same thing.

Still, I'd be lying if I said the back windshield didn't temp me. "Are they following us?"

Cool as ever, Mr. Mayhem said, "They are."

Unanswered questions spiraled through my mind. "It's almost like you wanted 'em to see us, but that doesn't make sense."

"No?"

"No. Right?"

His gray, almost translucent, eyes shifted to the rearview mirror. "Running Bear, please explain to Cat why I might want Killzme to spot us at their crime scene."

"To nip it in the bud."

"Precisely."

*Was it me, or did this make no sense?* "Nip what?"

Running Bear laced his fingers behind his head. "C'mon, Ghost Dog, you've been around long enough to know what we need to do."

All the oxygen in my lungs crystalized. "We're luring 'em into a trap?"

One slow nod of acknowledgment accompanied his smirk.

"Why?"

"Want this one, Shadow Wolf?"

"You're doing fine."

Running Bear leaned forward. "To buy time to get you out of Alaska before they call in reinforcements."

Again, Mr. Mayhem said, "Precisely."

But I still couldn't grasp the point. "Doesn't our leaving endanger your family?"

"How? My house is empty. Carolyne and the kids are at my folks, miles away from Dutch Harbor. As long as my wife does nothing stupid, no one will ever find them."

When I turned toward the driver's seat, the cold, hard truth hitched my voice. "What about *Shicheii*? The second we stop, war will break out. Killzme knows where the cabin is."

He winked. "Watch and learn, Cat."

The Caddy lurched into high gear. Banged a right. Then a left. Another right. And looped around. All these turns disoriented me, not to mention the speed, my fingers clawed into the armrest, praying to all that's holy we wouldn't crash.

The headlights trailed into the blackness. But instead of driving faster, he slowed for the Escalade to catch up. "Running Bear, would you mind assisting Cat?"

"Now?"

"Yes, please."

I rubbed the back of my neck. "Help me with what?"

Running Bear slid behind the driver's seat. "Come back here with me, Ghost Dog."

"What? Why?"

"You're still a target."

Voice rising in intensity, I thrust a hand at Mr. Mayhem. "So is he."

"Cat, please. Let us handle this."

"While I do what?" When the realization hit, I crossed my arms. "There's no way I'm goin' back in that trunk."

"Running Bear?"

"Sorry, Ghost Dog, but this is for your own good." In one swift motion, he pinned my arms to my side, and yanked me into the backseat.

"Not cool!"

He slapped down the hideaway door into the trunk. "It'll be easier for all of us if you got in on your own."

"No, dammit." Shoulders squared, I jutted my chin. "I won't go."

Piercing gray eyes reflected in the rearview. "Our rendezvous point is seconds away."

"Please, Ghost Dog. Don't make me do this. Just get in. I'll let you out as soon as I can."

"For the record," I hollered into the front seat, "this is a total bullshit move!"

"Noted. Thank you, Cat."

As I squeezed through the hole, a fiery blaze enveloped me from the inside out, my skin hot and tight. "Why'd I train my ass off? To hide like a little bitch while you guys kick ass?"

Inside the trunk, I stuck my head out the passthrough. "It's 'cause I'm a chick, huh? Haven't I proven myself by now? You talk about *Shicheii* not loosening the reins. You're doing the same thing! Well, I've got news for you, pal. I don't need or want your protection. I can defend myself, thank you very much. Where were you when I was chopping off Echo's dick? Huh? Huh? Oh, that's right. You weren't there!"

Running Bear leaned toward the rearview. "When she what?"

"Now is not the time nor the place to rehash this, Cat." The Caddy veered to the side of the road. "The weapons satchel is to your left. When the trunk rises, be ready to fight."

"See ya on the flop, Ghost Dog." He closed the hideaway door.

In the darkness, all my senses heightened, but the adrenaline coursing through my system muffled sound. If I didn't calm down soon, I might pass out.

Man, I had a bad feeling about this.

# Chapter 4

*"I am no longer accepting the things I cannot change. I am changing the things I cannot accept."* —Angela Davis

***1:40 a.m.***

Before the Escalade pulled to the side of the road, Mayhem and Running Bear fled into the forest, shedding their shirts to better blend into the shadows. He scaled one tree, his former protégé scaled another.

Together, they waited for the prey to arrive.

Four flashlights bounced to the rhythm of the henchmen's stride. A spherical luminesce scanned the wood line, but the light never rose above chest-level. Few had the wherewithal to search near the canopies.

An unfamiliar male voice pierced the silence. "Was Mutt with Redskin?"

Killzme's racist codewords.

"She's here, yeah." Another unfamiliar voice. "They both ran this way."

Amused by their ignorance, Mayhem sniggered to himself. Running Bear's loose hair created the perfect diversion. Grandmother Moon trickled a golden smolder through leaves as the henchmen split up to search the Alaskan wilderness.

His gloved fingers tightened around the knife handle.

Squatted in the next tree, Running Bear hand-signaled. *The prey is almost within reach.* When two henchmen strode beneath them, they leaped in unison.

Clung to the back of one poacher, Mayhem drew the blade across his throat.

Severed both external carotid arteries.

Jugulars too.

Before the dying man crumbled, he turned enough to bathe Mayhem's bare chest in blood. Another henchman bled out at Kuruk's feet.

Mayhem jabbed his chin. *Where are the others?*

Both shoulders rose.

The roar of more than one engine whirled him around. The Escalade and his Cadillac pulled into the road. Eyes blinking, he gaped.

*Cat!*

He sprinted into the street, leather soles slapping the pavement, vision locked on the Caddy, the heart thundering in his chest. Footfalls pounded the asphalt behind him. *Running Bear.*

The Caddy banged a right.

With Kuruk on his heels, Mayhem veered through the woods to hedge it off. Jumped streams and fallen timber, slapped branches out of his way. The moment he emerged on the street, the Caddy zoomed past.

He pushed harder, ran faster. Almost within reach, he hollered, "Cat, pop the trunk!"

"Ghost Dog—" Running Bear looped wide in case the Caddy took the next right. "Ghost Dog!"

Mayhem's gloved hand slapped the trunk, but he couldn't grab hold. A bloody handprint streaked the back emblem. "Pop the trunk, Cat!"

Is she still inside? Or did they find her?

Once he caught up again, he lunged, body-slammed the trunk, his fingers groping for a lip to hold. "Cat!"

The Caddy lurched into high gear. Zigged then zagged. And he sailed off the side, tumbling to the dark road. In seconds, he leaped to his feet and sped to a full-on sprint. Wind whipped his bare chest, the internal drive to save her pushing him harder, propelling him faster.

Cherry red taillights trailed into the darkness.

A thousand pounds crashed on him, and he fell to his knees, forearms curled around his head. Cat put her trust in him, and he failed her. How did this happen? The trunk was the safest place to hide.

Numbness branched through his system, a tsunami of tears threatening his resolve.

Running Bear patted his shoulder. "We'll get her back. Don't worry."

"If I let her fight beside us, she'd be safe now."

"You did what you thought was best, Shadow Wolf."

With an inferno raging inside him, he flung a hand to where the taillights vanished. "Look how well that turned out. I should be heading to Montana with Cat beside me." His heart collapsed in on itself. "If she crawls through that hideaway door..." He couldn't bear to say the words aloud.

"I've got an idea." On the keypad of his phone, Kuruk stabbed four digits before Mayhem stopped him.

"If you call her, you could further jeopardize her safety."

"It's a chance we'll have to take."

"Stop—We can't afford another mistake." Mind whirling for a solution, he withdrew his cell. "Cat's in my vehicle."

On the *My Cadillac* mobile app, he tapped Vehicle Locate. An address emerged. He flashed the screen at Running Bear. "No one steals my Caddy for long." Another address popped up. "They're still on the move. Let's go."

"On foot? They're miles away."

"Then I'll run all night. Killzme cannot have her." He jetted down the middle of the dark road, his mind replaying Cat's heart-felt words in the Arctic hours earlier.

*"I can't ever leave you because... you're the missing piece of my life puzzle."*

Why, oh, why didn't he tell her then? What if he never saw her again?

Running Bear shot out of the woods. Once he caught up, he grabbed his arm. "Let me help you."

Stopped, Mayhem's gaze shot to his tight grip.

He let go. *Smart move.*

"With all due respect, Shadow Wolf, you're not thinking clearly."

A pulse throbbed in his forehead, his chest swelled in a slow, controlled heave. "If you have a point, make it. Time is slipping away."

"Here me out. Please." Kuruk stepped back.

*Also, smart.*

"We're covered in blood. If the cops drive by—"

"Do you or do you not have a plan, Running Bear? If they take Cat back to that ship..." He couldn't even process the thought.

"I know a place where we can clean up. Maybe borrow a vehicle."

"Maybe?" Definitive answers helped, not guesswork.

"It's complicated."

Another conquest, no doubt. If Jacy Lee hadn't healed his sex addiction, Kuruk could have lost everything.

"Can you trust this mystery woman?"

"Yeah, she's good people."

"She better be, or blood will spill. Cat has sacrificed enough. I will not allow some woman to stand in my way of finding her." He checked the app. The address moved farther and farther away. "Go. Now."

When Kuruk took off, he chased him through the woods for three or four miles before he stopped behind a typical Alaskan cabin sided in planks. No lights inside or out.

"Wait here, Shadow Wolf." His tone portrayed confidence. "I'll give you the signal once I'm in."

Nothing about this felt right. "I don't like it. Too many variables. When's the last time you spoke with this woman?"

"About a year ago. It's all good."

He rocked back. "A year is a long time to wait in the wings for a married man."

"It's not like that. We're just friends. I told you, I'm honoring my vows."

"For Carolyne's sake, I hope that's true." He shooed him away. "Go. Time is not on our side."

Running Bear crept up the deck stairs, ran his fingers across the top doorframe for the spare key, then entered with no fair warning. Do friends let themselves into each other homes? Lovers might, but not after a solid year with no communication.

Ducked low, Mayhem crossed the backyard. Padded up the stairs, his back pressed to the siding, an ear cocked toward movement inside.

This hulk of a man muscled Running Bear out the door, the woman inside screaming obscenities.

Mayhem head-locked the stranger, his forearm squeezing his airway. "Release him."

The woman shouted, "I'm calling the cops!"

When the white man complied, Mayhem walked him inside. Kicked the door closed behind him. "You touch that phone, and he dies."

Palms up, a Native woman backed into the stove. "Who... are you?"

"Your worst nightmare or a trusted ally. Which do you prefer?"

"Ally." She collapsed in a chair at the kitchen table. "Whose blood is that? Are you here to kill us?"

"No, ma'am." He loosened his grip. "May I be completely transparent with you?"

Visibly trembling, she nodded.

"Thank you." He shoved the white man into the chair beside her. "Have a seat, Mister...?"

"Stapleton, Craig Stapleton."

He softened his tone for the frightened woman. "And you are?"

"Sadie Redfeather."

The surname surprised him. "Any relation to Jax and Patrice Redfeather in Kodiak?"

Her dark eyes lit up. "They're my folks."

Good news. She's less likely to turn in a family friend. "I know them well. Good people, your parents." He pulled out the chair across from them. "May I join you?"

Another nod, though with much less trembling.

"Thank you, Miss Redfeather. My sincerest apologies for disturbing you at such an ungodly hour." Elbows on the table, praying hands tapped his lips as he carefully chose his words. "Does Mister Stapleton make you happy?"

"Very." She flashed a diamond solitaire. "We're engaged."

"How nice. Congratulations to you both." Again, he hesitated. "Mister Stapleton, is it fair to say Miss Redfeather keeps your heart beating? That by presence alone, she parts the darkest of storm clouds? That her laugh carries a thousand rainbows? And together, no mountain seems insurmountable, no ocean deep enough to drown in?"

"Wow. Never said anything close to that—wish I did—but yeah. She's my everything."

"You're a lucky man." His heart ached. "I feel the same about a woman in my life. About forty minutes ago, someone stole my Cadillac with her inside."

A slow hand rose to the woman's parted lips. "I'm so sorry."

"I need to find her, Miss Redfeather."

"How can I help?"

"Is it possible to borrow your car?" From his jeans pocket, he withdrew his money clip and peeled off three crisp hundred-dollar bills. "For your inconvenience."

"Will you return it? I need it for work."

"Of course. You have my word."

"Ford Bronco parked out front. Take the spare key on the hook by the door."

"Thank you, Miss Redfeather. I appreciate your kindness more than words can express." Mayhem swung open the deck door. With a sneer at Kuruk, he whispered, "Behave yourself."

When Miss Redfeather spotted her friend, she rose. "Why didn't you just call me, Running Bear?"

"Sorry, Sadie." His head hung. "It'll never happen again."

"I have no problem helping you, you know that. All I ask is for common decency in return. You can't just barge in here anytime you feel like it."

"You're right. I should've called."

Her dark gaze skimmed their chests. "Should I ask why you two are covered in blood?"

"Please don't, Sadie."

With a heavy sigh, she regarded Mayhem. "You can wash up in the kitchen sink. I'll fetch you some towels."

"Very kind of you, Miss Redfeather. Thank you for your hospitality."

"Sadie speaks highly of you." Mr. Stapleton shook Kuruk's hand. "No hard feelings?"

"All good, dude. Treat her right. She's one of a kind."

After thanking the couple for their generosity, they showed themselves out. Behind the wheel of the Bronco, Mayhem holstered his iPhone on the dash.

One last address emerged on the screen. "Why would they stop on Henry Swanson Drive?"

In the passenger seat, Running Bear gestured up ahead. "Take Airport Beach Road to Amaknak Island."

"If you have some insight into where they're headed, I am all ears."

"Where on Henry Swanson did they park?"

A headache bloomed behind his eyes. "How on earth would I know where they parked? Honestly, Running Bear, I know it's late—early—but I need your head in the game."

"It is." He snatched Mayhem's cell from the holder.

Intermittent moonbeams shadowed the passenger seat enough to mask Kuruk's activity on the phone. Or, more importantly, why he grabbed it at all. Plus, Mayhem had to focus on the dark road ahead. If a deer leaped in front of the Bronco, it might destroy his one chance of finding Cat. Striking a moose could turn even deadlier, as the animal often landed in the driver's lap, killing both on impact.

Running Bear said, "Little South America."

"I am cognizant of that, thank you."

The shape of Amaknak Island resembled a miniature South America on a map, hence why the locals referred to the area as such. None of which helped narrow in on Cat's precise location.

"Tell me something I can use to find her. Or don't speak at all." The realization hit him hard, his ribcage squeezing the oxygen from his lungs. "Isn't the old military road off Henry Swanson?"

"About seven-tenths of a mile down, yeah. You know where it leads."

His Adam's apple rose and fell. "I do."

"Better step on it. If they find Ghost Dog and drag her out there—"

"Not helpful." When he stomped the gas pedal, the Bronco bucked in protest. "Call Klee. Tell him we're delayed and to wait till he hears from me. If Ferron answers, get creative. She cannot know about Cat's abduction."

"You want me to lie to Mama Hen?" He clawed back his hair. "She'll see right through it."

"I said, get creative. Not lie."

After more blustering, none of which helped the situation, he punched in the digits. "If Mama Hen finds out, I'm a dead man."

Mayhem snickered. "You're not wrong."

"Look—" He flashed the screen. "Ghost Dog sent her location." A moment later, Kuruk's phone chimed, as well.

As much as he desperately longed to believe Cat sent the text, he must weigh every possible angle. "Or they stole her phone to lure us into a trap."

"Fuck."

"The language isn't helpful, Running Bear. Though I concur with the sentiment behind it."

Where are you, Kitty Cat?

# Chapter 5



Trapped inside the trunk moments after they fled the Caddy, a low rumble loudened as the Escalade pulled in behind me. Nothing I witnessed by sight, but the ears didn't lie. Multiple boots struck the pavement. Though no one spoke. Which made it damn near impossible to determine the number of Killzme henchmen.

At least three. Maybe four.

Silence enveloped me. No fighting. No angry shouts. No signs of a struggle. Where'd Mr. Mayhem and Running Bear go?

In complete darkness, my breath shallowed, my heart working overtime, blood sluicing through my veins. For several minutes, I detected nothing outside.

Eerily silent. Ominous. Desolate.

Boots struck the pavement again. A car door slammed shut, followed by the weight of a man climbing into the Caddy.

*About time they showed.*

My fingers patted for the loop of the hideaway door. But then, the engine started. Why didn't anyone let me out? Mr. Mayhem would never leave me in the trunk. Neither would Running Bear.

Why didn't they speak? Sure, they both adopted the silent killer persona when necessary, but if they'd "nipped it in the bud" like they claimed, why wouldn't they release me? Or talk inside the Caddy?

The driving felt off, too. Mr. Mayhem babied his Cadillac. Well, except for the death ride earlier.

Maybe Running Bear drove. Why would he, though? Unless Killzme shot my faux husband. Nah. That man moved like a trick of light.

The silence nearly killed me. Something must be wrong.

To slow the endless spiral of scenarios—each one worse than the last, ending with a fatal chest wound leaving him bleeding out in the passenger seat—I inched open the hideaway door.

No one occupied the backseat.

Outside the vehicle, his husky voice called my name. What the hell? Nothing made sense. If the Caddy's in motion, why would he—? Maybe I imagined it. Or hit my head. I felt my skull for eggs or gashes. Nope. All good. So, if it wasn't me, then... Again, I cracked open the hideaway door.

The rearview reflected a white-skinned forehead, mousy brown hair, and caramel-colored eyes. Who the fuck is that?

Mr. Mayhem hollered, "Pop"—the motor and tires drowned out his words—"Cat!"

I twisted back to the darkness. *What'd he say?*

The weight of a body slammed the trunk above my head. "Cat!"

Jigsaw pieces snapped into place. Oh. My. God. Someone stole the Caddy. I scrambled to find a way out, my fingers darting across cold metal but unable to find the trunk release. My breath grew heavier and thicker, harder to catch, my heart slamming against my ribcage, my pulse soaring to two thousand beats per minute.

A gazillion things coursed through my mind in seconds.

The last thing he said was, "Weapons satchel is to your left." Where was I at the time? Right, right. With my head poked through the hidden opening. Aw, man. I'd said some awful things to him. What if I never saw him again? Would he know I shouted bullshit in anger? Or would my last words haunt him forever? If I died, he'd never know my true feelings.

In the future, I must do better… if I survived. Who's the driver? I'd never seen the guy before. Who would even have the balls to steal—

My breath caught. Killzme. Would they take me back to the docks? Or worse, the ship?

Dear God, no. I barely survived that nightmare, never mind my return trip to save little Tamak.

The loud voice inside my head screamed for me to do something—anything—to fight and not accept the inevitable. And so, I patted around for the leather satchel. Hang on. I smoothed my hand down the side of my knee-high moccasin. The lump of my iPhone arced my lips. A lifeline.

Once I clicked Location Sharing, I sent the text to both Mr. Mayhem and Kuruk.

But if either texted, the driver might hear the chime. If they called, Alanis Morissette would belt out *Ironic*. Man, that'd suck. To be safe, I put my cell on silent mode.

Maybe the driver didn't know I was back here. Then why steal the Caddy? Did punks carjack it for cash? If Killzme was behind this, how'd they slip past two Apache warriors?

With the flashlight app, I scanned the dark trunk. No latch release anywhere. None I could find, anyway. Leave it to my mentor to have a vehicle that didn't allow an escape.

From the weapons satchel, I snatched my favorite curved blade. With my folded legs beneath me, my back confined by the tight space, I prepared to lunge if anyone dared to open the trunk.

*You got this, Shawnee... right?* Even my inner voice had a questionable tone, which didn't help instill confidence.

Four deep inhales through my nose and exhales out my mouth steadied my breathing enough to slow the adrenaline. As part of my warrior training, Mr. Mayhem taught me mindfulness. A moment-by-moment awareness of thoughts, feelings, sensations, and the ability to stay attuned to the environment through a gentle, nurturing lens. Mindfulness also involved acceptance, the act of paying attention to thoughts and emotions without judgment or fear.

When one practiced mindfulness, all senses enhanced, enabling the dissection of the present moment without baggage from the past or concern for the future.

Not an easy feat while trapped inside the trunk of a moving vehicle.

*Shicheii* often harkened to reach *hozho*—the most important word in the Navajo language—loosely translated to peace, balance, beauty, and harmony. To be at one with, and part of, the world around us. Centered. Whole. Spiritual.

I found it easier to reach *hozho* if I practiced mindfulness first. So, I squeezed my eyes closed, my other senses heightened and aware.

Tires rolled over cracked asphalt. Tiny pebbles pinged off the undercarriage beneath me. The engine's steadiness and predictability lulled me into a false sense of security. Its continual purr reminded me of a lioness snuggled beside her mate, relaxing in the shade of an acacia tree to escape the midday heat.

Cigarette smoke seeped into the trunk and snapped my mind to high alert. The stranger coughed twice in quick succession.

A phone rang.

I curled my hair around one ear. *Please say something to help me.*

"Problem?" the driver said.

"All clear." The male caller's voice had a feminine quality. "Pull over up ahead. Any trouble on your end?"

"Not yet."

"Good."

"Zulu?"

Silence.

"Zulu?"

Silence.

"Prick."

The Caddy rolled to a stop. The engine shutdown. The driver's door opened, closed.

Footsteps approached the trunk, and my grip tightened around the knife handle. *C'mon, motherfucker. Touch me and die.*

From behind, someone yanked me back to the hideaway door by the hair. It was so forceful and unexpected, it threw me off my game. I swung at the disembodied arm, my knuckles topped with the curved razor-sharp blade.

Missed. Shit.

I swung again. This time, the knife nicked flesh. Probably didn't do much damage, but at least I hit him. When I swung a third time, I might've nailed the brachial artery, the major blood supply for the upper extremities—Mr. Mayhem taught me that—and wetness soaked the back of my scalp, hair, and shoulders.

"The bitch cut me." Driver's voice.

When he released me, I spun. Slashed the inner arm twice more before it retracted. If I did sever the brachial artery, he'd lose consciousness within thirty seconds. Die within ninety.

With both feet, I kicked the trunk. "Fight me like a man, you fuckin' pussy."

The trunk rose. And there stood three muscular guys, all dressed alike. Camouflage pants and olive drab t-shirts. The one with a belt tourniquet'd around his upper arm pitched toward me, and I swung to keep him away. Light from the trunk illuminated the face of the stockiest dude—dark buzz-cut, eye patch, goatee. A thick scar split one eyebrow in half.

"Hand over the weapon, Mutt." His confidence alluded to his rank among the men—boss.

"Make me, motherfucker."

He turned to a dirty blond with pockmarked cheeks. "Get her out of there."

"On it, boss."

That's the feminine-like voice on the phone. The driver called him Zulu. Killzme used the military alphabet for individuals, so the Z name showed the absolute bottom of the pecking order.

Ready to cut anyone who came near me, I cocked my arm.

In seconds, the boss trained a pistol on me. "Drop the knife, Mutt. Now."

Every time they used their racist codeword for me, flames licked my stomach liner. "I'll say it slow so everybody understands. Fuck. Off. Any questions?"

"This bitch is crazy." He chambered a round. "Drop the knife. Or die. Your choice."

"Alright, fine." I tore a page from Mr. Mayhem's playbook. "I choose death. Now what?"

In one fluid motion, the boss pivoted and kicked me square in the chest. When my head snapped back, the other two brutes dove into the trunk, pinned me down, and peeled back my fingers to pry the knife from my death grip.

During the scuffle, I chomped down on Zulu's neck, trying to bite his jugular as my mentor advised. He screamed like a little girl with hurt feelings and yanked me off his neck by my hair.

The driver jumped in to help. Together, they dragged me from the trunk, my arms and legs flailing, my body arching in protest.

I'd barely hit the ground when the driver stomped my temple. Tiny flecks of light danced before my eyes, and I curled into a ball, my forearms wreathed over my head. Multiple boots kicked my arms, legs, and spine.

"Enough." The boss shoved back his henchmen. "The buyer wants his merchandise in one piece."

"Bullshit order, Tango." *Thanks for the name, asshole.* "The bitch cut me for chrissakes. I'm bleeding like a stuck pig."

"Vic's right," Zulu said. "She ain't right in the head."

*So, if Vic's the driver—obvious by the belt limiting blood flow—and Zulu's the pockmarked dude with a high pitch, Tango must be the eye-patched boss.*

"Did I ask for your opinion?" *Tango again.* "If she dies, it's *my* ass on the line."

Vic tightened the belt around his bloody arm, his flounder-white skin growing pastier by the second. "She'll have plenty of time to heal on the way to Japan."

Japan? Aw, shit. They did plan to return me to the ship.

While they bickered, I scrambled to my feet. Hightailed it the hell out of there, sprinting in a zigzag pattern to avoid predictability—another tip from my mentor. The golden smolder of Grandmother Moon helped guide me but didn't provide enough light to clear every obstacle in my path.

Arms pumping, I jetted up a grassy knoll, the area bereft of trees.

I ran full force, moccasins trampling the barren tundra, and prayed for my survival. As long as I kept moving, zigzagging out of reach, at least I stood a chance.

Behind me, the stampede of boots closed in faster than expected.

*Please, don't let them catch me.*

# Chapter 6

*"She wears her scars like a warrior, for they are reminders of when life tried to break her. But failed."* —Unknown Author

*2:30 a.m.*

Mayhem wrung the steering wheel, his mind riddled with endless *What-ifs?* "Do the coordinates of Cat's shared location match the app?"

In a crackling tone, Running Bear said, "No."

"Distance between the two points?"

"Just over a mile." His thumbs worked the keypad. "Aw, shit. She's heading to the summit."

Mayhem's heart sank. The absolute worst place for her. Not only could they throw her off the embankment, a jagged drop onto the rocky coastline below, but no one would hear her cries for mercy. And her captors could do anything without fear of reprisal.

The mere thought of those men touching her drove him to mental places where he should never travel.

Once he turned onto Henry Swanson Drive, he instructed Running Bear to scan the left side of the road while he skimmed the right.

Soon, the Bronco's headlights brightened the Caddy.

Several car lengths away, he pulled over. Killed the engine. They stepped out. No words exchanged between them, both fully aware of the mission.

Mayhem gave the Caddy a cursory glance inside.

Unoccupied.

He opened the back-passenger door. Blood splattered the supple leather. The trail of crimson dripped down the pig skin to the carpet. A thick smear on the doorframe led to the trunk.

On the soil by his moccasins, arterial blood pooled.

Multiple boot prints and scuff marks showed a struggle took place here. He swiped gloved fingers through the blood around a bare spot where someone had lain in the fetal position.

*I'm so sorry, Kitty Cat.*

With a quick glance at Kuruk, he snatched the weapons satchel from the trunk. On the old military road, Mayhem hugged the shadows, continually scanning right, left, and down at his phone.

Her signal remained stagnant.

Running Bear hooked an arm for him to follow off-trail. Mayhem sprinted uphill, down the other side. The barren tundra showed no signs of life. A lack of flora worked against them. Much harder to stay incognito here. No trees to climb. No bushes to help blend them into the landscape.

Smart locale on Killzme's part. An ambush would be difficult.

He latched onto Kuruk's arm. "We need a solid plan in place before we continue. They could have a sharpshooter poised and ready to kill the minute we crest the next hill."

"Agreed."

"What if we looped around to Captains Bay?"

"It's steeper, but doable. I doubt they'd expect us to approach from there."

"Precisely. It will also allow us to stay low and out of sight longer."

"Lead the way, Shadow Wolf."

Mayhem circled wide. It'd take longer to reach her now.

Fight them, Kitty Cat. Help is on the way.

# Chapter 7



Mysterious side-by-side structures loomed in the distance. Haloed by moonbeams, the bi-level bunker drew me closer with promises of safety. If only that were true. In reality, I had no clue where I was, no destination in mind. Somehow, I shook my pursuers, but I was running out of places to hide. It was only a matter of time before they caught me.

Two structures built into the earth looked like they'd survived an apocalypse. Round, rusted metal chambers bore concrete doorframes and pipes over each entrance. All the structures had one way in and no way out, including the bi-level concrete bunker, but at least that had a space from one side to the other and across the front.

Might be my safest option. I careened uphill. Skimmed the area for Killzme's goon squad before slipping inside. Old. Rank. Damp. Mildew twitched my nose.

Was this a military site?

Remnants of four circular gun mounts crouched on a concrete platform. Something happened here a long time ago. The age of the buildings proved that. And so did the creep factor, the area emitting a chilling vibe as though tortured souls still lingered to give silent testimony of the strategic importance of Unalaska in U.S. history.

I wasn't sure how or why I formed that opinion, except for the tingle to my skin, tiny body hairs rising with each step farther inside. Did this place have a mass grave?

Male voices pierced the silence.

I backed into the shadows, my spine pressed to rough, cold concrete. As quietly as possible, I separated the Velcro of my moccasin pocket to slide out my spare knife—less lethal than my curved blade, but it was all I had.

"Check battery command," Tango said. "When you're done, help us search the ammo bunkers. She couldn't've gotten far."

No clue who he spoke to. And without the proper names for these buildings, I couldn't tell if one brute or two headed my way.

Boots hit the concrete pad at the entrance—only one set. Electrical currents charged through my veins, and my heart jackhammered.

In case I died, I prayed.

*O Great Spirit, whose voice I hear in the winds and whose breath gives life to all the world, hear me! I am small and weak. I need your strength and wisdom. Let me walk in beauty and make my eyes ever behold the red and purple sunset...*

The footsteps grew closer.

*Make me wise, so I may understand the things you have taught my People. Let me learn the lessons you have hidden in every leaf and rock. I seek strength, not to be greater than my brother, but to fight my greatest enemy—myself.*

One footstep, then another. Slow. Cautious. Deliberate.

*Make me always ready to come to you so when my life ebbs, as the fading sunset, my spirit may arrive without shame.*

One footstep, then another. Any second he'd find me.

I adlibbed the ending.

*Forgive me for what I must do to survive. And please—please—protect my family. If I must die to save them, it's okay. Just don't let me suffer for long.*

The footsteps stopped in front of me.

A slow smile raised pockmarked cheeks.

Without a word, I slashed open Zulu's throat.

Meaty hands groped for the neck wound as he stumbled backward.

I lunged onto his chest, stabbing him in the eye, twisting the knife to inflict the most damage. Warm blood soaked my face, chest, and thighs, but I didn't care.

Zulu melted to the concrete.

Bloody hair dripping wet, I stood over him.

He gurgled, gasping for air.

In a squat beside him, I whispered, "If you answer one question, I'll end your suffering. Blink once for yes, two for no. Got it?"

One blink.

"Is another team meeting you here?"

He blinked once. Death rattled in his throat. And the eye hooded.

"Was that a second blink?"

Blood leaked out the corner of his mouth.

"Zulu." I shook him. "Did you blink twice?"

Limp hands slipped off the neck wound.

Unbelievable. He couldn't've waited two more seconds to die?

Near the entrance, a pebble rolled across concrete.

Uh-oh. I tugged the handle of my knife. The blade wouldn't dislodge from Zulu's eye socket. I rubbed my bloody palms on my sweatpants. Tried again.

The damn thing refused to budge.

I set one foot on his forehead for leverage. Pulled and pulled, but my hand kept slipping off the slick, bloody handle.

*Shit. Without a weapon, I'm dead.*

By the time I straightened, I sensed a presence behind me. Please don't be—I peeked over my shoulder.

A bushy tail.

When I turned, an adorable little fox met my gaze.

"Hi," I whispered. "There's an old Apache legend about you and a mountain lion." Visions of my buddy, Karma, the cougar, fled through my mind. He'd love a juicy bite of poacher meat. "You wouldn't happen to have a friend with ya?"

The fox cocked his head.

"Not important." I swayed my hand toward Zulu. "Hungry?" I hopped atop the platform with the gun mounts. "Actually, you should probably leave too." I jutted a thumb over my shoulder. "Poachers."

As though he understood, he bolted in a flash.

Seconds later, a gunshot rang out.

I winced. *Please tell me they didn't shoot the little guy. Absolute monsters.*

Once I backed through the opening, my legs dangling down the outside wall, I inched lower and lower. When my moccasins hit solid ground, a hairy arm locked around my neck, the reek of his bloody sweat invading my nostrils.

A pistol dug into my left temple.

"I don't give two shits about the buyer." Vic's evil whisper chilled me to the bone. "If you struggle or scream, I'll blow your brains out."

# Chapter 8

*"The [American] Indian knew how to live without wants, to suffer without complaint, and to die singing."*
—Alexis de Tocqueville

**3:15 a.m.**

Mayhem climbed the embankment but stayed low. At the top, he lay flat against the rough tundra. Running Bear slithered to his side. Ocean salt tinged the evening breeze.

Darkness shrouded the two-tiered Base End Station. No movement inside either level.

Voice barely audible, Mayhem whispered, "Clear lower tier." From the weapons satchel, he withdrew the tomahawk. "I'll take the top."

"Copy that."

At the bunker, Mayhem crept through the entrance. Moonlight smoldered through the lookout space, the concrete hazed in a golden luminesce. He ventured farther inside.

A dead man sprawled on the floor, arterial castoff splattered the walls. Cat severed his throat with the knife lodged in his eye socket.

*Good girl.*

After withdrawing the blade, he kept it for her.

Bloody moccasin tracks led from the body to the gun mount. Cat's escape route. The trail led up the wall. He followed. At the top, he peered down at bloody toe smears like she'd suspended herself to drop to the terrain.

He mirrored her movements.

Boot prints indented the gravel. Someone waited for her to emerge.

Fatal mistake.

More tracks showed a widened gait. Evidence of walking with another person pressed to the boot-wearer's chest.

Dear God, no.

When Running Bear arrived, he whispered, "Clear," then followed Mayhem's gaze to the gravel. He understood the tracks.

*Cat's in serious trouble.*

They hugged the shadows to circle around the back of the first ammo shed, where they flattened on the mossy roof. Muffled male voices coiled inside, but he couldn't unscramble individual words.

Running Bear flashed two fingers.

*Two men.*

The wooden door opened below them.

"Do you copy?" A stranger held a phone above him, as if searching for a cell signal. The light illuminated an eyepatch.

When the henchmen turned, he and Running Bear ducked.

Into the ammo shed, he said, "Need to run back to the Escalade for the SAT phone. Don't let her escape."

"Gimme a break, boss. Where's she gonna go?"

As Mayhem's grip tightened around the tomahawk, he popped his eyebrows. Running Bear smirked. Once the boss hit the trailhead, they climbed down. At each side of the entrance, they waited for a beat.

When the other henchman didn't emerge, Mayhem kicked in the door.

A husky male whirled around with a belt strapped to his bloody arm, a pistol triangled in front of him. "Well, well, if it ain't the infamous Redskin, the bitch's husband."

With one step forward, Mayhem hurled the tomahawk.

The hatchet blade lodged in his Adam's apple. Sloppy gunfire ricocheted off the walls as he stumbled back. Mayhem ducked but continued his pursuit. Running Bear leaped onto a stack of old wooden crates. And dove. He muscled the gun away from the white man and shot him twice in the head.

Flawless technique.

He twisted left, right. "Where's Ghost Dog?"

She wasn't on the floor, nor under any debris. "Cat?" He wrenched out the tomahawk. "Cautious Cat!"

No response.

Kuruk flipped boxes. "Ghost Dog!"

No response.

"This shed appeared longer from the outside. Did it not?" With the end of the tomahawk, Mayhem knocked on the back wall.

*Thud. Thud. Echo.*

He chopped at the hollow spot while his former protégé kicked. Soon, they'd torn apart the first layer of wooden planks.

"Do you see her, Shadow Wolf?" Fear rattled his tone.

"Let me in there." Mayhem tore through the false wall enough to squeeze into the void. "Cat?" He spun left, right. "She must be here."

Running Bear lit up the space with his phone. "Where?"

Emptiness surrounded Mayhem. "Go check the other shed." Alone in the space, his gaze fell to the floorboards. The toe of his moccasin pressed a crooked board.

*Squeak, squeak, squeak.*

Down on his knees, he wedged the hatchet head under the board to pop it loose. Bloody raven hair peeked through, and stole his breath, his heart frozen mid-beat.

"Kitty Cat?" Tears waterfalled down his cheeks. "What did those monsters—?" He tore apart the floor.

Unconscious, she lay wedged in between the rafters, covered in blood.

"Kitty Cat?" Chest heaving in desperation, he pulled off his glove to sweep bloody hair off her beautiful face. "Sweetheart?" He pressed two fingers to her neck.

Thready pulse, shallow breath. Those monsters almost suffocated her to death.

If her neck's broken, moving her might kill her. But he couldn't tell the extent of her injuries without pulling her out. With no alternative, he slipped his hands beneath her—waited to see if she stirred—then lifted her out.

Cradled in his lap, he pressed his lips to her forehead. *Please don't let me lose her.* "Where're you hurt, darlin'?" No stab wounds. No bullet holes. Not on the front, anyway. *Where is all this blood coming from?*

"Ghost Dog!" Running Bear clamored closer. "Is she—?"

He passed the tomahawk. "We need to go. Now."

"Safest route is Captains Bay."

"Agreed." He carried her to the door. "Watch my six in case the boss returns with more men."

"Copy that. Go."

Mayhem sprinted past the two-tiered Base End Station, Cat's legs dangling over his arm, her head cradled against his bare chest, blood dripping down his skin. At the embankment, he glanced back. When Running Bear gave the "all clear" signal, he stepped over the ledge.

Once he traveled far enough down, he slowed to readjust her in his arms. Moonlight cascaded over her bloodied face.

Silently pleading for more time, he kissed her perfect nose. "I'm so sorry, Kitty Cat." Tears clouded his vision, his voice crackling with pain. "I never should have made you wait in the trunk."

Beneath closed lids, her eyes rolled back and forth.

He jostled her. "Fight through the fog, Cat."

As he reached the trail below, her lashes fluttered apart. Pools of electric emeralds gazed up at him.

Somehow, he wrangled his emotions under control. "Hey, you."

She said, "What?"

"How are you?"

"What?"

He curled her hair around her ears. Blood trickled out the right side. "Can you hear me, Cat?"

She stared at his lips. "Can I what?"

"Hear me." He raised his volume. "Can you hear me?"

"Kinda. I dunno."

"Are you reading my lips? Or can you hear my voice?"

"What?"

Oh, boy.

Running Bear slid down the embankment. "How's Ghost Dog?"

"See for yourself." Mayhem turned. "Say hello."

He brushed off the seat of his khakis. "Hey, Ghost Dog."

"What?"

"I said, hey."

Her eyes squinted at his lips. "What?"

When his gaze shot to Mayhem for answers, he turned to show her right ear. "Please do not alarm her. She's unaware of the injury."

He swiveled so she couldn't read his lips. "She doesn't know?"

"Not that I'm aware of, no." When Cat leaned closer to his mouth, he held a tight smile. "And it needs to stay that way for now."

"Won't she figure it out?"

He cradled her head against his shoulder. "Potentially, yes. Until then, let's not panic her."

"Hey, it's your funeral."

"I am painfully aware of that, thank you." Cat did not take kindly to being kept in the dark. What choice did he have? She just regained consciousness.

Mayhem trekked down the trail that led to the old military road. At the end, he jabbed a chin for Running Bear to take the lead. They must stay vigilant. If Killzme sent another team, an all-out war could break out, with casualties on both sides.

That, he could never allow. Under no circumstances would he let Cat sustain any more injuries. As it stood now, she'd lost the ability to hear in one or both ears—a disability that could prove disastrous in the wilderness, where she needed all her senses to function.

Perhaps the hearing loss was merely temporary. Once Jacy Lee evaluated her, they'd know more. For now, he kept her quiet. Panic or hysteria would only amplify this dangerous situation.

Following Running Bear, he crossed the old military road.

Bunker Hill and its surrounding tundra emitted an unnerving stillness. The summit's vantage point and Mount Ballyhoo were strategic locations for coastal defense during World War II. After the Japanese bombed Dutch Harbor in 1942, the U.S. Military mounted four 144 mm Panama guns at the two-tiered Base End Station—the area known as Hill 400 then—with the capability of firing in a three-hundred-sixty-degree radius.

As they neared Henry Swanson Road, Running Bear gestured toward a side trail. The Bronco might be down that end, but the Caddy was straight ahead.

"Take her, please." He transferred Cat into his arms. When her brow furrowed, he said, "I need to secure the Caddy."

"What?"

Nice and slow, he accentuated each word. "I. Will. Meet. You. Soon."

"Okay, cool," she said, as if she had no idea where she was or what she'd endured.

He and Running Bear exchanged a befuddled glance.

"Once she's safely in the Bronco, head to Miss Redfeather's house. I shall meet you out front."

"Copy that. What if"—he pressed her head to his shoulder—"she asks questions?"

"Sidestep."

"Ghost Dog doesn't like that."

"I am painfully aware of that, as well. Do the best you can."

"Be careful, Shadow Wolf."

"Always."

Running Bear veered onto the side trail.

Mayhem stayed straight. *O Great Spirit, please let them make it out safely.*

If Killzme made a move, Cat was in no condition to fight back.

# Chapter 9

*5:00 a.m.*

Behind a typical Alaskan cabin, dark reds burned the horizon, embered like coals in a fire, hastened only by dark charcoal clouds. Stripes of salmon interspersed through deep purple bands that warned of turbulence.

Hints of amber kissed the treetops, limbs reaching for Father Sky to celebrate the birth of a new day, the chance to fix yesterday's mistakes, the future full of possibilities. But darkness still cloaked the street. The in between time, as *Shicheii* called it, when the night yearned to reign longer.

From the passenger seat, I marveled at the riches of Mother Earth. "It's so beautiful." When I turned, I startled when Mr. Mayhem wasn't beside me. "Running Bear?" My gaze zipped across the front seat. "This isn't the Caddy."

He smiled.

"Whose vehicle is this?"

He pointed at the unfamiliar house.

"Say something."

Another smile.

"Why aren't you talkin' to me? Did something happen?" I twisted to peer into the backseat. "Where's Shadow Wolf?"

His lips moved but no words escaped.

"What's wrong with you?" A realization flooded my eyes with tears. "Is he dead?" I wailed. "Break it to me gently." I hiked my knees to my chest and rocked, my heart shredded like meat through a grinder. "Oh, God, he's dead. Isn't he?"

Running Bear tapped my shoulder. He said something, but I was so hysterical I didn't catch it.

"What?"

"He—"

Shaking my head, I fingered my right ear. Blood. What the hell?

He leaned closer, hot breath striking my left cheek. "He's not dead."

"Really? Then where is he?"

Again, he leaned forward. And I leaned back.

"What's up with you?"

Closer and closer, he moved. "Ghost Dog—"

"What?"

The hand signals confused me. *What's wrong with him?* I was this close to giving him a piece of my mind when my door flew open. Mr. Mayhem said something, but I didn't catch it. "What?"

He smiled. I smiled back. Then all the blood registered, his chiseled torso and one cheek bathed in crimson.

"Are you alright?"

Nodding, he swayed an opened hand out the door.

"Say something."

The hand rolled as if he wanted me to hurry, but I held firm.

"Tell me what's goin' on first."

"Cat, please." His lips formed the words, but no sound escaped.

Confusion rocked my senses. "Say that again."

"Cat, please."

"Why can't I hear you?"

I swear he rolled his eyes, like this wasn't news to him. When I parted my lips to question him again, he scooped me off the passenger seat, ushering me into the Caddy.

His lips mouthed, "I. Will. Explain. Later." He jutted a stiff finger downward. "Now." He motioned between us. "We." Two fingers waved down the road. "Must. Leave."

*What's with the hand signals?* "Why?"

Head rocking, he closed the door. Running Bear slid into the backseat.

Halfway down the road, a black Escalade appeared in the side mirror. Killzme. Shit. How long had they been following him?

Mr. Mayhem said something into the rearview mirror, but I only caught intermittent words. "Text. Meet."

Not sure what that meant.

When Running Bear spoke, I narrowed in on his lips. "Whatever you need, Shadow Wolf."

"Thank you." He glanced at both side mirrors. And soon, the Caddy slowed. He held up one finger, and I think he said something like, "Wait for my signal." Then he veered toward the wood line but didn't stop. "Now."

Running Bear rolled out, the door closing behind him. Heart in my throat, my gaze bounced from window to window, but I couldn't find him anywhere. "Where'd he go?"

He tapped my leg, mouthed, "He's fine, Cat."

"Are you sure?" I leaned halfway out the window to scan the dark road behind us, my hair wriggling in the wind like Medusa's snakes. "What if we ran him over?"

When he grabbed the back of my tee, I slipped into my seat. After two more sharp turns, he slowed enough for the black Escalade to catch up.

"Whaddaya doin'?"

He laced his fingers through mine, and somehow, I knew, deep in my core, he was allowing Running Bear time to pick up *Shicheii*, Poe, and Spirit Crow.

"Shit." I slapped my forehead. "I didn't pack."

He pulled me close, his cheek nudging mine to turn my head, minty fresh breath striking my ear. "Not to worry, Cat. He will gather our belongings. Now, could you please call your grandfather?"

"And say what?"

Again, he spoke directly into my ear. "Tell him we're delayed. Running Bear will pick him up, and we shall meet him at the rendezvous spot."

"You said you'd explain why I can't hear."

"And I will. For now, after you tell your grandfather to expect Running Bear, please pass me the phone. Remember, we cannot lie to an elder."

*Shit.* There's no way *Shicheii* won't know something's fishy.

# Chapter 10

*"If only our eyes saw souls instead of bodies. How different our ideals of beauty would be."* —Lauren Jauregui

***5:45 a.m.***

Once Mayhem shook their tail again, he banged a left into Klee's driveway, following the long, winding pavement to the hanger out back. While he cruised, his mind drifted back to Kimi's grave. To protect his loved ones, he'd forfeited a proper farewell. Though her soul had reincarnated into the angelic Spirit Crow, he'd miss the Sacred Land that held her Holy vessel.

Nor could he thank Odin for staying behind to guard the grave. He'd become a valued family member. Already, he missed his happy *gronks* and heartfelt song.

Why did Jacy Lee meddle with Killzme Corp? Couldn't he foresee this storm? As the largest animal trafficking ring in the country, hadn't they proven they'd kill to protect their bottom line?

Mayhem was not unsympathetic to his plight. As a powerful Diné Medicine Man, Jacy Lee could only handle so much. It simply was not in his nature to walk away from someone in need. Thus, the double murder plot had pushed him past his breaking point.

But at what cost?

In the future, he and Cat must take greater care to shield their elder from the uglier aspects of their missions.

"Hey." She searched for eye contact. "I sense sadness. You alright?"

My, her perception has reached remarkable new heights. "I am." Now parked, he reassured her with a gentle cup of her cheek, his lips stressing each word. "Thank you for asking, Kitty Cat."

"It's what we do, right?"

Grinning, he rocked a yes. "We do." While holding her gaze a moment longer, he wove all his fingers with hers to close their energy circle. "We need to wash up with the garden hose." He jabbed a chin at the outside spigot. "We also need to unload the trunk before Jacy Lee arrives."

"The arsenal of weapons?"

Closing their energy circle worked. Evidently, if they stayed united, she understood every word. "Our tools of the trade, yes."

"I'm on it." She leaped out the door.

Over the roof, he motioned for her to follow.

After they rinsed blood off their hair, skin, and moccasins, each went their separate ways to slip into dry clothes. Then they got to work.

While Shawnee loaded her arms at the trunk, he unlocked the padlock on the wide double doors of the hanger. Even without an explanation, she was handling her deficit remarkably well.

Perhaps she'd recalled the events leading up to the injury, and that brought her comfort. Or she stayed in denial. Difficult to determine which. Nor did it matter. Mayhem created ways around Kimi's ALS to help her live a full and happy life, and he'd do the same for Cat.

Inside the hanger, a high-end Cessna gleamed under florescent lights. It boasted a gorgeous tan-and-black interior, plush leather seats—four behind the two in the cockpit—and ample space for luggage and other belongings.

Shawnee lugged over various duffels and satchels to load in the cargo hold. The heavier, bulkier items he carried, all of which he tucked out of sight mere seconds before Kuruk's Jeep Cherokee rolled to a stop in the driveway.

With so little room left in the cargo hold, he instructed Running Bear to store the luggage behind the passenger seats. "Also"—he passed the key fob—"please have the Caddy detailed. Charge the card I gave you."

"Copy that."

"Thank you. I appreciate you more than words can express."

"No problem. I'll monitor the cabin and Sacred Land, as well."

"Above and beyond." Mayhem tucked him into a warm embrace. "We'll see you soon. Don't forget to update your phone."

Jacy Lee exited the vehicle. Deep creases in his forehead and around the eyes showed concern. Perched on his shoulder, Spirit Crow refused to acknowledge Mayhem, her head hung low, a pale bill resting on her chest feathers. Cradled in his arm, Poe shot Dad an icy glare.

"I realize this situation is less than ideal," he said to the sorrowful faces in front of him. "However, the quicker we leave Alaska, the safer we'll be. So, if you wouldn't mind boarding the aircraft, I'd greatly appreciate it."

Without a word, they headed into the hanger.

"Thank you."

No one turned or responded. This would undoubtedly be a long trip.

# Chapter 11

*11:03 a.m.*

During the flight to Montana, *Shicheii* examined my eardrums. He reassured me the hearing in the left ear would normalize soon. The right had damage from that scumbag, Vic, who fired his gun centimeters away. Not getting a straight answer about the severity didn't thrill me, but he might not know without in-depth tests. Which, he explained, would need to wait till we arrived at our destination.

With his sultry voice inside my head, he telepathically communicated like animals in the wild. Dodging questions about my injury sucked. To sidestep without lying, I steered the conversation in a new direction. And soon, we were having a true heart-to-heart about life and the future—a special talk we might not have had otherwise.

The elevation sent stabbing pain deep into my eardrums, but I sucked it up so I wouldn't worry him. My grandfather was such a loving, empathetic soul. If he discovered what triggered the series of events that led to my injury, he'd never forgive himself.

Mr. Mayhem must've called his name because *Shicheii's* warm gaze shot to the cockpit. When he refocused on me, his voice rang clear in my mind.

*Cheveyo was asking for a progress report. How did this happen, honey?*

"Umm, well..."

Again, his attention diverted to the cockpit. *Cheveyo needs you.*

"Okay. Thanks." When I darted into the cockpit, Poe had already stolen my seat, so I stood between them, a hand on the back of each headrest. "What's up?"

He gestured for me to lower my good ear to his lips.

"Our destination is up ahead." Minty fresh breath struck the side of my face. "Please prepare Jacy Lee and Spirit Crow."

"I'm on it."

When I turned, he latched onto my forearm.

Into my ear, he said, "Would you mind if Poe sat in your lap?"

"*Aack.*" I shot the little diva a glare. "Fine."

"Thank you, Cat. I appreciate your cooperation."

Poe tossed me the stink eye, and I stuck out my tongue. "Lemme tell *Shicheii* first." I pivoted. "We're landing. Are you buckled?"

*I am, honey. Thank you.*

"Okay, cool." I transferred Spirit Crow from an empty headrest into his lap. "For your safety."

When her bill parted, I imagined her usual cooing.

"Love you, too." I scooted into the cockpit. "They're all set." When I cleared my throat for Poe to move, the little bastard refused. "Fine. You'll crash when we land. Hope your new tail feathers don't fall out."

Appalled, the bill parted.

Mr. Mayhem shot me an icy glare of his own, then must've sweet-talked his beloved crow companion, because Pissy Pants climbed onto the window ledge. God forbid he let me pick him up.

Once I slid into the co-pilot's seat, Poe climbed into my lap. Tossed one more distrustful stare my way before sitting with his shiny black-feathered back to me. Friggin' diva needed an attitude adjustment.

Mr. Mayhem focused on something below us. What, I had no idea. All I found were wide swaths of unbroken wilderness.

Where'd he plan to land this thing? When the nose of the plane dipped downward, I could no longer hold in my concerns. "Where, umm...?"

No clue how he responded, but his demeanor didn't exactly ooze confidence, eagle-eyed on an invisible landing strip.

Not good.

On the descent, a tiny strip of dirt emerged through heavily wooded terrain. No way would he attempt to land there. He'd have to be out of his friggin' mind.

"Hope you're not planning to land on a hiking trail."

As usual, he ignored me.

"Seems like you're heading straight for it."

Sure enough, we came in hot—too hot, in my opinion. The tires slammed into the packed earth, the speed pinning me to the headrest, one hand seat-belting Poe. Tree branches whipped the wingtips, the whole plane vibrating beneath us.

I squeezed my eyes closed. *Please, don't let us crash.* Moments later, all movement ceased, but before I could even part my eyes, Poe stabbed my hand.

"Sonofa—" I let go. "Do it again, and I'll knock you into next week."

"And you wonder why he doesn't like you." With his mouth next to my ear, he lowered his forearm for his brat. Daddy's Boy stepped aboard, eyes thinned and glaring at me, ready to slice my throat when I least expected it.

"You're calling *me* out?" I didn't love the proximity of Poe to my face, but I rolled with it. "He started it."

"You are the adult."

"Just sayin'."

Dammit. Why'd I always end up in the doghouse? Pissy Pants probably did it on purpose. When I followed them out of the cockpit, Poe turned on his dad's shoulder, and I swear that crow winked at me. Friggin' psycho.

While Mr. Mayhem assisted me out of the plane—not that I needed the help, but my legs were still a little shaky from the landing—a middle-aged man with two long, leather-wrapped braids strolled toward us. Instead of greeting us, he approached my grandfather.

Did they know each other? When I covered my bad ear, voices pierced the silence. Not loud, but enough to decode what they were saying if I concentrated.

"Klee," *Shicheii's* pitch rose with excitement, "I haven't seen you in ages. How are you?"

"I'm well, thank you. It's so nice to see you." When they shook hands, a somberness rolled over the stranger's pronounced cheekbones and wide nose. "Ferron and I meant to reach out when we heard the tragic news, but we didn't know what to say. Too many years had passed between us. Please accept our deepest apologies. We should have called."

*Was he talking about the death of my parents? Who is this guy?*

"No need, my friend. Cheveyo told me you and Ferron were praying for us." They embraced. "Forgive yourself, Klee. No one blames you. Now, let it go. Human hearts weren't built to carry such a heavy burden."

*Blame him for what?* Unsure of what to make of this stranger, I hung back to let things play out. *Let go of what? Did he tell Red Buffalo where to find Mom and Dad?*

Mr. Mayhem sidled up beside me. "No."

"No, what? I didn't say anything."

"You didn't have to, Cat. It's written all over your face."

I gnashed my teeth. "Stay outta my head."

Leaning closer, he held my gaze. "He's family."

*Uh-huh, we'll see about that.*

When he pulled away, his eyebrows rose. Think Poe would stay out of it? Hell, no. That punk leaned forward to toss another scowl, and it took all my power not to knock him off his human perch. Instead, I swayed a defiant shoulder at him and his dad. Whatever.

With my bad ear covered, I refocused on *Shicheii* and the alleged family member. *Jury's still out on this guy.* Too bad I couldn't call Running Bear. He'd tell me the truth. But Mr. Mayhem said we couldn't have contact till he at least upgraded his phone. Even then, he claimed it wasn't safe with Killzme poking around. If they found out he knew our location, they might try to torture him for our whereabouts.

Good luck with that. Running Bear might be a lot of things, but he wasn't stupid or careless. Still, since he asked me not to call, I agreed.

"Great to see you, as always." Mr. Mayhem and Klee embraced. "Did Ferron decide"—unintelligible—"at the house?"

"You know her. Mama Hen wants everything perfect for you."

He chuckled. "Your wife is a saint."

"Klee"—*Shicheii* slung an arm around his shoulders—"I want you to meet someone." Arm in arm, they approached me. "This is my granddaughter. She's dealing with an ear injury." He said it the way some might break the news of a death in the family.

Klee's dark eyes widened. "Mourning Dove?" Not only could I read his lips perfectly, but I picked up on the timbre of his tone, his voice warm and inviting. "It's an honor to finally meet you. Cheveyo told us of your mentorship. I understand you're a quite impressive warrior in your own right."

*Aww, he said that?* "Thanks." I shook Klee's hand, my mind whirling with ways to dig for information. "Have you known each other long?"

"All his life, not mine."

"Did you know my mom?"

"Know her?" A smile brightened his face. "I wanted to marry her."

This guy could've been my dad? "Then why didn't you?"

"Oh, my, you're direct. All right. Fair question. The truth is, I never worked up the courage to—"

"Cat"—Mr. Mayhem slung his arm around my shoulders—"we do not have time for this conversation, I'm afraid."

*Shicheii's* voice emerged in my mind. *Cheveyo's right, honey. Leave the past where it is.*

*I'm sorry, but I can't. Not when it's about Mom.*

*Your feelings are valid, my love. When you're ready, we'll talk about it.*

"It was an honor to meet you, Mourning Dove."

Okay, so maybe Klee wasn't a bad guy. Still didn't explain his feelings for Mom or what scared him away. And who was he related to? Or did "family" mean close friend?

The jostle from my mentor jarred me out of the haze of endless questions. "Nice to meet you, too."

We all piled into a black Mercedes SUV with plush leather seats, tinted windows, and a dashboard that totally rocked with a huge built-in monitor, multiple vents, and a steering wheel built for speed. The interior's sleek design included a neon purple strip outlining key features across the dash, around the center console on both sides, and accenting each door.

What'd Klee do for a living? The guy obviously wasn't hurting for cash.

The house he drove us to amazed me. A log home nestled into the wilderness, the nearest neighbor multiple acres away. On the covered porch, a woman waited with an inviting smile and shiny dark hair pulled into a loose bun. A basket of vegetables sat beside her free-flowing skirt, the hem dangling above her bare feet. She wore beaded anklets and rings on several rose-polished toes.

To not miss a second of this conversation, I covered my bad ear.

"Nice to see you, darlin'." Mr. Mayhem kissed her cheek. "Why do you never age?"

"Stop." Giggling, she play-swatted his chest. She turned her attention to Poe, perched on his shoulder. "Aren't you a handsome little fella?" Her dark gaze shifted back to her longtime friend. Or family member. Not sure which yet. "He's the spitting image of Thoreau."

Mr. Mayhem's guffaw warmed my soul. "Isn't he? Poe's feistier than his father but no less impressive."

*Rattle, rattle. Rattle, rattle.*

Oh, please. Someone shoot me.

Why everyone swooned all over Pissy Pants, I had no clue. And sure, he might rock the gold jewelry, but it's only because bling glittered more on black feathers. Any corvid donning a three-hundred-dollar necklace and custom-made ankle band could do the same.

"Ferron"—he dragged me closer—"*this* is Cat. Rather, Shawnee." He stumbled over my name before adding, "Mourning Dove."

Huh. Did she make him nervous? Or did introducing me rattle him? Hmm... Maybe Klee and Ferron were his actual family members.

"Ohhh..." Her tone indicated they'd discussed me at length. "I've been dying to meet you." She hugged me so hard she almost cracked my ribcage. "Your mother had the kindest soul. What an exquisite woman, inside and out." She stroked my hair. "I'm sorry you lost her so early in life."

Something told me she meant every word.

Her warm palms cradled my face. "Now, I know you have your grandfather and Cheveyo as confidantes, but if you ever need a woman's perspective, I'm here for you, always and forever."

Her mothering nature left me speechless.

"I mean it. Don't hesitate to call. Anytime, day or night."

All I could manage was a simple, "Thank you."

Something about her was so inviting. Nothing I could nail down. Maybe her caring nature drew me in, or how sandalwood and jasmine caressed my senses when she neared, conjuring sweet memories of my childhood home. Or the way she swayed like a warm, gentle breeze, her aura radiating tenderness and love, trust and loyalty—a rock-solid foundation on which to stand. Or rest awhile, if someone in her flock needed a respite.

Did she comfort Mr. Mayhem when he lost Kimi? I wouldn't rule it out.

"If you haven't guessed, Cat," his raspy voice pulled me from my thoughts, "Ferron is our Mama Hen. She's also our sounding board and the voice of reason." His palms swept up and down her outer arms. "Thank you for such a magnanimous offer. Now"—he stepped back—"if you ladies will excuse me, I better move Jacy Lee along, or they might never leave the Mercedes."

"Don't blame him, Cheveyo. Klee can talk the varnish off a rocking chair." She snaked one arm around my waist. How she knew to position herself to my left, I had no idea, but she seemed fully informed. "Let me show you where everything is so you'll be comfortable here."

I stopped mid-stride. "We're staying here?"

"Cheveyo didn't tell you. Why am I not surprised? Men." With a slight shake of the head, her eyes rolled upward.

*Love her.*

"To answer your question, yes. Consider this your home away from home. I wish we could stay to help you acclimate, but I'm afraid Klee and I need to head back to Dutch Harbor soon."

"You don't mind us staying here without you?"

"Why would I?" She acted like handing over her property was a perfectly natural thing to do. "You're family."

If *Shicheii* and Mr. Mayhem taught me anything, it's that Native People cared for one another in a way Caucasians did not. No matter the miles between them, the community rallied around each other, celebrated achievements, danced and sang and prayed for the betterment of all. If one family suffered, everyone shared their pain. A camaraderie unlike anything I'd ever experienced.

The farther I ventured into my destiny, the more I learned I'd never again feel alone, isolated, or abandoned. In a sense, I'd finally found my way home.

Wooden trusses with black and gleaming brackets braced the rich pine ceiling and cathedral-high log walls of the great room, with thick natural beams. A glass wall showered sunlight across high-end floors.

Ferron gave me the full tour.

At the top of the stairs, the second level split into an opened loft on one side, a bedroom suite on the other. At the end of the hall, the great room's glass wall continued straight up. We stopped to bask in the wooded landscape backdropped by mountain ranges.

The California king in the upstairs bedroom surprised me, as did the spaciousness. Log bureaus and dressers matched the headboard, loveseat frame, and single chair in the corner.

She led me downstairs to an overstuffed sofa, matching loveseat, and leather chair—all chocolate-brown—with red-plaid toss pillows, a silhouette of a bear paw stamped dead-center, same as the area rug. A black pole extended from the second floor into the first and held a tangled knot of antlers, tiny white lights woven through bone.

With a never-ending eyeful, I low-whistled. "What a gorgeous home."

"Aren't you sweet." She gave me a light squeeze. "Thank you, Mourning Dove. Come. I'll show you the kitchen. Do you like to cook?"

"Um, no, not really. *Shicheii* does, though."

Too polite to say, "I know," an inner light brightened her flawless skin as she escorted me into an outstanding chef's kitchen with charcoal granite counters and matching island, glass-fronted wood cabinets, and a copper sink. A breakfast nook nestled in the corner, the seats covered with thick, red-plaid cushions. The stovetop held six burners, two ovens built into a stone feature wall. And the smoky-glass-fronted fridge—also built-in—might be the fanciest I'd ever seen.

Which was saying something. As a former cat burglar, I'd prowled through many high-valued homes.

On the kitchen wall hung a primitive wooden plaque with a leather-skinned face.

"What is that?" I didn't dare touch it. "Looks antique."

"This is an ancient war shield carried into battles by one of my ancestors."

"To stop bullets?"

"Arrows, mainly. And to redirect larger projectiles like spears."

"So cool." Why could I hear her so well? Was my left ear clearing already?

I padded across the slate kitchen floor, trying to absorb the kindness of handing over a house like this.

"Klee and I grocery shopped yesterday. Do try the vegetables from my garden." She set the basket on the island. "Freshly picked this morning for you."

"Ferron, I don't know how to thank you."

"Honey"—she smoothed her hands down my hair—"I realize this is a lot to absorb, but I have loved you since birth. Your mom sent photos of every birthday, every achievement, no matter how minor. When the dark times hit, Cheveyo and I prayed for you to find your light. Now, look at you. You're a gorgeous, intelligent, confident woman in your prime."

She locked me in another bear hug. "I'm so tickled you're here, Mourning Dove."

By the time she'd finished showering me with love, I was so overwhelmed. Tears brimmed my eyes, and I could only nod. It took a while for me to wrangle my emotions under control. "Can I ask you somethin'?"

"Of course."

"Is it strange that I reference him as Mister Mayhem?"

"Not at all. Many do. We earn names throughout life. Some represent an achievement—Cheveyo earned his epithet for being an impressive and frightening warrior who showed no mercy to the enemy—others symbolize a person's attributes, like Mourning Dove, Cat, or Ghost Dog."

She knew my Apache name?

"Those who meet or form bonds during that period will often refer to the person by the name given to them. In simpler terms, your use of Cheveyo's epitaph does not differ from him calling you Cautious Cat. It allows you both anonymity in public spaces. In private, I'm sure Cheveyo would answer to just about anything. He's an accommodating soul."

"When we worked undercover in Alaska, I called him sugar bear."

"Adorable." She tittered. "How'd that go over?"

I glanced over my shoulder to ensure he wasn't heading our way. "Between us, I think he kinda liked it."

Her smile couldn't stretch any wider. "Cheveyo's a good man. Who knows where destiny might take you two?"

Did she feel the chemistry between us?

"I'm glad you felt comfortable enough to ask."

For some reason, I got the impression no question was off-limits.

"Klee and I feel blessed to play a minor role in your becoming."

"Whaddaya mean?"

"Many never walk their true path, opting instead for the easy road. Smooth, safe, careful to avoid speed bumps. Fulfilling one's destiny is difficult and complicated and rife with challenges, but you and Cheveyo are chasing rainbows for a better tomorrow. And that, sweet Mourning Dove, is truly commendable. Your darling mother is so proud."

Is? Not was? Could Ferron speak to the dead?

# Chapter 12

*"What's broken can be mend-
ed. What hurts can be healed.
And no matter how dark it
gets, The Sun will rise again."*
—Unknown Author

*Monday, 12:33 p.m.*

Behind the wheel of the Mercedes, Mayhem drove his family back to the high-end bush plane. "I'm pleased we visited awhile. Thank you for staying to welcome Cat. It meant a lot to me to see you two bond last night."

In the passenger seat, Ferron emitted a dispirited somberness. "She knows more than you think she does, Cheveyo."

An empty pit widened inside him. "How much more?"

"She's close to unraveling the pieces you've withheld. You best tread lightly. She's cued in on you. It wouldn't surprise me if your hearts beat in synchronicity."

He smirked. "Some may call that a necessity. We do work as a team."

"You can hide from yourself but not from me." A wave of sandalwood and jasmine struck him as she leaned over the middle console to not be ignored. "I see you, Cheveyo. Even more than you think I do."

"Is that so?" She still hadn't backed away. "I wonder if you nudged Cat in the right direction."

Only then did she slide over.

Klee's neck craned around the passenger seat to speak with his wife. "Please tell me you didn't."

"She deserves the truth." Her tone chilled. "All of it, no matter how painful."

"Never have I lied to her, Ferron."

"I don't doubt that—it's not in your nature—but it still does not absolve you from telling her. Mourning Dove has more layers than an onion. How long do you plan to peel her?"

Ooh, that woman knew right where to push. "For as long as it takes."

"To what end?" Her voice boomed. "Her destruction?"

Stunned silent, her words slapped him across the face.

"That's unfair, darling." Again, Klee came to his rescue. "Cheveyo would never let that happen."

Near the plane moments later, Mayhem slid the shifter into Park. "With all due respect, Ferron, if you truly believe I would let Cat self-destruct, then you don't see me at all."

Her breathy exhale showed annoyance. "Once again, you two have misinterpreted my words. Men." Her head shook as she exited the vehicle.

Mayhem followed her to the cargo hold, where he and Klee transferred weapons and supplies to the Mercedes.

When he returned to the plane to bid Ferron farewell, she refused his affection.

"Tell her, Cheveyo. Or I will."

An invisible bullet sailed through his core. "I presume this is your line in the sand?"

"It is."

"What if you're wrong?"

"I'm not."

As much as he longed to believe her, he couldn't risk it. "I need more time."

"Are you planning to retrieve the Caddy when you're done here?"

"I am."

"Come for dinner. You'll tell me all about your chat then. In the interim, stop blaming yourself. You did the best you could under impossible circumstances."

The memory wilted him inside. "What if Cat doesn't see it that way?"

"You won't lose her, Cheveyo." Embracing him, she whispered, "Your destinies are intertwined."

Mayhem's iPhone vibrated in his pocket.

"Give Cheyenne my love."

While she and Klee boarded the aircraft, he withdrew his cell. The caller ID showed his daughter's name. Even after all these years, Ferron's intuition still surprised him.

"Cheyenne?" The mountains toyed with cellular signals. "Cheyenne?"

The call disconnected.

With the dark cloud of despair baring down on him, he leaned against the Mercedes. How would Cat have any inkling about the events of that night? Did she sense his guilt? His anguish? The closer they became, the more this secret crushed him.

How much did Cat trust him? Surface level, perhaps. She had difficulty in that area, and for good reason. Most everyone in her life had let her down.

Oh, how he longed to be the man she could count on, lean on, turn to in her darkest hour. How could he expect unconditional trust with this haunting secret lingering between them? Ferron was right. The only way to progress—together—was to reveal the one thing he never wanted her to know.

The Cessna taxied down the dirt runway.

Mayhem tapped a Dunhill International Red on the leathered face of his gold cigarette case. The first drag filled his lungs. Exhaling a billowed plume conjured images within the smoky haze, fleeting glimpses of how his talk with Cat might play out. Where he'd take her. How to broach the subject in the kindest way possible. More importantly, how their conversion might end.

Could she forgive him? Or would she consider his actions unforgivable?

# Chapter 13



Why do we judge an animal's intelligence by our ability to understand them?

The jet lag combined with sleeping in a strange bed wore me out. Ferron and Klee were generous hosts, but I couldn't relax with the palpable tension between the two most important men in my life. Though Mr. Mayhem masked it well, I could tell *Shicheii's* meddling still pissed him off.

For fresh air, I moseyed down the stairs of the covered porch. Rubbing my tired eyes, I ventured into the yard with my head down, my mind whirling with the chaos of leaving Alaska and my subsequent talk with Ferron, windswept hair shielding my face.

A low rumble shook the earth.

A spade-shaped hoof stepped into my sightline.

Frozen mid-stride, it took me a minute to work up enough courage to raise my head. *Please let it be a deer and not a…*

My gaze inched up the burnt sienna legs and furry culottes of an American Buffalo. All the oxygen in my lungs escaped. Dirt, pollen, and grasses coated a straggly beard and wet nose. Furious eyes bulged out the sockets—a six-foot impenetrable wall of rage deadlocked on me.

I couldn't move, couldn't breathe, my moccasins rooted to the grass. Frozen in place, I fell under his thrall. Two feet separated me from the most Herculean land mammal in North America.

A gazillion things coursed through my mind in seconds.

*Shicheii* taught me how to gauge a Bison's mood. If the tail hung loose and switched, the animal felt relaxed. Not so with the enraged individual towering me. His tail flexed upward, the fluffy end bent forward like a scorpion. The hair on his ginormous shoulder hump hackled. Even his thick, grayish-black tongue stiffened, the muscular organ protruded out his mouth, long strings of saliva dripping from black lips.

Uh-oh. Not good.

Why, why, why, why, why did I leave the porch? No one even knew I strolled outside. If I'd stayed near the stairs, the Bison's near-sightedness might help me. Not now, while he stood close enough to kiss. Everything about his demeanor screamed our chance encounter flipped a sullen and disgruntled switch.

When he snorted, a watery mist smacked my face, lashes fluttering to clear the phlegm.

*O Great Spirit, please don't let my journey end this way. I might deserve it after all the crap I've pulled over the years, but I'm not ready to die. Not yet. The Innocent Ones, including the pissed off individual in front of me, count on us to stop their destruction.*

Foot after careful foot, I backed away. The closest tree stood about ten feet behind me, to the right of the covered porch. If I made it there in time, I might survive this encounter. Keyword—might.

Slow and steady, I expanded the distance between us. If I tripped, it'd be game over. At that point, I could only play dead, even though the act probably wouldn't fool him. If I made it to the tree, I could climb. Then I might have a shot of escaping his wrath.

The little voice inside me screamed for me to do something—anything—before the inevitable unfolded.

*Move your ass, Daniels!*

I whirled around.

Inside the log home stood Poe. The wall of windows shielded him from the danger breathing down my neck. Think he'd call for *Shicheii*? Hell, no. That punk couldn't wait to see me gored by two pointed horns.

Time chugged.

One arm flexed forward, the other back, my legs moving but not gaining traction fast enough. The stench of rotten eggs, wet clay, and santal assaulted my sinuses. I couldn't scream without startling the ginormous beast behind me. I also couldn't gain enough speed to outrun my pursuer. American Buffalo sprinted at thirty-five to forty miles per hour. They hopped high fences and even swam. The only thing they couldn't do was climb.

Please let me reach the tree in time.

A hair-raising bellow shot over my shoulder, hot breath parting the back of my hair. Why wasn't anyone stopping this? Would my family find me sprawled on the ground, impaled through the heart? How'd this happen? I only stepped out for fresh air. Why'd that piss him off?

Cloven hooves clamored behind me, the earth quaking from one ton of fury.

*Love you, Shicheii.*

An enormous head scooped me off my feet. My legs dangled down his muzzle, my ass cushioned by thick curly fur. In a split-second, he flung me twenty feet in the air, conifer branches and a cloudless sky strobe-lighting as I dropped. When I slammed against solid ground, the force knocked the wind out of me, and I rolled to my back, arms flapped open like Jesus on the cross.

In total surrender, I gulped the air. Braced for another strike. Or stomped to death.

Cloven hooves stampeded away, Mother Earth vibrating beneath me.

Still couldn't move.

Pain spindled up my spine, a deep throb pulsated through my limbs. Father Sun's rays reached for me, spears of sunlight heating me from the inside out, my body temperature rising higher by the second. Trickles of sweat needled my scalp, watery eyes leaking past my temples. Even my hair sagged, long strands plastered across my nose and chin.

*Ca-caw, caw, caw, caw, caw!*

Now Poe alerted? Friggin' psycho probably enjoyed the show. If I could find the strength to crawl to my feet, I might be tempted to yank out all his new tail feathers. Sadly, that'd have to wait. My body ached from head to toe. But if I didn't summon the power to rise soon, I could die out here.

What if the Buffalo left to notify his herd? Or worse, a massive grizzly or Wolf pack found me. No way wouldn't they partake in a free meal. And yet, there I lay. Easy prey for predators in the thick forest around the log home.

*Aw, shit.*

Monstrous wings circled overhead. One bird from the pack of six swooped low for a closer inspection. Its bald head sent shockwaves through my system. Vultures. Fuck. They're such efficient feeders, they could pick prey clean in less than thirty minutes. Some went one step further and devoured the bones as well, to ensure they didn't waste a morsel.

During the flight from Alaska, Mr. Mayhem shared another of his "fun facts"—translated through *Shicheii*—as though he'd foreseen this moment. If he did, a little heads up would've been nice. He told the story of a female hiker who'd fallen off a cliff in France. Griffon vultures consumed her corpse in forty-five minutes flat. Rescuers only found bare bones, shredded clothes, and shoes.

All my nerves fired at once, my body twitching from electrical impulses rocketing through my veins.

Did Griffon vultures patrol Montana skies? Golden and Bald Eagles called this region home. And neither shied away from an easy meal. Common ravens also scavenged. If we hadn't left Odin behind, he'd notify the kettle of vultures to leave me alone.

'Course, he would've also alerted a lot sooner than his psychotic crow cousin. No doubt about it, Poe enjoyed every second of my torment. Hell, he probably still watched from the window, munching on a fruit cup, praying to the crow gods to eject me from the family once and for all.

Total opposite of his mom, who would've immediately called for help, even waited with me till they arrived. Plus, she'd shower me with feathery head rubs and preen my hair. Not Poe. After one brief series of caws, he stayed uncharacteristically silent. Punk.

*Hey, how'd I hear him?*

A car door slammed shut.

*Oh, my God. I caught that, too. Shicheii's right. My left ear's already clearing. Still nothing but crackling in the right, but at least I wasn't totally deaf.*

Footfalls pattered closer.

"Oh, my." Gray, almost translucent, eyes gazed down at me, his soft stare connecting with my soul, my labored breath relaxing into an easy rhythm. A long single braid dangled in front of his shoulder, loose strands tickling my neck. "How are you, Cat?"

"If we're being totally honest, I've had better days."

A smirk lingered right below the surface. "Welcome to Yellowstone."

"For the record, I don't find the humor in this at all."

"Too soon?" His throat cleared. "Noted."

If this was day one of the mission, I could hardly wait for day two.

# Chapter 14

*"One day you will realize that material things mean nothing. All that matters is the well-being of the people in your life."*
—Leon Brown

*12:50 p.m.*

"Where were you?" Shawnee whined. "He almost gored me to death."

"And you call Poe a drama queen." Mayhem slid one arm under her neck, the other under her knees, and carried her to the porch.

The log home sat near the West entrance of Yellowstone National Park. A perfect haven. Far enough from the action to keep their family safe, close enough to stop the hunt.

"Jacy Lee will want to assess your injuries. Where does it hurt, Cat?"

"Everywhere."

Not at all helpful. Regardless, he footed open the screen door. Inside, he lowered her to the overstuffed sofa, her slender frame enveloped in chocolate-brown leather, nature's supple yet durable material. Under her head, he slid a toss pillow.

At the bottom of the stairs, he called up to the loft.

Soon, Jacy Lee leaned over the railing, two long gray braids dangling mid-air. "Mourning Dove? Oh, my goodness. What happened?"

"Please don't panic," Mayhem said. "Cat had an unfortunate run-in with—"

"A Buffalo attacked me, *Shicheii*."

A loud gasp coiled off the pine walls.

Mayhem smoothed his lips. "If the big fella meant to hurt you, you'd be in a lot worse shape." When he regarded his elder and spiritual leader, his head would not stop rocking. "No outward signs of injury. However, she did strike the ground quite hard."

"How do *you* know?" Her tone dripped with ire. "What'd you do, watch from the driveway?"

His eyebrows lifted on their own. "Have you learned nothing from our time together?" A cord twanged in his neck. "When I pulled in, you were riding the Buffalo's head. What I did do was scare him away, so he didn't trample you to death. You're welcome."

"Oh. Thanks."

"Perhaps we should work on your trust issues today."

For weeks, he'd been sculpting her into an impressive warrior. But some days, she fought him every step of the way. When that woman dug in her heels, she outright refused to listen to reason.

Though Cat's unfortunate encounter did not bode well for the upcoming mission, one could hope this wasn't a preview of the days ahead. With the hunt scheduled for Friday and limited intel on the whereabouts of the trophy hunters, time was a commodity they couldn't waste. Visiting with Klee and Ferron already put them behind. Any more delays could prove disastrous.

Jacy Lee pounded down the stairs, the leather soles of his moccasins slapping the exquisite barnboard flooring. At the sofa, he scooted onto the cushion beside her, his aura radiating a controlled panic.

"Can you hear me, honey?"

"In my left ear, yeah."

"Wonderful." His warm smile lingered on her a moment. "How did this happen? I thought you'd meet me in the loft."

"I needed to clear my head before I unpacked, but I got distracted and didn't realize I walked right up to him."

"All right, my love." He cupped her cheek. "First, I put away all your clothes, hung Carolyne's wigs on the hook in your closet, and laid your robe on the bed."

One of these days, Jacy Lee should treat her like a grown woman, but nurturing her helped his guttural ache from missing the last thirty-some-odd years.

Bravo to Running Bear for having the wherewithal to pack his wife's wigs. Masking Shawnee's signature style added to the illusion of their cover story, the subject of which Mayhem hadn't broached yet. The details might not resonate right away.

Jacy Lee raised her "broken in" tee to her sternum. The woman had an endless supply. Gentle fingers walked across each rib to feel for fractures. "We've briefly discussed Bison before. Do you remember how important they are to their ecosystems?"

Clever man to divert her attention. For now, Mayhem let the charade continue. But if they didn't gather intel soon, their window might slam shut.

"What fascinates you most about this Sacred Animal?"

"Hmm," she said as though time was not a factor.

Perhaps he should help move things along. "Buffalo's spade-shaped hooves till the soil as they roam grasslands, and their footprints create mini nurseries for native plants, such as blue grama, sand dropseed, and little bluestem. They also transport plant seeds in their thick fur, their dung fertilizing them after they fall. When they graze, they act as pollinators, their long beards dusting flower blossoms."

"Oh, I know," she said as though Mayhem hadn't said a word. "How their wallowing behavior benefits other species."

Bison wallows—natural depressions in prairie land created over time as the animals rolled in mud to seek relief from biting insects or shed winter coats—altered the landscape and formed microhabitats that collected water which insects, amphibians, and reptiles used as homes. These mini watering holes also offered other wildlife a convenient place to stop for a drink.

"Mm-hmm. Impressive, aren't they?" Jacy Lee rolled the bones of her wrists, elbows, shoulders, and knees. "When we restore Buffalo to grasslands, songbirds thrive."

Mayhem glimpsed the loft. "Speaking of songbirds, where is Spirit Crow?" He spun back to Poe, still on the floor in front of the window. "Have you seen your mother?"

"Cheveyo, she fell asleep in the loft. She looked so peaceful, I didn't have the heart to wake her."

Poe hopped up to the armrest of the loveseat. Once he drew Shawnee's attention, he fell back into the seat cushion, legs kicked in the air, wings parted like her arms. Not a terrible impression of the incident outside. Little rascal. Mayhem chuckled.

As usual, she took the bait. "Ha. Ha." Sarcasm punctuated her words. "At least I didn't get a hair transplant... on my ass."

Jacy Lee gasped. "Mourning Dove—"

"What? He started it, *Shicheii.*"

By the time Jacy Lee glanced over his shoulder, Poe was on the armrest, preening his flight feathers like a good boy. "She didn't mean to insult you, child. You look dashingly handsome with your new tail feathers."

*Rattle, rattle.* Poe's love language.

"Roll onto your stomach, please."

Jacy Lee slid the toss pillow out from under her, his fingers walking up and down her spine.

"Vesper and grasshopper sparrows are more abundant where Buffalo inhabit grasslands." He continued the exam, hands smoothing over her hips, shins, and ankles, testing each joint with the softness of handling a rare feather. "Magpies ride atop Bison, picking insects out of their fur, while sharp-tailed grouse and burrowing owls benefit from the way they mow down vegetation, revealing access to the prairie floor. That one species ecologically benefits half a million square miles of wildlife."

"You're the coolest, *Shicheii*."

Chuckling, dimples dotted his cheeks. "What I failed to mention is their unpredictability. Their hair-triggered temper manifests in a split-second."

Mayhem mumbled, "Cat learned that lesson the hard way."

Jacy Lee stayed focused on her. "We owe a great deal to the American Buffalo. Most especially, our respect and kindness. For centuries, our People lived in harmony with these Sacred Animals."

"Until the white man moved in," Mayhem added. "In the annals of American history, there is no greater destruction of a single species than the Buffalo's senseless slaughter. Another dirty little secret they'd prefer to keep hidden."

She peered around her grandfather. "How many did they kill?"

"Story for another time, Cat." When she learned this truth, it may hit harder than other stories they'd shared about the mistreatment of their People. With hours slipping away, they couldn't afford to waste time on an in-depth discussion. "What is your assessment, Jacy Lee?"

"Mostly soft tissue contusions. No fractures."

"Splendid. Thank you." Mayhem strode into the kitchen, returning moments later with the PC, which he set on the coffee table in front of Cat. "Please search the local five-star hotels for reservations under any of the names on our list." Back in Alaska, they'd compiled a list of Killzme members and/or close associates.

"But I was just attacked."

"Attacked is an overdraw, wouldn't you agree?"

"No. I wouldn't." She flung a hand at the wall of glass. "He threw me twenty feet in the air for cripes' sake."

The height was closer to ten, but why squabble over a minor point?

Poe mocked her with another impression of falling backward into the loveseat. Only this time, he added a screech as he fell. Flawless rendition.

"It's not funny, you freak o' nature. *Shicheii*," she whined, "he's doing it again."

Mayhem darted to the loveseat. "Come, handsome. Let's wait for Cat on the porch."

Jacy Lee rose. "Cheveyo, may I have a word, please?"

After hours of traveling and another sleepless night, this was the last thing he needed. "Certainly."

Mayhem palmed open the screen door for the man who befriended him as a child. The man who never judged. The man who for decades loved him unconditionally and never revealed his secrets to anyone, even if it put him in jeopardy to hold his tongue. And so, when his elder asked for anything, he granted the request.

Out on the porch, Jacy Lee slung his arm around Mayhem's shoulders. "How does a nice hot cup of tea sound?"

"What can I do for you, my friend?"

"Is it possible for you and Mourning Dove to rest today? Neither of you have slept much lately, and her right eardrum concerns me."

Valid point. "What if we stayed on the property? Will that work?"

"It would."

"Consider it done. Keep in mind, if we make little headway, we may need to leave later tonight."

"Understood. Thank you, Cheveyo. As a mentor and a man, your empathy knows no limits." He jostled him. "How about that tea?"

"Sounds heavenly. Thank you."

Inside, Shawnee still hadn't left the sofa, clearly hoping Jacy Lee had talked him out of working today.

Alas, Mayhem's forthcoming instructions might not land well. "Please join me, Cat."

"But…"

"Go on, my love." Jacy Lee mussed her hair on his way into the kitchen. "I'll bring your tea out when it's ready."

"Alright, *Shicheii*." Head hung, her moccasins dragged across the barnboard floor, her lackluster demeanor grinding Mayhem's back molars.

When she slogged out to the porch, Poe caped his wings, waited to draw her attention, then fell back into the thick cushions of the chair.

"Hope you strangle on that gold chain."

"I beg your pardon."

"You're calling *me* out?" She flung an angry hand at her adversary. "What about him? He's done nothing but impersonate me since we got here, and I'm sick of it."

"She has a point, bud." Mayhem pulled out her chair before lowering into his. "Though your acting skills are top-notch, please refrain for now. We have work to do."

Her fingers raced across the keyboard. Moments later, she spun the PC. A list of hotels filled the screen. "There's four friggin' pages here. What about Elliot's briefcase? Was the ledger in it?"

A novel idea skipped through his mind. "Please stand, Cat."

"What?" She leaned out of reach. "Why?"

"This blatant distrust of yours is becoming an issue." He hustled down to the dirt driveway, rummaged around the cargo area of the car—obsidian black metallic Mercedes G-Wagon with peak performance for rugged terrain—snatched duct tape from the duffel bag, then rejoined her on the porch. "Please stand with your hands behind your back."

"What? Why?"

He sighed. "Do you trust me, Cat?"

"Yeah."

"Then you have nothing to fear."

Eyeing him with suspicion, she crossed her wrists. Once he bound her arms behind her back, he slid a chair to the railing. "Please step up here."

"On the railing? What if I fall?"

If she only knew. "Ghost Dog," he said, using her Apache name to remind her how to move—silent and surefooted, "please trust the process."

When her moccasins balanced on the railing, albeit unsteady, he hustled down the stairs. Rather than stand still, she tracked his movements. "Where're you goin'?"

On the ground below the porch, he said, "Don't concern yourself with my actions. Please turn and face the house."

"Can't you just gimme a hint?"

"Cautious Cat," his tone deepened, "face the log home. *Please.*"

"Fine." She followed his directives. "Now what?"

Raising his voice so she could hear him, he said, "Fall back."

Her gaze shot over her shoulder. "Run that by me one more time?"

"Fall. Back."

"Why?"

"It's a trust exercise."

"Will you catch me?"

"I will."

"What if you don't?"

"Have I ever let you fall, Cat?"

"Ever?" she said, digging through their sordid history. "I can think of a couple times."

Now was not the time to discuss past regressions. "You will fall off that railing. Don't make me do this the hard way."

"Fine—" Her tone held a bite of indignation.

"On three. One... Two..."

"Wait—" She glanced back. "Can't we talk about this?"

His gaze sidled to Poe. Though no words exchanged between them, he lunged at her, talons out to push her off the railing, the high-pitched shrill startling her enough to lose balance.

When Cat fell, he caught her, gently lowering her feet to solid ground. "Good. Again."

As she stomped up the stairs, Jacy Lee backed out the screen door with a serving tray of three mugs, the thermal-lined pitcher, and honey pot.

Before he questioned the restraints, Mayhem explained. "We're working on building trust." Another idea flitted through his mind. "Care to assist?"

"Very much. What can I do to help?"

"Do you recall the exercise you asked me to do in my youth?"

Dimples dotted both cheeks with his smile. "You remember that, Cheveyo? You couldn't have been more than five or six years old."

"Of course. It's one of my fondest memories of you."

"Mine, as well." He leaned over the railing. "I am deeply sorry for notifying Cynthia and Elliot. It was not my place to do so."

"Thank you. I'm pleased we cleared the air."

"As am I, Cheveyo. You deserved an apology much sooner." His warm gaze lingered as he stepped up to the railing. Crossed his arms over his chest, like he'd instructed Mayhem to do as a child, and faced the log wall. Without prompting, he fell backward with complete confidence. All the while, Shawnee watched in amazement.

He caught his lifelong friend. "Cat, please note his lack of hesitancy." He turned to Jacy Lee. "Do you feel up to switching roles?"

"Of course. Whatever you need."

"Thank you." Up the stairs he trod. On the railing, he grabbed both shoulders then leaned back. Jacy Lee caught him before he struck the ground. This amazed Shawnee even more, her mouth gaped wide as though she couldn't trust her eyes.

Without prompting, Poe hopped up to the railing next, turned toward the log wall, and fell back into Dad's arms. "Flawless as ever, bud. Thank you for the demonstration" Mayhem smooched his feathery cheek, wisps tickling his skin. "As you can see, Cat, we all have complete trust in one another. Why don't you? After all we've endured together, your blatant mistrust confuses me. Have we given you reason to doubt our sincerity?"

Her stiff shoulders slumped. "No."

"And yet, your actions say otherwise." Praying hands tapped his lips. Perhaps he should elaborate. "Relationships must stand on solid foundations with enough strength to weather any storm. Otherwise, they crumble."

Her whole body pleaded for forgiveness. "Please don't give up on me."

"Might I make a suggestion, Cheveyo?" After Mayhem acknowledged with a nod, he continued. "Do you agree Mourning Dove's past has given her plenty of reasons to remain guarded?"

"I do."

"Perhaps the trust fall is too advanced. What if I led you both in a few basic exercises? Then build from there. It may be advantageous in the long run."

He's right. This issue was too important to ignore. "All right, Jacy Lee. We are in your capable hands."

"Please unbind my granddaughter's wrists first."

He cleared his throat. "Certainly." Once he assisted Cat down from the chair, he slashed off the duct tape with a knife. "Where would you like us, my friend?"

"Remove your shoes and join me at the hammock."

When they sat to yank off their moccasins, she whispered, "Why does he want us barefoot?"

"It's good for the skin to walk on Sacred Soil, which soothes, strengthens, cleanses, and heals. The electrical impulses from Mother Earth also boosts endorphin levels."

"He wants us happy?"

"Starting from a place of joy and peace produces better results."

"Can we bring our tea?"

If only. "I'm afraid not."

At the hammock in the yard, Jacy Lee instructed them to stand on opposite sides facing one another. "The only way to climb up is to mirror your partner's movements. If you don't, you will fall."

*Clever, clever man.* "And the rules?"

"You may use nothing but each other for leverage. And you must stay on your own sides of the hammock. Questions?"

Mayhem stayed quiet.

"Honey, the only way to succeed is to trust Cheveyo."

"I do."

"Then you shouldn't have a problem with this exercise. I'll leave your tea capped just in case. Good luck." After kissing her cheek, he gave Mayhem a quick smile before strolling to the porch.

"Why'd he leave?"

"Evidently, he believes this might take a while. Let's prove him wrong." He extended his arms. Interlocking their fingers closed their energy circle. "For this to work, we must maintain eye contact throughout the exercise. I'll move slow so you can mirror me."

"Okay, cool. I'm ready."

Gazes locked, he raised his left leg.

She followed.

Nice and slow, he rested his knee on the hammock. And she mimicked his movements. "Apply light pressure on the count of three. One... Two... Now."

The moment she added her full weight, the hammock flipped, and they crashed to the ground.

"Light pressure, Cat." Rising, he brushed dirt off his jeans. "Do you understand what I mean by 'pressure'?"

Her shoulders sprang to her ears. "Not really, no."

"Then, why, pray tell, did you not ask me to expound?"

"Cheveyo," Jacy Lee called from the deck, "she won't trust the process if she believes failure is not an option."

"How right you are, my friend." He took a moment to inhale a deep cleansing breath. "I apologize, Cat. My tone was uncalled for."

"Apology accepted."

"Thank you." He held up his hands, and she threaded her fingers through his. "When I said 'light pressure' I meant a fraction of your weight."

"Got it."

Since she seemed sure of herself, he raised one knee. When she did the same, the hammock wobbled beneath them. "Stay with me, Cat." Without prompting, they lifted their legs in unison. "Perfect."

The hammock shook hard and fierce.

"This is the tricky part. If we don't sit back on our heels at the exact same time, we will fall."

"Got it," she said, but far less assured than he'd hoped.

"Bend at the waist." Their upper bodies grew closer. "Hold." He stared into deep pools of electric emeralds. "And... lower." On the descent, her gaze sidled. "Cat—"

The hammock twisted, bucking them off, and they crashed to the ground. On the porch, Jacy Lee waved while sipping his tea. Even Poe and Spirit Crow looked amused.

All the long hours of late intensified every strike of Mother Earth, each crash harder than the last.

After two more failed attempts, Jacy Lee bustled into the yard. "Might I make a suggestion, Cheveyo?"

"Please do." Or this exercise might take all day.

"Even with closing your energy circle and full eye contact, you've fallen out of sync with one another. Did you two have an argument?"

"Not that I recall, no."

"Honey, are you upset with Cheveyo?"

"No. I just don't wanna let him down."

Perhaps she sensed his guilt. Ferron said she was close to unearthing the past. Or did she feel pressured by him? That wasn't his intention at all. Quite the opposite. He championed her success.

"Ahh, there it is," Jacy Lee said. "Now we've reached the root of the problem. The fear of disappointing Cheveyo has thrown you off balance. You must find your center, find *hozho*." He gestured to Mayhem. "Please join us over here."

Now on the same side, Jacy Lee told him to crawl onto the hammock. "Lay back and relax."

Mayhem followed his instructions.

"Your turn, honey."

"My turn? For what?"

"Cuddling boosts oxytocin, the trust hormone."

It's also the love hormone for couples in a relationship. "Jacy Lee—"

As though she'd read his mind, Cat said, "*Shicheii*, Spirit Crow's right there."

"I will speak to her about it. Time is a factor, no?"

Mayhem admitted, "It is."

"Then cuddling is the fastest way to strengthen trust. Now, please do as I ask."

Without another word, she stretched out beside him on the hammock, her head resting on his biceps.

"It won't work unless you face each other."

He flipped onto his side. She did the same.

"Do you two not know how to cuddle?" He slung Mayhem's leg over hers. "Hold her close, Cheveyo."

He pulled Cat into his chest.

"Much better. Don't move till I return."

Once Jacy Lee left, she raised her head, the tips of their noses touching. "This isn't awkward at all."

"If you'd fallen off the railing like I asked, we'd be enjoying a nice breakfast and a hot tea about now."

"Yeah. In hindsight, I can easily see where I went wrong. So," she said to fill the uneasy silence. "Did you and Running Bear ever do this exercise?"

"Never had a reason to. He fell off the railing."

"Yeah, this one's on me for sure."

Jacy Lee called out, "No talking, you two."

She whispered, "On the plus side, you smell really nice."

He kissed her nose. "As do you, Kitty Cat."

"No talking!"

# Chapter 15



S till on the hammock, Mr. Mayhem whispered my name, waking me from a dead sleep, my face buried in his chest. "Don't. Move."

Those two words ignited all the nerve endings in my body. "What? Why?"

"Promise me you won't panic."

Only then did snorts, coughs, and grunts materialize. "What the hell is that?" A crick stiffened every muscle in my neck. "I gotta raise my head."

"I don't mean to alarm you, but a Buffalo herd surrounds us."

Oh. My. God. Not again. "When you say herd—?"

"At least eight individuals. Perhaps ten."

"Fuck. Not good."

"The language is not helpful, Cat."

"I disagree. If ever there was a time to swear, this is it." The neck pain worsened. "I gotta straighten."

"Can you raise your head without shaking the hammock?"

"I think so."

"I need certainty, I'm afraid. Can you do it or not?"

"Pretty sure, yeah."

"Are you certain, Cat? If you startle even one individual, the herd will charge. And we are not in any position to defend ourselves."

"I can do it. *Sheesh...*" Inch by careful inch, I raised my head. Now, we lay face-to-face, our noses touching like before. The Bison chatter intensified, and all my tiny body hairs hackled, my voice low and whisperous. "Where's *Shicheii*?"

A massive Buffalo lumbered behind him, and I gaped. On his massive hump sat Poe, gazing down at us, bill slightly parted like he'd caught us in the throes of passion.

I whispered, "Problem."

"I'm aware."

Maybe he sensed the Buffalo, but I seriously doubted he knew about Poe. If that punk took a hissy fit, he could easily startle the herd. Man, that'd suck.

"Stay with me, Cat."

When I stared into his eyes, my heartbeat slowed, my pulse even and steady, our surroundings fading away as I fell deeper and deeper into his pupils. With Levaughn and other past lovers, this position led to a make-out session. I tried to ignore the tingly sensation, but the warmth of his body next to mine enhanced the intimacy tenfold.

*Did he do this with Kimi? Man, they must've had amazing sex. I wonder if he's hung like a—*

His eyebrows popped high.

I mouthed, "Sorry."

*Was Running Bear right? Did danger turn me on? Maybe. Because man, am I—*

In my mind, his deep, raspy voice rang clear. *Cat, please do not let your mind wander.*

*Stay outta my head. How 'bout that?*

*It's difficult in our current position.*

*Where's Shicheii?*

*That I don't know. I fell asleep.*

*And you didn't strangle me? Huh. Progress.*

Startling him awake could turn deadly fast. Learned that little tidbit the hard way.

"I don't hear 'em anymore. Do you?"

*Ca-caw, caw, caw, caw, caw!*

"Thank you, Poe," he called out.

*What if it's a trap? It'd be just like that punk to—*

Without warning, his grip tightened around me and he flipped us out of the hammock.

On the covered porch, *Shicheii* backed out the screen door with a serving tray. "Oh, good. You're up."

I whirled around. "Did he plan this the entire time?"

"Oh, yes. Yes, he did."

*Shicheii* looked awfully pleased with himself. "Did you two have a nice nap?"

"We would have preferred not to forfeit our free will."

"He's right, *Shicheii*. Not cool." *Although, kinda hot.*

"You had no plans to rest today. And you both needed it. I will not sit by while you abuse yourselves." He waved us up the stairs. "Come eat before it gets cold. I made fresh teas, as well."

On the porch, my snuggle partner pulled out my chair before lowering to his. "Thank you, Jacy Lee."

"You're welcome." He set a tinfoil-wrapped plate, napkin, and silverware in front of us. Then rose as though he forgot something. "Excuse me for a moment, please."

While we waited at the outside table—teakwood, according to my full-time mentor, part-time fake husband—I swished the dipper through the honey, its clay pot and matching mugs adorned with four Sacred Colors of black, white, yellow, and blue. Because *Shicheii* made the serving set on the reservation years ago, we took it everywhere we went.

In the yard, my grandfather crisscrossed cut lumber within the firepit encircled by white stones, like the one at Mr. Mayhem's cabin in Jackson, New Hampshire. Soon, timber crackled and popped, smoke billowing up to the heavens.

No matter where we traveled to, *Shicheii* ensured we had a Sacred Fire burning nearby. Representative of the Central Fire, the heart of a Hogan, it aligned with Polaris—aka the North Star—added protection, and opened a doorway to the spiritual realm, where we could connect and commune with our ancestors.

Though I hadn't reunited with lost loved ones in the flames, *Shicheii* said I had the ability within me. Too bad I didn't know how to access it. I'd give anything to chat with Mom again.

Stomach rumbling, I peeked under the tinfoil on my plate, but before I caught a good whiff, Mr. Mayhem stopped me. "I wasn't gonna start without him. Just curious what he made."

The mug hovered in front of his lips, steam billowing up his face. "While we wait, would you mind checking on Spirit Crow? She's still in your room."

Shit. He's right. She never slept this long.

Inside, I darted to the staircase, then stalled. What if she's sick? Did Kimi's reincarnation come with an expiration date? If anything happened to her, none of us would recover.

My moccasins clamored up the treads.

In the loft, Spirit Crow nested in a folded blanket near the pillows. "Hey, you." I crawled onto the mattress, and her inner eyelid parted. "Are you okay?"

*Coo...* Her soft tone wasn't normal.

"*Shicheii* made brunch. Are you hungry?"

Her bill sank to her chest feathers.

My heart ached for her. "You miss him, huh?"

She refused eye contact—also uncharacteristic for her.

"I'm sure he's fine. Running Bear won't let anything happen to him."

A yelp escaped her bill, shattering me even more.

*Shit, shit, shit.* "Alright, gimme a sec."

Downstairs, I snatched my phone off the coffee table, and raced back into the loft. "I shouldn't be doing this." Deep sadness radiated off every feather, so I called Running Bear on FaceTime.

"Hey, Ghost Dog." His pearly teeth gleamed in the sunlight. "Can you hear me alright?"

"Yeah, my left ear is clear.

"And the right?"

"Still crackles and pops. But I'm okay." A quick glance over my shoulder ensured privacy. "Did you update your phone yet?"

"Who's asking, you or Shadow Wolf?"

"Me. Doesn't matter. Umm…" A breeze from an opened window feathered strands of hair across his face. "Are you driving?"

"I just left the cabin. Did I forget to pack you something?"

"No." My gaze sidled to Spirit Crow, my insides twisting more and more. "Did you, uh, see Odin there?"

"Yeah. We ran a perimeter check together. Sacred Land is secure."

"Cool, cool. Good to know. Err… Is there any way you could drive back there?"

"What do you need, Ghost Dog? Spit it out."

I couldn't betray Spirit Crow by spilling her secret. So instead, I aimed the camera at her.

"Copy that. Let me pull over."

My leg drummed the mattress.

"Say hi, bud. Someone misses you."

Raven eyes peered into the screen. *Gronk, gronk, gronk.*

Spirit Crow's head popped up. *Coo… rattle, rattle. Coo…* Her talons pawed the phone, and tears pooled in my eyes.

Even Running Bear scrubbed a hand over his face, muttering, "Damn allergies."

Not sure what transpired between them, but judging by the body language, they had quite the conversation. Both were downright giddy, bouncing in place, feathers fluffed with excitement.

*Gronk, rattle, croak. Coo… whisper, whisper. Coo…*

"Mourning Dove?" *Shicheii's* voice carried up the stairs. "Come eat while it's hot."

"Be right there." I blew Odin a kiss, whispered, "Gotta go, Running Bear. Thanks a bunch."

"Any time. See ya on the flop, Ghost Dog."

When I lowered my forearm for Spirit Crow, she climbed aboard. "Probably best if we kept this on the down-low."

A definite yes rocked her head.

With Spirit Crow bundled in my arms, I boogied down the stairs. When I burst out the screen door, Mr. Mayhem rose from the table, chivalry alive and well in his world. "Sorry I took so long. Nature called."

"Huh." His head tilted to one side. "Did you not find her in the loft?"

"I did."

"Did you venture across to my room?"

I sucked my teeth. "No. Why would I?"

"You stayed in the loft the entire time?"

"Yeah. Why's it matter?"

"The loft has no bathroom."

"You're right, Cheveyo. It doesn't."

*My own flesh and blood agreed!*

With the full attention of everyone at the table, including Poe, who traced me up and down with disgust, heat incinerated my insides.

"See my confusion, Cat? Where exactly did you answer nature's call?"

*Shit, shit, shit.* When I parted my lips to confess, Spirit Crow hopped down to the table, hips wiggling, tail feathers swishing as she melted the heart of her husband.

"Did you enjoy your nap, sweetheart?"

*Coo... rattle, rattle. Coo...*

And just like that, I'd jumped off the hot seat. Girl power.

The first bite of *Shicheii's* eggs Benedict lowered my eyelids, cheesy hollandaise sauce and cooked spinach slipping across my tastebuds. The toasted English muffin had the perfect snap of crunch, adding to the chorus of yolky goodness.

Mr. Mayhem raised a sideways fist in front of his mouth. "You've outdone yourself, my friend."

"Truth." I swallowed. "This might be my new favorite."

A blush swept across *Shicheii's* cheekbones, warm chestnut skin hued with added red. "Thank you both. I'm glad you're enjoying it."

Fork tines scraped high-end plates as I devoured brunch like I hadn't eaten in days. Chugged my orange juice—freshly squeezed by my grandfather's loving hands—and slammed the glass tumbler on the table a lot harder than I expected.

*Brrp...* My shoulders sprang to my ears. "Oops. Excuse me."

Lifting his head from his bowl, yolk dripped off Poe's bill, beady dark eyes slitted like he wanted to stab me.

I stuck out my tongue. And sure enough, his father caught it. Without a word, one hand slid the PC in front of me. Translation—Get to work. 'Course, he'd add a "please." Mr. Mayhem was many things but impolite wasn't one of them. Didn't matter who he spoke to. Even poachers got a "please" and "thank you" right before he murdered them.

To say "complicated didn't describe him" was an understatement. That man stood in a class of his own—a freakishly impressive Apache warrior, dispenser of justice, spokesman for equality, and the most generous, compassionate, and loving human on the planet, especially when we're alone.

The list of hotels filled the screen.

I scoured reviews for familiar names. No luck at the first place, nor the second and third. With hundreds of reviews, both negative and positive, it'd take days to comb through this info.

And so, I abandoned the search. Much quicker to hack hotel records. Because hotels in general offered free Wi-Fi to guests, they inadvertently opened vulnerabilities that someone with expert tech skills like *moi* could exploit. But without a password to access the network, this plan required a lot more time and energy than I had.

Mr. Mayhem and I had been down this road before, so I used hacker terminology to avoid questions from *Shicheii*. "Can't deploy an evil twin without a password."

"Try guest in all caps followed by a random room number. Are you focused on five-star establishments?"

"Yep." I brought up the first hotel, but the PC was out of network range. "We're too far away."

"How close do you need to be, Cat?"

"Within thirty feet worked last time. Wanna take a ride?"

"Hmm." While dabbing his lips with the napkin, his gaze sidled to *Shicheii* for a hot second. "I gave my word we'd spend most of our day on the property."

"Why?"

My grandfather reached across the table. "You're still healing, honey."

"But *Shicheii*, I can't do my job from here. We'd only be cruising through Yellowstone. What's the big deal?"

"Aren't you sore from the Buffalo incident?"

"I mean, yeah, I'm bruised, but it goes with the gig. Besides, it's not like we'd be doing anything strenuous." At our ages, we hardly needed permission to leave, but we both honored our word and respected elders. So, I tossed my best puppy dog eyes. "The Innocent Ones need us."

For several grueling seconds, *Shicheii* held my gaze, clawing through my subconscious. "You'll stay in the vehicle?"

Mr. Mayhem's throat cleared. "Neither of us can make that promise, I'm afraid. We must follow leads as they arise."

"Fair enough, Cheveyo." Though he agreed, I could tell he wasn't thrilled. "Poe, however, may not accompany you. Too much activity could undo the imping procedure."

"Hahahahaha..." Hand on my stomach, I laughed so hard I snorted, joyful tears watering my eyes. "His tail feathers could fall out?"

A mind-numbing screech rattled my eardrums.

"Not nice, Mourning Dove. Come, child." Before Poe attacked—been there, done that, got the scars to prove it—*Shicheii* scooped him into his arms. "Let's clean you up a bit."

"Friggin' psycho needs an attitude adjustment." When I swiveled back to the table, Mr. Mayhem's icy stare drilled deep.

Yep, pissed him off, too. Shit.

# Chapter 16

*"Crow's lesson is to work...
Walk without fear, even if the
way is not clear... Trust your
intuition and the animals that
cross your path to guide you."*
—Kym Dunbar, Soul Wolf
Journey

**4:44 p.m.**

After Cat changed into more appropriate attire—she could not enter a high-end establishment in a ratty t-shirt with sweatpants hiked to her knees—Mayhem cruised through the West gate of Yellowstone. "Thirty-five dollars for a seven-day pass. What a bargain."

She flipped open the PC. "Thought for sure they'd search the cargo area."

"For what?"

"Oh, I dunno." Her focus never left the screen. "All the weapons you packed?"

"It's perfectly legal to carry firearms into the park. What you cannot do is shoot."

That remark drew her attention. "Even in self-defense? What if you're attacked? You still can't fire?"

"Correct. Otherwise, trophy hunters could use the false narrative to kill the wildlife here."

She scratched her cheek. "Then why bring a gun in the first place?"

"Therein lies the rub. If the Innocent Ones step over the boundary line, the State of Montana allows hunting. In fact, they encourage it."

"How far over the line?"

"Not far enough. Here's the wrinkle. If the victim backtracks onto federal land after being shot, even if the hunter fired after the individual left the park, Yellowstone's no hunting policy applies, and game wardens may level charges."

With her focus diverted to the screen, her fingers raced across the keys. "Well, now we know how Killzme plans to smuggle in rifles for the hunt. They can do it right in the open."

Part of his soul collapsed. Greater Yellowstone politics left vulnerabilities for monsters like Killzme Corp to exploit, and the Innocent Ones who called this vast landscape home paid the ultimate price.

The road weaved through tunnels of lodgepole pines, past sprawling prairies and Mother Earth's most inspiring jagged rocks and hot springs. Yellowstone had a soul, an effervescent pulse of life found nowhere else in the lower forty-eight.

Though darkness and uncertainty hung over this mission, breathtaking beauty surrounded them. "Silencers would also not be out of the realm of possibilities. Unless, of course, Killzme bribed a game warden or two."

Never did she lose focus, her expert tech skills continuing to amaze him. When she was in her element, she rarely failed to uncover the enemy's secrets.

Though he appreciated her hard work, stealing a moment to allow the spirit to feast on such a rich bounty was equally important. "Cat, you're missing spectacular views."

Up ahead, a Buffalo herd gathered in the road.

He braked to offer them a wide birth. "Allow a minimum of twenty-five yards between you and the wildlife here, including deer, antelope, pronghorn, bighorn sheep"—he gestured toward the herd—"and these magnificent creatures. For bear, moose, and wolves, the park recommends a separation of one hundred yards."

"How're we supposed to save the Innocent Ones from a hundred yards away?"

"I gave you the park's recommendations."

"Meaning?" Outside her window, one of the senior Bison stopped for a peek inside. "Shit—" She sprang over the middle console and into his lap. The steering wheel wedged her against his chest.

"Is this a preview of our time here, Cat?"

"No." Tsking her tongue, she scooted to the middle console. "Think he's the dude from this morning?"

"Doubtful."

"I dunno. He looks really familiar. Maybe he recognizes me."

"Cat, please." He pinched the bridge of his nose. "I cannot pull away with you hovering over the shifter, and the visitors behind us are growing restless."

"Tough luck. They weren't attacked this morning."

*Creator, please hold my tongue, so I cannot wield it like a weapon.*

With the herd safely across the street, Mayhem increased speed. The Benz cruised around the next bend, where a gorgeous moose stepped off the asphalt into the forest, his fifteen-point rack still encased in velvet.

Magnificent specimen.

Rather than revel in the tranquil beauty, Shawnee stayed glued to the PC. "How will we know who's involved in the hunt? We haven't even found where it is yet."

"Hence why we first need to locate their hotel. With the crowds and distance between each lodging, we have little time to waste." His gaze strayed back to her. "How are you, Kitty Cat? I apologize for not asking sooner." Ferron's demands made him question things he shouldn't. "You've had a difficult few days."

"I'm good." Her bright smile fluttered his heart. "Warriors don't break, we bend."

*There she is.* "Yes, we do, darlin'."

In true warrior fashion, she veered back to the mission ahead. "Do we even know what time Friday?"

"We do not. However, the park bustles with visitors during the day. Which narrows our window somewhat. The predators

Killzme plans to slaughter are most active between dusk and dawn. Thus, the trophy hunters will most likely wait for nightfall."

"Complete and utter scum."

He concurred.

"If we gotta search every hotel, this might take a while. Elliot's briefcase didn't help?"

"I haven't had a chance to dig through it with Jacy Lee's hovering. The last thing we need is for him to question how we obtained Elliot's belongings."

"Did you bring the briefcase with us?"

"I did. We'll pour through the contents once we stop, which I cannot do with the line of traffic behind us. How many hotels are on the list?"

"Sixteen."

The amount made little sense. "All five-star establishments?"

"No. The cheaper places are either three-star or campgrounds."

"Then we can safely exclude those. Killzme will want the best for their clients."

"I started scratching 'em off earlier but wanted to check with you first."

Impressive to have the wherewithal to jump ahead. "How many have you excluded?"

"Eight."

When another herd lumbered into the road, Mayhem braked. "Let's try to whittle down the list while we wait. May I?"

Once she passed the PC, he scrolled through the list. "The Old Faithful Inn is the park's most popular hotel. Also keep the Snow Lodge, the Canyon Lodge, and Lake Yellowstone Hotel and Cabins."

"That's it? Only four?"

He returned the computer. "For now."

"Works for me. Bringing up the websites now." The keys clacked in her lap. "Uh-oh." The fingers increased speed, her unwavering dedication on display. "Damn. Only one offers Internet access, Lake Yellowstone Hotel."

"Hmm. That does pose a problem, doesn't it? Good thing you changed." With a wink, he shifted into Drive. Though he hadn't foreseen this roadblock, it made sense for hotels to keep the focus on the scenery and wildlife. Most people visited Yellowstone to escape from daily life. "Please read me the exact wording."

"For which one?"

"All four."

"Alright. 'There is no air-conditioning, TV, telephone, or radio. No cooking is allowed. All rooms and cabins are non-smoking and non-vaping. Select cabins are pet friendly. There is no Internet service at Old Faithful Inn.'" She tapped a few more keys. "Same wording for the Snow Lodge."

"Then we may have to rent suites."

"So? We work outta hotels all the time. What's the big deal?"

"I meant, we may have to rent multiple suites, one at each lodging. At least for a night until we find them."

"Must be nice to throw money at a problem."

A surge of heat swept up his neck. "Are you implying I gained my wealth through nefarious means? I'll have you know, I earned every dollar. Unlike you, my parents couldn't afford to leave a trust. Have you even checked your account balance?"

"Why would I? I don't want a dime of that blood money."

"The negative connotation is unfair. Your mother went without to build the trust for you. That's love, Cat, not blood money."

Teary eyed, she said, "I'd rather have my parents."

"I know, darlin'." His tender stroke of her hair soothed her enough to focus her attention to the screen. "Does either hotel offer a business center?"

"No, but Lake Yellowstone Hotel does. That's where the ethernet is."

"Hard wiring doesn't surprise me. Cell coverage is spotty throughout the park."

She raised her iPhone. "No bars."

"The park limits coverage to preserve the wilderness."

"Damn. Just lost the hotspot connection."

Once they neared Lake Yellowstone Hotel and Cabins, more commonly referred to as Lake Hotel, he slowed the Benz. "Did the signal return?"

"Yep. Park out front so I don't lose it again."

"Yes, ma'am."

Her fingers danced across the keyboard. "The 'please' was implied."

"Common courtesy is never implied, Cat. You either practice good manners or you don't."

She sighed like she had better things to do. "Guest plus a random room number doesn't work. I tried several."

"Because the Internet is in the business center. Okie doke." He banged a U-turn. "We better head into town."

"But we just got here. Whaddaya need? Are we stopping at home first? How're we gonna find the poachers if we leave?" She slapped the dashboard. "Hello?"

"Oh, look." He pointed out the windshield. "Antelope."

The appearance of wildlife scrubbed the hard edge off her demeanor. "Aww, the baby's so cute. *Shicheii* would love him."

"*She* is a doe." Now that he'd stalled the endless stream of questions, he explained the next steps. "Because you cannot penetrate the network—"

"Me?" A splayed hand spanned her neckline. "What about you? Last I checked, we were a team."

"Pleased you're paying attention." He winked. "Without access to the network, *we* may have to secure a suite to obtain log-in credentials. First, however—"

"What if someone recognizes us? We don't exactly blend."

Mayhem stayed silent.

"Why aren't you answering me?"

"I'm waiting for the next flurry of questions."

Her arms crossed. "Fine. I'll shut up."

"I appreciate your sacrifice." Again, he winked. "You are correct. Without a list of participants, we have no way of knowing who might attend the hunt. Hence why we first need to head into town."

A blank expression stared back at him.

"Note the pause for your response."

"What if Elliot has the list in his briefcase?"

"As a disposable employee, I highly doubt it, but we shall do our due diligence." After parking at the side of the road, he hustled to the cargo area for the briefcase. Upon his return, he passed it to Cat.

While he veered into traffic, she fumbled with the hasps. "It's locked."

"And the problem is?"

"It's locked."

"Then your cat burglary skills should come in handy, no?"

"Gotta sledgehammer on ya?"

"A sledgehammer." He scoffed. "No alternative with a little more finesse?"

"It's the quickest way in."

"*Au contraire.* How many digits does the lock require?"

"Three."

"Try eight-oh-two."

"What is that?"

"Date stamp of the wedding photo on Cynthia's dresser."

"Wow. You're good."

"You are too kind, Cat." A flush warmed his cheeks as he steered around the bend. "Thank you."

All too often people used dates to help them remember passcodes to combination locks. The common practice made them predictable. And thus, easy victims of theft.

When she dialed in the date, the hasps popped open. "I'm in." Digging through the paperwork, she made quite the mess.

"It would behoove us to keep things in order."

Smiling, she jiggled a ledger in the air. "Lookie what I found."

"Good job, Cat. Let's hope Elliot took copious notes. In the meantime, our objective is clear—gain access to the business center. Are you up for a little roleplay?"

Her smile beamed even brighter. "Always."

A tingle zipped up his spine.

Prepare, Entitled Ones, for she is the judge and jury for your unforgivable sins. And I, dear trophy hunters, am your executioner.

# Chapter 17

***5:40 p.m.***

Parked in the driveway of the log home, Mr. Mayhem suggested we ask *Shicheii* if he needed anything in town. Poe and Spirit Crow perched on the porch railing, watching an unkindness of ravens fly from tree to tree. Stupid name for such brilliant birds.

All excited about new pals, Poe bounced on his pipe cleaner legs. But when he hopped down to the yard to play, enormous ebony wings flapped straight for him.

Uh-oh. I cringed. This might not go his way.

Sure enough, the lead raven buzzed his head. Another joined in, then another and another, all divebombing Poe to deliver a warning—leave their domain or risk the consequences. Spirit Crow cooed from the railing, but it made no difference. More and more ravens scolded and mobbed Poe till they'd forced him back to the porch.

Now with total control of the yard, they weren't going anywhere. If Poe even thought about venturing beyond the stairs,
they'd make him regret it. Mr. Mayhem said first offense was a
broken wing. Second offense? Death.

Though the little diva and I'd had our issues, my heart broke for
him. So, before we left the Benz, I tapped his father's arm. "Isn't
there something we can do?"

When he tore his gaze away from the window, tears teemed his
eyes. "To help Poe?"

I sloughed off a quick shrug. "Hurts to be excluded."

"Sounds like the voice of experience."

"Everyone's cruel to foster kids, even the teachers, like somehow
we chose that lifestyle."

"I'm so sorry, Kitty Cat. If I had known—"

I flashed a flat hand. "This conversation isn't about me."

"It can be, if you need to talk about it."

Poe sat on the top stair. Head hung, ebony wings slumped,
pinion feathers dragging on the deck boards.

"Look how sad he is."

"Your beautiful soul never ceases to amaze me, Kitty Cat. Thank
you for considering his feelings." He turned back to his faithful
companion. "Though gut-wrenching to witness, I'm afraid they
must work it out on their own. Humans have no business meddling in corvid rivalries."

"So, we just let 'em just treat our family like garbage?"

The eyebrows rose. "If you have a suggestion, I'm open to ideas."

"I don't... but I bet *Shicheii* does."

"Brilliant." He snickered. "It'll also focus his energy elsewhere."
*So he doesn't wonder what we're doing.*

Normally, Poe flew straight to his dad's shoulder the moment we crossed the yard. Not today. He just stood there, staring at his oversized crow feet.

"Hey, bud." Mr. Mayhem swept him into his arms, but Poe still refused eye contact. "Would a juicy fruit cup raise your spirits?"

The yelp almost destroyed me.

"Not cool." I waved a stiff finger at the ravens, still mocking Poe from the trees. "He just wants to play with you."

All at once, they scolded *me* with harsh, throaty caws. Uh-oh. Was I the enemy now? Hope not, or I could kiss my ass goodbye. I'd been on the wrong side of corvids before—namely Poe and his brothers, Edgar and Allan—and I certainly wasn't in a hurry to do it again. I'd barely escaped with my sanity.

The minute I strolled through the door, *Shicheii* used the standard Diné greeting. "*Yá'át'ééh*, my love." He kissed my forehead. "How was your trip?"

"We saw a ton of wildlife."

"How nice." His warm smile bathed me in unconditional love. "Yellowstone has one of the few intact ecosystems in the country."

My partner-in-crime patted his shoulder. "*Yá'át'ééh*, my friend."

"What happened, Cheveyo?" With the depressed crow in our midst, he released me. "Come, child." He cradled Poe like an infant, and Pissy Pants laid it on thick with his whimpering and shit. "Uh-huh." Poe rambled on and on. "Uh-huh." *Shicheii* strode toward the kitchen. "Well, that wasn't very nice. Was it?"

My gaze snapped to Mr. Mayhem. "He speaks crow?"

"It boggles the mind why you are still unaware of his abilities. He does not speak crow, per se. He listens to the language of spirits. The body the soul inhabits is irrelevant."

"Wow." My jaw slacked. "Just... wow."

Slight grin. "Quite a remarkable gift. Is it not?"

"Geez, I guess." *What else could Shicheii do?*

"More than you know."

*I wasn't talkin' to you. Stay outta my head!*

Chuckling, he strode into the kitchen.

Rather than watch two grown men swoon over a crow who had them both wrapped around his toothpick legs, I strolled out to the porch.

Angry vocalizations swallowed the yard. Goosebumps sheathed my skin, but I'd be damned if the local unkindness would barricade *me* indoors. So, all casual like, I rested my forearms on the railing beside Spirit Crow. Not sure if she was trying to soothe the ravens or reveling in their presence.

"Hey, you."

*Coo...*

*Only one? Not good.* "They remind you of Odin, huh?"

Her inner eyelid closed for a hot second, but her gaze never left the ravens, now playing tag through the woods.

"I know, me too. Sucks he couldn't come with us." I peeked through the glass wall into the great room. "Wanna call him real quick?"

That drew her attention, stunning blue eyes wide with hope.

"Alright, but only for a sec. Gimme some sugar, babe." Her talons tapped my raised palm. As I brought up FaceTime, I skimmed the great room again.

Running Bear answered right away. "Hey, Ghost Dog. What's up?"

"Um, is Odin still with you?"

"Does she need to speak with him again?"

"We both do."

"Have you told Shadow Wolf about these calls?"

"No, and it needs to stay that way."

"Copy that." The image changed to his washboard abs as he spoke to someone off-screen—I'd had worse views—but I couldn't make out what he said. Seconds later, Odin peered into the camera.

"Hey, buddy." My voice rose ten octaves. "Someone wants to say hi." I aimed the phone at Spirit Crow.

Like before, her talons pawed his image. *Coo... rattle, rattle. Coo... Whisper, whisper.*

A deep gurgling croak rose from the speaker, his love language pitched, his volume increased. *Kuk, kuk, kuk. Gronk, gronk.*

Odin was so vocal, he drew the attention of the raven gang and, apparently, earned us a few brownie points. With Odin and Spirit Crow calling back and forth, I feared Mr. Mayhem might overhear the chatter. So, for the third time in a matter of minutes, I surveyed the great room. Sure enough, he headed our way.

"Sorry, but we gotta go," I whispered. "Thanks, Running Bear."

"See ya on the flop, Ghost Dog."

The second I slid my phone into my moccasin's inner pocket, the screen door swung open. "Jacy Lee needs a few ingredients from the grocery store." Quick stroke of the crown feathers for Spirit Crow. "You look happy, sweetheart."

*Rattle, rattle, coo...*

"Cat and I shan't be too long. Poe conned Jacy Lee into frying bacon." He palmed open the door. "Care to join?"

No one had to ask her twice. Snow-white wings angled through the doorway.

He crossed the yard, with me following like a lost cub.

In the Benz, we cruised through a quaint town. Shops framed both sides of the street, sidewalks bustling with visitors.

Once he parked in front of a bridal boutique, he hustled around the front bumper to open my door.

"Thanks, hon." Stepping into my role for our husband-and-wife routine, I slipped my hand into his.

"My pleasure, darling."

Our arms swung between us as we moseyed to the sidewalk like any other happy couple on vacation. But when he reached for the boutique door handle, I braked.

"Why're we here?"

"The groom is rarely involved with choosing the wedding gown, I agree. However, those same principals don't apply for a renewal of vows."

Did I get swept into an alternate universe? "Our what?"

A bubbly blonde woman bustled over to greet us. "Welcome to A Day to Remember."

*What the hell is he thinking?*

"Thank you, Missus…"

"Anna's fine."

"Pleasure to make your acquaintance, Anna." He tipped the fedora. "This is—"

"Kai." I hugged his arm. "And my sweet *Gaagii.*"

Anna's hand fluttered toward her eyes, as if to halt the production of joyful tears. "Beautiful names for a gorgeous couple."

Beside me, my faux husband probably wondered how I nailed our new aliases without even a stumble.

During the flight to Montana, *Shicheii* asked me to choose two baby names, one for a boy, one for a girl, even though that ship had sailed after a dangerous atopic pregnancy. Both Diné names, Kai meant willow tree whose spiritual properties included protection and healing, and *Gaagii* meant raven.

Not sure why or how we got on the subject, but he said if I believed I could be a mother someday—really believed, deep in my soul—the Holy Ones might bless me with a miracle.

Honestly, my lifestyle never screamed stability, so I really had no business dreaming about it. Hell, even my relationship with Detective Levaughn Samuels had ended, with him thousands of miles away and clueless about my warrior mentorship. When we were in Alaska, I called him one night. My heart didn't beat for him anymore, and he deserved to know.

Once Mr. Mayhem and *Shicheii* re-entered my life, Levaughn and I drifted apart because of my inability to share details about my life. But how could I? If he knew my partner and I protected wildlife by any means necessary—even murder—he'd turn us in. It wasn't in his nature to look the other way, and I admired him for it. Probably always will.

Though the break-up was an emotional conversation, he said he'd always love me, and he understood. We agreed to meet in person when I returned to Massachusetts, but I couldn't give him a date. Instead, I set him free to move on with his life. He's a good man who deserved happiness.

Plus, with the innate sense of belonging lately, motherhood crossed my mind from time to time. And when it did, I never envisioned Levaughn as the baby daddy.

Farther into the boutique, Anna said, "Would either of you care for a glass of champagne before we get started?"

*Started on what?* Last I checked, my faux husband was already married... to a crow. Okay, so, maybe it wasn't a legal union after Kimi died. Whatever. The point is... Did I have one?

"Sounds lovely, Anna." His deep, raspy voice jarred me from my thoughts. "Thank you."

Three champagne flutes later, I found myself standing on a block in a wedding gown, with a wall of mirrors in front of me and an overjoyed blonde lady touching me everywhere. And I mean everywhere, as she tucked and pinned mountains of material. Meanwhile, Mr. Mayhem stayed on the other side of the boutique with Anna's husband, Joe.

How'd this benefit the Innocent Ones? And why the hell weren't we searching for the hotel? Nothing made sense. But what I could do? We were in too deep to turn back now.

I shot back flute number four. "Anna, can we stop for a sec?"

"Sure. The ladies' room is in the hall."

"Thanks." With the mile-long train slung over one arm, I jetted past the bathroom and straight into the men's section. There he stood in front of a full-length mirror with an old guy fiddling with the hem of his tuxedo pants.

"Ahem."

In the reflection, he said, "Problem, darling?"

"Why am I wearing this?"

He bent toward the guy at his ankles. "Could you give us a few minutes, Joe?"

"Take the room. I'll check in with my wife. Holler when you're ready."

"Will do, Joe. Thank you."

After he left, Mr. Mayhem led me into the corner behind racks of suits. "Speak your mind, Cautious Cat."

"Look at me." I swung my arms wide. "It's too much. The ruffles and poofy things. It's all just too much."

"Did you explain to Anna you and I are already married?"

Tight fists topped my hips. "Are we, though?"

"As far as they know, we are. Thus, a wedding gown with a full train is a bit over the top."

"Thank you. That's what I'm talkin' about."

"What would you like to wear to renew our vows?"

Man, he's such a talented actor, I couldn't separate fact from fantasy. When he played a role, he rarely broke character. And so, I played along. "I dunno, like a swanky leather and lace combo."

The eyebrows lifted. "You've given this some thought. White, ivory, or...?"

"Black."

"Nice." Quick nod of approval. "Would you like me to help you find a dress?"

"Could ya?"

"Certainly."

"Can I ask you somethin' real quick?"

"Of course."

I whispered, "Why're we doing this?"

"You tell me. How might a wedding—or in our case, a renewal of vows—benefit the mission?"

"I honestly have no idea."

"Mull it over. Let me know on the drive home. Now"—he offered me his arm—"shall we, darling?"

How would a wedding benefit the mission?

# Chapter 18



**6:55 p.m.**

After he and Shawnee left the wedding boutique and stopped at the grocery store for Jacy Lee, they finally headed home. The trip took longer than expected, though at least they had a solid cover story in place.

"Have you determined why the bride and groom personas benefit us, Cat?"

"Nope. You're gonna have to gimme a hint."

"Fair enough. What do you feel when you meet a couple who plan to marry?"

"I dunno. Happy?"

"And?"

"Excited for them."

"Precisely. Of all the special occasions, a wedding or renewal of vows sparks joy and excitement in everyone the couple encounters, regardless of whether they know them. Now, if you worked at an establishment that caters to the public, who might you be more apt to assist—a couple on vacation, business types, or a bride and groom planning their special day, and in a broader scope, their future together?"

"The bride and groom."

"Did you base that decision on *your* emotion associated with marriage, or the emotion of two strangers?"

"Mine."

"Precisely. When a cover story stirs a visceral response in others, they are far more likely to grant requests that may otherwise seem suspicious or odd. For example, asking to tour the banquet room to set the right tone. Access to the computers for last-minute arrangements. Or to search off-trail in the park for the ideal wedding photo background. All three requests make perfect sense for a bride and groom."

"Wow." Her head shook as though baffled by why she hadn't made the connection sooner. "We could invent excuses for just about anything."

Now she's catching on. "Correct. The hotel may even relax their check-in and checkout policy for us."

"When's our wedding?"

He grinned. "Saturday night."

"What about guests? We don't have any."

"Hence why a renewal of vows fits better."

"It kinda seems more romantic too, like eloping."

"Precisely."

"Err... Question. If we recite vows in front of a Justice of the Peace or whatever, wouldn't we legally be tying the knot?"

"We would. Hence why we must leave before that point."

"Even with fake names?"

"Depends on your view of marriage, I suppose. If you and I recite vows to one another in the presence of Creator, do our names matter? He knows who we are."

"Good point."

"So, unless you intend to marry me, the charade cannot continue to the altar."

"I dunno." She sloughed off a half-shrug. "I could do a lot worse."

She wasn't serious. Was she? "There's a fatal flaw in your argument, Kitty Cat. A marriage is built on trust."

"Oh, here we go." She slapped her forehead. "I'm telling you I trust you. Why do I gotta fall off the railing to prove it?"

"Because words are easy. Actions speak volumes."

Silence enveloped the Benz as he pulled into the driveway. In the yard, Jacy Lee chatted with the local ravens. Poe still hadn't left the porch, which meant he'd made little headway.

Parked, he killed the engine. "Please wait for me to get your door."

"Why? We're home."

"Please, Cat."

An audible exhale showed her annoyance. "Fine."

"Thank you." When he swung open her door moments later, he extended his hand, whispered, "Slide the briefcase out."

With a slight nod, she set her hand in his. As she rose, she dropped the briefcase in line with the tire. Perfect placement.

At the hatch, he gathered the shopping bags.

"Do we hide our cover story from *Shicheii*?"

"The man suggested the hammock exercise. I doubt a fictional narrative will faze him."

"Good point. What'd he hope to achieve, anyway?"

*Did she mean—?* "Are you insinuating he had ulterior motives beyond a nap?"

"There are simpler ways to force us to rest."

He hadn't considered that. *What are you up to, Jacy Lee?* "Interesting."

"Right?"

"You two look happy." Dimples dotted both cheeks when Jacy Lee held open the screen door. "Did you remember the almonds, Cheveyo?"

"I know better than to return without them."

In the kitchen, Mayhem set the bags on the granite island.

While his lifelong friend unloaded the groceries, he mulled over the most acceptable excuse to leave the property. Normally, Jacy Lee had no problem with their comings and goings, but the Buffalo incident rattled him, evident by the immediate construction of the Sacred Fire. The flames created a barrier between the log home and aggressive wildlife.

"What're you making, *Shicheii*?"

"A little something special for you and Cheveyo."

"Not necessary, Jacy Lee. You spoil us enough."

"Nonsense." He swatted away the comment. "Do you have something to do for an hour or two?"

That solved one problem. "We could go for a run, so Cat can familiarize herself with the landscape."

"If we're goin' for a run, I need to change."

"As do I."

"It's settled then." He shooed them out of the kitchen. "Take care of my granddaughter, Cheveyo."

"Always, my friend."

At the top of the loft stairs, Cat stalled. "Hey, um, your bedroom has a bathroom, right?"

"It does."

"Can I change in there? The loft has no door."

"That does pose a problem, doesn't it? Let me fetch a change of clothes. I'll dress in the loft. After our run, we should switch rooms. These sleeping arrangements make little sense with a woman in the house."

"For the record, I love chivalry."

*Adorable.*

When he strolled out of the bedroom moments later, Cat stood in front of the full-length window, gazing out at the wilderness.

Behind her, he breathed her in. Crisp and fresh, hints of citrus and earthy tones rose through his senses. "Stunning view, isn't it?"

"Wicked." She lingered a while longer. "Do you ever get nervous?"

"Nervous?"

"Yeah, I mean... What if you get shot? Or worse?"

"Nothing will happen to me, Kitty Cat." He rested his chin on her head. "I've been fighting the good fight for a long time."

When she turned, electric emerald eyes peered up at him. "I get that, but Killzme wants you dead. Since they plan to sell me, it at least gives me a chance to escape."

Their gazes locked.

"Say something."

"We cannot control the actions of others. What we can control is our response."

"I get that, too, but how do you not worry about the genuine possibility of death?"

"Through trust."

"Ugh." Her head shook. "Why does every conversation circle back to that?"

"Because it's important, Cat. Trust in your training. Trust in your partner. Trust in Creator and Holy Ones. It's a vital building block. Without trust, we have nothing."

His words struck the right chord because her stiff shoulders relaxed into the moment. "Fine. I'll fall off the damn railing."

He winked. "Looking forward to it."

She strode into the bedroom, muttering, "Yeah, yeah."

What he failed to mention was he couldn't reveal his secret without first knowing she fully trusted him, or he'd risk losing her forever.

# Chapter 19



Shirtless in buckskin pants like mine, Mr. Mayhem leaned against the railing, with the phone pressed to his ear. "Thank you, June. My bride and I shall see you soon." He disconnected. "I booked us a suite at the Lake Hotel."

"When do we check in?"

He grinned. "Whenever we arrive."

"Cool. Cover story's working already." I jogged down the stairs, but he didn't follow. "Thought we were going for a run."

Without a word, he dragged a chair to the railing.

"You're not gonna let this go, huh?"

His stare held all the things he wanted to say, words he'd never spoken, an aura that beckoned me closer. And so, I climbed up to the railing.

"Cross your arms over your chest, please."

He scuttled down the stairs. "Ready when you are, Cat."

"On three." My pulse pounded against my skin. "One... Two..."

*Shicheii* appeared in the screen door and broke my concentration.

I rolled the bones in my neck, shook out my arms, then re-grabbed my shoulders. "On three, ready? One... Two..." I glanced back to make sure he was still in position. "You're gonna catch me, right?"

"I am."

"Okay, here we go. One... Two..." Again, I hesitated.

"May I make a suggestion, Cat? Don't count. Just let go."

"Cool, cool," I said all casual-like, as though this exercise didn't bother me. Nothing could be farther from the truth. "Do I close my eyes or...?"

"Whatever makes you more comfortable."

Comfortable? Not even close.

My gaze sidled to my grandfather. If I didn't fall, I'd fail him, too. So, I inhaled a deep breath—exhaled—and leaned back into nothingness.

He caught me mid-air. When he lowered my feet to the grass, his raspy voice whispered in my ear, "Nicely done, Kitty Cat."

"Thanks."

Applauding, *Shicheii* burst through the doorway. "I am so proud of you, Mourning Dove."

My smile couldn't stretch any wider. "Thanks."

It might not seem like a big deal to some, but my past gave me plenty of reasons not to trust. The few times I did, life proved me right, resulting in a thick protective wall few could penetrate. Safer that way.

All of which these two incredible humans knew all-too well. Their devotion never wavered, their patience and understanding unmatched. But to continue my journey, I must break free from the chains of my past. Not easy—baby steps, as my mentor would say—but tonight, I took a giant leap in the right direction.

"Have fun, you two." *Shicheii* scuttled inside, the screen door slapping shut behind him.

"Stay close." He jogged toward the Benz. In one swift motion, he snatched the briefcase off the driveway and kept moving while I ran beside him to block in case my grandfather looked out the window. We both hated to keep things from him, but we had no choice.

Partway into the thick wilderness, he slowed. "Until you learn the landscape, let's not tempt fate."

"Aha. So you *do* worry."

"There's a vast difference between concern and caution. By familiarizing ourselves with our environment—or in my case, re-familiarizing—we are exercising the latter while gaining life-saving knowledge. For example, tell me what's around the next bend."

"It's a trick question. It's too far away."

His stiff arm stopped me cold. "You can't tell me anything? Nothing?"

"When we get closer, I can."

He lowered the briefcase. "Why not now?" Behind me, his gentle hands shielded my eyes. "Listen."

"But my right ear—"

"Shh... listen."

Birds flitted from tree to tree, rustling leaves in their wake. Chipmunks chirped, their *chuck-chuck* call often mistaken for birdsong—*Shicheii* taught me that. Repeated scrapings, rapid clicks, and squeaks alluded to a robust squirrel community, and bleats and snorts from deer and antelope.

All at once, the chorus of chatter silenced.

My body stiffened into concrete. "There's a predator nearby."

"Correct. Which one?"

A *mah* pierced the air, followed by a *hish*, then another *mah*. "No clue."

His hands lowered. "You don't recognize the vocalizations?"

"Should I?"

A sly grin emerged. "Does Karma ring a bell?"

"Cougar. Aww, I miss my buddy."

"Perhaps you'll make a new friend." He slung a loose arm around my neck. "Let's give him a wide berth so he doesn't feel threatened."

Clouds rolled overhead when we reached the foot of a mountain, but he didn't seem concerned about it, so I kept my mouth shut and followed up a steep incline. Were we hiking to the top?

When the trail jackknifed, he switched the briefcase to his left hand to extend his right. "Careful, Ghost Dog."

Dropping my Apache name was his subtle hint to watch where I stepped as he pulled me higher and higher. The elevation pained my eardrums, my right-side crackling and popping, my head light and airy, but I couldn't show it without failing the exercise. So, I slapped on a smile and continued, sheer perseverance driving me to scale the friggin' cliffside. Which, by the way, nobody else dared to do, hikers noticeably absent from this area.

Gee, I wonder why? No big predators up here, but with a storm moving in, traversing rocky terrain wasn't what I'd call safe. Stones tumbled off the rockface at a steady pace.

The flat plateau diminished the fear of falling to my death. Gotta admit, he chose the perfect spot.

Had he come here before? No one could deny his close relationship with Klee and Ferron—so much so he had his own bedroom in their home. Maybe this was his favorite thinking spot.

Aww, how sweet to share it with me.

Seated on the rock, he said, "Speak your mind, Cautious Cat."

"How'd you find this place?"

"When or how?"

"When?"

He smiled. "Years ago."

"Do you come here a lot?"

"Every time I'm in town."

"Alone or...?"

"For the past few years, I have."

Kimi died over a year ago, but she lost mobility from the ALS long before then. "She used to come here?" Once a loved one passed, it was bad luck to speak their name aloud.

"She loved this spot."

"I see why." Heart wrenching, my gaze settled on the horizon. "It's beautiful here. Serene."

"That it is, Cat." He stared in the same direction. "That it is."

"How's Cheyenne?" His daughter, who I last saw at Kimi's memorial in Jackson, New Hampshire.

"She's well, thank you."

"How does she feel about Spirit Crow's return?"

That got him to face me. "I haven't told her. Do you think I should?"

"Doesn't Spirit Crow help you cope?"

"Yes and no." He re-faced the horizon. "She prevents me from moving forward with my life. At other times, I can't imagine a day without her. It is a torturous seesaw I'd hate to inflict on my daughter. Have you noticed she's beginning to favor the lifestyle of the body she inhabits?"

"Yeah." My calling Odin probably didn't help matters. "I'm so deeply sorry for the part I played."

"You have nothing to apologize for, Kitty Cat. These are extraordinary times. We navigate the best we can with highly volatile emotions and deep connections that only intensify the difficultly. If we do right by one, we may hurt another. We can try to widen our perception to predict how our actions may affect everyone involved, but failure is inevitable. It's not a simple home life."

"Maybe not, but I wouldn't change a thing about where we are now."

His coy smile gave me hope. "Nothing at all?"

Did he mean us? I couldn't get a read on him. "No one ever promised us an easy life."

"How right you are." His soft gaze lingered on me a moment longer before his attention turned to the briefcase. "Let's see what intel good ol' Elliot has to offer."

He passed me a stack of file folders.

When I flipped open the top cover, I said, "Odin still needs to come home, though."

He leafed through the ledger. "Agreed."

My inner cheerleaders applauded. They silenced as my eyes bulged at the words scrawled across the paper in my hands. Held hostage by the savageness of Killzme's plan, I couldn't speak, couldn't breathe.

"Dare I ask what you found?"

The more I read the more my stomach knotted. "They're hunting Buffalo."

His expression blanked. "Not wolves, grizzlies, and lynxes?"

"In addition to them. The hunt spans the weekend, from Friday to Monday. Each day focuses on a different species, with cash prizes for the winners. Largest kill. Trickiest kill. Cleanest kill. At the end of the massacre, participants vote for the best overall in two categories, most skilled and—" I swallowed. "Most skilled and—" Tears tumbled down my cheeks. "And most—"

"Harvested."

I nodded, my chest rallying against a tidal wave of sadness. "We can't let anyone win that title."

"We won't."

"If Killzme offers cash prizes for a four-day massacre, imagine the size of the group? How are me and you gonna go head-to-head with that many poachers?"

He smirked. "Tactfully."

"I don't find this funny."

"Nor do I."

"Then what's the smirk for?"

"The challenge." His elbow nudged mine. "You don't find monster slaying the least bit exhilarating?"

"Alright, maybe a little."

With his arm hooked around my neck, he kissed my cheek. "There she is."

An hour later, after loading all the paperwork in the briefcase, I rose. When he didn't stand with me, I followed his sightline.

Cloud cover squashed the horizon, shadowing vibrant pinks and peaches into ghostly hues, their brilliance hidden beneath. The impending storm signaled a harder road ahead, the air tainted by the scent of rain—a prophecy of the war to save the Innocent Ones before Killzme Corp tore apart the natural splendor of Greater Yellowstone, including all that it stood for, all that it was, and all that it could be for future generations. A breathtaking representation of wild spaces, where the voiceless roamed free and the evil acts of man laid dormant, beaten and dead, never to rise again.

Or would this mission turn into the battle that finally broke us?

# Chapter 20

*"It is hard for me to understand a culture that not only hates and fights his brothers but even attacks Nature and abuses her. Man must love all creation, or he will love none of it."*
—Chief Dan George

*9:00 p.m.*

Cat's scream snapped his attention away from the sunset. As she sprang backward, he latched onto her wrist, her feet slipping off the ledge, the force dragging him, his feet groping for leverage. The briefcase sailed off the mountainside with her, papers raining like snowflakes.

With a firm grip on one of her wrists, he looped his free arm around a protrusion of rock near the edge.

Sheer terror crossed her face, her body dangling mid-air. "Don't let go."

"I would never." He scanned the rockface. "See the crevice below me? It's about even with your hips."

Tears streamed in lines out the corners of her eyes, raven hair blowing beneath her, her widened gaze straying left and right and above him. "Tell *Shicheii* I love him."

"Tell him yourself. I am not returning without you." Knuckles blanched from his tight grip, his muscles strained from supporting dead weight. "Focus on me, Cat. Wedge one foot in the crevice for leverage, then climb."

Her free hand latched onto his forearm.

"You can do this."

Frantic, her legs bicycled mid-air. "Oh, my God, I'm gonna die. This is it. This is how it all ends. If I don't make it, I need you to know how I feel about us."

Negativity would not benefit her. "Ghost Dog—"

Her focus snapped to attention.

"Step into the crevice. Now."

Without a word, she followed his directives. The heaviness of her weight decreased somewhat. Even more so when she planted both feet on the rockface.

"Excellent. Now, climb."

Never had he witnessed such buckling knees, like her legs rubberized, and she no longer controlled them. "Eyes on the prize, Ghost Dog."

Her frantic gaze locked with his.

"Good."

Little by little, she climbed higher.

"Excellent." He leaned farther over the edge. "Wrap your arm around my neck, darlin'."

"But I gotta let go of your arm."

"Understood. You can do this."

The moment she hooked his neck, he pulled her. Together, they fell back on the flat-topped surface. She crawled away from the ledge, settled with her spine against the mountain, legs stretched out in front of her.

Still flat on his back, he took a moment to slow the adrenaline.

A Billy mountain goat loomed on the ledge above her. Males had a wider horn base, a "roman bulge" on the nose, and longer face and horns than females. Billies also traveled alone, like the curious individual staring down at them.

"Cat?"

"Yeah?"

"What startled you?"

"Some big white furry thing, with hollow black eyes and devil horns."

He sat upright. "The big fella above you is a mountain goat. They're docile creatures with a long history in the area."

She flattened to the rock wall. "He's above me?"

With an audible exhale, he pinched the bridge of his nose. "Cat, please. We cannot lose any more intel because of your knee-jerk reactions to unfamiliar wildlife."

"I almost died, for fuck's sake, and you're worried about the briefcase?"

He winced. "Language, please."

"Just sayin'. You could show a little more compassion for what I just went through."

Oh, boy. Here we go. "You're alive and well."

"Not the point. Maybe if you warned me mountain goats lived around here, he wouldn't've scared the crap outta me."

"Fair enough. I apologize for the oversight. How are you, Cat?"

"Besides the crackling in my right ear?" She grimaced. "Alright, I guess."

"Pleased to hear it." When he rose, she followed, her gaze ping-ponging between him and the mountain goat. "Shall we proceed?"

"Waitin' on you, partner."

Only she could regain complete confidence minutes after falling off a mountainside, as though her skill and perseverance was what saved her. "Oh, Cat, what will I do with you?"

She strode toward their exit route. "Hey, don't hate the player. Hate the game."

"Again, that expression has nothing to do with this scenario."

She looped one leg over the edge to climb down. "I know, but it fits."

"Does it?" Following her, they soon reached the bottom, where they picked up the hiking trail. "Veer right, please."

"I know."

The bite to her tone was unnecessary, but he stayed silent. Already, it'd been a long day, and it still wasn't over.

The hazy moon lingered overhead, its beams unable to penetrate thick canopies of leaves. In the meager trickles of light, she felt around for his hand. Laced her fingers with his, her chewed nails clawed into his skin—a sure sign of fright.

"Almost home," he said in the hopes of comforting her.

"I dunno how I feel about leaving the briefcase behind. What if someone finds it?"

"I don't like it any more than you do, but we ran out of daylight. It's safer to salvage the contents in the morning."

"If *Shicheii* hadn't planned this special dinner, we at least could've given it a shot."

"Not to worry, Cat. The breath of a new day puts everything into perspective. Until then, stay positive. Nurturing us is Jacy Lee's love language. We're blessed to have him in our lives."

"No, I know. Didn't mean it like that. His timing needs work, though."

He chuckled. "That trait runs in your bloodline."

She slapped his arm. "Ha ha. Everyone's a comedian."

He led her around the last bend in the trail.

Flames tongued the night air. Orange sparks leaped past the ring of stones, firelight blazing a path through the woods, the Sacred Fire guiding them home.

Jacy Lee sat on the top stair of the porch beside Poe, whose bill hung low, wings slumped in defeat. Spirit Crow leaped off the railing to greet them. Soft rattles emanated through the amber luminesce as she neared, ultimately landing on his outstretched forearm.

"Hello, sweetheart." He smooched her feathery cheek. "How are you?"

She nuzzled into his neck.

On the porch, Poe raised his head, his neck missing the tricolored gold braid. Oh, my. "Jacy Lee?"

As he stroked Poe's back, he explained, "One of the local females lured him into the yard."

"Oh, boy."

"Evidently, it was an ambush. The big male pinned him down while another stole his necklace. It was awful, Cheveyo. Just awful. They were heckling him during his escape."

With a yelp, Poe dove into Dad's arms. Soft whimpering muffled against his bare chest. Cat's watery gaze lowered to Poe, one hand slapped over her mouth, a slight shake to her head. Her empathetic reaction only made Mayhem more emotional.

Oh, how his heart bled. "It's all right, bud." He cradled him in one arm, much in the way one carried a football. "You're just as handsome without the necklace."

Another gut-wrenching yelp escaped.

"I know it's difficult, bud." Tears blurred his vision. "Once the novelty wears off, the ravens will leave it in a tree somewhere. It may take some time, but we will find it. If the necklace remains beyond our reach, I'll buy you a new one. How does that sound?"

Poe's guttural cry snapped his last heartstring.

"If Odin was here, this never woulda happened."

Spirit Crow leaped off his shoulder, angelic wings headed straight for the screen door, which Jacy Lee opened.

"Thank you, Cat. Now she's upset, as well."

A defiant shoulder swayed. "Maybe you shoulda thought of that before leaving him behind."

"Not helpful. We have already established my error. Have we not? The rehash only stirs emotions to a boiling point."

"Maybe next time when I make a suggestion, you'll listen." She stomped up the stairs and into the house.

*Ooh, that woman...* "Why am I always the bad guy?"

Jacy Lee's silence spoke volumes. Seconds later, he strode inside, as well.

Alone at the table, Mayhem uncapped his tea, crossed his ankles out in front of him, and leaned back in his chair. Tensions ran high tonight, which did not bode well for the week ahead. Soon, all the lights in the house blackened.

Did everyone go to bed? What happened to the special dinner Jacy Lee allegedly prepared?

Between the time change and the lingering jet lag, he could not settle. Instead, he paced, the deck boards creaking under his weight. Family issues aside, they still had a job to do. But he couldn't check into the hotel without Cat.

With no alternative, he strode into the house. Perhaps a good night's sleep would benefit everyone. Life had a funny way of improving in the morning.

In his dark bedroom, he stripped off his buckskin pants and slid into bed, his tired bones sinking into the mattress, his head melting into the pillow. As he drifted into a deep slumber, a disembodied hand slipped across his abdominal muscles.

Startled awake, instinct took over.

In one swift motion, he pounced on the intruder. One arm pinned the forehead while he death-gripped the throat, his fingers squeezing the airway. Hands clawed at his face and chest, but he refused to let go.

Once the intruder went limp, he leaped out of bed. Flicked on the light.

And there lay Cat, out cold on his pillow, drool dripping down her chin.

Uh-oh. As this was not the first time, she would undoubtedly hold this incident against him.

Why was she in his bed?

# Chapter 21



A cool, wet washcloth dabbed my forehead, down my cheek, and across my neck. "*Shicheii*?"

Mr. Mayhem's deep, husky voice said, "No." His palm cradled the back of my head, a glass pressed to my lips as he raised me far enough off the pillow to drink. "Tiny sips, Kitty Cat."

A sharpness scratched my throat like I'd swallowed glass, so I pushed his arm away. "What happened?"

"Tiny sips." Again, he pressed the tumbler to my lips. "Here we go."

This time, I slapped his arm away. "I don't want it. My throat's killing me. What happened?"

"Well, I thought you'd learned not to startle me awake, but evidently not." He sat back on his heels, a sheet draped over his bare lap. "How are you?"

"Hey, um, are you—?"

"Cautious Cat, I thought I was alone. In my bed. What I choose to wear or not wear is not up for debate. A better question might be why you are here."

"Whaddaya mean? You said you were cool with switching rooms."

"Without fair warning?" His head rocked, tilting like I'd spoken a foreign language. "You walked away without a word. How on earth did you expect me to know what bedroom you entered?"

"If you bothered to check on me, you woulda."

"Oh, is that the game we're playing now? You walk out, and I'm expected to chase you? Hate to disappoint, but I am not that man. If you cannot express yourself without storming away, then—"

A fist clenched in my stomach. "Don't say it."

Another tilt of the head. "What words do you fear?"

"That you'll leave."

The hard lines around his eyes softened, and our souls danced. My heartbeat quickened to a fast *pitter-patter, pitter-patter, pitter-patter*.

"I would never abandon you, Kitty Cat. Never."

Emotions heaved my chest, tears spilling over the rims of my eyes. "Promise?"

"Why do you still feel so unworthy?"

"I dunno."

He yanked me into his chest, held me tight, and I blubbered all over his shoulder.

"Sorry."

"Hey." He pulled me away, his thumbs wiping my tears as quickly as they fell. "You have nothing to apologize for." He kissed my forehead then nose. "I'll sleep in the loft tonight."

When he swiveled to leave the bed, I latched onto his arm. "Wait—"

The raised chin prompted me to continue.

"Wanna have tea first?" My empty stomach roared like a lion. No way didn't he catch it. "The honey might help my throat."

"May I put pants on first?"

*Ahem.* "Sure."

After crawling out of bed, my nightshirt twisted and tight, I tried to act natural by looking anywhere but at him. "Cool, cool. So—"

"I'll meet you in the hall, Cat."

Translation—*Please leave my room.* "Probably best."

When I swung open the door, there stood my grandfather in his robe, two gray braids reaching for his waist. "Mourning Dove?" He peeked around me at Mr. Mayhem, still in bed, the blankets halfway off the mattress, a strip of sheet draped over his bare lap. "Cheveyo?"

I doubt either of us inhaled. He could easily misinterpret this as the scene of wild sexcapades.

The silence lasted ten years.

"Cat and I hit a snag in our sleeping arrangements."

"I see." He stole another eyeful of the bed. "Quite the miscommunication, by the looks of it."

"That it was. What can I do for you, my friend?"

"I came for the nest. Or didn't you notice Poe and Spirit Crow weren't in the room?"

"Honestly, it was quite dark when I slipped into bed. Are they all right?"

"They're upset, Cheveyo. As am I. Those ravens were so cruel. And Odin's absence is not helping matters."

"I am cognizant of that, as well. I'll have a talk with Poe in the morning." His throat cleared. "Cat, would you mind fetching the nest?"

*So he didn't have to rise buck-assed naked.* "Sure."

When I passed the nest to *Shicheii*, I led him into the hall. "We were gonna have tea? Wanna join us?"

"No, thank you, honey. I'm still trying to console Poe and Spirit Crow."

I pulled the door closed behind us.

"Let me ask you, honey. How did you raise her spirits earlier?"

I led him farther away from the bedroom door. "I called Running Bear on FaceTime so she could chat with Odin."

"FaceTime?"

"Y'know, the video call like we used in the Arctic."

At the top of the stairs, he framed my face in warm palms. "Is there anything you want to tell me?"

"*Shicheii*, nothing happened, I swear. We planned to switch rooms after supper, but then we didn't have supper, and I thought that meant his room was mine now, but I left without discussing it with him, and I guess he assumed I went to sleep in the loft."

"And Cheveyo's undressed because...?"

"What he wears to bed, or doesn't wear, is none of our business."

"You're right." He kissed my forehead. "Goodnight, my love."

"Night, *Shicheii*."

Before heading downstairs, I slipped into spandex short-shorts. Only wearing a nightshirt allowed mosquitos too much access. By limiting the soft-skinned areas for the females to bite—the males of the species didn't consume blood—it gave my crotch some protection.

Plus, at least now, we wouldn't end this night with an unintentional gap shot.

# Chapter 22

*"Love is something you and I must have. We must have it because our spirit feeds upon it. Without love, our self-esteem weakens. Without it, our courage fails. Without love, we can no longer look out confidently at the world. Instead, we turn inwardly and begin to feed upon our own personalities, and little by little we destroy ourselves." —Chief Dan George*

### *11:30 p.m.*

On the porch, Mayhem's conversation with Ferron crushed his spirit. If Cat couldn't find it in her heart to forgive him, he might never see her again. He couldn't return to a solitary existence. Not now. Not after how close they'd become. Creator never built humans to walk alone.

Beside him, her delicate hands cupped her mug, her eyes sparkling in the moonlight.

If this turned into one of their last nights together, he must make it unforgettable. So, he rose. "Dance with me, Kitty Cat."

"What? Where?"

"In the yard. Under the stars."

"Now?"

"If you'll do me the honor, yes."

"What kind of dance? You've only taught me two."

"Freestyle. No right or wrong steps."

"But there's no music."

"O ye of little faith." He hooked his phone to Ferron's portable speaker. "Hello" by Lionel Richie filled his screen. Perfect. He pushed pause before it played. "Come on. It'll be fun."

Her expression still held hints of suspicion. "Is this another trust building exercise?"

"It can be. Or we can simply surrender to the music. Do you have a preference?"

"Surrender."

"Then we shall."

"Alright." She smiled. "Ask me again."

With his hand extended, he offered her a slight bow. "May I have this dance, milady?"

"Sure."

On their way down the stairs, he tapped Play on his phone.

In the moonlight, he held her close, her back aligned with his bare chest, their arms breathing—in... out... in... out—with wide sweeping motions. Her scent reignited a spark he could no longer deny. His leg lifted hers. On a slow pivoted twirl, her silky hair caressed his neck and shoulders.

When the lyrics began, he spun her to face him. His thigh prodded hers backward, every sliver of him longing for her to feel the power behind each word.

At the first "hello" he lifted her, his arms curled around her sculptured thighs, her delicate fingers resting on his shoulders, her long tresses dangling down at him, their souls dancing as closely as their bodies.

In total surrender, she fell back on his hand, swaying like a warm summer breeze. He rolled her into his arms as they spun—slow and rhythmic—the backs of his fingers stroking her arm.

He walked her backward, a cougar stalking his mate. Tenderly, he tucked her hair behind her ear. They arced back, forward, back, forward.

He lifted her higher now—a slow, sensuous pirouette—her grace stealing his every breath. As the tempo picked up, they glided across the grass. Their bodies expressed all the things they couldn't say. On the next lift, she draped her body across his chest, united and twirling, her essence connecting to the deep recesses of his soul, her soft skin glistening in the moonlight.

When he dipped her for the last time, their gazes locked, two breathing as one. Heart swelling with endless love, he glanced down at her lips.

*Squeak, squeak.*

The screen door. "Jacy Lee?" he called out.

Shawnee melted off his arm.

"Kitty Cat—"

"Go." Flat on her back, she waved him toward the porch. "I need a minute, anyway."

"Jacy Lee," he called again, but his weight shifted from leg to leg, wavering whether to pick her up or chase her grandfather.

"My apologies, Cheveyo." He slinked out to the porch, his face wet with tears. "I didn't mean to intrude."

"Intrude?" *How much had he seen?* He extended a hand to Cat, who still hadn't moved.

Meanwhile, her grandfather's emotions bubbled over.

"Talk to me, Jacy Lee. Why are you upset?"

"That—" He cupped his mouth, fresh tears tumbling over his fingers. "That dance..."

Oh, boy. He did not approve. Mayhem's breath caught.

"What I just witnessed was the most beautiful, heartfelt expression of love. You two took my breath away. I forgot how much I missed watching you dance, Cheveyo."

A warmth filled him deep inside. "I haven't danced like that in a long time."

"Because you stopped having a reason to." His gaze sidled to his granddaughter. "Now you do."

"Jacy Lee..."

"Mourning Dove, I..." He swept away tears. "I never knew you could move like that, honey."

"If we're being totally honest," her voice was soft, emotional, "neither did I."

"I don't understand, honey."

"I surrendered to the music... to the moment... to him."

*They both did.* "She's quite remarkable."

"That she is, Cheveyo." Pure love emanated from his aura. "And so are you." He seemed to shake off the emotion. "Well, you're certainly in sync now. Goodnight, my loves. Don't stay up too late."

The somber tone ached Mayhem's heart. "Jacy Lee..."

Cat must have also picked up on it. "Maybe we should turn in, too."

"Good idea. I'll sleep in the loft. We'll transfer over our belongings in the morning." As he held open the screen door, he whispered, "Thank you for the dance, Kitty Cat."

One finger stroked down his chest. "Anytime, sugar bear."

# Chapter 23



Knocking at the bedroom door startled me awake. My gaze shot to the bedside clock. Shit. I overslept.

"Honey," *Shicheii* called, "may we come in?"

"Coming." On my way to the door, I stubbed my toe on the bedpost and pain lasered up my shin. Before he knocked again, I hopped. When I opened the door, my grandfather's gaze lowered to my raised foot.

"Are you all right, my love?"

"Yep." I added weight to the leg. "Is it time for morning prayer?"

"It is." My dance partner dragged open the full-length curtains to expose a balcony I never knew existed. He swayed one hand out the sliders. "After you, Cat."

In the early morning darkness, my grandfather recited the opening prayer in Athabaskan. My faux husband played a Native flute.

The wood added a specialness to the notes while *Shicheii* and I sang to the Holy Ones.

Sprinkling corn pollen into the early predawn dimness, my grandfather prayed for our well-being, our safety, and our defeat of the Natural World's enemies. It was so uplifting and heartfelt, my chest heaved with gratitude.

Soon, pinks splashed across the horizon by Creator's loving hands. Magenta emerged. The colors brightening, widening, and spreading like the barbs of a feather.

"O Great Spirit, may Cheveyo and Mourning Dove never stop dancing. Their steps honor the simple pleasures of life, of unity, of family. Thank you for opening my eyes to love at its purest form."

*Aw, man. Why, Shicheii, why?* Dragging my teeth down my upper lip, my gaze strayed to my dance partner, who fingered his shirt collar like he needed air.

To end the awkwardness, I said, "In the name of all my relations, I pray."

Mr. Mayhem said, "A'ho."

"What?"

"Comparable to Amen."

"Why am I only learning this now? I've been saying, 'In the name of all my relations, I pray' this whole time."

"Don't be angry, honey." *Shicheii* chuckled. "It was so cute, we didn't have the heart to set you straight."

I flung up my hands. "Unbelievable. What else don't I know?"

My dance partner sniggered. "Plenty."

"For the record, I don't find the humor in this at all."

His throat cleared. "Noted."

With morning prayer completed, I followed them down the stairs and out to the porch, where *Shicheii* poured homemade wild tea into three mugs.

"Could you cap mine, honey? I need to get breakfast ready."

"Sure."

Mr. Mayhem lifted halfway off the chair. "Let me get the door for you, Jacy Lee."

"I can manage on my own, thank you. Sit. Relax." All smiles, he scuttled inside.

An awkward silence hung in the air.

I drizzled honey into my tea, my mind reliving the sensuousness of last night. "So... should we talk about that dance?" *Or what might've happened if Shicheii hadn't interrupted us.*

"If you need to, we can."

"Nope." The wrong words might halt the fantasy replaying on an endless loop. "All good."

"What we should discuss is our plans for today."

"Don't we need to check into the hotel?"

"We do."

I tried to act natural when this intimate new wrinkle was anything but. "Cool, cool."

After another awkward moment, he whispered, "Kitty Cat, I asked you to dance last night because—"

*Shicheii* backed out the door with a serving tray. *Man, he had shit timing.* "Made your favorite, honey."

I held my dance partner's gaze. "Smells amazing, *Shicheii.*"

He broke eye contact first. "Indeed, it does."

The eggs Benedict were better than sex. Well, not quite. But damn close. My eyes rolled closed, and I couldn't stop the soft moan before it escaped. By the time I shook out of the love bubble, Poe stood across from me, beady eyes slitted like he wanted to rip out my throat. The never-ending glower ended when he pushed his bowl next to his literal meal ticket.

*Kiss ass.* "Where's Spirit Crow?"

*Shicheii* blew on his tea. "Napping in your room."

Mr. Mayhem's napkin dabbed his lips. Seconds later, his chair slid backward. "I better check on her."

Only I knew the real reason for her depression, so I shot to my feet. "I'll go."

"I appreciate the kind gesture, Cat, but I wouldn't want your meal to get cold. If the moan was any indication, you were clearly enjoying it."

"You heard that?" I swiped away my comment. "Not important. I'll bring it with me." I raised my plate. "Problem solved."

"Are you sure?"

"Positive." I headed for the door, but he beat me to it, his palm flattened on the screen to hold it open. Never once did I tire of chivalry. "*Shicheii*, can you cap my tea, please?"

"Certainly, my love."

When I passed Mr. Mayhem, he thanked me. And I waved over my head. "No problem."

On the second floor, I tapped on the bedroom door. Inside, Spirit Crow slept on the nightstand in the handcrafted nest *Shicheii* built for her and Poe, her bill tucked into her angelic chest feathers.

"Hey." I lowered to the edge of the mattress beside her, my plate in my lap. "We're worried about you. Are you alright?"

A light coo barely registered.

"Should we check on Odin one last time?"

She perked up.

"If you-know-who finds out, he will kill me. You know that, right?"

The saddest blue eyes pleaded with me to understand.

"Okay, fine." I called Running Bear on FaceTime. Only this time, he didn't bother to answer first. Instead, Odin peered into the screen. I giggled. "Hey, bud. One sec." The moment I set my iPhone in the nest, Spirit Crow sprang to life.

*Coo... rattle, rattle.* She bounced up and down. *Coo...*

*Gronk, gronk.* He matched her motion. *Kuk, kuk, kuk.*

While they chatted, I shoveled in cheesy hollandaise sauce and poached eggs, yolk spilling over cooked spinach and grilled English muffins.

*Whisper, whisper. Coo...*

*Gronk, gronk, gronk.*

Was this a romance thing or...? I didn't dare ask, nor did I want to know. None of my business, really. Plus, I loved them both. If I learned the truth, I might have to choose a side, especially if Mr. Mayhem found out.

Regardless, she deserved happiness, too.

Odin leaned closer to the screen. Spirit Crow did the same. Their inaudible whispers—used in the wild for communication between family members—barely pierced my good ear. Every now and then, Spirit Crow peeked over her wing at me, and I couldn't figure out why.

Soon it became clear these two were planning something. What, I had no clue, but I knew conspiring when I saw it. Were they talkin' about me? Sure seemed like it. Was she filling him in on our cuddle session in the hammock? My heart collapsed. Did she watch us dance?

*Whisper, whisper.* Glance back. *Whisper, whisper.*

Crap. *It's the hammock, I think.* Probably didn't look good when we fell asleep in each other's arms. Though, in all fairness, we'd been working nonstop for weeks chasing Killzme scumbags. And sure, we spent a lot of time together. Like every minute of every day. Still. What partners don't? They're called work wives for a reason. At least, that was the lie I'd tried to believe till the dance shattered the illusion.

All casual like, Spirit Crow stepped to one side, and Odin stared straight at me.

*Kuk, kuk. Gronk. Whisper, whisper.*

Her body blocked the screen. *Coo... coo... Whisper, whisper.*

Okay. No way did I imagine that. They really were talking about me. About us.

Even though I'd devoured every morsel on my plate, they were bouncing again, and I didn't have the heart to break up the love-fest.

The door flew open, and there he stood. "What on earth is going on in here?"

Uh-oh. The jig's up. "I can explain."

When he plucked the iPhone from the nest, Odin ducked off-screen. "Running Bear—" Seconds felt like days till he appeared. "Have you updated your phone?"

Without a word, he jiggled a new iPhone, still in the box.

"Cautious Cat," he said in a tone that matched his mood, but didn't turn to face me, "have we or have we not discussed security concerns?"

"We have."

"And what is the one thing I asked you not to do?"

"Call Running Bear."

"Why?"

"Because Killzme could track his old phone."

He still couldn't look at me. "Which would jeopardize his entire family. If the new phone is still in the box—though why boggles the mind—what phone did you call?"

Head hung, I squeaked out, "The old one."

"Correct." Only now did he turn. "After everything you endured on that ship to save his son"—one hand thumped his chest—"my godson," his voice boomed, "why, why, why, why, why would you risk his life?"

Running Bear's voice rose from the speaker. "Shadow Wolf, Ghost Dog was only trying to—"

"Hook up your new phone." He punched End.

*Gulp.*

"How many times have you called him?"

As he loomed over me, I could not stop blinking. "A couple."

"Twice?"

I chewed my lower lip. "Three times, but only because Spirit Crow was so depressed."

He whirled toward the nest. "Is that why you've been moping around?"

Her bill hit her chest feathers.

"Sweetheart, why didn't you come to me? I would never have left Odin behind if I'd known how you felt about him."

*Coo... coo... coo...*

"I miss him, too. Look, if he makes you happy—"

"I probably shouldn't be here. Doesn't sound like my business." Neither glanced in my direction as I backed toward the door, but I still jutted a thumb over my shoulder. "I'm gonna go drink my tea."

Damn. These family dynamics got more and more complicated by the minute. If we didn't find some common ground soon, Killzme might win this war.

# Chapter 24

*"Healing doesn't mean the damage never existed. It means the damage no longer controls our lives."* —Akshay Dubey

***7:30 a.m.***

Spirit Crow's affection for Odin did not surprise or upset him. Rather, she set him free to follow his heart.

In the kitchen, Jacy Lee scrubbed the dishes in the sink, even though a perfectly good dishwasher crouched under the counter beside him.

"Any objections to Cat and me leaving for our morning run?"

"Not at all, Cheveyo. Her training is important."

"Where is Poe?"

"Back in the nest with his mother."

Mayhem slung an arm over his shoulders. "Do you and I need to discuss last night?"

"Not right now."

"Are we all right?"

While turning toward him, Jacy Lee dried his hands on the dish towel suspended from the waist of his jeans. For several moments, he didn't speak. "You're wrong about why Spirit Crow returned."

He rocked back. "I am?"

"She's always loved you, Cheveyo. And always will. This, you know."

Mayhem's mind spun. "I don't understand."

"What's more likely? That she returned to protect her family, knowing full well you are more than capable in that regard, or couldn't she rest without ensuring your happiness?"

Lips parted, breath tangled in his chest. The right words stayed beyond reach.

"Is there anyone else who could fill her shoes?"

"That's the last thing I want." Surely, he wasn't insinuating women were interchangeable. "Cat blazes her own trail."

Dimples dotted both cheeks. "That she does." He cupped Mayhem's cheek. "You didn't need my blessing last night, and you don't need it today. Follow your heart, Cheveyo. It has never failed you."

Emotions swelled his chest. "Jacy Lee..."

With a simple nod, he returned to the dishes. "Better not keep my granddaughter waiting. She's not the most patient creature."

Chuckling, Mayhem patted his back. "How right you are, my friend."

"I have one request, however."

"Name it."

"Tell her, Cheveyo, sooner rather than later. We were wrong to withhold that story. She has a right to know."

*Did Ferron change his mind?*

Cat darted into the kitchen. "Know what?"

"Hi, honey."

She kissed her grandfather's cheek. "What do I have a right to know?"

Mayhem froze, body board stiff, his gaze shifting between them. He couldn't tell her now. Not yet.

Jacy Lee stroked her hair. "Have I told you how proud I am of you?"

"Only every single day." She embraced him. "Love you, *Shicheii*." She jabbed a chin at Mayhem. "Ready to go?"

He swayed an opened hand at the archway. "Lead the way."

"Love you both." Turning back to the sink, Jacy Lee waved over his head. "Enjoy your run."

After trekking through the woods, Mayhem led her to the foot of the mountain. No briefcase, no scattered papers.

Cat scratched her cheek. "You sure we're in the right place?"

"Evidently not, though why remains a mystery." His gaze crawled up the mountainside. "The plateau is directly above us. We may have to scan from there. Do you recall where the briefcase landed?"

"I was a little preoccupied with death."

He pinched the bridge of his nose. "You did not almost die."

"Says you. That's not at all how I remember it."

He chuckled. "Why doesn't that surprise me?"

"Hilarious." Her expression said anything but. "Why don't I stay here, and you can direct me where to go?"

Why hadn't he thought of that? "Brilliant idea."

She flipped her hair over one shoulder. "I thought so."

"Humility is a much nicer look, wouldn't you agree?" Without waiting for a reply, he hiked up the mountain.

On the plateau, he peered over the ledge—a continual scan of the landscape below. Where'd she go? Hands cupped around his mouth, he called down, "Cat—" But sound waves had a difficult time traveling downhill.

A fair-skinned arm waved from a tree canopy's bushy leaves.

What on earth—? Did the wildlife spook her again? About twenty yards to her right, sheaths of paper rolled with the breeze.

"Cat, head West—"

She didn't move.

A little louder, he called out, "Head West, Cat!"

When she still did not budge, he let out a breathy exhale. Hopefully, she brought her cell.

He dialed.

She answered on the second ring. "I'm not moving till you get down here."

"This was your idea. Was it not?"

"Well, yeah, but—"

"Then what is the problem?"

"Can you please come down here?"

"Mountain goats again?"

"I don't care what you say. Those devil horns and soulless black eyes freak me out."

"Oh, Cautious Cat..." They didn't have time for this. "Stay put. I'll be right there."

Minutes later, he stood under the tree. She lowered down the trunk. Together, they gathered all the paperwork, some sheaths chewed apart by wildlife, others entirely consumed. The only item they hadn't destroyed was the ledger. Its cover bore a few bite marks but was otherwise in good shape.

Cat pressed a pile of shredded paper to her chest. "Maybe we can piece it together."

"Potentially. It may be advantageous to try." He leafed through the ledger. "Did Cynthia ever mention how long Elliot worked for Killzme Corp?"

"No. He pretty much kept her in the dark. Hang on." Her eyes angled upward, as if to recall a specific conversation. "She said Elliot went out on his own around the time they bought the cottage."

"Do we know when they purchased the property?"

"No, but I can search public records for the deed. Why's it matter?"

"Knowing when his employment started will tell us if we have the complete records."

"Gotcha. Okay, I'll get started as soon as we get home."

With Jacy Lee hovering? Too risky. "Let's wait till we check into the hotel."

One shoulder swayed. "Works for me."

"Pleased we're on the same page."

*9:03 a.m.*

At the main entrance to the Lake Hotel, automatic doors opened for them to stroll into the lobby. Cat wore a fitted skirt, heels, and a vibrant red blouse, long ebony hair extensions covering her cherry tresses, the ends dangling past her slim waist. He missed her emerald eyes, now disguised by dark brown contacts.

Mayhem could no longer don his usual fedora. Thus, he wore two braids across the sides that wove into three in front of each shoulder, and round, smoky sunglasses. Behind him rolled two suitcases, one hard-shell, the other soft-sided.

At the front desk, he smiled to draw the attention of the middle-aged clerk with no nameplate. "Might you be June?"

"Yes." She glanced down at the lapel of her blazer. "Sorry." She patted both pockets like she'd lost something. "And you are?"

"Mister Thunderhawk. We spoke on the phone."

"The groom?"

He draped his arm around Cat. "And the woman who completes me."

"Aww, so sweet." Tittering, her hand sided her mouth. "He's a keeper."

"That's why I'm marrying him." She patted his chest. "Again."

"You're a gorgeous couple, if you don't mind me saying so." The keyboard clanked. "Are we still charging the card on file?"

"Yes, please."

"All right, Mister and Missus Thunderhawk. You're in the Presidential Suite." She passed one keycard to Mayhem, another to Shawnee. "Can I help you with anything else?"

"Yes, please. Is it possible for us to use the business center to check on the arrival times of guests?"

"The Presidential Suite has Internet access for five dollars per hour." She passed a card with the network name and password. "It's a little slower than Wi-Fi but should fit your needs."

"Thank you, June. You've been most helpful."

"My pleasure, Mister Thunderhawk." She leaned toward Shawnee. "You're a lucky lady."

She giggled. "You should see him dance."

"Oh, I would love to. Will you need a room to practice in?"

"Err... what?"

He tried to cover for her slip of the tongue. "What my wife meant was—and please correct me if I'm wrong, darling—we dance under the stars. Alone. In the moonlight."

"We do, and it's amazing." Her gaze hollowed, as though reliving last night. "I've never felt more... more..."

June said, "Loved?"

"What?"

"You've never felt more... loved?"

"Oh." His "wife" peered up at him. "Um."

After a long pause of silence, June said, "Well, it sounds romantic."

Cat held his gaze.

He jostled her. "Kai?"

"Huh?"

"Shall we head to the suite?"

"Right." Ever so slightly, her head shook. "Yeah. Absolutely. We need to jump online and make sure Dad made it to the plane alright."

"Good idea." He re-focused on the clerk. "Thank you, June."

"Enjoy your stay."

Cat's reaction surprised him. Perhaps they should discuss the dance.

# Chapter 25

*9:15 a.m.*

My faux husband held open the door to the suite as I strolled inside. "How'd you get a credit card in a different name?"

"Klee loaned it to me."

"His last name is Thunderhawk?"

"It is."

"Love it."

Rolling the suitcases into the bedroom, he chuckled. "Pleased you approve."

A cardboard basket stood at the foot of the mattress on a chocolate-brown blanket, packed with a stuffed black bear, brochures with photos of Greater Yellowstone, and room service menus.

"Look how cute this is." I shook the stuffy at him. "Can we keep it?"

"Of course. You probably have the same basket in your room, as well."

"Really? We never get souvenirs."

"You have a robe from Thorn Hill that you're awfully fond of."

"Yeah, but I swiped that."

He unloaded the PC and MacBook from the hard-shelled suitcase. "Cat, you did not steal the robe. The inn included it in the room charges."

"Says you."

"Because it's true."

"Okay." I exaggerated a wink. "We'll go with that."

And he laughed—hard—his head in a continual wag. "Never a dull moment."

"C'mon, let's check out the rest of this place." I darted into my room, with a king-sized bed and private bath. Sure enough, there sat another basket with a stuffed black bear. Now I had two. Because I never had much on the cold streets of Boston, I loved stuffed animals as an adult. Each one held a story.

The kitchen had a mini-bar, dorm-sized fridge with complimentary soft drinks inside, empty cabinets, and a countertop for food prep, even though the hotel didn't supply appliances or silverware and forbade cooking in the rooms.

The upholstery of the living room didn't thrill me—stripes of puke green and brown—but the hard cushions of the pullout couch and matching loveseat were a lot more comfortable than they appeared, which I discovered by bouncing on each one.

The cozy table-for-two was a nice touch. Mahogany. Possibly cherrywood.

In the en suite bathroom, I stopped mid-stride. White subway tiles lined the shower/jet tub combination and ran halfway up the walls. But what really got me was the thick marble vanity and towel rack—also white—with an inlaid sink and rich cedar-framed mirror, triple lights suspended above.

I poked my head out the doorway. "You gotta see this bathroom."

"Nice?"

"Snake's hips."

He leafed through the ledger. "I'll take your word for it."

"No, you gotta see this."

"If you insist." He strode into the bathroom. With a cursory glance, he said, "Very nice." After a quick grin, he moseyed into the living room then lowered to the loveseat, his full attention on the ledger.

I chased him. "What's so interesting?"

"Elliot might not have been as naïve as we thought. It appears he kept insurance."

I plunked down beside him. "He found dirt on Killzme?"

"Evidently." One finger pointed to a line in the ledger at the back of the book. "Recognize the initials?"

"C.W." I flipped through my mental rolodex. When it finally hit me, I gasped. "No."

Big smile. "Yes."

"Chip Worthington?"

Back in Jackson, New Hampshire, he killed and dismembered Chip Worthington after finding his home office lined with stuffed zebra heads, lions, pangolins, elephant tusks, rhino horns, and every other species in the Animal Kingdom, including crows.

So. Many. Crows.

Friggin' scumbag deserved to pay for his sins. Burying his body parts twice—long story—wasn't the highlight of my trip, but whatever. If it weren't for good ol' Chip, we would've never known about Killzme Corp.

"Chester was his given name."

"Potato, po-tah-to." I swiped away my comment. "Why the letters and numbers next to his initials?"

"Must be a code of some sort."

"Then don't we need a cipher?"

"We do."

Was it me or did he skip important pieces of this revelation? "Then... how do you know it's insurance?"

"Why else go to these extremes to conceal intel?"

"Good point."

"Thank you."

I flipped open the PC. "Still need the cipher before it's useful to us."

"I am painfully aware of that."

My fingers raced across the keyboard. "Bringing up property records for Unalaska. Can you text me the address?"

"The cottage is on—"

I flashed a flat hand. "If you text it, I'll have the correct spelling and what-not."

"As you wish." He thumbed the keypad of his phone. "Sent."

"Thanks."

"Perhaps you should search the hotel registry first."

"It'll just take me a sec to find the deed. I'll do it after."

"I really think the hotel registry should be our top priority."

I sighed loud enough to make my point. "I'm almost there."

"All right, Cat. Would you like a bottled water or tea?"

"Is it *Shicheii's*?"

Air sucked through his teeth. "No. I got sidetracked and forgot to ask for a few bundles."

"No worries. How 'bout a mimosa?"

The eyebrows lifted. "That I can do." He strode halfway to the door, where he stopped and glanced back. "Care for any refreshments while I'm out?"

*Man, I love chivalry.* "Absolutely. Surprise me."

He smirked as though reading my mind again. "As you wish. Please don't forget to check the list against the hotel registry."

"I'm on it. Geez... gimme a sec."

"The snark is unwarranted, Cat."

Maybe I got a little heated, but I was working as fast as I could. If Elliot had dirt on Killzme, we needed to find it ASAP. The list of guests could wait.

The door clicked shut moments later. While I waited for him to return, I dug through the various owners of Cynthia and Elliot's vacation home. When the current deed-holder's name emerged, my breath halted.

Killzme Corp owned the property for at least the last decade. Maybe more. How many animals had they slaughtered in ten friggin' years? I figured they weren't a new corporation. They had their shit too nailed down, their rich, entitled asses fully covered. But I never expected they'd been trafficking wildlife for this long.

What would Elliot use as a cipher? Hmm... I flipped through the ledger.

Found nothing.

Maybe it's in the paperwork. From the file folder, I laid all the shredded documents on the coffee table. To assemble the jigsaw puzzle, I matched ink, lettering, and approximate age of the paper.

Forty minutes scrolled by, and I'd still only completed sections of pages. Mr. Mayhem hadn't returned yet. What's the hold-up? It wasn't like him to go MIA.

Wavering back and forth, I ultimately shot him a text.

> *R U OK?*

Text bubbles *pulsed… pulsed… pulsed…*

> *Are you worried about me, Cat?*

> *No. Just didn't know where you were. How's the mimosa coming?*

> *Apologies for the delay. Ran into an old friend.*

Fuck. I never checked our list of Killzme employees against the hotel registry. But I sure as shit wasn't admitting it through a text.

> *Do I know this friend?*

> *Time is a factor, Cat. Please join me. Suite 250.*

Uh-oh. Not good.

> *On my way…*

What would I walk into? Pretty sure "friend" meant enemy.

By the time the elevator doors parted on the second floor, my adrenaline had maxed out, my insides fluttering like dragonfly wings. Suite 250 was only about twenty feet away.

Heart hammering my chest, I raised a fist to knock.

Mr. Mayhem swung open the door, grabbed me, and yanked me inside. "I presume you know who's in the other room?"

"No." I sucked my teeth. "How would I?"

Piercing gray eyes tunneled into my soul. "Did you or did you not check the hotel registry?"

"Oh. Um. Well, not exactly."

When the eyebrows arched, my heart almost leaped out my chest.

"But I did start piecing together the paperwork."

"Let me see if I understand your logic." Praying hands tapped his lips. "Knowing I left the room to fetch you a mimosa, you thought it'd be safer to work on paperwork rather than check to see who I may run into. And—oh, I don't know—shoot me a text to warn me ahead of time?"

Aw, man, I really stepped in it this time. "Well, when you say it like that..."

"Please correct me if I'm wrong. I don't wish to put words in your mouth. Was that your thought process?"

"No."

"Correct. You did not consider my safety at all."

Those words cut me deep. "I'm sorry. You seem so indestructible, I guess it never occurred to me." My whole body pleaded for forgiveness. "I hate when you're mad at me."

"I am not mad, Cat. Disappointed, perhaps a bit hurt, but angry? No."

*Aw, man. That's worse.* I kicked the carpet.

"Where is the PC now?"

Teeth dragging down my upper lip, I raised a robotically slow thumb over my shoulder.

"Back in the suite with your shoes?"

Head hung, I nodded.

"Follow me, please."

When I rounded the corner, I didn't dare peek around him, vision locked on my bare feet while a man screamed behind a gag.

"Pipe down, Mister Russell, and you may survive this encounter."

Who? Oh. My. God. He had Rupert Russell, CFO of the Killzme Conservation shell company, hogtied on the bed.

Where'd he get nylon rope? Did he carry a roll in his leather blazer? Or did he grab it before he left the room?

All I managed was, "How?"

"Did we get here? Well, Mister Russell recognized me the moment I stepped into the elevator."

Aw, shit. Not good. "Did he say he recognized you?"

"He didn't have to, darling," he said, playing the husband role. "Recognition flashed in his eyes. I am not blind."

"O... kay." Still wasn't totally onboard yet. "And then what happened?"

"I invited him for a chat."

I flung an opened hand at the hostage. "You hogtied him."

"Correct. He chose anger over civility. What would you have me do? This is the monster who sold you to the highest bidder."

A lightning rod pierced my core. "Not Witherspoon?"

"Mister Witherspoon tacked the bounty to our heads. That is true. However, Mister Russell finds donors with deep pockets. Or in your case, a buyer who was all-too willing to dish out a cool million for a sexual slave. Make no mistake, darling, if I hadn't reacted when I did, he would have immediately notified his associates. And you and I would lose our safety net."

What could I say? "Thanks. I think."

"You're welcome. Now, could you please check the hotel registry? We cannot afford any more surprises."

"I'm on it." I spun to leave, but he hooked my arm. "Whaddaya doin'? I need the PC."

"We've wasted enough time. I'm certain our guest would be more than willing to loan you his computer. Isn't that right, Mister Russell?"

The hostage rolled from side to side, struggling to break free from the intricate lacing of rope. But that only made things worse. The cool part about Mr. Mayhem's expert hogtie—or concerning part, depending on how one looked at it—was, the more the victim struggled, the tighter the ropes got.

This scumbag would've been better off staying still. Which, in all fairness, my faux husband explained to no avail. Some poachers just didn't listen.

He spun the handle of his hunting knife. "Do you need me to repeat the question, Mister Russell?"

Frightened baby blues bulged like he hadn't comprehended his words.

"Do you mind if my wife borrows your laptop?"

More unintelligible screaming.

"Thank you, Mister Russell. We appreciate your sacrifice." He gave me a cheeky smile. "See? No problem at all."

Didn't sound like that to me, but whatever. "Where is it?"

"With his luggage, I presume. He hasn't unpacked yet."

"Which is where, exactly?"

The haughty stare made me back out of the bedroom. "I'm, uh, gonna look around."

"Good idea. Thank you, darling."

The palpable tension in that room could've asphyxiated a six-hundred-pound man. But how else would he keep us safe? Why hadn't he killed him yet? What was he waiting for?

Man, I could go for that mimosa about now. Or better yet, a few shots.

# Chapter 26



**11:11 a.m.**

As the prey continued to struggle in the restraints, Mayhem settled in the upholstered chair beside the bed. "Mister Russell, if you refuse to concede, you will strangle to death. Thus, unless you wish to end your life today, I suggest you relax."

The thrashing subsided.

"Are you willing to have a civil conversation with me now?"

The restraints had tightened to a point that made head movement impossible.

"Blink once, and I shall help you."

The prey blinked. Mayhem severed the rope running from his flabby neck to his ankles. Meaty shins dropped like dead weights.

"Roll onto your back, please."

Without even a muffled yelp, the hostage obeyed.

"Thank you." He loomed over the prey. "I shall lower the gag, but know this, Mister Russell. If you scream or call for help, I will end you. Am I clear?"

He nodded.

"Splendid." Once he untied the bandana from around his head, he slapped a gloved hand over his mouth. "You may speak only when instructed to do so. Do you understand the rules I have set forth?"

Another nod.

"Did you organize the upcoming hunt?"

When he lifted his gloved hand, Mr. Russell said, "Not my job."

"Fair enough. Then what is the name of the organizer?"

"Killzme Conservation."

He covered the liar's mouth. "Killzme Conservation is a shell company, a fabrication. Smoke and mirrors to cover your illegal trafficking activities and appease the public. Please do not insult my or my wife's intelligence by insinuating otherwise."

The man had the audacity to snicker.

Nostrils flaring, Mayhem stole a moment to pet the beast within. "What is the name of the individual who organized the upcoming hunt?"

"Luther Abbott."

"He's a middle manager, is he not?"

"Yes."

"Then he does not act alone. Who gave Luther Abbott the order?" When he lifted his hand, the prey refused to speak. "Do you need me to repeat the question, Mister Russell?"

"Yes."

"Who ordered Luther Abbott to organize the upcoming hunt?" He leaned in close. "Before I allow you to speak, I should caution you. Rarely do I ask a question without some inkling of the answer. If you lie or skew the truth, you will die." He lifted his hand.

"I gave the order."

"Then you—you, Mister Russell—are the organizer of the hunt."

"Yes."

"Thank you. Now, you've taken a step in the right direction."

Cat barreled into the room. "Problem."

"What sort of problem?"

"A time-sensitive one."

Mayhem regarded the prey. "Will you excuse us for a moment, please?" He took two strides toward the door—stopped—then pivoted to the un-gagged hostage. "Are you capable of silence, Mister Russell?"

He nodded.

"Do not disappoint me." He ushered Shawnee into the living room. "What is the problem, Cat?"

Panic registered on her face. "This is an adjoining room with another suite."

"And?"

"The COO, Asher Ferguson, booked the other one. He checks in at noon."

"Today? Within the next ten minutes?"

She flashed clenched teeth. "Yep."

"Hence why I asked you to check the registry. But no, you had better things to do." Mumbling under his breath, he paced in circles, his mind whirling with scenarios of how things might play out. "I need more from you in the future, Cat."

"I know. I fucked up. How can I fix it?"

"First, the colorful language is not helpful."

"You're right." Her palms flashed. "Sorry."

An audible exhale escaped.

"Whattawe do?"

"I'm thinking."

Another flash of the hands. "Do your thing."

"Could you please watch the hostage while I formulate the best course of action?"

Splayed fingers slapped her chest. "Me?"

The squint to his eyes got her moving.

"Okay, alright, I'm goin'."

"Thank you, darling."

"Can I have the knife... hon?"

"Certainly." He cautioned her against stabbing the prey. "I am not done questioning him."

"Got it."

As she strolled into the bedroom, his head would not stop rocking. If she'd checked the registry, neither of them would be in this position. One hostage was manageable. Two might arouse suspicion. However, these two particular men were awfully chummy at the gala in Alaska. One could argue they'd fled to a more lucrative opportunity. If they stayed in touch with the middle manager, they could potentially leave the hotel unnoticed.

Hmm, that may work.

Cat's voice carried through the suite. "What the fuck did you just say to me?"

He bounded through the doorway. "Problem, darling?"

"Yeah, he's a filthy pig."

"Is he?" Flames licked his stomach liner as he invaded the hostage's personal space. "Are you bedeviling my wife, Mister Russell?"

"No, sir."

She jutted an angry hand at the prey. "He's a fuckin' liar."

"We have already established that. Haven't we, Mister Russell?"

The hostage stayed mute.

Smart. He was in no mood. "What did he say to you, darling?"

"Err…"

"Will it upset me?"

"Definitely."

"Then let's circle back. I need to step out for a few minutes. Would you feel more comfortable if I fully restrained him?"

"Hundred percent."

"As you wish." After re-hogtying the hostage, he plucked the knife from Cat's grasp. "What time does Luther Abbott check in?"

"Three o'clock."

He pointed downward. "This floor?"

"No. He booked a cabin out back."

A little thrill zipped up his spine. "That'll be fun."

Giggling, she followed him into the living room. "Probably the wrong time, but I could really go for that mimosa about now."

"Apologies for the oversight, darling. The champagne, juice, and strawberries are in the refrigerator. Help yourself."

"Wait—" She teed her hands. "How'd you capture him while carrying all that stuff?"

With a slight grin, he winked. "I'm a man of many talents. Are you not aware of that yet?"

She smirked. "Humility's a much nicer look. Wouldn't you agree?"

He laughed. "Touché, Cat. Touché."

Waving over his head, he strode toward the door separating the two suites. "See you soon."

# Chapter 27

*12:15 p.m.*

There I was, sitting on the loveseat in an animal trafficker's suite, sipping champagne—I skipped the O.J.—from a glass flute filled with strawberries. As I scrolled through his laptop for something we could use to our advantage, a body, or bodies, slammed against the adjoining door.

Moments later, it flew open. And I almost spilled my drink.

My pretend hubby manhandled Asher Ferguson into the room, restrained against his chest, a sharp blade leveled to his throat. When he walked the dirtbag by the loveseat, a warm smile crossed his lips. "Tasty? The strawberries looked nice and fresh."

Still blew my mind how he normalized situations like this. "As a matter of fact, they are. Want me to make you one?"

"A cocktail sounds lovely, thank you." He muscled the dude toward the bedroom. "Stop struggling, Mister Ferguson, or it will not end well for you." He kicked the door close behind him.

I called out, "Need help in there?"

"All set, darling. Thank you."

Why didn't that surprise me? Rarely did he need my help with the restraint part. Though he did enjoy my company during interrogations. I kinda liked them, too. What I could've lived without were the burials. Man, they sucked. I doubted I'd ever get used to being elbow-deep in human remains. The stench alone killed me.

At the makeshift bar, I filled his flute with fresh strawberries and cold champagne, bubbles crackling and fizzy. I also took the opportunity to top off my glass.

Perfect.

When I returned to the loveseat, he backed out of the bedroom.

"Everything alright in there?"

"Fine." He jabbed a chin at the flute. "Is that for me?"

"Yep."

"Looks scrumptious." He sipped from the rim. "Thank you."

"Least I could do." I lowered to the cushions. "I know you're busy, but can you sit for a sec?"

With a quick glance back at the bedroom door, he sat on the armrest beside me. "I always have time for you, Kitty Cat."

*Aww... so sweet.* "So, I've been poking around, seeing what dirt I could kick up, and found this list of codewords. Since it's a shared file in Google docs, it piqued my interest."

I angled the screen to let him view the document. "I know what aloo or potato, kola or banana, striped t-shirt, Australian teddy bear, white, black, and red mean." Musk deer, elephant tusk, tiger skin, a live koala, ivory, rhino horn, and helmeted hornbill beak, respectively. "Whaddaya think fleece blanket, gray hoodie, and warm rug stand for?"

"In what context are they used?"

"See here?" I highlighted the objective. "Wording for pop-up ads."

Animal traffickers sold illegal wildlife, and parts thereof, right in the open through pop-up ads. The website host and other visitors stayed clueless because of the randomness of the language, which continually changed to keep anti-poaching organizations at bay. Buyers looking to purchase animal parts simply had to search for the codewords, and the websites returned corresponding ads.

This disgusting practice spilled into social media as well. Because anyone could open an account and set it to private, poachers gained the upper hand. The good guys, like TRAFFIC and other anti-poaching groups, needed to friend these fake accounts to gain access to their content. But if they never bought products, they got booted. No lurkers allowed, which made policing the wildlife trade almost impossible. When they shut down one account, another popped up in its place under a different alias.

And the no-win situation continued to worsen by the hour. It wasn't even a matter of days anymore, never mind months or years.

My faux hubby set his flute on the coffee table. "Let's ask our guests."

"Think they'll tell us?"

Quick wink. "Pain is a marvelous motivator."

I sniggered. "Lemme guess. The foot thing again?"

"It's effective."

"You're not wrong." Back in the day, he used a similar technique on me—long story—and it scared me half to death. All thanks to Poe, by the way.

He swayed a gloved hand toward the bedroom. "Shall we, darling?"

"Right behind ya, hon." I shot back my drink. "Please don't ask me to sit behind Russell. The pig pissed himself."

He chuckled. "Mister Ferguson is the weakest link. We'll start there. Please bring the laptop."

I sleeved the PC under one arm.

When we approached the bed, the two scumbags cowered. Didn't look so tough now, did they?

"Good afternoon, gentlemen. And I use the term loosely, considering neither of you rise to that title. My wife has questions. You shall respond without hesitation, malice, untruths, or skewing the facts. And above all, show respect. If you fail to do so, you will experience unbearable pain. I will not end your lives quickly. Rather, your suffering will continue for hours. Questions? Now is the time to ask."

Neither poacher made a peep, two blank stares glued to their captor—Mr. Mayhem excelled at holding everyone's attention—and I could barely contain my glee, secretly loving every minute of their torture, like they did to innocent animals.

"Silence is a good sign," he said. "As I previously told Mister Russell, cooperation goes a long way with me. If you continue to behave, you both may survive this encounter."

Total bullshit but hope helped extract valuable information.

He reached for Ferguson, who let out a frantic cry, muffled by the bandana stuffed in his mouth. Mr. Mayhem removed Ferguson's left loafer and black dress sock then rolled the pantleg over his pasty white shin to a boney knee.

Not sure why. Maybe he wanted Russell to have an unobscured view of the damage inflicted on his buddy.

Cradling Ferguson's bare heel in a gloved hand, he pressed the tip of the blade to his foot arch. "This long band of muscles is called the fascia. If severed with the nerves, mind-numbing pain will flood your system in a matter of seconds. The excruciating agony that follows is unlike any you've experienced. Unless, of course, someone has previously set you on fire, Mister Ferguson?"

He rocked a firm no.

"I suspected as much. Darling, when you're ready, please begin."

"Should I show him the list or...?"

"If you think it would be advantageous to do so, sure."

"Might be easier."

"Then by all means, the floor is yours."

I angled the screen so the scumbag could read it. "See this list? I'm not worried about the top half." Meaning, the familiar codewords. "I'm interested in these."

Mr. Mayhem said, "You'll need to remove his gag, darling."

My upper lip curled and twitched. Why'd I always get stuck with the gross jobs? With two fingers, I dragged the bandana out of the poacher's mouth, my head turned away to avoid having to witness the strings of saliva and whatever else.

Afterward, I showed him the PC again. "What do fleece blanket, gray hoodie, and warm rug mean?"

The hostage's bulging eyes shifted to Russell, who rocked a defiant no.

Not smart.

"My wife asked you a question, Mister Ferguson."

Again, the dude glanced at his compadre.

"I see you'd rather do this the hard way. Okie doke." The tip of his razor-sharp blade pierced the skin, and Ferguson cried out. "Once I rip straight down, you will lose the ability to form a coherent sentence. Shall I continue?"

"No—please. I'll tell you what you want to know."

"Hey." I snapped in the scumbag's face. "I'm asking the questions here."

Mr. Mayhem's nose crinkled with his smile.

"Fleece blanket is a Bison hide."

"Gray hoodie?"

"Wolf."

"And warm rug?"

"Grizzly."

"Wait, wait, wait." I could barely make sense of the ruthlessness. "You're slaughtering all these animals for their skin?"

"And trophy heads. It's a lucrative business. We could cut you in. Couldn't we, Rupert?"

Still gagged, his buddy rocked a yes.

"I don't give two shits about the money. What the fuck is wrong with you people?" I slapped him across the face. And he actually had the balls to return a glower. So, I sucker-punched him. Blood poured from his nostrils, but I couldn't stop. I hit him again and again and again. "Gimme the knife!"

"No can do, I'm afraid. Not while you're heated, darling."

I shook my sore knuckles. "This fucker needs to die."

"I don't disagree. However, we never fight from a place of anger."

"Well, maybe we should." I thrust my hand at the two scumbags on the bed. "In case you haven't noticed, they're winning this war."

He waved me closer. "Let's talk in the other room."

"Fine—" I rammed the bandana down the poacher's throat. "Move an inch while I'm gone, and you're a dead man. *Comprende*, muthafucker?"

"You've been clear about your intentions, darling." His head jabbed toward the doorway. "Shall we? Now? Please?"

I gnashed my teeth. "Coming, hon."

In the living room, my adrenaline wouldn't slow. The mere thought of all those suffering animals drove me to pace in circles, one hand clawing back my hair.

"Hey—" His V-shaped frame blocked my well-worn path, the leather gloves now folded neatly on the sofa arm. "Breathe with me, Kitty Cat." He inhaled a deep breath through his nostrils, exhaled out his mouth. "Join me, please. You'll feel better."

But I couldn't. Not yet. Still too pissed off.

His palms cradled my face. "Tell me what you need, darlin'."

Tears bubbled to the surface, and I dove into his chest. "We're fighting a losing battle."

"Perhaps." He stroked the back of my head. "Regardless, the Innocent Ones need us."

"How're we gonna protect 'em?"

Two fingers lifted my chin. "One dead poacher at a time."

Instant tingles shot to all the right places. *Man, he's sexy. Why am I so turned on right now?*

He grinned.

"You're in my head again, huh?"

The grin morphed into a chuckle.

"For the record, I don't find it funny."

More laughter busted loose. "Not even a little?"

I slapped his chest. "Stop. What I thought is embarrassing."

"Adorable."

With a fist planted on my hip, I said, "Puppies are adorable."

"Would you prefer irresistible? Stunning? Tigress?"

A flush of heat swept up my neck. "All of those work." *Man, I wanna rip your clothes off so bad.*

"Do you?"

*Oh, you have no idea.*

For several moments, he stared deep into my eyes. "We should work on your timing."

On my tippy toes, I gave him a quick peck on the lips. When his eyebrows lifted, I sloughed off a half-shrug. "Gotta problem with that?"

His stare grew deeper and more intense, but he didn't speak.

The silence nearly killed me.

*Aw, shit. I shouldn't've done that. He doesn't feel the same way. But that dance... those lyrics... How'd I misread—?*

Mid-thought, he lifted me, pulled me closer, and my legs curled around his waist. A muscular hand slid up my back and sifted through my hair. With a slight pause, his gray eyes connecting with my soul, he kissed me with so much passion, it melted every single bone in my body.

The longer his tongue swirled with mine, the less I could hang on—my arms limp, my crossed ankles losing their grip. If it weren't for his tight embrace, I could've easily landed on my ass. How sexy would that be?

When the kiss intensified even more, I let go, falling deeper and deeper under his spell. He could do just about anything without my objection. I was complete Jell-O in his hands. I might've also blacked out a little, which only dawned on me when our lips parted.

Someone pounded on the door.

My mind snapped back to reality, my legs and arms re-tightening around him, my voice low and whisperous. "Whattawe do?"

Nothing ever rattled him, not even a stranger trying to barge into the suite.

"I hope I've sufficiently silenced any lingering self-doubt, Kitty Cat," he whispered with a little nose nuzzle.

"Um, yeah." I blushed all over. "We're good."

He winked. "Pleased we're finally on the same page."

"Me too."

The knocking grew louder, angrier. Whoever was out there needed Russell and Ferguson ASAP, and they weren't willing to leave.

"May we return to work now?"

"Absolutely." When he lowered me to the carpet, I ripped off the love goggles.

"Thank you."

"No, thank you." Giggling, I shuffled my bangs into place. Dragged my fingers through the sides of my hair, angling wisps toward my face. "Whaddaya need me to do?"

He slipped his powerful hands into the gloves. "The unexpected visitor is not room service, nor any other hotel employee."

"Agreed."

"Ideally, Misters Russell or Ferguson should answer the door."

"How?"

"You let me worry about that." He glanced left and right. "Where might the laptop be?"

My stomach collapsed. "I left it in the room. If they notified their men, we're screwed."

"One problem at a time. Check the recent activity while I get Mister Ferguson ready."

"I'm on it." I raced into the bedroom, with the best kisser in the world on my heels.

Though the laptop hadn't moved, and both scumbags were still in the same position as when we left, I sensed suspicion from my honey bun. I mean, partner-in-crime. Probably best to follow his instincts since I couldn't rely on mine after that kiss.

While he tested the tightness of Russell's wrist bindings, I flipped open the PC, my fingers darting across the keyboard.

"Any suspicious activity, darling?"

"Not yet."

"Please let me know if or when that changes." He dragged the bandana from the poacher's mouth. "You have a visitor, Mister Ferguson. Any idea who?"

"Must be Luther."

"At this hour?" For a hot second, his gaze shifted to the alarm clock. "Mister Abbott checks in at three. Correct?"

"Rupert and I told him to meet us for drinks ahead of time."

"I see. Will he leave on his own?"

"Doubtful. He has nowhere to go."

The hunting knife urged the poacher off the bed. "Please stand."

"Why?" Ferguson cowered. "I've obeyed every command."

"Relax. If you continue to follow my directives, you have nothing to fear."

"Just don't screw it up, or you'll die. Brutally." I flipped my hair over my shoulder. "Right, hon?"

Mr. Mayhem grinned. His luscious lips parted, but before he had a chance to spit out a response, a stranger's voice carried through the suite like Luther found a way inside.

*Shit.* Didn't the door automatically lock? Or did he bribe a maid to let him in?

"Boss," he called out, "are you here?"

While Mr. Mayhem grabbed hold of Ferguson, I clomped across the mattress to lock the bedroom door.

In a low, raspy whisper, he said, "Tell him you and Mister Russell are otherwise engaged and don't wish to be disturbed."

"But he'll think we're lovers."

"Would you prefer a bloodbath?"

"Luther," Ferguson hollered through the door, "we're on an important conference call overseas. Wait for us in the lounge."

Mr. Mayhem whispered, "We may be awhile."

Ferguson repeated the line.

"I just need five minutes, boss. It's important."

With a firm grip of the hostage, he withdrew a pointed dagger from an ankle sheath. Once he tossed it to me, he gestured for me to threaten Russell into compliance.

Whatever he whispered in Ferguson's ear worked, because the scumbag's frantic gaze shot to his buddy on the bed.

Mr. Mayhem untied his wrists.

"Five minutes is all I have to spare," the hostage called out.

"Great. Open the door so we can talk face-to-face."

After untying the rope from around the hostage's ankles, he hid behind the door with a death grip on Ferguson's arm, black leather stretching the knuckles thin.

When Mr. Mayhem grabbed the doorknob, Ferguson glimpsed his compadre again, the dagger in my hand mere centimeters away from Rupert's eye socket—quickest route to the brain, according to my sexy faux hubby.

In the next moment, Ferguson seemed to steel himself, ready and willing to play the role of a lifetime, as outlined by his captor, with one minor change. But then, Mr. Mayhem tore open the dude's dress shirt, buttons flying in all directions.

Good luck with the conference call excuse now, asshole.

It took all my power not to laugh out loud, my lips wiggling against the surge of hilarity. Say what you will about Mr. Mayhem but no one could deny how much he enjoyed his work. Some might not appreciate his amazing sense of humor like I did. Almost daily, he cracked me up, especially when he was in his element. Like now.

"Time is money, Luther." Ferguson tried to act natural with his hairy white chest and ginormous nipples exposed, shirttails untucked, and a paisley-print tie still knotted around his neck. "What is the problem?"

Smiling like the spokes-cat Chester Cheeto, Mr. Mayhem winked at me. I had to look away, or I'd burst out in hysterics.

A long pause of silence fell between the two so-called men as though Luther couldn't make sense of the false narrative.

"Err..."

"Luther—" Ferguson's voice deepened.

The sweat on his forehead alluded to hot sex. Super surprised he held it together at all, considering he and Russell were top dogs in the shell company. Maybe Killzme Corp, as well.

"Now, you're down to four minutes. What is the problem?"

"Hey, no judgments here," Luther said. "You do you."

And I almost died, my body rocking with silent laughter.

*Keep quiet, Daniels, or all hell will break loose.*

# Chapter 28

*"Raise your words, not your voice. It is rain that grows flowers, not thunder."* —Rumi

***1:18 p.m.***

More and more, Mayhem's patience thinned while waiting for Mr. Ferguson to regain control of the conversation. Behind the door, he squeezed the prey's arm.

"Three minutes, Luther. How much time do you intend to waste?"

"Sorry, boss. One of the game wardens has cold feet."

"Then handle it."

"But he wants more money."

"Pay him. Is that all?"

"Pay him?" Luther's tone pitched. "But Rupert said—"

"As COO, it's my job to allocate funds, not Rupert's. Now, if there's nothing else, I need to return to my conference call."

"Everything alright, boss? The doctor's here if you need him."

What an odd thing to say under the circumstances. This group used codewords for everything, from daily operations to covert missions. Could "doctor" mean "send help"?

"I'll phone him after the conference call. Thanks for stopping by, Luther."

The response raised even more suspicions. Leery of a surprise attack, Mayhem locked the door. To remind the prey not to speak, he tapped a straight finger to his lips.

When Mr. Ferguson's mouth parted, Mayhem hooked his neck, his gloved hand forcibly muzzling him.

The suite door clicked shut a lot louder than normal, as though Luther Abbott wanted to ensure everyone heard his departure. His gaze strayed to Cat. She returned a silent no. Evidently, she hadn't fallen for the staged exit, either.

The middle manager—point person for the muscle—must possess some intelligence. Though Killzme employed sinewy armed henchmen to act as shields for the quote-unquote "important members," none rose to the level of boss. Except Luther Abbott.

Before the interrogation could progress, Mayhem must confirm who was or was not inside the suite. Thus, he ordered Mr. Ferguson to sit on the foot of the bed while he cleared the other rooms.

Luther kicked in the door, with a pistol drawn. Thrashing in the restraints, Mr. Russell screamed behind the gag. Cat clobbered him over the head with the clock radio.

*Interesting technique.* He'd given her the dagger. Why, pray tell, would she choose an appliance over a perfectly good knife?

Mayhem threw a roundhouse kick to Luther's face, and he fell backward, the gun tumbling across the carpet.

For a moment, their gazes flicked between the pistol and each other.

Luther scrambled, but Mayhem beat him to it. With the 9mm now aimed at his adversary, he chambered a fresh round. If forced to shoot, the racket of gunfire inside the hotel would cause a panic, with guests stampeding to find the nearest exit. That'd draw the attention of the authorities.

Police weren't ideal in this line of work. Successful warriors operated in the shadows, safely under the radar of legalities.

Though he didn't shy away from ending Luther's life, he first offered him a choice. "Tell me what I want to know, or I will kill you. Brutally. When I'm done, even your family won't recognize you. Do you understand the two options?"

Luther's gaze strayed to his boss frozen on the foot of the bed.

"I wonder, Mister Abbott. Will you choose the simple path or the road fraught with obstacles?" He sniggered. "Namely me."

"Hey—" Cat piped up. "What am I, chopped liver?"

"My apologies, darling. They should fear you as well." *Adorable.* "Do you have a preference between the two options?"

"Think he gave the Innocent Ones a choice before blowing their brains out?"

"My wife does raise a valid point, Mister Abbott." He swapped the gun for the knife, tapped the blade on a gloved hand. "Karma is a factor here."

In his peripheral, the unbound poacher rose to escape. Mayhem spun, the blade severing Mr. Ferguson's throat, blood arcing across the carpet as he collapsed.

Mayhem swung his arms wide. "Let the fun begin."

When Luther lunged, he ducked, and the poacher sailed over his head. Unfortunately for him, he refused to stay down. Luther swung a switchblade, the tip slicing Mayhem's dress shirt.

He pressed a hand to his abs. Blood stained his glove. With a snide snicker, he said, "If I allow you to look back on our time together, remember this moment as when you made the fatal error."

A stiff hand sliced the air above Luther's head. "I've had it up to here with your bullshit, Redskin. And that goes double for your bitch wife."

Heat excoriated his insides, and he hurled the hunting knife, the blade tumbling through the air. But Luther had the wherewithal to jump out of the way.

"Cat—"

She clomped across the mattress. Without a shared word between them, she passed the dagger.

Luther dove to attack her.

Another fatal mistake.

One punch knocked the middle manager off his feet. Now straddling the hips, Mayhem struck him again and again, shattering his nose, cheekbones, eye sockets, and the jaw in several places. Bloodied and battered, the prey waved a weak hand in surrender.

Still on top of him, he leaned in real close, his chest heaving with adrenaline. "Don't you ever lay your filthy hands on my wife." The dagger he drove through his eye socket.

Cat's voice rolled over his shoulder. "Err... problem."

His gaze shot to her.

"Russell escaped."

He whirled around.

Empty bed.

"He couldn't have gotten far."

From the floor, she raised pieces of cut rope and the hunting knife. "Yes, he could."

Mayhem yanked the dagger from the dead man's skull, rummaged through his pockets for his phone, passing the device to Shawnee. "Don't forget to change the passcode, Cat."

Her thumbs worked the keypad. "Not my first rodeo."

"Work on the run, please." He ushered her out of the bedroom.

"Wait—" She dug in her heels. "What're we doin' with them?"

The two bodies.

"They're Killzme's problem now."

In the living room, Mayhem gathered the flutes, bowl of strawberries, and the bottle of champagne. All of which contained their fingerprints. If they didn't leave ASAP, another Killzme employee might arrive.

"Don't forget the laptop, Cat."

She showed him the PC under one arm. "Way ahead o' ya."

At the door, he skimmed both ends of the hall. No guests, but the gears of the elevator climbed toward the second floor. They darted for the exit, slipping inside moments before the elevator dinged.

While guarding Shawnee from behind, they clamored up the stairs to the third floor, where she stopped to poke her head out the door.

When she turned, her gaze dropped to the bloodstain. "You're bleeding."

"Are we clear to proceed?"

She reached for the wound, but he angled out of her grasp. "Did Luther stab you?"

"Cat, please. I appreciate your concern, I really do, but we need to head back to the suite."

"Well, excuse me for caring."

Oh, boy. Here we go.

She checked both ends of the hall. "Clear. Stay close so I can block your bloody shirt."

"Will do. Thank you."

Outside the Presidential Suite, she stopped. "Shit. Forgot my keycard."

He angled his arm out of the way. "Right front pocket."

"So, just like, stick my hand in there?"

He gave her a sly grin. "Unless you don't trust yourself to behave."

"Not funny." As she rooted around in his pocket, she glanced everywhere but at him, a blush crawling up her neck. "Got it."

The green light flashed thrice.

In the foyer, she unloaded his arms. "Now can I see the wound?"

"Fear not, Kitty Cat. It's only a scratch."

"You gonna show me or what?"

"We have more pressing matters to intend—"

When she tore open his shirt, she stunned him silent.

"Stop putting yourself last." Bending low, she examined the wound. "That's more than a scratch." By the hand, she tugged him toward the bedroom. "Gotta clean it so it doesn't get infected."

He rather enjoyed her assertive side. "Yes, dear."

In the bathroom, she ordered him to lean against the vanity while she darted into the bedroom. Seconds later, she returned with the first-aid kit. Water ran in the sink as she soaked a folded washcloth.

In front of him, she dragged a padded stool. Dabbed the wound with the gentleness of tending to a newborn. "Does it sting?"

"No."

"Would you tell me if it did?"

*Doubtful.* Instead, he grinned. "The coordinates of the hunt should either be on the phone or Mister Russell's laptop."

"Why give scummy poachers the respect of calling them mister?"

"Because I do not allow others to skew my values, manners, or change who I am as a person. Common courtesy is important to me."

"I see what you're sayin' but..." She rang out the bloody washcloth. "I need time to get past what they've done, what they stand for, and what they continue to do."

"Fair enough."

"And sure, I let my emotions get the better of me now and then. Maybe that's just who I am. I don't see myself changing anytime soon."

"Nor would I ever want you to, Kitty Cat. I like who you are."

Blushing, she play-swatted his chest. "Stop."

The smirk he forced down. "Interesting technique with the clock radio. May I ask why you chose an appliance over a weapon?"

Her lips smoothed into a straight line. "It worked, didn't it?"

"Well, let's review. Where might Mister Russell be now?"

"If you have a point, make it. Otherwise, hush." The warm washcloth dabbed across his abdominal muscles. "I need to concentrate."

"Yes, ma'am."

"You know I don't like that."

His heart swelled. "Yes, dear."

# Chapter 29

*2:03 p.m.*

After washing the wound, I squirted one of *Shicheii's* concoctions into my palms and smoothed the lotion across his twelve-pack abs. And sure, I might've taken my time, my fingers dipping into and out of muscly ripples.

So. Many. Muscles.

"Kitty Cat?"

In my happy place, I kept massaging the lotion into his skin. "Yeah?"

"Though I appreciate the thoroughness to which you work, I am certain you've sufficiently disinfected the wound. Along with my chest, for some reason."

"Oh." I jerked back, his bronze torso glistening in front of me. *How much can one woman take?* "Sorry. Didn't mean to go that high. Should I cover the wound or let it breathe?"

"In this case, cover. First, however, it may be advantageous to seal it closed."

From the first-aid kit, I raised a fresh tube of superglue.

"That's the one. But I can manage if you'd rather dig into the devices."

"No, no. I'm good right here." Squeezing the skin together, I drew a line of superglue. As I blew on it, my gaze flicked up at him for a millisecond, praying he couldn't read my filthy thoughts.

The grin he returned pretty much destroyed any hope of that.

*Puppies, kittens, and rainbows. Puppies, kittens, and rainbows.*

Once the glue dried, I covered the wound with the longest gauze pad in the first-aid kit, smoothing my fingers around the edge to get the adhesive to stick. But it kept lifting from all the lotion.

"We may need to add tape," he said.

"Probably." Once I secured the gauze in place, I sat back to admire my handiwork. "Looks good. *Shicheii* will still wanna take a peek when we get home, but at least it won't get infected now. How's it feel?"

"Perfect. Thank you."

"My pleasure." *Literally.* When I rose, I acted all casual-like. "So, what's our next move?"

"Besides combing through the laptop and phone?"

*Shit. Get your head in the game, Daniels.* "'Course. Goes without saying."

"We also have some tough decisions to make. If Mister Russell doesn't flee the area—or even if he does, I suppose—he will alert his men to our presence at this hotel."

"So? He doesn't know we booked a suite."

"True. However, it's a safe assumption."

"Not necessarily. For all he knows, you coulda followed him from the airport. What floor were you on when you two ran into each other?"

"Lobby."

"Perfect. Then you could've easily just arrived."

"Hm. Valid point."

"*He* may not feel safe staying here, but I don't see how it changes anything for us. It's not exactly our first time being surrounded by killers."

"So, to clarify, you would prefer to stay put?"

"Yeah. Don't you? We're in the perfect spot, with a clear view of the lake and cabins out back. Plus, no maid service for four days. Why would we leave?"

"Some would call the understaffing a negative."

"Yeah, but it works for us. Less chance of anyone going through our stuff."

"Maids don't normally rummage through guests' belongings."

"Never?" I swiped away the question. "If we leave, June will have a connipshit."

"Connip... *tion.*"

"Whatever." I huffed out a breath. "The point is, the woman is more excited about our wedding than we are."

He chuckled. "Poor June will be awfully upset when we skip out early."

"Right?" I laughed, too. "Aw, man, I'd love to see the look on her face."

The phone rang in the bedroom, and I froze.

As usual, he stayed calm. Unfazed. Total opposite of me.

He smoothed a hand across my scalp. "Breathe, Kitty Cat." And then, he just strode into the bedroom like this was an ordinary day and we hadn't left two dead poachers on the second floor.

"Yes?" he answered. "I see." He paused, listening to the caller. "What time Friday?" A brief second or two passed. "Uh-huh. Understood. Sounds reasonable enough. Let me check with Kai, and I shall call you—" His gaze landed on me. "You'd rather hold. Certainly. One moment, please."

With the mouthpiece covered, he lowered the phone to waist-level, whispered, "Do you have a problem with moving the ceremony to Friday night?"

"Won't we be a little busy?" The hunt started then. If we didn't get the jump on Killzme, they could wipe out an entire herd before we arrived.

"In theory, yes."

"Not in theory. In reality."

"June is waiting for an answer."

"Why do we need to reschedule?"

As he raised the phone, I swear his eyes rolled. "Kai says she needs to check with the caterer and what-not, but it shouldn't be a problem." When he paused again, his gray eyes widened. "A wedding concierge? Not that I'm aware of, no."

I whispered, "If a concierge is a planner—"

"Complimentary?"

Waving my arms like a referee calling a penalty, I wagged my head from side to side—a clear sign of a hard pass. Or better yet, a "hell, no."

"More than generous, June. Above and beyond, really. Thank you. Kai will be thrilled."

When he hung up, I planted tight fists on my hips. "Did you just agree to a wedding planner?"

"I did, yes."

I flung my hands in the air. "Why, when I clearly said no?"

"She didn't give me much choice."

"Thought we always had a choice."

"Cat, please don't weaponize my words." Two fingers pinched the bridge of his nose. "Do you or do you not agree a solid cover story is vital now?"

"Well, yeah, but—"

"Then what is the problem? If a wedding concierge allows June repentance for her oversight, the least we can do is accept her generous offer."

"What kinda oversight?"

"A scheduling error. Evidently, another couple booked the banquet hall for Saturday night over a year ago."

"To get married or...?"

"Does it matter?"

"Kinda, yeah."

His arms crossed. "Explain."

"If we're the only bride and groom, June will view us as guests of honor. She'll bend over backward to make sure we're enjoying ourselves. But if there's another couple, the special treatment flies out the window. And with it, the love that blinds her to our activities."

His eyebrows arched.

"Still got a couple major problems, though. Like reciting vows in front of God."

With a lingering gaze upward, I could almost hear the gears turning in his mind. "What if we hired an actor?" He flashed a flat hand, urging me to let him finish. "If Jacy Lee speaks with the Holy Ones beforehand and an actor stands in for the marriage officiant, then the ceremony becomes more like a play. A production, if you will, that looks real to an outsider but absolves us from any spiritual or legal entanglements."

"Wow, you're good. Think *Shicheii* will go for it?"

"If we frame it correctly, with a heavy emphasis on the stakes if we fail, I don't see why not."

"How's it gonna look real without guests?"

"One problem at a time, please. We first need to find the location of the hunt."

"I'm on it." I darted into the living room. On the sofa, I snuggled in with the laptop and phone.

Ten minutes later, my fake husband strolled out of the bedroom in crisp jeans, his fingers buttoning up a deep burgundy shirt. "Are you hungry?"

*Starving.* "I could eat."

"Why am I not surprised?" He chuckled. "Room service may not be available at this hour, but I'd be happy to fetch lunch for us."

"Could you grab me the champagne and strawberries before you go?"

"Certainly." He returned moments later with a ready-made cocktail. "Are you peckish for anything in particular?"

*Peckish?* I sipped from the flute. "Surprise me, but don't go nuts with the fancy stuff."

"Perish the thought." He slid on his round, smoky shades—a favorite of mine, and good coverage for his recognizable eyes. "Are we any closer to a location?"

Strawberry bubbles trickled down my throat. "I found a file that looks promising, but it's encrypted."

"Perhaps you'll have better luck with the phone?"

My fingers raced across the keys. "Wanna see where this leads first."

"All right, then. I shall leave it in your capable hands. See you soon."

Once the door clicked shut, I blocked out all distractions, my full attention on the screen, logging keystroke after keystroke. Kilzme messed with the wrong cat.

If they're stupid enough to store files on a laptop—much safer on an encrypted external drive—I'd uncover their dirty little secrets.

"Yessss..." I blew on my talented fingers. "I'm in."

When the first document filled the screen, I leaned in, my head cocking at the evidence. *What the hell is this?*

# Chapter 30



***3:11 p.m.***

Unwilling to tempt fate, Mayhem waited for their lunch order at the deli within the hotel. Crowds of vacationers flooded the front desk. Some checked-in after a fun-filled day in the park, others just arrived in Yellowstone.

A stocky man with a dark buzz-cut and goatee stood back from the counter as though waiting for a friend to get his room key. What drew Mayhem's attention was the eye patch. The boss of Cat's abductors wore an identical one.

Mayhem raised the camera of his phone, enlarging the face for a closer view. A thick scar split the stranger's eyebrow in half.

Hmm... interesting. It was not out of the realm of possibilities for a Killzme sentinel from Alaska to travel here with Luther Abbott. After all, he'd first encountered Misters Russell and Ferguson there as well.

"Order's up for Thunderhawk," the attendant called out.

Rousted from his thoughts, he darted to the counter.

"You're all set. Napkins and silverware are in the bag."

He stuffed two twenties in the tip jar. "Thank you kindly."

After he'd snaked around the crowd of exhausted toddlers, teenagers glued to their phones, and bickering parents, the stranger with the eye patch had vanished from the lobby. Mayhem hustled out the main entrance. In the distance, the two men strolled around the corner of the building, heading for the cabins out back.

Cat's hunch was spot-on. Luther Abbott kept his men close.

Behind the hotel, Mayhem lit a Dunhill International Red. Though a new hairstyle and sunglasses hardly constituted a disguise, confidence helped to persuade onlookers to adopt the correct perspective. In this case, he looked like any other Native guest who slipped outside for a cigarette. Nothing more, nothing less.

The two men continued toward the rustic cabins. After reaching their destination, they chitchatted awhile on side-by-side porches. When they entered individual units, Mayhem scrawled a mental note of the cabin numbers painted above the doors. A comparison to the hotel register would identify both men.

Once he stubbed out the cigarette on the sole of his shoe and pocketed the charred butt, he entered the hotel through the back exit. Rather than risk another hiccup in the elevator, he double stepped it up the stairs to the third floor.

Outside the Presidential Suite, he inserted the keycard. Cat whipped open the door, panic splashed across her face. To ease her unrest, he said, "Honey, I'm home."

No laughter, nor even hints of joy.

*Oh, boy.* "Problem?"

"I dunno. Maybe." After checking both ends of the hall, she fastened the bolt lock behind him. "Gotta show you somethin'."

"On the devices?"

"Yeah."

He strode straight for the table-for-two in the living room, where he unloaded the bag. "Whatever it is, we'll deal with it."

"What... are you doin'?"

He offered her a warm roast beef sandwich. "Mayo and cheese, correct? I also ordered you French fries instead of salad, though I'd be happy to share mine if that doesn't appeal to you." When he smiled at her, she returned a blank stare. "Would you prefer Waldorf's chicken salad on a multigrain roll? Toasted, of course, with—"

In slow motion, her arms crossed.

"Cat, if you have something to show me, please bring it to the table so we can eat."

Without a word, she soldiered to the loveseat. Returned moments later with the laptop, and slapped down the phone.

"If you don't tell me why you're upset, I can't fix it."

She popped a French fry in her mouth, her full attention on the phone. "There's a meeting tonight. The coordinates lead outside the park."

He poured vinaigrette dressing on the salad. "Near which entrance?"

"West."

Oh, boy. Now her demeanor made sense. "May I?"

Once she passed the phone, she hovered over his shoulder while he clicked the coordinates for the map and enlarged the area around the red marker. Klee and Ferron's house was at least five miles away, but Cat would have no way of knowing that.

"Your grandfather is safe."

"It's not next door?"

"No."

Audibly, she exhaled. "Thank God."

He peered up at her. "Are you happy with the roast beef or...?"

"Yeah, perfect." She settled in the chair across from him. "I *will* take half that salad, though."

"Of course."

"Just kidding. I'm good." Cheeks packed with savory beef, she reopened the laptop. "Found somethin' strange. Not sure what it means, though."

When she spun the screen, he leaned closer, narrowing in on an image that jerked him back. "How dare they..."

"What is it? What're they planning?"

How could he share this devastating truth? When they first arrived in Montana, Jacy Lee laid the groundwork for a much longer conversation. One that might tear apart her tender heart. It'd certainly shatter some illusions.

Even after all she'd seen and heard, she had difficulty reconciling her two worlds. Understandable. The knowledge that her paternal side targeted her maternal ancestors with this level of malignant cruelty could only escalate her inner turmoil.

*We are the sum of our parts, after all.*

Creases of concern deepened between her faux chocolate eyes. Why would Killzme target these specific individuals? Revenge for his and Cat's interference? Or did they have a more sinister plan in mind?

As though sensing his despair, she reached for his hand. "Please tell me what's wrong."

What was the kindest way to broach this subject? If only Jacy Lee was here to help her absorb the ruthlessness.

"Does it have anything to do with what *Shicheii* said earlier?"

No. That'd be an even tougher conversation. With a halfhearted grin, he didn't respond.

She slapped the table. "Say something."

If he broached the subject, it'd rob her of well-needed sustenance. Thus, for now, he stayed silent, a tsunami of heartache threatening his resolve.

# Chapter 31



During all our missions, mealtime became a respite from the chaos, a chance to allow our bodies to rest and digest, and our minds to unwind. So, he insisted on pleasant chitchat rather than discuss the stuff I found. In his view, and mine most days, meals signified relaxation and thankfulness in the surrounding beauty.

After lunch, I dragged two chairs out to the cozy balcony while he mixed cocktails. This wasn't a celebration. Far from it. Judging by his reaction to the photo and attached documents, I had a feeling I'd need a stiff drink to get through this conversation.

Two tumblers in hand, he strolled out to the balcony. "No schnapps, but I found Kahlua." He passed me a cocktail. "I whipped you up a popular drink from the eighties."

"What's it called?"

He chuckled.

I stole a sniff. "What's in it?"

"Ketel One Vodka, Irish cream, Kahlua, amaretto, and half-and-half."

"What's it called?"

"Does it matter? Try it."

"What the hell. You only live once, right?"

"Usually." He meant Spirit Crow, who defied the odds by resurrecting as a different species.

Unwilling to touch that subject, I sipped from the rim, ice clattering against the glass. "Wicked good."

He propped crossed ankles on the railing. "Pleased you approve."

"You're really not gonna tell me what it's called?"

Another chuckle. "Screaming Orgasm."

"Oh." Now his reaction made sense. "Awkward."

"Hence why I tried to avoid it."

Like a teenage girl, I could not stop giggling. But my amusement soon died when I turned toward him. His gray eyes held so much sadness and pain, enhanced by the hollowed stare at the horizon, his heart breaking before me. I laid a gentle hand on his forearm. "Whatever it is, I can handle it."

"Never have I doubted your strength, Kitty Cat."

"Then tell me. Please..."

With a quick wan grin, his gaze returned to the horizon. "Thousands of years ago, before the time of Buffalo and antelope hunting, our ancestors were dangerously malnourished. A plant-based diet couldn't sustain them. One day, Coyote climbed a prominent ridge to search for food."

"Coyote? As in, the shape-shifting trickster who scattered the stars?"

"One and the same. In the distance, Coyote spotted a humble abode with a fenced-in yard. A large Buffalo herd grazed within the enclosure. This discovery surprised Coyote. He thought someone had hidden the animals, which he felt was unfair because his People neared the brink of starvation."

He stole a quick sip. "For many moons, he watched the house. Until one day, he spotted a man, his wife, and their young son at the homestead. Their daily chores included caring for the herd. Late one afternoon, Coyote raced back to the village to tell the community what he'd seen. He also offered to help free the herd."

That rarely worked out well. "Did they believe him?"

"They did. The chief's son agreed to go with Coyote. So, the following day, they trekked back to the prominent ridge, where they had lain flat in the brush to surveil the property. The herd hadn't escaped. However, the surrounding fences were too high to climb, too strong to knock down. The chief's son didn't know what to do. Coyote suggested tricking the young boy by shapeshifting into a dog to gain access to the property. The ploy worked."

"Why do I feel like he screwed up?"

As if I hadn't said a word, he continued. "Once the family had fallen asleep, Coyote, in dog form, charged the Buffalo, barking and nipping at their legs. This, of course, spooked the herd, who stampeded to the safety of the house, but they trampled through the doorway and out the other side. The family woke during the chaos but were helpless to stop the herd. Soon, the father realized his son's dog wasn't a dog at all but Coyote, the trickster."

The tale captivated and intrigued me. Every animal had their own story.

"From then on, Buffalo roamed the grasslands."

"Coyote did a good thing for a change."

"He did. For thousands of years, American Indians relied on Buffalo for everything, from food, clothing, and blankets to shelter and spiritual worship. We consider them relatives. They are part of us. We are one, bonded by respect and admiration. When we admire a Buffalo, we don't see a big, furry animal. We see life. We see existence. We see hope. We see prayer. More importantly, we see a future for our young, and for those un-born."

"Don't worry. Killzme won't get away with this."

"You don't understand." He shot back the last of his drink. "Sit with me, Kitty Cat."

Once he dragged the chairs out of the way, he lowered to the deck boards. In front of him, I sat cross-legged, our hands woven at chest-level, knees touching to close our energy circle.

The sad smile lingered on his lips. "When the so-called settlers arrived, sixty million Buffalo roamed the grasslands of North America, freely grazing and cultivating the land. Thirty million on the Great Plains alone, and an integral part of daily life. Our People have always had a deep-rooted, spiritual connection to the Buffalo and always will. It's ingrained in our bloodline, heritage, and culture."

His shoulders squared. "The white man figured out their importance to us. Thus began the largest-scale slaughter in U.S. history, spouting rhetoric like, 'Kill every Buffalo you can. Every Buffalo dead is an Indian gone.'"

When my chest heaved, he squeezed my hands. But that only made me more emotional, awash in his sadness and devastation. "What'd they do?"

Tears somersaulted down my face as he recounted stories of hide hunters lining up in rows with their rifles, how the U.S. Military backed their efforts, and how the Buffalo never ran away. From years of sacrifice for Native People, and the honor bestowed for their selfless act, they couldn't predict the malicious destruction that awaited them.

"From the mid-1860s through the Battle of Little Bighorn and beyond, tragic conflicts ensued between the U.S. Cavalry and Native tribes. The Indian Wars were well underway, during which our People outwitted and outlasted the Cavalry's tactics. Their efforts kept them at bay for a while."

When he paused for a deep breath, I mirrored him. "Though many died, they refused to allow the white man to deliver a final deathblow. Around this time, the Transcontinental Railroad pushed its way across the Plains. Once completed, the Cavalry moved its men and equipment deeper into Indian Territory to help wrangle Natives onto reservations."

I held on tighter. "Why'd they hate our ancestors so much?"

"Ignorance and greed. They didn't speak their language. They didn't pray their way. What they didn't understand, they destroyed."

"Why, though? Who cares if someone's culture, lifestyle, or spirituality differs from yours? I don't get it."

"Nor do I, Kitty Cat." Another deep breath followed. "The discovery of gold in Idaho and Oregon in the 1860s led to similar conflicts, which culminated in the Bear River Massacre and Snake

War. In the late 1870s, another series of armed conflicts occurred in Oregon and Idaho and spread East into Wyoming and Montana."

*Greed really was the root of all evil. That and ignorance.*

"Generals Sherman and Sheridan believed if the soldiers eradicated the Buffalo, our ancestors would have to surrender. If herds roamed the Great Plains, so did American Indians, with our deep-seated symbiotic relationship. It wasn't unusual for the generals to provide the rich and influential opportunities to travel West and hunt Buffalo with the Cavalry. Military commanders had full license to kill as many Buffalo as possible to quote, 'do their part' to gain control of American Indians."

Oh, my God. This story got worse by the second.

"Some hunters used these majestic creatures for target practice, killing massive numbers in a day. They didn't even want the meat." Confusion and despair crackled his voice. "Skinned, rotting red carcasses and sun-bleached bones littered the Plains. The hides they sold for three dollars and fifty cents apiece."

*What the—?* "That's it?"

"Sadly, yes. With inflation, it still only amounts to roughly eighty-five dollars."

"They slaughtered Buffalo to earn only a few bucks?"

"And to 'do their part' to starve our ancestors into submission, yes. The Buffalo's mistreatment rubs against our values, culture, and traditions. Never would we commit such vile acts. Yet, in settler's eyes, American Indians were nothing more than—quote—*godless savages*, unintelligent, uneducated, and undervalued as humans."

A squeal escaped my lips, tears sheening my skin. My Caucasian ancestors caused these monstrosities, choosing commercialism, greed, and hatred over millions of innocent lives, animals with souls and culture and family who loved them.

Of all the stories about the white man, this one cut me deepest because of its disgusting hidden agenda—to rid the nation of Native Americans—to murder the best part of me.

"By 1889, only five-hundred-twelve Plains Buffalo had escaped the ravages of westward expansion, market demand, and a deliberate effort by the U.S. Government to force our ancestors to submit to the white man's superiority and assimilate to their culture, religion, and language by forsaking their own. Or die of starvation. Many chose the latter. Others surrendered. In 1900, Congress finally outlawed the killing of any animal in Yellowstone National Park. However, by then, the damage had already been done."

The story rocked my chest, my emotions spiraling.

"When the European market pivoted due to the scarcity of Buffalo, hide hunters became skull gatherers. The smell of death remained, however. And soon, trophy hunters lusting for a bust to display on their wall whittled the last five-hundred-twelve down to less than two dozen."

Confusion scattered my thoughts. "But we saw that many yesterday."

"We did. Due in part to traveling road shows and Smithsonian displays, which led to the Buffalo Nickel."

"You lost me."

"Once the public viewed the animals up-close, they could no longer support all the killing. By 1933, twenty-two Buffalo grew to four thousand. One-hundred-twenty lived in protected herds in forty-one different states, half of which were national herds. Some were even born in the National Preserve here in Montana.

The American Bison Society made plans to disband protections and declared the Buffalo safe from extinction. What they never understood was the intricacy of ecosystems. You cannot save an animal without also preserving their habitat."

"Right. *Shicheii* said the same thing."

"The following Spring, the National Herd birthed seventy-five calves. One of which was all white with blue eyes. A genetic rarity. They called him Whitey for a while." His eyes rolled. "To us, a white Buffalo holds spiritual significance. His birth was a gift from Creator. Extremely sacred. White Buffalo have spiritual power and meaning. Big medicine, it's called. And that's precisely what the local tribes named him, Big Medicine."

"Aww, cute." Did this tale have a happy ending of sorts? I didn't dare ask.

"By presence alone, Big Medicine offered hope to all American Indians, his message clear. We will weather this storm. We will persevere. We will prosper."

"Love that." *Did he skip parts of the story, or did I miss something?* "How does the Buffalo Nickel fit?"

"It's a fun fact."

I suppressed the eyeroll. "Alright, lay it on me."

His soft chuckle nourished my wounded soul. "On March 4, 1913, the government introduced the coin into circulation. One side shows the profile of an American Indian. The other side shows an American Buffalo. However, it's all an illusion. The model for the Buffalo Nickel was a large male named Black Diamond. Though the coin portrays wilderness and freedom, Black Diamond lived in a cage at the zoo. Later sold to a butcher, processed, and sold for his meat."

I slapped a hand over my mouth. "Please tell me that isn't true."

"Wish I could, Kitty Cat." He hesitated a moment. "When the average American looks at the coin, they see a symbol of wilderness when in fact, the five-cent-piece celebrates its wanton destruction. Why use our image and the Buffalo on this nickel?"

"I dunno. Maybe the white man grew to love the Buffalo in his own twisted way?"

"Which begs the question—Why do they destroy the things they claim to love? Mister Worthington used the same language for the crows he slaughtered, stuffed, and displayed as trophies."

Slapped by the memory, I still didn't understand why the photo and document upset him.

"How are you, darlin'?" He thumbed away my tears. "That was a lot to absorb."

"I'm okay, I think."

"Need a hug?"

"No, but clearly you do."

Chuckling, he pulled me into his chest. When his grip loosened, he thanked me. "Now that you have the backstory, I'll show you the significance of what you found." When he stood, he extended his hand.

"Is it worse than the backstory?"

"It could be."

What could be worse than the mass destruction of millions of animals?

# Chapter 32



**5:10 p.m.**

Mayhem led Cat to the laptop on the table, where he enlarged the photo she'd found.

She rubbed her eyebrow. "Are they bones?"

"Skulls, specifically."

The image showed a man—arrogant and proud—standing atop a mountain of sun-bleached Buffalo skulls. Another man stood on the ground in front of the mountain of death to show the aftermath of lost lives numbering in the millions.

"It's an old photograph taken amidst the conflicts."

"Why would Russell save this to his computer?"

"To add validity to this document." He clicked the attachment. "When private landowners preserved the last remaining Buffalo, many bred them with cows. Today, the U.S. is home to over three-hundred-fifty-thousand Bison. Natives oversee twenty thousand. Twenty thousand more live in protected federal and state preserves. The rest exist in private herds, confined like cattle, fattened in feedlots, and raised for slaughter."

Her forehead dropped into her hand.

"Until Buffalo can live and roam free, we haven't restored them at all. Instead, the white man created a very special grass-eating zoo creature. To turn them loose to live how Creature intended, where they thrived for thousands of years with our People, is the only way to repair the damage."

A pang throbbed his temples. "Here's the wrinkle to that argument. Only the herds who escaped to Greater Yellowstone and those on tribal land possess the ancient bloodline of the individuals involved in the mass extinction."

"Please don't say that's who Killzme is targeting."

"I'm afraid so. They plan to finish what their forefathers started. What better way than to offer cash prizes in a competition?"

A slow hand rose to her heart. "Is this our fault?"

"What do they call me, Cat?"

"Redskin."

"And you?"

"Mutt."

"Because they know of your mixed heritage. Who are we fighting to protect?"

"The Innocent Ones."

"And?"

"The Natural World."

"Why?"

"For future generations."

"Precisely. Now, if you were an arrogant white man of privilege, you might misconstrue our objective."

A gasp escaped her mouth. "They think we're only protecting our People."

"Correct. Their ignorance blinds them to the fact that we're working for all of humanity, not only indigenous communities. However, the entitlement mindset supersedes logic. If Killzme slaughters the offspring from the ancient herd, they will cause irreparable damage to Natives everywhere. The Buffalo as we know it, deep in our soul, in our bloodline—as every single one of our ancestors knew it—will cease to exist. Thus, deliver a kill shot to you and me."

Fresh tears bloomed in her eyes and her chin dropped. "Oh. My. God. Just when I think Killzme can't get any eviler..."

"Unfathomable, I agree. Yet here we are. This may be our most important mission to date."

"Understood."

This next subject may be a little delicate, so he started slow. "Kitty Cat?"

She raised her watery gaze.

"We need to draw an obvious line between personal and work."

"Agreed." She hesitated. "Can I ask you somethin' first?"

*Why did he always brace for that question?* "Certainly."

"Did your wife do this work?"

"In the field?" He scoffed. "Good Lord, no."

"But she seemed so involved in all aspects of your life."

"She was, mostly."

"What's that mean, exactly?"

His mind fled back in time. "I knew what she wanted to hear and protected her from the parts she preferred not to know."

"Like we do with *Shicheii*?"

"We shield Jacy Lee a touch more than I did with her, but yes, similar."

"So, our thing is unfamiliar territory for you?"

"It is."

"Hmm." Her eyes sparkled. "Good to know."

"Hence my reluctance."

"You didn't seem reluctant downstairs."

Her quick wit never got old. "That was an icebreaker."

"Wow." She stroked her neck. "It's one helluva icebreaker."

"Cautious Cat"—he barely withheld a smirk—"we're veering out of work-mode."

Her throat cleared. "Right." She snapped up the phone. "I also found the coordinates for the hunt." She showed him the satellite map. "Bastards tried to hide it with invisible ink, but Mister Genius kept a copy in his photos."

*Luther Abbott.*

Mayhem reached for the phone. "May I?" Enlarging the image showed an area deep in the wilderness. "What time does the hunt start?"

"Ten-thirty."

"It'll be tight." June rescheduled the ceremony for nine p.m., but the hunt was a good forty-minute hike from the nearest trail. "Between now and Friday, we need to run this route multiple times, under different weather and light conditions, until we can almost do it blindfolded."

"Fun," she said with a mouthful of snark.

His cell vibrated in his pocket. When he checked the caller ID, Jacy Lee's name appeared. "What a pleasant surprise," he answered. "Is everything all right?"

"Fine, Cheveyo. I can't call to say hello?"

"Of course, you can. Would you like to speak with Cat?"

"Have you told her yet?"

Pressing the phone tighter to his ear, he strolled out of the living room. "Jacy Lee, what is the urgency?"

"Ferron called."

Ooh, that woman would not rest. "And?"

"And nothing. She sends her best."

"Mm-hmm. Is there anything else I can help you with? Cat and I are working."

"What time will you be home for dinner?"

He released an audible exhale. "When would you like us there?"

"Six, please."

"Jacy Lee, it's after five, and it's a thirty-minute drive."

"Perfect. We'll see you then. Tell Mourning Dove, I love her."

"Jacy Lee?" He pulled the phone away from his ear. Blank screen.

Cat prowled closer. "Did he just hang up on you?"

"He did."

To keep from laughing, her lips curled around her teeth.

"We've been summoned for dinner."

"Huh. He never does that."

"No, he doesn't."

"Uh-oh. What'd *Shicheii* do now?"

"Good question."

Jacy Lee, what are you up to?

**6:01 p.m.**

When Mayhem pulled into the driveway, Poe was modeling his new tail feathers—a slow swagger across the railing that warmed every cockle of Dad's heart. As he and Shawnee crossed the yard, Jacy Lee oohed and ahhed and Spirit Crow cooed. Poe lapped up every morsel of praise.

Little Rascal.

"Hey"—Cat nudged his arm, her voice a low whisper—"how'd he get his bling back?"

Only then did the gold necklace register. Hence why Jacy Lee called. He'd planned a celebration for Poe. The local ravens veiled the trees in black feathers.

Such a glorious sight. "Looks like he made some new friends, as well."

"Aww... *Shicheii* fixed everything."

*Gronk, gronk, gronk.*

Mayhem's gaze shot to the porch. "Odin?" Sure enough, he perched on the railing, celebrating their reunion with a serenade, high and low notes in perfect harmony.

"Look who's here." Her pitch rose with excitement. "Hey, buddy."

Missing pieces of this jigsaw puzzle still escaped him. "How—?"

When the screen door flapped open, Mayhem's mind spun even more. "Running Bear?"

What on earth was going on here?

On the porch, Cat threw her arms around Kuruk. "I can't believe you're here."

*Neither could he.*

"Easy handling the merchandise, Ghost Dog." Grinning, his pectoral muscles danced beneath his tight t-shirt.

"Ugh." She shoved him away. "You're impossible."

Chuckling, Mayhem patted his shoulder. "Nice to see you, handsome." He pulled out Cat's chair before lowering to his. Hands steepled over his empty plate, he regarded Jacy Lee. "Is this the reason you called?"

He raised a large wooden bowl. "Salad?"

Cat's emerald eyes shifted between Mayhem and her grandfather.

"Almost forgot. Silly me." Jacy Lee darted inside, returning moments later with a bottle of wine and three long-stemmed wineglasses. "Shall I pour?"

"Not necessary, thank you." With his hands still steepled over his empty plate, his attention turned to Kuruk. "Though I'm pleased to see you, Running Bear, why are you here?"

He scooped salad on to his place. "Jacy Lee told Mama Hen about the Buffalo hunt, so I figured you could use some help. Can't believe they'd target the sacred lineage."

Speechless, he and Cat gaped at each other. "How did you—?" His gaze strayed to Jacy Lee, whose dimples deepened with satisfaction. "How long have you known about this?"

"Gee, let me think." From a second casserole pan, albeit smaller, he spooned harvest chicken into three bowls for Poe, Spirit Crow, and Odin.

By baking a smaller portion of the meal, he avoided adding onions and other ingredients that harmed corvids.

"The Holy Ones showed me shortly after our arrival while I was praying for a healing for Mourning Dove."

Her fork clattered against the plate. "Is that why I can hear?"

Grinning, he patted the top of her hand.

Rather than fall prey to Jacy Lee's clever tactic to change the subject, Mayhem stayed on point. "Before or after I drove Klee and Ferron to their plane?"

He raised the bottle. "Wine?"

"Jacy Lee," his tone hardened, "I would appreciate a response."

"Don't interrogate me, Cheveyo."

"I'm not." His head would not stop rocking. "I asked a simple question that has still not been answered."

His elder scanned the table. "Would anyone like gravy?"

Immediately, Poe pushed his bowl toward one of his favorite humans, whom he viewed as his personal chef.

Mayhem slapped the table. "Jacy Lee—"

All three corvids shot him the stink eye.

"Before. All right, Cheveyo? Before."

He swung his arms wide. "And you shared the vision with Ferron instead of me?"

"*Shicheii,* I love you, but he's right. You shoulda told us."

As though she and Mayhem had overreacted, Jacy Lee shook out his napkin. "Cheveyo asked me not to meddle, and I honored his wishes."

"By summoning Running Bear?" Heat rose in his chest. "He has a family to protect." Another inconsistency occurred to him, and his gaze landed on his former protégé. "How did you even get here?"

"Mama Hen."

The nonchalance to his tone confused him even more. "She flew you to Montana?"

"Don't be ridiculous, Shadow Wolf. Mama Hen can't pilot a plane." He took one heaping spoonful of casserole, then another. "Pass me a glass, please." He jabbed a chin at the wine. "You gonna pour or...?"

Why could no one see the recklessness of this? Without crucial intel, the odds turned in Killzme's favor.

"Y'know what?" Shawnee swiped the bottle off the table. "I think I'll join you."

"You don't even like wine, Cat."

"It's better than nothin'." After overfilling the glasses—a decent vintage needed room to breathe—she slid a goblet in front of his plate. "Take a hit o' that. Fix ya right up."

Why the change in demeanor? "Are you not the least bit concerned about your grandfather's meddling?"

"Not really, no. Our family's whole again. Besides, we do need the added manpower."

Valid point. While he swirled his wineglass, Odin pushed his bowl next to him. "Hey, bud." He stroked his sleek back feathers. "Glad you're home."

*Gronk, gronk, gronk.*

Flavors burst from the first bite of Jacy Lee's casserole, his palate alive with cranberries, sweet potato, Brussels sprouts, wild rice, and almond, the chicken cooked to perfection with a hint of paprika, thyme, and broth. The ideal meal to dampen any lingering doubts.

Mayhem thanked his lifelong friend. "It's a work of art. Truly."

"He's right, *Shicheii*. Freakin' amazing."

With a packed mouthful, Running Bear jutted out a thumbs-up.

"Thank you, all." He blushed. "So, did you and Mourning Dove have a nice day at the park?"

What an odd question. "We're working, Jacy Lee. Not sightseeing."

"How will you ever nurture your relationship if you don't have any fun?"

Mayhem choked on his wine. All the coloring in Cat's face drained in an instant.

And Running Bear perked up. "Your what?"

When his gaze slid to Spirit Crow, Poe caped his wings to block his mother, his bill parted in disbelief.

The right words escaped him. With another sip of wine came clarity. "Our cover story is a bride and groom renewing their vows."

"Yeah, uh, it, uh, gives us freer rein. Y'know, without... people... y'know, asking questions and shit." She gulped down the wine.

Oh, boy.

Running Bear's gaze shifted between them. "Uh-huh." He shrugged. "Makes sense."

Hawkeyed on Jacy Lee, Mayhem said, "Is there something you'd like to discuss in private?"

"No, Cheveyo. I'm fine. Thank you."

To sidestep this conversation, he changed the subject. "Cat found the location of the hunt."

Big smile. "Did she?"

"She did. In fact, we're heading there later tonight. Running Bear, please join us. We could use your help."

"That's why I'm here."

"We have an errand to run first, where you could also assist."

Nodding, he shoveled in the casserole.

"Splendid. Then it's settled. Who returned Poe's necklace? Did you mediate the feud between him and the locals?"

After a quick glance over his shoulder at the massive unkindness of ravens, Jacy Lee lowered his voice. "They refused to listen to reason, Cheveyo. Odin handled it shortly after he arrived."

*Gronk, gronk, gronk.*

Warmth flooded his system. "You are a welcome ray of sunshine, bud. Thank you." Spirit Crow hadn't made a peep, nor did she greet him or Cat. "You're awfully quiet, darling."

Cat said, "I'm eating."

Mayhem winced. "I was speaking to—"

Her palms flashed in surrender. "My total bad. The right ear's still giving me a little..." She shoveled in another fork full of casserole.

Oh, boy.

As much as he adored this family, somehow his home life had gotten even more complicated. If Jacy Lee was right about Kimi's reason to return, did she complete her mission here?

He swallowed hard. Please no. He's not ready to say goodbye, nor to deal with the aftermath of her departure.

# Chapter 33



Watching the sunset with *Shicheii* was the second highlight of my day. The whole family lounged on a tribal blanket in the backyard, munching on popcorn. Spirit Crow and Odin nuzzled and cooed in my lap while I marveled at one of the pinkest skies ever created. Poe perched on his dad's crossed knee, his beady-eyed gaze fluctuating between the sunset and the two lovebirds, eyes thinning at me like I had something to do with turning his mother's head.

"*Shicheii*?"

In an instant, Poe faced front. *Ah-ha!* Found his weakness.

"Yes, my love?"

After a side-glance at Poe, I said, "Do sunsets hold special significance? They feel as spiritually meaningful as a sunrise."

"They are." He gave me a one-armed squeeze. "The sunset symbolizes the end of a chapter in one's life and hope for a new beginning. For those in mourning, the sunset helps them connect to a deceased loved one and shows how to restore peace and harmony in their lives. Do not drown in grief, for a new journey awaits."

*Shicheii* smiled at his dearest friend. "Isn't that right, Cheveyo?"

"Indeed, it is." Grinning, he returned a wink. "A sunset also stands as proof—no matter what transpires during the day, it ends on a beautiful, heartfelt note of encouragement, with the promise of a new dawn."

Running Bear peered around his former mentor. "Do you plan to finish that, Ghost Dog?"

"I was gonna." I popped a kernel in my mouth, melted butter slipping across my tastebuds.

My faux hubby bumped his elbow. "Looks like you've finally met your match."

I snarled. "What the hell's that supposed to mean?"

"Shadow Wolf just called us pigs."

"I said no such thing." When he rose, he cradled Poe in one arm. "Thank you for a beautiful evening, Jacy Lee. Now, if you'll excuse me, I need to gather a few supplies and change." Gray eyes glanced me up and down. "Is that you plan to wear, Cat?"

Well, "Yes" was obviously the wrong answer. "*Shicheii*, did you get a chance to wash my buckskins?"

"I sure did. They're on a hanger in your room."

"You're the best." I kissed his cheek. "Thank you."

Mr. Mayhem said, "Let's meet out front on the porch. Ten minutes?"

"Sounds good." I passed my bowl of popcorn to Running Bear, who'd already dressed in warrior gear—buckskin pants with fringe down the outer seam, like our team leader wears, and a tight black tee to show off his chiseled physique, his dark hair down and loose. "You're getting my popcorn in protest."

"Makes no difference to me." He clawed out a handful. "See ya on the flop, Ghost Dog."

"Yeah, yeah." I headed for the backdoor.

Later, after our usual hugs and kisses for *Shicheii*, my grandfather professing his love for each of us, we piled into the Benz. Perched on the middle console, Poe shot daggers at me every chance he got.

"What *is* your problem?"

He glanced me up and down with disgust.

"Hey, bud." His dad stroked the brat. "Come sit with me."

Poe hopped into his lap, a satisfied glance back at me like he'd won his father's affection.

Friggin' diva needed an attitude adjustment.

Mr. Mayhem angled the rearview mirror to speak into the backseat. "Cat found Killzme's rendezvous point. We're headed there now. Did Odin find a replacement to guard the Sacred Land?"

*Kimi's grave.*

"His buddy who helped escort Little Man to the dock is there. Don't worry. It's secure. Just checked the cameras a few minutes ago."

The mere mention of that ship sent tremors up my spine.

"Perfect. Thank you."

Within fifteen minutes, we cruised a lonely side street framed in thick forestry, a few houses set back from the road, visible only through trickles of moonlight. Darkness overshadowed the area, except for periodic mailboxes snapshotted in the cylindrical spheres of headlights.

Though the idea of tromping through unfamiliar terrain didn't thrill me—night predators stalked the woodlands—I rolled with it. This mission was too important for me to panic over wildlife, who couldn't separate bad guys from good. But since my two Apache warriors didn't seem bothered at all, their innate calmness kept my nerves from firing.

At the trunk, Mr. Mayhem armed himself with multiple knives and the tomahawk. I grabbed a bigger, sharper knife for the shin pocket of my moccasin, my favorite curved blade sheathed in the small of my back.

While Running Bear withdrew his long-range rifle case, he said, "No bow, Ghost Dog?"

"Why? I miss the target more than I hit it."

"She had a stance issue." He patted my back. "Your aim is improving, Cat."

Total bullshit, but I appreciated the positive feedback.

"However, with Poe here, it may behoove us to leave it behind." His nose crinkled. "Wouldn't you agree?" On his shoulder, Pissy Pants thinned his eyes as though the incident happened yesterday. "Practice and perseverance breed success."

"For the record, I only clipped one tail feather. Running Bear did the most damage."

Pitch rising, Kuruk flung a stiff hand at Poe. "He flew into my shot."

Our team leader patted down the tension. "All right, you two. Let's not zing accusations. What's done is done."

I mumbled, "Just sayin'."

"And I hear you, Cat." The piercing stare shut my mouth. "Now, the rendezvous point is a half-mile away. I suggest we get a move-on."

"Copy that."

I concurred. "Right behind ya."

"Running Bear, if you could trail her, I'd appreciate it."

"Copy that." He sloughed off a shrug. "The Oreo."

"Precisely."

"The... Oreo?" I firmed a hand on my hip. "Why am I the cream filling? 'Cause I don't have a penis?"

He winced. "No, Cat. You are still in training."

"Oh." *Should've known. He's far from a sexist.*

Through the darkened woods we trekked single file. As much as I hated to admit it, I felt a lot safer sandwiched between two Apache warriors. Maybe not bulletproof, but damn close.

A hair-raising screech stopped me mid-stride, my heartbeat quickened to a fast *pitter-patter, pitter-patter, pitter-patter.* Quaking aspen leaves trembled as we passed. Night owls slalomed through the trees, oarlike wings emitting a *whoosh* with each stroke.

To my left, sticks crunched under heavy paws. Or hooves.

Bear?

Moose?

Wolf?

Before I figured it out, Running Bear clamped a hand on my shoulder, whispered, "Get out of your head, Ghost Dog."

"How do you—?"

He leaned closer to my ear. "You're as rigid as an iron rod. Concentrate on breath control."

"Listen to him, Cat," he tossed over his shoulder. "He's been where you are."

"I'm on it." To Running Bear, I mouthed, "Thanks."

Acknowledgment came with another pat.

The invigorating freshness of pine helped me regain control, diminished only by the strong lemony pineapple fragrance of Douglas firs—my mentor taught me that—as we neared a bend in the trail.

"Lights up ahead, Shadow Wolf." Behind me, Running Bear's cool tone prevented my adrenaline from spiking. "Where do you want me?"

Mr. Mayhem stopped to point through the canopies of leaves to a higher altitude, but no clue where. "That ridgeline should offer you an optimal vantage point."

"Copy that." Within seconds, he vanished among thickets of trees.

As we hiked side-by-side, his comforting fingers wove through mine. Poe rode his outer shoulder. Fine with me. If he blamed me for all the shit that went down recently, there wasn't much I could do about it. Maybe in time, he'd forget.

Yeah, right. Who was I kidding? Crows held grudges forever, even passed down mental snapshots of "dangerous faces" to future generations. Learned that little tidbit the hard way. Friggin' psycho.

Once I reconnected with *Shicheii* and Poe begrudgingly witnessed genuine affection forming between me and his dad, he stopped spreading nasty rumors about me. Spirit Crow also persuaded him to cut the shit. His hatred still lingered, but at least I could leave the house without fear of retaliation from an army of taloned soldiers.

Been there, done that, got the scars to prove it.

When we rounded a bend in the trail, a massive barn loomed in a wide-open expanse of land. An endless line of ATVs and pickups parked out front, floodlights spotlighting the X'd double doors. Darkness shadowed the back half, but without trees it wouldn't be easy to approach.

"How're we gonna get close enough to see inside?"

"The lack of vegetation is problematic, I agree." Before we reached the trailhead opening, he stopped me. "Do you recall how you accessed Mister Worthington's yard?"

Stomach crawl. "Yeah. Why?"

"We may have a similar opportunity here." From his moccasin boot, he withdrew a compact. But instead of makeup inside, three sections held black, light charcoal, and red face paint. After dipping two fingertips into black, he dragged them down my face and neck. "With this paint, I will transform."

Raising my bangs, I echoed his words.

"A rebirth, with new responsibilities, new obligations, new relationships."

Again, I repeated the mantra.

He smudged the lines with his thumbs, then added light charcoal, his gentle touch swirling across my skin.

"What about the rest of me?" Because of my mixed heritage, I was a lot whiter than him.

"You could probably manage those areas on your own, no?"

"Nope." Let's see him wiggle out of this one. "Can't see what I'm doing. You'll have to do it." I stared up with a sly smirk. "Unless you don't trust yourself to behave."

Grinning, he slapped dollops of dark and light paint into his palm. Massaged his hands together, our gazes locked till he lifted my chin to tilt my head back.

The first touch sent warmth and tingles everywhere, but I tried not to react. His hands smoothed across my upper chest, two fingers sliding down the crease of my cleavage, and lowered to my abs, where he drew jagged lines from the bottom hem of my halter to my waistline.

I bit my lower lip, my mind imagining the best possible scenario, even though I promised not to mix work with personal. But that kiss was so friggin' hot. It's sheer torture to stop there.

"Turn, please."

Warm palms ran across my shoulder blades, two fingers trailing down my spine. When he massaged the paint into my skin, I forgot where I was for a second, and arced my back like a cat in heat.

*Aw, shit. Get it together, Daniels. Just stop thinking about it.*

My eyes flashed open to a spitting mad crow, who didn't hesitate to show me exactly what he thought of my impure imagery. When he bill-tapped his gold ankle band, I translated just fine.

*Tick-tock, bitch. The second Dad turns his back, I'll claw your filthy eyes out.*

My moccasins shuffled backward. "I... uh... can probably do my arms."

"All right, then." He smeared paint across his face and down his neck—a disorientating black-gray swirl that looked creepy as hell.

"Is that how you did mine?"

"It is."

"Sick. I love it. What about my handprints?"

He coated his palm in blood-red paint, then pressed his hand across my mouth. Another handprint grabbed my shoulder.

Though he'd earned many more than me, he only wore one tonight—four fingers spanned his left cheek, the palm masking his lips, and the thumb stood erect on the opposite side. Not only did handprints signify bravery in battle, but they also acted as psychological warfare to the enemy.

When he put the compact away, he chuckled to himself, the head rocking like he didn't know what to do with me. "Ready for a little fun, bud?"

Poe cawed his acceptance.

"The SD card in your special ankle band is already active. Are you clear on what to do?"

Like a good soldier, his bill lowered, raised.

The device really belonged to his brother, Edgar, but Poe wore it when we needed video evidence. Plus, he loved the added bling of a second ankle band. When his dad put it on him at the house before we left, the added swagger churned my stomach acids.

"Excellent. Please be mindful of wildlife. Sounds like a robust community here."

He probably meant the owls—the arch enemies of crows.

With one last never-ending glare at me and his dad, Poe flew straight to the barn. He stopped at a side window, his enormous crow foot pointed at the glass, working the edges to capture video of the men inside.

His father beamed. "Flawless as ever."

"I mean, it's not rocket science."

The eyebrows lifted. "You don't find him the least bit impressive?"

"Right this second? Not really, no. Ask me again when all my hair grows in."

Back in Alaska, after my misplaced arrow clipped off one of Poe's two remaining tail feathers, he viciously attacked. Damn near scalped me, too. Luckily, I had enough hair left to cover the bald spots. If it weren't for his father and *Shicheii's* quick response, the damage could've been much worse. Still could if I didn't stop lusting over his dad.

Sidestepping my remark, he swayed an opened hand at the clearing. "Shall we proceed?"

At the tree line, I led while he guarded me from behind. Hunched low, we ventured into the darkness. At about the halfway point, headlights turned into the long dirt driveway, and we hit the ground.

Compacted dirt scraped my elbows as I headed toward the barn—commando-crawl style—with my feet propelling me forward.

Now and then, I froze when flashlights slashed the darkness above me, Killzme's henchmen skimming the landscape for intruders.

Elbow after elbow, we made our way to the back of the barn, where we slinked to an upright position, our backs pressed against the rough barnboard. Concealed in the shadows beside me, he hand-signaled to Running Bear, watching our every move through his telephoto rifle scope.

Far in the distance, a tiny red light blinked *on... off... on... off* to show his precise location.

Though it appeared miles away, for an expert sharpshooter like him, it didn't matter. The dude could probably wipe a freckle off a chipmunk before it reached the burrow. Not that he would. He respected wildlife as much as we did.

Inside the barn, chatter engulfed the space, but I couldn't make out specific words among the plethora of male voices. Poe fluttered down in front of us, and almost gave me a friggin' heart attack. The second he landed on his father's forearm, he kicked out his leg.

He whispered, "I can't check it now, bud."

The leg shook again, insisting for him to watch the video.

"I'll check the footage as soon as I can. Thank you." He scanned the backside of the barn.

No windows. No entry point, except for a hay door near the peak.

Before he got any ideas, I whispered, "Too high."

"Doable."

"It's really not."

"It's no higher than the steakhouse window."

*Aw, man. That's one stunt I'd rather not repeat. If he wasn't so convincing and freakishly strong, I could've easily kissed the pavement.*

"The barnboard siding should be easier to climb, no?"

"Y'mean, easier for *me* to climb."

"I do, yes."

*Why, oh, why am I agreeing to this? Have I not tempted fate enough?*

"Let's just get it over with." Exhaling loud enough to make my point, I climbed him like a ladder till I stood on his shoulders.

With both hands under my moccasins, he bench-pressed me straight up over his head. My fingers clawed into the wooden framework, my feet crawling upward.

At the hay door, I slid open the bolt lock, stopping when the activity got too loud. When I eased it open a crack, my breath froze.

*Oh. My. God. What is this?*

# Chapter 34

"*Traditional Healers and Elders say the Great Spirit works through everyone, so that everyone has the ability to heal, whether it's the mother who tends to the scrapes of her child, a friend who eases your pain by kind words, or the Healer who heals your illness. Everything that was put here is healing—the trees, the Earth, the animals, and the water.*"
—Native American Wisdom

### *10:30 p.m.*

W hen Cat climbed down, her entire body trembled as she insisted for them to leave right away. Though Mayhem couldn't grasp the urgency without intel, he never doubted she'd seen something horrific.

After everything they'd witnessed from Killzme Corp, what could frighten her to this extreme?

"C'mon—" She pulled his hand. "We gotta get outta here."

Mayhem didn't budge. "You head back. I'll catch up."

"No way. I'm not leaving without you." She reached for him, but he angled away.

"That was not a request, Ghost Dog." Using her Apache name helped to snap her out of the panic.

Without a word, she dropped to the soil, careful to stay low and out of sight.

Flattened against the siding, Mayhem inched toward the corner of the barn.

A handheld radio squelched to life. "Tango to Yank. Do you copy?"

"Go for Yank."

"Did you clear the rear?"

"Heading there now."

Cat was midway to the trailhead. Exposed and vulnerable, with no way for him to warn her.

He slid the curved blade from its sheath.

Waited for the footsteps to approach.

Static from the handheld pierced the night.

On the roofline, Poe spread his magnificent wings. Mayhem stepped into the open. The henchman reached for a pistol on his waist.

Mayhem pounced. A quick one-two slash of the blade severed both carotids, and he ducked beneath the arc of blood, pulsing out the prey's neck.

By the armpits, he dragged the well-built sentinel behind the barn. A second henchman in fatigues rounded the far corner, gun drawn. Running Bear put him down with one perfectly placed headshot. On the ground, his body writhed, the nervous system still reacting to a fatal injury.

At the opening to the trailhead, Cat rose. Sensing her panic, he signaled for her to stay put.

From the waistband of the dying man with severed throat, he snatched the radio, squeezed the side button. "Clear."

Tango said, "Good. Continue with the perimeter check till you hear from me again."

The gurgling intensified, the poacher choking on blood. A tomahawk strike to the larynx silenced him forever.

"Copy that," Mayhem said into the radio.

Across the field, Cat's mouth gaped.

His breath caught. She, of all people, knew the stakes. Why did his actions surprise her?

Time slowed.

For years, he'd hidden the darkness from Kimi, who never wanted to know *how* things got done, just that he'd solved the problem. As much as he'd desperately loved her, he prayed his relationship with Cat could be different.

Evil only responded to evil. If his motives stayed pure, he'd commit any brutal act to safeguard his People, the Natural World, and every innocent soul within it.

Once Cat shot him two thumbs-up, his breath relaxed into a peaceful rhythm.

*There she is.*

Poe fluttered down to his forearm. "Thank you for the assist, bud." He smooched his feathery cheek. "Did you spot any other obstacles that require my attention?"

No reaction meant no.

"Splendid." He lifted Poe to his shoulder perch. As they trekked toward the trailhead, he whispered, "One of these days, you must forgive her. She's important to me."

Poe whipped his face away.

"She's family, bud."

He leaped off his shoulder, flew straight to his adversary, his talons skimming her raven hair, cherry tresses nestling back into place.

Uh-oh. Not again. Mayhem jogged to catch up.

"Keep your mitts off me, you fuckin' freakshow."

He winced. "Language, please."

"You're calling *me* out?" She thrust an angry hand at Poe, now perched on a low tree limb, preening his flight feathers. "What about him?"

He smirked. "*He* doesn't use foul language."

Clearly unhappy with his response, her upper lip twitched. "Just keep your psychotic pet away from me."

"Pet?" He rocked back on his heels. "Hardly. Poe is his own man." The scowl caused him to tug at his shirt collar. "I shall speak to him about boundary lines."

"Thank you." Her tone still held a bite of indignation.

While he led her along the bend in the trail, he slung a loose arm around her neck. "Please tell me what you witnessed back there."

"It was awful, but I dunno what it all means yet. Still tryin' to piece it together."

He jostled her. "Let me help you."

"Can you gimme a few minutes?"

"Of course. Take all the time you need."

Silence rode the still night air as they ventured farther into the forest. When they crested the hill, Running Bear had beat them to the Benz.

Clearly thrilled with his performance tonight, he leaned against the quarter panel. "Did you see that shot?"

"I did." Mayhem gave him a congratulatory pat on the shoulder. "You haven't lost your touch."

"Ghost Dog?" He searched her face for answers. "Are you alright?"

A nod rocked her head, but she didn't speak.

"She's still processing what she witnessed."

"The caged Buffalo?"

His heart stalled. "The what?"

"If I didn't know better, I'd swear he was Black Diamond."

Mayhem whirled toward Shawnee. "There's a live Buffalo in the barn?"

"With red paint on his horns, yeah." Tears washed straight lines through the face paint. "They're poking him with poles."

"Cat, why on earth didn't you tell me sooner? If they are torturing an animal, the last thing we should do is leave."

Kuruk clamped a hand on his shoulder. "Shadow Wolf, there must be thirty, forty men in there. The line of vehicles extends to the street. You're the one who says to choose our battles wisely."

"Unacceptable." A blaze raged inside him. "They are torturing one of our relatives." He whirled back to Cat. "What is this about painted horns?"

Her shoulders sprang to her ears. "I dunno. They're red."

His heart sank. "Marked for death."

"Then we definitely can't leave." She raked back her hair. "What if he's from the ancient bloodline?"

"I have no doubt he is. Perhaps even part of Black Diamond's lineage. Killzme needs familial DNA to target the correct herd."

"Then we definitely gotta go back."

"Thank you." He blew back a few loose strands dislodged from his braids. "But first, we need a rock-solid plan in place." When he didn't find any signs of hesitancy, he said, "How are you, Cat?"

"Lost it for a few back there, but I'm okay now, I think."

"You think, or you know?"

"I'm good."

"Pleased to hear it." Plausible scenarios rolled through his mind. Thirty or forty armed men were a lot to deal with at once. "What were you wrestling with?"

"Huh?"

"You said some aspects confused you. The caged Buffalo is one puzzle piece. What else?"

"Oh, um..." For better recall, she closed her eyes. "The equal sign crossed out and the number fourteen."

Kuruk said, "Shit."

"If you have some insight, Running Bear, please share."

"I dealt with a few of these guys in the military. Nasty bunch. The first symbol means 'not equal' and the number fourteen stands for fourteen words."

"Which are?"

"It'll piss you off."

"Try me. Time is a factor here."

"Okay. Don't say I didn't warn you. 'We must secure the existence of our people and the future for white children.'"

Inner flames flashed his eyes wide. "We're dealing with a white supremacy group?"

"Oh, dear God." Cat slapped her mouth. "The guy in the orange robe and hood." Her gaze hollowed. "That's a... a... Klan meeting."

"Shit." Running Bear massaged the back of his neck. "Orange is the color of the Grand Dragon, a high-ranking leader within the national *and* state organizations."

"Then unmasking him should remain a top priority."

*Ca-caw, caw, caw.* Poe shook the ankle band at Dad.

"Please don't interrupt, bud. I told you I would review the footage, and I shall."

He kicked his leg toward Running Bear.

"I don't have the reader on my phone. Your dad will check it when we get home."

Foot lowering to his shoulder perch, Poe slumped in defeat. Mayhem raised his spirits by ejecting the SD card, which he tucked between his cell and phone case. A scratch of the chest feathers also helped.

"I don't get it," Shawnee said. "Doesn't the Klan only hate black people?"

"No, Cat. Their hatred runs much deeper. White supremest groups target so-called immigrants, including Natives—the only natural born Americans—even though their own ancestors weren't born here. Anyone outside their race, creed, and warped values has a bullseye on their back. The reason you've never heard of the Klan targeting our People is because many don't view our murders, rapes, or the defiling of our children as human tragedies."

A pained groan emerged from somewhere deep inside her. Mayhem reached to comfort her, but she backed away.

"My inner struggle isn't a battle you can win for me. I need to face it on my own."

"Fair enough, Cat. If I can help in any way, please let me know."

"Me too, Ghost Dog."

"Thanks." The back of her hand dried her eyes. "Did I smudge my handprint?"

Head rocking, he chuckled. "The heart of a warrior." Something still made little sense. "Cat, if I asked you to identify the race of the iceman, what would you say?"

"Can't be a hundred percent with just a profile view, but he looked Asian."

"That was my impression, as well." Praying hands tapped his lips, his mind puzzling together the jigsaw. "No one else wore a robe or hood?"

"Not that I saw, no, but the loft floor blocked most of my view."

He jabbed a chin at Running Bear.

"I saw no hoods through the scope."

"Interesting." Mayhem contemplated various way to handle this situation. "Okie doke. Our main objective is this. Free a caged Buffalo in front of thirty to forty armed Klansmen."

Easier said than done.

# Chapter 35



*11:25 p.m.*

Since the scumbags stopped poking the Buffalo—a two-thousand-pound animal crammed into an iron-barred cage meant to hold a creature half his size—we all flattened side by side on the gambrel roof of the barn to wait till the ATVs and pickups left. A few would probably stick around, but that'd be a lot more manageable.

If the Buffalo wasn't trapped inside, we could bomb the place—solve our problem once and for all—but we weren't willing to kill or maim an Innocent One.

Every animal matters.

While we waited on the rooftop, Mr. Mayhem's fingers wove through mine.

I leaned closer, whispered, "You're breaking your own rule."

"No. I am offering comfort to a team member."

"Are you holding Running Bear's hand?"

"He doesn't need comfort right now."

I slid my hand out of his. "Then neither do I."

Through the face paint, his nose crinkled with his smile.

Most of the vehicles cleared the driveway, but we held our position, ears cocked for movement below.

When Mr. Mayhem tapped my arm, I crawled to my feet. Using hand-signals, he instructed Running Bear to cover the West side of the roof. I took the East while he secured the front and rear.

That man moved like firefly flickers. Silent, fast, and unpredictable.

Below me, I didn't find anyone or anything.

When Mr. Mayhem darted toward the front of the barn, he glanced back at me. I signaled all clear with a double thumbs-up. Across from me, Running Bear used one stroke of X'd forearms to note a lack of henchmen below him.

Would've been nice to learn *that* signal ahead of time. Much cooler than my geeky impersonation of the Fonz from *Happy Days*.

Mr. Mayhem stared at movement below, but I couldn't tell who or what from my vantage point. I jabbed a chin at Kuruk, but he didn't catch it—too focused on our fearless leader, who inched closer to the roof's edge like he planned to jump.

With a roll of his hand for Running Bear, he unsheathed his knife.

Something was about to go down. What remained a mystery, but I'd be damned if they left me out of the action. Jumping off a building? Admittedly, it wasn't my favorite thing to do. Last time didn't quite go as planned.

Whatever. After one more quick scan of the East side, I charged for the front. Running Bear met me there.

Now poised on either side of our team leader, we all peeked over the edge.

Three men smoked outside the closed double doors. The dude below me blew a plume above his head, and his black eye patch transported me back in time.

The trunk.

The train tracks.

The bi-leveled bunker.

And that asshole, Vic, who thought it was an absolute riot to fire a gun next to my ear.

Was he here, too? Or did my protectors kill him at Bunker Hill? We never discussed what happened there. Not in detail, anyway.

I backhanded Mr. Mayhem's rock-hard chest, and he lowered his ear. "That's Tango," I whispered, my voice barely audible, "the boss from Bunker Hill."

The nod indicated the news didn't surprise him. He leaned close enough to kiss me, mouthed, "Jump on three."

I pointed down at Tango.

Another nod.

"But he's the guy who—"

Without a word, he traded places with me, mouthed, "Better?"

What could I say, no? It wasn't *his* fault Tango flew in for the hunt.

His fingers counted down the three-count.

The second my toes left the roof, I had a bad feeling I'd misjudged the angle. Sure enough, I sailed over the poacher's head, bounced off a hay bale, and crashed on the packed dirt in front of the dude's military boots.

Not my greatest entrance ever. Dammit.

Inch by inch, my gaze crawled up camouflage pants to the barrel of a pistol aimed at my face. The dude didn't even acknowledge the two badass warriors beating the shit out of his buddies.

"Bitch," he said, chambering a fresh round, "either stand the fuck up or suck my dick."

With a bloodied and battered poacher by the throat, my faux husband's head turned uber-slow. The ferocious glower showed he'd unleashed the beast within—dangerous, deadly, and merciless.

To hold Pistol Guy's attention, I said, "I've mulled over your two options. Since I have no need for a toothpick, I guess I'll stand."

Mr. Mayhem released Tango, the eye-patch dangling from his ear as he collapsed against the barn. He threw a roundhouse kick to the back of Pistol Guy's head, spinning him around, the gun skidding across the dirt, military boots stumbling back into me.

We crashed to the ground. Two hundred pounds of semi-conscious weight sprawled on top of me, stubble from the back of his buzzcut needling my bare skin.

The sheer force of Mr. Mayhem's first punch reverberated straight through him—and by extension, into me—my ribcage rattling in the quake.

This guy's toast.

He heaved the scumbag off me. Down on one knee, gentle fingers swept hair off my face with the tenderness of stroking a child's cheek. "How are you, Kitty Cat?"

"I'm okay. The hay broke my fall."

Slight smirk. "When I said jump, I meant straight down."

"Yep, I know. Overshot my mark."

His nose crinkled. "Little bit."

Behind him, a gun fired twice in quick succession. And I froze, my eyes bulging from the sockets. Footfalls slapped the soil, yet he remained unfazed, his full attention on me.

Running Bear emerged beside him, long hair dangling below his face. "You okay, Ghost Dog?"

"She hit the ground quite hard. Could you assist her while I—" He jabbed his head toward Pistol Guy, moaning on the ground behind him.

"I've got her." Kuruk slung my arm around his neck. "Go."

"Thank you."

Running Bear raised me to my feet. Not that I needed the help, but my legs were still a little shaky from the fall.

Mr. Mayhem soldiered straight to Pistol Guy. "Hello, friend. Let's discuss how to speak to a lady. Shall we?" With a chokehold, he dragged the dude toward the barn. Long, deep gouges marked the dirt from the scumbag struggling to break free.

"Even you gotta admit, that's friggin' hot."

Running Bear threw his head back and laughed. "I knew this shit turned you on. Finally learned to lean into it, eh, Ghost Dog?"

"Big time."

"So"—his elbow nudged mine—"Shadow Wolf rock your world yet?"

My entire body blushed. Thank God for face paint. "No."

"Then what'd Jacy Lee mean by 'your relationship'?"

"Oh, that? He watched us dance."

"In the house or...?"

"No. Outside. In the moonlight. Under the stars."

He glanced back at the barn. "This is the real deal."

"Whaddaya mean?"

"Shadow Wolf doesn't dance with just anyone, Ghost Dog. Do you have any idea how many women threw themselves at him while his wife was sick? Might be easier to list the ones who didn't. And after she died? Forget about it."

Another glance at the barn. "Thing is, he wanted no part of it. Never once did he give any woman a second look. I couldn't understand it until Carolyne said he'd probably closed that chapter of his life. He loved, he lost her, and that was that. Acceptance helped him heal, I guess."

"Heartbreaking." Pieces of my soul ached. "What changed?"

"You, Ghost Dog. You."

I laid splayed fingers on my chest. "Me? What'd I do?"

"You're unapologetically you, and he admires that. So do I, by the way."

"Aww…" I kicked the dirt. "Thanks."

"Plus, you keep him on his toes." He chuckled. "What you did specifically to win his heart? It's probably the culmination of many moments. You two have a long history."

True. Our affection for one another had been building for a while. We both ignored the chemistry out of respect for Spirit Crow, but once she fell for Odin, she ignited a spark we couldn't extinguish.

"Wanna know a secret?" My turn to the check the barn. "You can't tell anybody, though."

Two bloody fingers X'd his heart.

"He kissed me today."

A sly grin lifted his lips. "How was it?"

"Melted every damn bone in my body."

Again, he laughed. "Believe me, that man is just getting started."

"Whaddaya mean?"

Another quick glance at the barn. "If you ever repeat this, I'll deny it. I mean it, Ghost Dog, don't throw me to the Wolf."

I X'd my heart. "I would never."

"All right." His voice lowered to a whisper. "Shadow Wolf knows the sweet spot of every pleasure point in a woman's body."

Lashes fluttering, my jaw unhinged from its joints. "How do you know?"

"I just know, okay?"

"No way. You can't drop that bomb without details."

"Let's just say, I heard it from a reliable source."

"His wife?"

He nodded yes. "She and I used to talk. A lot. About everything. No subject was off-limits. I had a closer relationship with her than my own family. Losing her nearly killed me." His voice crackled with grief.

"Anyway…" He checked the barn again. "The night before my wedding, she convinced Shadow Wolf to teach me a couple new moves. But only two. Even she couldn't get him to reveal all his tricks."

How would he teach—? Unable to envision that scene, I abandoned my attempts for something he said earlier. "How many pleasure points are there, exactly?"

"A lot more than you think. And Shadow Wolf knows how to manipulate every… single… one."

Full body tremors gyrated through me.

"Word of advice? Let him control the pace. Be patient. He's worth the wait."

I brushed my shoulder against his. "Thanks, Running Bear."

"'Course." He mussed my hair. "I got you, sis."

The barn doors flew open, and there he stood, shirtless, blood smattered across his chiseled chest and abs. "What are *you* doing? Get the truck, please." He jutted a gloved thumb over his shoulder. "The big guy has suffered enough."

For a minute, I wasn't sure who he was talking to until my confidant stepped forward. "Keys?"

"Visor." The icy stare indicated he'd told him once already. Maybe he did, and I missed it. "Cat, you're with me."

When he soldiered into the barn, I jogged to catch up. But I couldn't prepare for what awaited me. The first step inside drained every pocket of air from my lungs.

The scumbag who disrespected me slumped in a wooden chair, two eyeballs dangling near his chin by bloody cords. If that wasn't dramatic enough, he'd sewn his lips together—probably with fishing line from the broken pole beneath him—and chopped off both hands, blood pooling on the floor.

Mouth agape, I seesawed between satisfaction and unease. In the end, I rolled with the flow. "That's different."

In front of side-by-side tool chests, he searched for something specific, but I had no clue what.

"I offered Mister Smith the chance to tell me what he most admired about women."

"Didn't go well, I take it?"

He rummaged through the drawers. "Let's just say he won't be ogling another lady. Nor will his filthy mouth spit vitriol, the vile pig."

Didn't take a genius to figure out why he chopped off the dude's hands. Whether Eyeball Guy, formally known as Pistol Guy, outright confessed to rape remained unclear, but I wouldn't rule it out.

The lack of blood on his crotch spotlighted the difference between men and women. I would've gone straight for his manhood. Wouldn't be the first time. Inside, I snickered. Scumbag deserved it.

A guttural groan escaped his sealed lips.

My breath stalled. "He's alive?"

"Not for long." He opened and closed four more drawers. "Would you mind checking the loft for feed, please? The big guy hasn't eaten in God-only-knows how many days."

"I'm on it." Hesitating, I swiveled left and right. "Where's Poe?"

When he turned, a sly grin emerged. "Why, Cat, do I detect concern in your tone?"

I tsked. "No."

"Then why ask for Poe's whereabouts?"

"Okay, fine. Maybe I'm the tiniest bit concerned. I can't help it. There're a ton of owls around here. No matter how crazy he makes me, he's still family."

The hard lines softened around his radiant eyes. "Your beautiful spirit never ceases to amaze me, Kitty Cat." His gaze lingered on me a while longer before he shattered the moment with, "Feed bags, please."

"I'm on it."

He returned to the tool chests, tossed, "Thank you" over his shoulder.

Metal clanged against metal as he searched one drawer after another. Still no idea why, but I had to focus on my job.

At the top of the stairs, I banged a left into the loft. Hay bales lined the back wall, more scattered in the middle of the space, additional racist symbols hidden behind them.

I called out, "Do Buffalo eat hay?"

"No grain up there?"

"Still lookin'." When I heaved a few bales out of my way, Poe squawked. Moments later, the little diva swaggered into the open. "What're *you* doin' here?"

Wings spread, he spring-boarded from the floor to the railing to the air.

"See ya, punk." I moved broken saddles, boxes, and more hay. "There's no order to anything." In the far corner of the loft, a burlap sack slumped against the wall. Once I hefted the forty-pounder to my shoulder, I headed for the stairs. "Found somethin' that might work."

In seconds, Mr. Mayhem padded halfway up the treads. "Let me get that for you, Cat."

I swayed out of reach. "I got it. Weren't you looking for somethin'?"

"Bolt cutters."

"Did you find 'em?"

"I did." His arms extended toward the sack, then retracted. "Are you certain I can't help you? Looks rather bulky."

Teeth clenched, I hardened my tone. "I said, I got it."

A slight grin arced his lips. "If you change your mind, please let me know."

"Would you give Running Bear the same offer?"

His muscular chest deflated. "Is it so terrible to want to help you?"

"No. Unless it segregates me as the weaker sex."

"Darlin', you are far from weak. In fact, you might be the strongest of us all."

How did he always find the right words? "You're not wrong." The weight of the sack bared down on me. "Now, please get outta my way. I'm working here."

His gloves flashed in surrender. "Yes, ma'am."

He knew damn well I hated "ma'am". Probably why he booked it down the stairs.

In front of the cage, I dropped the sack. "What's in here, anyway?"

When he slit the burlap, apples spilled onto the concrete floor. "These should do nicely."

Perched atop the cage, Poe squawked.

"Wait your turn, please." He offered the fruit to the big guy, who gobbled it right down. Poor baby was starving.

Before giving him another apple, he sliced a wedge for his spoiled brat. "Under normal circumstances, Cat, hand-feeding wild animals is never a good idea."

"Really?" I said with a mouthful of snark. "Woulda never guessed by his buddy throwing me twenty feet. He seemed so friendly right before he almost gored me to death."

Laughter coiled off the walls. "Ohhhh, Cat." Head wagging, he headed for the double doors. "Never a dull moment." Motioning to Running Bear, he directed him to reverse into the barn.

"Hey, can I feed him?"

"Once he parks the truck, I'm sure he'd let you. Running Bear rarely passes up food."

Gotta admit, that one was pretty funny. "I meant the big guy."

He chuckled. "Just move slow. No sudden movements."

When I stuck my hand through the bars, the truck released a loud *beep, beep, beep* as the trailer reversed into the barn. White rimmed the startled Buffalo's bulging eyes, and he thrashed inside his prison. Backing away, I dropped the apple before he crushed my hand. Even Poe leaped off the cage.

"Three more feet," Mr. Mayhem called out. "Stop." The rumble of the motor ricocheted off the walls, panicking the Innocent One even more. "Kill the engine."

Silence encompassed the barn.

Running Bear jumped out the driver's door, but the enclosed trailer still stood several feet from the cage.

I had to speak up. "How do we get him from the cage to the trailer?"

"We run him," Mr. Mayhem said. "Preparation is key to ensure his safety as well as ours. Would you mind checking Mister Smith's pockets for keys?"

*Aw, man. I always got stuck with the gross jobs.* "Eyeball Guy?"

"Problem?"

"He's all slumped over and shit."

"If he's too heavy to move, I could ask Running Bear to handle it."

I sneered. "I got it."

"Splendid." He winked. "Thank you, Cat."

I marched over to the bloodbath. Behind me, I swear Poe snickered. Friggin' psycho enjoyed every second of my torment.

"We need one more vehicle, Running Bear."

"Copy that."

With my head turned to one side, I reached into the dead guy's pocket. Empty. Shit. I moved to the other side.

From behind me came, "Need help, darlin'?"

He'd never let me live down the speech on the stairs. "Don't you have somethin' better to do than watch me?"

A sensual gaze lingered on me. "I enjoy watching you."

Blushing, I play-swatted the space between us. "Stop."

An SUV reversing into the barn spun him around. Over his shoulder, he said, "Any luck with those keys, Cat?"

When I finally pulled out the keyring, blood saturated my hand. "Got 'em."

Running Bear hopped out of the vehicle. "Right here, Ghost Dog." He clapped for me to throw the keys, but my slick fingers shortened the gap between us. The keyring clanged through the iron bars, skidding to a stop beneath the big guy.

When our team leader turned, my neck turtled in my shoulders.

"Oopsie."

Without taking his steely eyed gaze off me, he said, "Poe, please correct Cat's error."

That's all the punk needed to hear. He slipped between two iron bars and snatched the keyring from beneath the big guy. The egomaniac showed off with a slow strut from hoof to hoof like he was all that and a bag of chips. Crows and Bison had a symbiotic friendship.

Once he swaggered out the cage, his dad swooned all over him. "Thank you, handsome."

And again, Poe's gaze strayed back to me. This competition for his father's affection better end soon, or I might be tempted to knock him into next week.

Running Bear parked a gold Chevy pickup opposite from the SUV, creating a blocked alleyway for the Buffalo to run through.

My mentor tossed me a rope. "If you could hop into the trailer, I'll instruct you from there."

And so, I did.

"Thank you. Tie one end to the inside gate and pass the rope through the slot." The trailer had a hard top with gaps down each side for ventilation, large enough for air, small enough not to trap his horns. A Buffalo's thick coat could cause them to overheat in the summer. Probably a blessing we moved the big guy at night.

After I followed his instructions, I jumped down to the floor. "Now, what?"

"When he runs into the trailer, pull the gate closed behind him."

"Got it."

"You must be quick. If he escapes, we could be in real trouble."

"Got it."

For a moment, he studied me. "Questions? Now's the time to ask."

"Nope. Got it."

"All right." He sounded unconvinced. "Running Bear?"

Kuruk raised the rope tied to the cage door. "All set here."

"Cat?"

"Ready."

"On three." His gaze shifted between us. "One... Two... And release."

When Running Bear pulled the rope, the cage door flung open. But the Buffalo didn't move. He just stood there.

"I was afraid of this." Mr. Mayhem strode to the back of the cage. "All right, big guy. Let's get you moving in the right direction. Does anyone have a suggestion for how to move a one-ton animal?"

"Actually"—I raised my hand—"I do."

"Let's hear it, Cat."

"*Shicheii* said Montana cops blast AC/DC to get stubborn bulls off the road."

"AC/DC," he repeated, again unconvinced. "Any specific song?"

"Yep. *Hells Bells.*"

He and Running Bear exchanged a dumbfounded glance.

"Worth a shot, Shadow Wolf."

"Okie doke. Can't hurt, I suppose." On his phone, he scrolled and scrolled. "*Hells Bells*. Hold your positions, please." He fiddled with the volume on the side. "Here we go."

With the speaker aimed at the big guy's butt, he pressed Play. The Buffalo didn't budge for the bell tolling, nor the rhythmic beat of cymbals, or even the riff of Angus Young's guitar. But the second Brian Johnson's iconic voice broke through the music, he galloped straight into the trailer, the power of his stride vibrating the floor. I yanked the rope to trap him inside, but he bucked against the gate.

The strength of this animal was unlike anything I'd ever experienced. Praying he didn't escape, I dug in my heels. "Little help here."

In two leaps, Mr. Mayhem was at my side. With gloved hands on the rope, he told me to close and lock the trailer in case the big guy crashed through the inner gate.

Once we'd trapped him inside, my partner-in-crime anchored the rope. "Excellent work, you two. Cat, brilliant plan. Thank you."

"Ah, y'know..." Pretty damn proud of myself, I flicked my hair off my shoulder. "Just doin' my part." On the sly, I gave Poe the side-eye. *Let's see you try to top that. Who's his favorite now?*

The slitted glare said I'd soon regret stealing his spotlight.

*Gulp.*

# Chapter 36



***Wednesday, 12:20 a.m.***

Mayhem drove the truck with the Buffalo secured in the trailer.

Beside him, Cat gazed out the passenger window. She sighed. "What a beautiful night."

"That it is."

On the middle console, Poe stayed quiet. It'd been a long day for everyone.

Running Bear followed in the Benz. Without a slop sink in the barn, no one could wash up before leaving, which heightened the danger of this excursion. If the police stopped them, explaining the blood splatter and face paint might be tricky.

What choice did they have? He refused to leave behind a tortured animal. Every individual from the ancient herd was in serious peril. If his team failed, the one pure bloodline would cease to exist. And that, Mayhem could never allow.

"Where're we takin' him?"

"Back to his herd in Greater Yellowstone."

"Should we name him first?"

*Adorable.* "Sure, if you'd like."

One finger tapped her chin. "How 'bout Hope?"

"Don't you think it's a smidge too feminine?"

"Probably, but his name should reflect what he stands for, like an ambassador for his People."

"How about Resilience?"

"Love it. We'll call him Resi for short."

Warmth spread through his chest. "Resi has a nice ring to it, Kitty Cat."

"We should name all the Innocent Ones we save."

*Such a beautiful heart.* "Good idea. Let's add that to our list of goals."

Poe backed against the stereo, gaze shifting between the two of them, clearly dismayed by the trajectory of their relationship. Nor was he pleased with the affection between his mother and Odin.

Mayhem patted his thigh. "Sit with me, bud."

Poe hopped into his lap, nuzzling a gentle cheek against Dad. Mayhem caressed his crown feathers.

"What if we can't find Resi's herd?"

"At least he'll be home. Had we freed him at the barn, he might never have reunited with his family. That said, night releases are tricky with wolves in the area. We need a well-lit clearing."

"Err…" Her voice stalled as they neared the park. "How're we gonna get through the gates?"

"That's trickier." To draw Running Bear's attention, he stuck his arm out the window.

The Benz pulled alongside the truck, the passenger window already down. "Problem?"

Holding up traffic wouldn't work. "Park in front of us, please."

Once Mayhem veered to the side of the road, Poe hopped up to the middle console to allow him space to exit.

At the hatch of the Benz, he met Running Bear. From inside the go-bag, he withdrew a travel pack of hand wipes to spot clean blood off his former protégé. Without face paint, it made more sense for him to handle the ruse.

Mayhem scrubbed the final bloodstain off his neck. "You're a high-ranking official for the Crow Indian Reservation. The big guy is part of the exchange program."

"Don't I need paperwork?"

"Not if you handle things properly. Use your charm."

"Copy that."

"Please don't raise anyone's hopes. You've broken enough hearts." The scowl drove home his point. "Under no circumstances can the warden approach the truck. If she wants to check the welfare of the bull, she may do so, but do not let her come to my or Cat's window."

"Copy that."

From his money clip, he peeled off two one-hundred-dollar bills. "This should cover any related fees. Questions?"

"No."

"How are you, Running Bear?"

"Good." He cracked the bones of his neck. "I'll handle it."

"I know you will." With a slight grin, he patted his shoulder. "See you on the other side."

"Copy that."

Back in the truck, Mayhem unwound his braids. Easier to mask the blood and paint with his hair down.

"What's happening?"

"Cover story to get us into the park."

"Which is?"

He sighed, though for different reasons than her's earlier. "Might we discuss this later, Cat?" The truck rolled closer to the gate. "I need to focus."

"Should I worry?"

"No." What he failed to mention was many things could go wrong. "Running Bear knows what he's doing."

The Benz pulled up to the guard shack.

Mayhem dropped his chin, allowing his hair to shield his face. "Please swivel toward me, Cat. The handprint draws the eye."

Soon, her long, cherry-streaked hair masked her paint, along with her vision. "What's happening?"

"He's speaking with the game warden."

"How do you think it's goin'?"

"Body language looks good. Hold your position, please." He dragged Poe into his lap. "They're headed our way."

"What? Why?"

"Part of a game warden's job is to check on Resi's wellbeing. Don't panic. Running Bear will not let her near us."

The trailer door opened.

A female said, "What an impressive male."

"Thank you. You're not so bad yourself."

*Oh, boy. This was not the time for a flirtatious tête-à-tête.*

The game warden tittered. "I meant the bull."

Running Bear chuckled. "Just playing with you. There's something about a woman in uniform that drives me crazy."

*For goodness sake.*

Giggling, the game warden closed the trailer. Moments later, they strolled by the passenger window.

Back at her post, she waved both vehicles through the gates. The bright overhead lights illuminated the truck's interior as they cruised into the park.

In the side mirror, the warden did a double-take. Another vehicle diverted her attention before her curiosity caused problems.

Fifteen minutes later, after winding their way through the park, Mayhem found an ideal spot for release. A quick flash of the high beams signaled for Running Bear to pull over.

Outside the truck, the sweetness of lodgepole pine rode a gentle summer breeze. A galaxy of starlight shimmered overhead, diamond flecks almost close enough to touch, Grandmother Moon hovering above as if orchestrating their movement in the night sky.

"Kitty Cat—" He corralled her to lean against his chest, his arms curled around her slim waist. "Look up."

Her head reclined on his shoulder. "Amazing."

"Isn't it, though."

A few strides ahead, Running Bear also stopped to admire Yellowstone's natural splendor, loose hair dangling behind him.

In the distance, Mayhem caught movement in the moonlight. "Hate to cut this short, but we need to move fast." He hustled to open the trailer. "Cat, please get into position to untie the rope."

"Is that Resi's family?"

"Potentially, yes. It's *a* herd, nonetheless." Lone individuals had a difficult time fending off Wolf packs. A herd offered safety. "Running Bear—" He peeked around the corner of the trailer, whispered, "Stay with her in case she needs help."

"I heard that."

"I said, *in case* you need help, not that you do."

"Uh-huh."

*Women.* "On three." Mayhem climbed onto the roof. "Ready?" He glanced over the side of the trailer at his team. "One... Two... And pull."

When Shawnee tugged the rope, Running Bear grabbed the end to help disengage the gate. Like before, Resi did not leave right away. Mayhem jumped up and down above his head, startling him enough to charge out of the trailer.

Cat cheered. "Run, Resi, run."

Celebratory grunts filled the space between Resilience and the herd—vital communication to stay in contact with one another.

Mayhem's heart swelled with joy. *You're home now, buddy.*

On the end of the trailer, he sat above two impressive warriors, legs dangling mid-air. While the herd reunited, Running Bear draped his arm around Cat. "This is what it's all about, Ghost Dog."

*Precisely.*

He peered upward. "What do you want to do with the truck and trailer?"

"Slash the tires." Mayhem hopped down to the ground. "I'll disable the motor."

Little doubt existed that Killzme would return for another member of the herd. Somehow, he and his team must stay one step ahead. How to accomplish that task remained just out of reach. For now.

# Chapter 37

*1:10 a.m.*

When we pulled into the driveway at home, I was still buzzing from freeing Resi. "I'm too wound up to sleep."

My faux hubby shot me the love eyes. Biting my lower lip, I took my time to admire every single inch of him.

Running Bear said, "Well, that's my cue to leave."

"Thank you for all your hard work tonight." He passed a sleeping Poe between the seats.

"I've gotcha, bud." Kuruk cradled the brat like an infant. "Catch ya on the flop, Ghost Dog. Don't do anything I wouldn't do."

Alone at last, he leaned back against the driver's door. "I could make us tea or..."

"Or?"

The hesitation lasted forever. "I could show you Heaven."

*Did he say—? Nah. No way I heard that right.* "Run that by me one more time."

"Ferron has a secret hideaway called Heaven."

"Ooh, sounds amazing." I tried not to react. "Does *Shicheii* know where it is?"

"Not that I'm aware of, no."

I could barely contain my giddiness. "Okay."

"You'd like me to take you to Heaven?"

*Best. Line. Ever.* "Are we off the clock?"

A seductive grin crossed those luscious lips. "We are."

"Then yes. Absolutely."

He winked. "I'll get your door."

"All yours, sugar bear."

Chuckling, he climbed out of the Benz.

*Oh, my God! This is it! It's finally happening! Breathe, Shawnee, breathe. Don't appear too eager. Just play it cool.*

By the time he opened my door, I'd regained some control, but I still needed to work on dampening my excitement before he saw right through my cool façade. One major problem arose, though. We were both still covered in paint and poacher blood. Not exactly how I envisioned a passionate night together.

With my hand in his, I rose from the passenger seat. "Does Heaven have a shower?"

"It does. That reminds me." He darted to the hatch, where he withdrew a go-bag from the cargo area.

On the back-quarter panel, I drew tiny hearts. "So... is the shower big enough for two?"

"Aren't you jumping ahead a bit?"

My finger froze mid-heart. *Did he just turn me down?*

"No, darlin'. I most certainly did not."

We trekked through the dark forest in silence, my mind working to unscramble his words. Jumping ahead was an odd thing to say, unless he didn't envision the same night I did. But he also said he wasn't turning me down, which left me even more confused. How could both things be true?

Grandmother Moon—higher and brighter now—illuminated the path ahead. Hand in hand, we hiked for a while. Where was this place? Nothing but thick woodlands surrounded us.

And then, he just stopped. "We've arrived at Heaven's door."

I swiveled left and right. "Where?"

"Look up."

Halfway up the trunk of a massive oak, a treehouse nestled in its branches. "No way. It's totally hidden."

"Wait till you see the interior." He let go of my hand. "Are you comfortable waiting here while I climb?"

"Why can't I go with you?"

"I'd planned to fetch the rope ladder for you."

I flashed a flat hand. "Lemme stop you right there. Don't start treating me like some delicate little flower. We climb trees together all the time. I don't need a ladder to go twenty feet."

"No, darlin', you most certainly do not. But would you like one?"

"No, thank you."

Bending toward the trunk, he wove his hands together. "How about a boost?"

"That I'll take." Once I slid in my heel, I pushed off, scaling the tree in seconds flat. *Hope there's alcohol in there.* I looped my leg over the decking, rolling under a wired railing that was near-invisible from ground-level.

The quality of the treehouse blew me away. Made from all natural materials, Heaven had to cost a fortune to build.

Was this Ferron's version of a she-shed? Sanctuary? Meditation spot? Or love shack?

On the deck, he pressed below the frame of an octagon window above the door, moonlight streaming through stained glass. A board popped loose, a key hidden inside the secret compartment.

Amazed, the right words escaped me. I'd always envisioned a passionate night with him would have magical elements, but a place like this never entered my headspace. Only he would bring me to a high-end treehouse.

The mere thought of sex heated me from the inside out. While he unlocked the door, I leaned back to check out his ass. Just a little peek. It wasn't like I was mentally undressing him or anything.

Okay, alright, maybe I was, but the way those buckskin pants hugged his muscular thighs and firm butt cheeks sent my mind on a pleasure cruise. Not to mention the view from the front. Mm-mmm. Yummy.

Images of that day at the pond in Unalaska spiraled through my mind. A sheen of water coated his flawless skin, ripped abs and chest glistening wet, and those defined V-like indentations that curved around each hip bone, like flashing arrows pointing to his manhood beneath the towel.

I should've jumped him then, but Poe outright refused to leave us alone. Plus, we'd just dumped three dead poachers in a watery grave so... probably the wrong time.

When he opened Heaven's door, sandalwood and jasmine whispered across my cheeks. He lit several votives on the windowsill, but it wasn't till he ignited the wick of four candles in copper wall sconces that I marveled at the design and décor.

Reclaimed barnboard, pine, and cedar lined the walls and ceiling, pitched high and steeply angled to prevent a snow load. The textured atmosphere invited peace and tranquility, and solar power allowed off-grid privacy.

Granite countertops, identical to the ones in the log home, lounged below floating shelves made of natural-edged wood, upside down wineglasses, mugs, and tumblers on top. Closed cabinetry crouched beneath the counters and sink, with the coolest brushed nickel faucet, hot-and-cold handles, and side spray.

Stacked beside a cushiony futon, oversized floor pillows towered four high to provide a wide-open space beneath the stars, which I only discovered after he remotely opened the shade of an oversized skylight.

"What an amazing place."

"Now you know why Ferron named it Heaven." He strolled into the kitchen area. "Care for a cocktail, Kitty Cat?"

"Thought you'd never ask. Where's the bathroom?"

He pointed out the only other room. "Light switch is by the door. Did you want your drink now or after your shower?"

"I'll take it with me."

"As you wish." He blended peppermint schnapps, Kahlua, and milk—my favorite combo—in a metal shaker, all of which he poured into two glass tumblers filled with ice.

When he neared, my heart petered out. "Peppermint White Russian, milady?"

"Thanks. Don't mind if I do." I reached for the drink, but my hand trembled.

"Kitty Cat, are you nervous?"

"Alone with you in this setting? Kinda, yeah."

His gray eyes squinted. "Does our age difference bother you?"

"I wouldn't've made the first move if it did. No, not at all. How far apart are we?"

"Almost fourteen years. I'm fifty."

"You don't look it, but I figured as much because of Cheyenne."

"She's younger than you, Kitty Cat. I don't correct Jacy Lee because it wouldn't do any good. He sees souls, not ages."

"Must run in the bloodline. So do I."

He smiled, but it faded when his forehead furrowed. "Are you nervous because of the mentorship? You owe me nothing."

"I know. We've already drawn a clear line between the two, so I'm not sure why..." *Does he think he's the problem?* "Look. I respect you as a mentor, but when we're alone or at home, I only see you as man." *A smokin' hot beefcake.* "Superficial stuff doesn't matter to me."

"Then we've narrowed down the list of possibilities." With another hesitation, he played with the ends of my hair. "What if I said intimacy doesn't necessarily lead to making love? Would you feel more secure?"

"Isn't that the point?"

"No." His head cocked like I'd spoken French. Or he was silently judging my past relationships, none of which were any good aside from Levaughn. "Let's remove that expectation altogether. Now how do you feel?"

As much as it pained me to admit, my stiff shoulders relaxed. "Better."

"Good." He kissed my nose. "Clean towels and clothes are in the duffel. Enjoy your shower, darlin'."

When I shut the bathroom door, I mentally kicked myself.

*What's wrong with me? I'd been lusting over this man for weeks. I finally get the chance to sleep with him, and what do I do? Chicken out. Even worse, I made him question how I felt about him.*

The waterfall showerhead sent warm water rushing over me, soothing my tense muscles but little else.

*He probably wishes he never brought me here. Dammit. This isn't how I imagined our first time. Somehow, I gotta make it up to him. He doesn't deserve my brokenness. What does he even see in me? He could have any woman he wanted.*

And it wasn't like I didn't want to sleep with him. I absolutely did. But I panicked. Why, oh, why did I let my nerves get the better of me?

After I slipped into his black button-down shirt and a fresh thong from the go-bag, I strolled out to the deck, where he lounged in a chair, ankles crossed on the railing, head reclined to admire Father Sky diamondized with stars.

"Is that my shirt?"

"Yeah. Do you mind?"

"Mind?" Surprise filled his tone. "Not at all. You wear it well."

I dragged over a chair. "Hey, about before, I didn't mean to imply I didn't want to sleep with you."

He passed me his cocktail. "Do you mind if I shower before we discuss this?"

"Not at all." Probably easier to talk without the paint and poacher blood, anyway. "I just don't want you to think—"

"Please allow me a few minutes?"

"Yep." Shit. Couldn't get a read on him. He acted like his normal self, but how could he not be disappointed?

The longest minutes of my life ticked by before he returned. Shirtless, barefoot, and in fresh jeans, he'd pulled his long, wet hair back into a low braid. The clean face instantly settled my nerves. Maybe that's what threw me earlier.

He extended his hand. "Join me, Kitty Cat."

God, I loved how my pet name rolled off his tongue. I'd follow this man anywhere.

With our fingers woven together, he led me into the living room, where he'd positioned two oversized pillows on the floor, surrounded by a wide ring of candles, wicks dancing in hot wax.

"Did you burn sage?"

"I smudged the room." His nose crinkled. "Too much?"

"No, it's nice. Just didn't expect it."

I stepped into the ring of flames.

Across from me, he sat back on his heels, hands folded in his lap, his full attention on me. "Now, what did you want to tell me?"

"I, um—" My mind blanked. "Not important, I guess."

"It was important enough for you to approach me on the deck. It's important now."

"Yeah, but"—my gaze strayed to all the effort he put into creating the perfect ambiance—"you worked hard to make it nice for me."

"Lighting a few candles entitles me to what exactly?"

"Well, when you say it like that..."

"Allow me to explain, Kitty Cat." His voice remained soft, caring. "Whether women realize it, societal rules scar them early in life. Parents tell children to hug and kiss relatives they barely know. Few set out to supersede their child's right to choose, but that is the message they're sending when they instruct a young girl to show affection to virtual strangers."

"Never thought about it like that before. I just figured parents wanted family and friends to feel at home."

"They do. But at what cost? Impressionable children don't yet possess the wherewithal to read signals. All they know is it is polite to offer hugs and kisses if they want to or not. To be fair, there's rarely any malicious intent. Most parents would never intentionally harm their kids."

"Can't say the same about foster parents."

"You've endured more than most, Kitty Cat." Concern flashed in his eyes. "Do you want to talk about it?"

"No. Maybe someday, but not now. I can't yet."

"Fair enough. You let me know when that changes."

"Just tell me one thing."

"Name it."

"Did you make that scumbag suffer?"

He smirked. "Brutally."

"For me?"

"Yes. And for Little Rain. And for all the other little girls he abused over the years."

"Did the coward confess to what he did to me?"

"Monsters like him rarely do." A tear escaped the corner of his eye, showing me how deeply our past affected him. "Any other questions about that night?"

I rocked a no. "I'm good. Thanks for doin' that."

"I will let no one hurt you like he did, sweetheart. They'd have to kill me first."

"I know, and I love that about you."

The warm smile veered the conversation back on track. Whatever he had to say seemed important to him.

"These continual demands to hug or kiss virtual strangers implant a seed that girls carry into adulthood. Same message—others may control your body—only with much higher stakes." As if searching for the right words, he hesitated. "Have you ever had a lover pester you for sex?"

"'Course. All women have."

"And did you give in?"

"Usually."

"Why?"

"Because it's easier than fighting about it."

"On behalf of all men, I am truly sorry." Somehow, I knew he meant every word. "Let's dispel the myth once and for all. No man has the right to use a woman's body as a sexual object. Without consent, it is rape, plain and simple. Conversely, when a woman retains her power, both parties benefit."

*Love the sound of that.*

"If you retain nothing else, remember this. You control who touches you. Not a boyfriend, nor a lover, or even a husband. Signing a marriage certificate does not forfeit your right to say no. Or say yes and change your mind later."

Never heard any of that before. From any man. Or woman, for that matter.

"Those same principles apply to me and everyone else on Mother Earth."

Not sure where he was going with this, but I'd be lying if I said it didn't intrigue me. His raspy tone made me want to jump his bones. "Got it, tiger."

Grinning, he swept my hair behind my shoulders. His hands lowered to my shirt, where his fingers froze on the top button. "May I?"

With my breath hastened, I nodded.

"Consent is a verbal response, Kitty Cat."

"Yes."

"Do you know what you're consenting to?"

"Unbuttoning my shirt."

"Yes. And only that."

A seductive smile warmed my face. "Got it."

Staring deep into my eyes, his fingers worked the buttons nice and slow, like time didn't exist. The lower he got, the more he turned me on. He hadn't even touched me yet. And already, I could barely contain myself.

# Chapter 38

**Time unknown.**

When he rose to his knees, I followed. He unbuttoned the bottom button, and I bit my lower lip, my breath enhanced by anticipation.

With the lapels in both hands, he whispered, "May I remove this?"

"Oh, yeah." By now, I was all in. "Absolutely."

The shirt he swept behind my shoulders, the sleeves slipping off my arms as it floated to the floor. Normally, I wasn't comfortable exposing myself like this—face to face without kissing—but he nurtured me in a way I'd never experienced before. He respected me, empowered me, even revered me. Giving consent opened a whole new doorway inside, a secret passage I never knew existed.

Inches apart, his bare chest radiated heat. "You are a vision, Kitty Cat. Flawless inside and out. May I touch you?"

*Man, that's hot.* "Dear God, yes."

"If at any time you want to stop, say the word and I'll back away. You have all the power."

"Love the sound of that."

"It's true."

"I know. Still love hearing it."

Off to his side, his palms rubbed together. Slow, methodical, without ever losing eye contact with me. Was he warming them? Or creating energy?

A grin lurked right below the surface as he slid two fingers up the outside of my arms.

"You're driving me insane."

His smile grew. "In a good way?"

"Oh, yeah. Big time."

His muscular hands slid up the back of my neck, and electrical impulses pinballed through me. With circular motions, he added pressure to certain spots on my scalp, and sheer unbridled passion flooded my system, my eyes rolling closed on their own.

He pulled me closer, whispered, "Let go, sweetheart. I've got you." Releasing his grip let me recline on his forearms. Tender kisses on my neck almost sent me over the edge, and I let out a soft moan. He kissed under my jawline and straight down my throat to the soft crevice between my collarbones. All the while, his fingers never stopped massaging my scalp.

When his magical hands slipped out of my hair, he brought me upright. Stared into my eyes, our chests heaving in unison, our souls connecting on such a deep, personal level.

"Kiss me," I whispered, pleading for more.

"Not yet." His fingers walked from my chin line down to my chest, where they froze above my breasts. The seductive "May I?" soaked me in white-hot passion.

"A thousand yesses. Don't stop."

The pressure lightened when he followed the curves of my breasts, circled inward, again and again, slow and rhythmic, goose-bumps sheathing my skin, my nipples rock-hard and throbbing, aching for him.

Suspended between ecstasy and anticipation, I disregarded everything except this moment—the here and now—his touch sending me into a frenzy, warmth enveloping every fraction of my soul. He could've done anything without my objection, yet he exuded nothing but safety, respect, and love. This amazing superpower entranced me.

His fingertips circled the outer rim of my areolas, and an explosion erupted inside me, my head falling back.

"May I?"

Not sure what he meant, but I agreed anyway. "Oh, yeah, absolutely."

His tongue followed the same route as his fingers then swirled around the first nipple, and I moaned louder. When his tongue moved to the opposite breast, the first flicker of an orgasm curled my toes, strengthened in intensity, and tremored up my thighs.

His mouth parted mine, and I came harder, longer, his powerful arms holding me as I convulsed and twitched. The passion-fueled kiss continued till every one of my muscles relaxed.

When our lips parted, my eyes flashed open. *Did I just climax without him ever touching my—?*

Gray eyes sparkled in the candlelight. "You did."

*How embarrassing. He must think—*

"Kitty Cat"—he gave me a little nose nuzzle—"an orgasm is one of the truest forms of compliment."

"Then you're welcome."

We both cracked up at that one.

"Thank you," he said.

"My pleasure. Literally." Neither of us could stop laughing. Both downright giddy, actually. "Seriously, though. That might be my favorite... y'know... ever."

"Darlin', this is only the beginning. The appetizer if you will."

By now, my bottom lip must sport a permanent bite mark. But I couldn't help it. He was so damn sexy with all those chiseled muscles glistening in the candlelight.

"Do you want to stop, Kitty Cat?"

"No."

In a low, seductive tone, he whispered, "Tell me what you want."

"My turn."

"To...?"

I was practically growling. "Explore... every... inch of you."

The eyebrows rose. "Is that so?"

"Mm-hmm." I warmed my palms like he did as we rose to our knees. The palpable heat and energy between us intensified to smoking hot. "May I?"

"May you what?"

"Touch you."

"You may."

Staring deep into his eyes, I ran my fingers along the hairline of his forehead, down the sides, then across his firm jawline. I drew a straight line from his brow, down the bridge of his nose to the soft crevice atop his upper lip.

When I leaned closer, my mouth hovered a millimeter in front of his, anticipation building in my toes. "May I?"

"No, you may not."

"What?" I jerked away. "No?"

"Not yet."

"Why? I want to kiss you."

"Your wants don't obligate me to explain. Nor do my wants obligate you. That's the power of consent."

"Okay, I see how this works." The chance of a no turned me on even more. "May I kiss those sexy eyes?"

"You may."

I pressed my lips to one closed eyelid, then another. Once he refocused on me, a slight grin emerged.

*He likes that. Good to know.*

I dragged my hands down his chest, and his nipples stiffened, arousing me even more. Before my mouth contacted his rock-hard pecs, I asked, "May I?" my breath labored, intense.

"You ma—"

He didn't even have time to spit out the word before I indulged, my tongue swirling around his nipple, my palms smoothing across his chest and down his arms, my fingers dipping into the creases of every single muscle.

I pulled away to raise his hand by the wrist. "May I?"

"May you what?"

"Lick."

"Oh, my." For a half-second, he lost balance. "You may."

My tongue licked up his palm, swirled around each finger, and I engulfed the longest one to the knuckle. His fluttering eyelids gave him away.

*Gotcha.* There wasn't a man alive who didn't love anything oral. A loud pop sounded from the suction breaking as I slid my mouth off his fingertip, and his body responded with a jerk.

Next, I pushed him to recline so I could lower to his ripped abs. I'd been dying to fondle these puppies, my excitement barely contained. Each long band of muscle appeared as defined as the previous, and I licked my way across every single one, pausing in between to tongue the creases, even where I super glued the skin.

With my fingers on the button of his jeans, I said, "May I?"

"You may."

Now, my inner cheer squad refused to shut up. The girls hooped, hollered, and cat-called, and some got downright filthy with their language as I worked the zipper nice and slow.

I stole a moment to slide my tongue down those curved creases around the hip bones I'd been admiring for weeks. Held the band of his boxer briefs with my teeth and yanked off his jeans.

Eyes widening at the outline of his manhood—so massive the cotton thinned to near-transparent—I ran a teasing touch along the shaft. Almost made it to the lip of the helmet before he interrupted me.

"Aren't you forgetting something?"

*Consent. Shit. What if he said no?* With my finger frozen mid-shaft, I asked, "May I?"

Breathlessly, he whispered, "May you what?"

*God, I love this.* "Release the—"

The ring of his cell phone stopped me cold.

My gaze shot to him. His gaze shot to me.

Second ring.

"Might be important, Kitty Cat."

*Fuck. So close.* After I dug the phone out of his pocket, I glimpsed caller ID. "Damn. It's *Shicheii*."

Third ring.

"We cannot ignore an elder."

"I know." With the phone leveled in my palm between us, I stabbed the speakerphone button.

"Everything all right, my friend?"

"Hope so, Cheveyo." As deeply as I loved my grandfather, he sure knew how to suck the passion out of a room. "I peeked in on Mourning Dove, but she wasn't in bed. Nor were you. Did you two work late in the park? Running Bear's in bed."

"We're also on the property. My apologies, Jacy Lee. We should have left a note. Neither of us could sleep, so we went for a stroll in the moonlight."

*Not a lie. We did walk through the woods to get here.*

"Aww, how nice. Are you on your way home? I just made tea."

My forehead fell against his chest, and he stroked my hair.

"We are."

"Great. I'll see you soon. Tell Mourning Dove, I love her."

"Will do."

When the line went dead, so did my chances of ravishing him. Defeated, I snatched my shirt off the floor. "I'm just gonna say it for the both of us. His timing really sucks."

Chuckling, he zipped his fly. "Go easy on him, Kitty Cat. He means well."

"Guess we're sleeping apart again."

"Sleep?" Another chuckle. "Morning prayer starts in less than an hour."

"What?" My gaze roamed around the treehouse for clock but never located one. "We've been here for hours?"

A tender kiss pecked my lips. "We have."

I melted into his warm embrace, his heart thumping beneath my ear. Not sure how long we stayed in each other's arms, but it was the perfect way to end the most intimate, empowering, sensual night of my life.

When we broke apart, he kissed me again. This time, with a lot more passion, silently showing me how much he cared. No one had ever made me feel this way, like I was the most cherished woman in his world, like he had a blind spot only I could fill, and he loved me beyond words.

No one could deny he and Kimi had a truly special marriage. Perhaps that's why Spirit Crow pushed us together, because she knew he wasn't the type of man who'd feel whole living a solitary existence. He had too much love to share.

Still, I'd never disrespect her by fawning all over him. The less she knew, the better. If she believed she'd completed her mission, she might leave. And neither of us could bear to let her go.

As we strolled through the woods hand-in-hand, the taste of his silky-smooth skin and soft lips lingered on my tongue. I needed more of him, all of him, for an entire uninterrupted night.

"So... wanna talk about a raincheck?"

"Are you in a hurry?"

"Now that I know what you're packin'? Yeah. Kinda."

He laughed. "I don't recall consenting to that?"

"Oh, you'll consent. You're not the only one with a bag of tricks."

"Innuendos make it awfully difficult to flip off the switch, Kitty Cat."

"Sorry." I swayed one shoulder, mumbled, "Not sorry."

He swept me right off my feet and into his arms, raining kisses down my neck.

But two could play his game, so I pushed him away. "I don't recall consenting to this?"

Big smile. "May I?"

"No, you may not. Unless you wanna discuss a raincheck."

"All right. Let's see. How about after we stop thirty-some-odd Klansmen and safeguard the ancient herd?"

*Shit.* Those words severed the band of my love goggles. "You're right. We should focus on the Innocent Ones."

He stopped to lower me to the ground.

"Wait—" I might not get another chance soon. "I want one last kiss."

He swung me in front of him, and my legs curled around his waist, my arms draped over his muscular shoulders. His magical hand slid up the back of my hair, and immediately reignited the fire between us. Kissing me, he backed me into a tree.

As the palpable heat intensified, I grinded against him, my mind envisioning the best possible scenario. No idea how long his tongue swirled with mine, but I never wanted him to stop.

Poe's incessant caws coiled through the predawn stillness, and he pulled away. *If it's not one cock-block, it's another.* At this rate, we might never reach heaven. And I didn't mean the treehouse.

Holding my gaze, he didn't release me right away.

"You gonna put me down or...?

"I need a minute."

*Oh. Not all of him got the memo.* "The grinding?"

"To be fair"—his gaze sidled for a hot second—"it's an effective move, and impossible to resist."

I exaggerated a wink. "Good to know."

Though we had a perfectly good suite at the Lake Hotel, we'd already agreed to work there, not play. If we didn't separate personal from professional, Killzme might catch us off-guard.

Now, I understood the sacrifices warriors made. It wouldn't be easy by any means, but we had no choice. Too many innocent lives depended on us.

"So," I said, allowing us to flip the switch to work-mode, "what's on the agenda for today?"

"The hike from the hotel to the hunting grounds is roughly forty-five minutes. We need to shave that time in half."

"How're we gonna make it in twenty-two?"

Once he lowered me to the ground, he dragged tree debris out of my hair. "Searching for an alternate route is the safest option."

On the trek home, his strong fingers slipped through mine.

"So, basically, we're spending the day trudging through the woods."

"A few hours, at least."

All traces of passion vaporized in an instant. "Can't wait." Not.

As we neared the log home, the Sacred Fire splashed an amber glow on the porch. With Spirit Crow and Odin on the railing, I dragged my fingers from his.

Dead in his tracks, he stopped. "You are not the other woman, Kitty Cat."

"I know. But she's right there."

He grabbed my hand. "Nor are you second best."

The moment Spirit Crow leaped off the railing, my heart froze mid-beat. Light cooing settled my nerves. When she landed on my shoulder, her feathery crown nuzzled against my neck.

"Love you, too."

"Thank you, sweetheart." She switched shoulder perches to shower him in affection. "You look happy."

*Coo... coo... coo...*

Few could endure this unusual arrangement, but it spoke volumes about who Kimi was in life. They did the best they could with the shit hand life dealt them. It's only because their love was so pure, so real, so mature that we all reaped the rewards. Never in my life had I met two more incredible souls. And now, he and I opened a new chapter.

*How'd I get so lucky?*

"Fate, Kitty Cat. Fate."

"Stay outta my head." My gaze strayed to Spirit Crow. "So annoying when he does that."

As he chuckled, I swear she winked at me.

### *6:15 a.m.*

After morning prayer on the balcony, the colors of the sunrise brighter than ever before, we all settled around the table on the porch, pigging out on *Shicheii's* eggs Benedict, crispy bacon, and a fruit cup filled with cubed cantaloupe, honey dew melon, strawberries, and red grapes.

As usual, Odin had pushed his bowl next to my love machine. Poe ate beside his meal ticket—aka my grandfather—and Spirit Crow sat with me. No one dared go near Running Bear, who engulfed his food like he hadn't eaten in months.

Mayhem—I dropped the mister—dabbed his lips with the napkin. "Truly magnificent, my friend. I appreciate all your hard work."

The dimples in *Shicheii's* cheeks deepened. "Thank you, Cheveyo. I'm glad you enjoyed it." He folded his hands in front of him. "Mourning Dove, I was thinking, perhaps you and I could tend to the garden after breakfast. Ferron asked if I could take care of it. Can we spend a little one-on-one time together, honey?"

Everyone froze—corvids and humans alike—all waiting for my response. When an elder requested one's company, they rarely got turned down. But we'd already planned to head into the park early. That busybody June might get suspicious if we didn't show at the hotel.

"Umm..." To buy time, I chugged my orange juice, freshly squeezed by my grandfather's loving hands. *What's the right move here?*

After like ten years of everybody staring at me, my love machine saved me with, "As long as we head into the park by eight, we should be fine, Cat."

"Cool. Then I would love to spend time with you, *Shicheii*."

"Wonderful, honey."

"In fact," Mayhem said, "why don't you let us tackle the dishes, so you'll have more time."

"Thank you, Cheveyo, but that's not necessary."

"We insist." A hard stare landed on his former protégé. "Don't we, Running Bear?"

"Huh?" He choked down a mouthful. "Oh. Absolutely. We got it, Jacy Lee."

"Well, if you insist..." *Shicheii* rose fast, like he couldn't wait to get started.

*Guess I'm done eating.* I pushed away my plate.

"Poe likes to help." He wiped cheese sauce off the brat's bill. "You don't mind, do you, honey?"

"But I thought it was just gonna be you and me." The fiery glare from Poe could've burnt down villages. "Okay, alright, you can come."

This should be fun with no sleep.

# Chapter 39

*"Thoughts are like arrows.
Once released, they strike their
mark. Guard them well. Or
one day, you may become
your own victim."* —Navajo
Proverb

*8:15 a.m.*

With Cat half-asleep in the passenger seat of the Benz, Mayhem cruised through the gates of Greater Yellowstone. "You can come out now, Running Bear."

To keep his cover story intact with the female game warden, he'd ducked into the cargo area until they passed the guard shack. He crawled over the headrests, slipping into the backseat. "How many wardens and rangers does one park need? We already passed about ten."

"Takes a village to protect wild spaces."

"I understand that, Shadow Wolf, but it doesn't make it any easier to veer off-trail?"

"*Au contraire.* Our cover story creates the perfect illusion for suspicious minds."

"Great for you." He scoffed. "What about me?"

"You, my impatient one, are the wedding photographer."

"Without a camera?"

Mayhem's gaze flicked to the rearview mirror. "Klee loaned us his old equipment."

"Is that who you called before your nap?"

In an instant, Cat rousted, her bloodshot eyes aflame with anger. "You slept?"

"For about an hour, yes." The air grew thick and hot. "You were out back in the garden with Jacy Lee."

"How is *that* fair?"

Her snarl raised his Adam's apple. "Why don't you rest while Running Bear and I check out the route."

"Really? That'd be amazing."

"All you ever have to do is ask, Cat. One day you will believe that."

Fifteen minutes later, he parked at the Lake Hotel. "Allow me to get your door, please."

"Too tired to open it, anyway."

Once she rose to her feet, he leaned over the passenger seat. "While I escort Cat to the suite, if you could monitor the cabins out back, that'd be helpful." Earlier, he'd brought Running Bear up to speed, including the incident with Luther Abbott and the hunters who occupied the cabins.

"Copy that. Sweet dreams, Ghost Dog. See ya on the flop."

Sleep-deprivation gripped her, evident by the weak wave.

The automatic doors slid apart to allow them entry into the lobby. As they passed the front desk, June called out, "Missus Thunderhawk" but Cat didn't react. "Yoo-hoo, Mister and Missus Thunderhawk?" When Mayhem stopped, she darted around the desk. "Oh, I'm so glad I caught you."

"Nice to see you, June. What can we do for you?"

"I called your room earlier, but no one answered."

"Correct." The clerk's remark did not warrant an explanation. Lately, they answered to too many people already.

To remind him to put the cover story above personal grievances, Cat squeezed his hand. "We got up and out early."

*She's right. What matters most are the Innocent Ones.* "We found a beautiful spot to watch the sunrise. Didn't we, darling?"

"Mm-hmm. Absolute heaven."

"Sounds romantic." June swatted the air. "I just adore you two. Have you seen Old Faithful erupt?"

"Not yet." With time as a factor, he hurried her along. "I presume you stopped us for a reason?"

"Right. Silly me. I booked the cake tasting for ten-thirty. It was the only time Chef Franklin had available before Friday. Oh, and the wedding concierge will arrive at noon."

"What in the actual fff—?"

Before Cat exploded on this woman, he slung his arm around her, stopping her mid-rant. "Where might these appointments be, June?"

"Here in the hotel."

"Where, June? Where?"

Her sensible shoes shuffled backward. "Are you upset with me, Mister Thunderhawk?"

"Of course not. You've been most helpful. However, in the future, we'd prefer to create our own schedule."

"Certainly, sir. I apologize if I overstepped."

"It's fine." Shawnee rested a soothing hand on her shoulder. "Just tell us where we need to go."

"The premier restaurant for the cake tasting. Banquet hall for the wedding concierge."

"But the ceremony will be outside, right?"

"Outside?" Her voice pitched.

*Brilliant idea, Cat.* "Is that a problem, June? We prefer a natural environment."

"No, sir. I'll make the arrangements."

"Splendid." He tucked a crisp hundred into her palm. "Thank you for all your hard work. Now, if you'll excuse us..."

"You can count on me, Mister and Missus Thunderhawk."

As they strolled farther into the lobby, he waved over his head. Their legs moved in unison across the hardwood. Oriental rugs spaced feet apart formed a runway, edged with square columns, the muted floral designs subservient to centuries-old architecture.

Guests occupied many of the upholstered sofas and chairs, framing the ample walkway, simple but elegant lights suspended above. Father Sun reached through oversized windows that faced the lake.

*Inspiring view.* "June is becoming a problem, Cat."

"Gee, ya think?" Her upper lip twitched. "You better be back for those appointments. I'm not doin' this crap alone."

The brashness of her tone allowed for only one response. "Yes, dear."

An uneventful elevator ride to the Presidential Suite was a pleasant change of pace. While he held open the suite door, Cat stopped short in the foyer.

"Guess what we forgot?"

Mayhem's mind raced.

"We never checked the footage from Poe's ankle band."

His stomach sank. For the first time, their two worlds collided, romance and passion overshadowing the mission. "Hence why business and pleasure rarely mix well."

Bloodshot eyes searched his face for answers, as though she'd leapfrogged over Heaven and plummeted into the worst probable scenario. "What're you sayin'?"

"Nothing close to the lies you're telling yourself. I meant, we must do better."

She picked at her chewed cuticles. "Oh."

"Speak your mind, Cautious Cat."

"I'm so freakin' exhausted, I'm over-analyzing things I shouldn't."

"Fair enough." He kissed her nose. "Get some rest. I'll meet you at ten-fifteen."

"Wait—What about the video?"

"Not to worry. I'll handle it."

"But—"

Did she fear being alone in the suite? After all, killers stalked the grounds.

He slipped his arms around her waist. "Tell me what you need, Kitty Cat."

"Can you maybe review the footage here for a few minutes?"

"For you? Certainly. Would you mind if we stayed on the balcony so I can monitor Running Bear?"

"I'll grab a blanket and meet you out there." She darted into the bedroom.

Moments later, while he leaned over the balcony railing, skimming the grounds of the cabins out back, she returned and patted the decking, the two chairs pushed to the side. When he lowered, he sat with his back against the vinyl exterior. Cat curled up with the blanket, her head resting on his side, his arm draped around her.

After sliding the SD card into the reader on his phone, he fast-forwarded past the drive and their trek through the woods. The video replayed Poe's flight to the barn, his talons clawed into the windowsill, then wobbled while he repositioned his leg.

Toward the back of the barn, rows of white-hooded Klansmen sat in folding chairs. Around the edges stood members in black robes—called Knighthawks, the security team.

The separation of ranks explained why Cat hadn't spotted the others. And why, through the scope of his rifle, Running Bear only caught sight of Resi, caged in line with the window.

How many other white supremacy groups did Killzme have ties to? And why would an Asian leader conduct business this way? Unless the iceman wasn't aware of his board members' allegiance.

Valuable intel. No wonder Poe was so insistent.

At the front of the barn in orange satin, their leader had his back turned while he prepared his hood of hatred. Poe moved enough to capture a quick profile.

Mayhem leaned in as the Grand Dragon rotated, the hood rising to slide over his head. He paused the footage. With two fingers, he enlarged the image.

"Hello, Mister Russell." A little zing tingled up his spine. "How nice of you to stay in the area."

When he glanced down, Cat was sound asleep.

"I've got you, sweetheart." He bundled her and the blanket in his arms, carried her into the bedroom, and tucked her under the covers with her head on the softest pillow.

Never once did she wake.

Mayhem padded out of the suite. Double checked the lock before hustling to the back stairwell. Running Bear met him at the rear exit outside.

"Anything to report?" Mayhem asked.

"Not yet. Racist pigs must sleep in."

"Does that surprise you?"

"Nope. Hate's a heavy emotion to lug around."

"Evidently." The insight made Mayhem smile inside. "And they have the audacity to call *us* savages. The irony astounds me."

As they trekked into the parking lot, Running Bear slowed his stride. "How is the photographer ruse gonna work without a bride?"

"She's resting while we find the perfect backdrop for wedding photos. Why should she trudge through the woods?"

"Copy that."

At the Benz, he passed Kuruk the tripod and camera.

They snaked through crowds of early risers eager to experience all Greater Yellowstone offered. The natural hot springs, the geysers, the rock and sandstone structures created over centuries, and the ever-shifting landscape beneath their feet from an active supervolcano.

If humanity continued to jeopardize the Natural World, the volcanic eruption could cause irreversible damage worldwide. Pyroclastic flows—a high-density mix of hot lava blocks, pumice, ash, and volcanic gas—would gobble up the closest states to Yellowstone, while falling ash would affect many other areas in the U.S., the totality of which would create climate issues on a global scale.

Once they ventured far enough off-trail, deeper into the thick forest, Running Bear again slowed his pace. "Do you have any idea how much she loves you?"

Appalled, he stopped mid-stride. "Frankly, our personal life is none of your business."

"I respectfully disagree, Shadow Wolf. Ghost Dog is family. And so are you. My family *is* my business."

"If you have a point, make it. We have work to do."

"Her outer strength hides brokenness inside."

"I beg your pardon." *The audacity.* "Cat is far from broken. How dare you insinuate otherwise."

"Look. I love Ghost Dog, too, but she is, Shadow Wolf. Mama Hen showed me how much pain she carries around. I honestly don't know how she functions day to day."

An invisible arrow sailed through his heart. "Then we'll heal together."

"Good. She doesn't need any more scars."

"You underestimate her, Running Bear. She's a survivor like you." He still sensed reluctance. "Why voice your concerns?"

"That's not at all what I'm doing. You two are made for each other."

*Ferron got to him.* "Did Mama Hen mention anything else?"

Kuruk's gaze roamed everywhere but at him. "She told me about that night."

*Ooh, that woman was like a pup with a squeaky toy.* "She had no right."

"Have you told Ghost Dog yet?"

"No." He released a pained groan. "I planned to tell her last night, but her nerves got the better of her, and we needed to have a different conversation."

"About consent?" His eyes thinned. "Thanks for giving Carolyne that speech. Now I need to ask permission to touch my wife."

"As you should." He hiked deeper into the forest.

Running Bear grabbed his arm. "You won't lose her, if that's what you're worried about."

Mayhem's gaze lowered to his tight grip, and he let go. Smart man. "Did Mama Hen tell you that, as well?"

"Yes, but that's not how I know. From the moment I met Ghost Dog, I saw how she looks at you."

*Oh, that's rich.* "Then why, pray tell, did you even entertain the thought of trying to sleep with her?"

"I'm weak." His arms swung wide. "And you're impossible to read." His voice hardened. "Don't turn this around on me. Tell her, for chrissakes. You've delayed long enough."

A hard breath petted his inner beast as he stepped closer to invade Running Bear's personal space. "You are dangerously close to crossing the line."

Palms flashed in surrender, he backed away. "Not my intention at all. What Mama Hen showed me freaked me out. I had no idea Ghost Dog endured years of abuse."

"Cat doesn't need or want your pity."

"I was there when she boarded that ship to save my son." One hand thumped his chest. "I know what she means to you. This secret must be eating you up inside."

"What's the alternative? Shatter everything we've built? This subject is extremely delicate for her."

"Ghost Dog is one of the strongest people I know. Trust her."

"I do."

"Then tell her. It's robbing you two of having a beautiful life together."

His heart throbbed. "Could you keep Jacy Lee away from the firepit tonight?"

"If that's what you need, sure." He patted Mayhem's shoulder. "You're doing the right thing, Shadow Wolf."

"If this backfires..."

"Jacy Lee and I will catch her if she falls."

"Let's hope it doesn't come to that."

They strode up the embankment. At the top, Mayhem froze mid-step.

Five feet away, an enormous male grizzly pumped up and down on the bark of an ash tree, using the trunk as a backscratcher. Cued in on their scent, the bear waved his nose in the air.

Kuruk said, "We mean you no harm, my grandfather."

Mayhem winced. If the grizzly hadn't spotted them, they might have escaped unscathed. Alas, that was no longer an option.

# Chapter 40



***10:20 a.m.***

*Where the hell is he?* Mayhem was never late. Nor would he ignore my texts. But with limited cell towers in the park, I couldn't be sure he'd received any of the messages I sent.

"Unbelievable," I muttered, rising from the table where I'd pieced together most of the chewed paper from Elliot's briefcase. Because I didn't have time to pour through the pages for the cipher—had to meet the frickin' chef in ten minutes—I snapped photos of each bizarre image and accompanying words. No clue what it meant yet.

Did Cynthia and Elliot have kids?

With or without my faux hubby, I couldn't blow our cover. So, I speed-walked to the elevator. Since it took forever to arrive, I ducked into the stairwell. My footfalls ricocheted off concrete walls as I clamored down the treads, my hand running the railing.

At the door to the main floor, I scanned for familiar faces. Namely, trophy hunters from the endless pool of guests.

Without photos, all I had were the names of those who booked cabins or the most expensive suites. The one thing that separated poachers from other guests was their fondness for military attire. Killzme used fatigues as uniforms to show their alliance to the wildlife trafficking organization.

Inside the hotel restaurant—super fancy, which didn't help settle my nerves—a flaming redhead approached me in a chef jacket and hat, a hairnet pulled over a full ginger beard.

"Missus Thunderhawk?" he said in a pitch much higher than I expected.

"Call me Kai." I shook his freckled hand. "And you are?"

"Chef Franklin. Will the groom be joining us?"

"Um, yeah. He's running late. But we can start without him."

"Please make yourself comfortable." He gestured toward a table near the kitchen. "Once you choose a cake, we'll discuss design."

Design? What'd I know about wedding cakes? "Sounds good."

"Excuse me, please. I'll fetch the samples."

While I waited for Chef Franklin to return, my leg drummed the padded chair. What if the guys ran into the Klansmen? A spotter must be trailing the ancient herd. How else would they know which animals to shoot? Did all the Buffalo in Yellowstone have the same bloodline?

Probably not. Otherwise, why capture Resi? Unless Killzme used him to whet their clients' appetite. Complete and utter scum. Anyone who abused an animal for fun deserved a bullet to the brain. Or better yet, a knife to the throat.

When Chef Franklin returned, he carried a serving tray full of cake slices. As he unloaded each dessert plate, he set them in a row. "Do any flavors hold a special significance for your relationship?"

*Huh?* "Not sure what you mean."

"Gone are the days of traditional vanilla, chocolate, lemon, strawberry, or butter cream. Unique flavors are now a dominant trend in the dessert world."

*Did he answer my question?* "To be honest, my husband is so much better at this stuff than I am." Didn't help that the chef remained standing.

"Is there a flavor you and he gravitate toward?"

"We burn sage. Does that help?" *Where the hell is he? I'm drowning here!*

"Why don't you taste test a few, and we'll go from there."

"Okay, cool. Lay 'em on me."

The squint to his baby blues increased the speed of my leg.

"I mean, sounds lovely." Adopting Mayhem's persona helped me regain some dignity. "Thank you, Chef Franklin."

When he slid the first cake in front of me, he handed me a dessert fork. "Peanut Butter Cup is a sweet, salty, nutty, decadent delight that checks many boxes. Layered with chocolate cake, peanut butter buttercream, and chocolate and peanut butter ganache, it's topped with Reese's peanut butter cups."

The moistness of the cake melted on my tongue. "Really good," I said through the mouthful. "Sold."

"Don't you want to try any of the others?"

"Probably should, right?"

He set the next slice and fresh fork in front of me. "Give your wedding a fun French panache with a citrusy splash of Grand

Marnier. The cognac provides dimension to simple cake flavors and adds a special *je ne sais quoi*."

I raised a forkful. "So, what you're sayin' is, there's booze in here?"

The blank stare almost compelled me to dive under the table.

The restaurant door swung open, and in swaggered the sexiest man alive in a long leather trench coat and his smoky shades. "Apologies for the delay, my love." He kissed my cheek. "Chef Franklin, pleasure to make your acquaintance." They shook hands. "What did I miss?"

"I was just explaining how the Grand Marnier adds a French panache to the wedding cake."

"May I?" When I slid the slice to him, he took a tiny bite like a cake connoisseur, dabbing his lips with a cloth napkin afterward. "The cognac adds a nice little *je ne sais quoi*, doesn't it?"

Chef Franklin lit up, and I half-expected him to throw his arms around my faux hubby. "I could not agree more. Shall I add it to the list of potentials?"

"Please do." He slung his arm around my chair. "Did you find a favorite, sweetheart?"

The tenderness of his tone immediately soothed me. "The Peanut Butter Cup is really good."

"For a wedding cake?" His nose crinkled. "What if a guest has a peanut allergy?"

What guests? Last I checked, we didn't have any.

"Glad you're here." I slid my hand to his thigh for leverage to scoot closer. Wetness froze my palm mid-stroke. *Please don't be—*I peeked under the tablecloth. Blood soaked through his jeans. *Is he hurt?*

"Sultry Chocolate is a sexy little number I think you'll enjoy." Chef Franklin set the slice in front of my honey bun, and he slid the plate to me.

"My wife has final say, not I, Chef Franklin."

"Understood, sir." He passed me a fresh fork. "Kai, this cake—"

"Kai?" He rocked back. "Why the informality with my wife?"

"She asked me to call her—"

"You will address her with the same respect you've given me." His tone chilled. "Is that clear, Chef Franklin?"

"Yes, sir. My apologies, Missus Thunderhawk."

When it came to me, he didn't let anyone step out of line. "Let's just keep things rolling."

"Understood, madam. As I was saying, this cake offers dark chocolate, cabernet curd, fresh raspberries, and French buttercream."

The first bite had our names written all over it. "You gotta try this, hon." I fed him, and the eyebrows lifted. "Amazing, right?"

"Very nice."

"Add it to the list please, Chef Franklin. Then pick one more. We've got another appointment to get to."

"Understood, Missus Thunderhawk."

While the chef belabored over which cake to choose, I mouthed, "Are you okay?"

The slight nod indicated yes, but something still felt off. Not sure what yet.

Another clean fork accompanied the next slice. "Strawberry Champagne leans toward the more sensual side of wedding cake flavors."

"I like the sound of it already. What's in it?"

"Dark chocolate raspberry cake... Quite scintillating to the senses, I might add."

*This dude really needs to get out more.*

"Combined with a layer of strawberry champagne cake, it's one of the more romantic confections."

Cheeks packed with deliciousness, I rocked a definite yes. "Oh, yeah. This is it." I fed a forkful to my honey bun. "Clear winner, right? We love champagne and strawberries."

He smiled. "We do."

"I'm gonna make your day, Chef Franklin. Use this cake with any design you want, but don't go nuts with poofy things."

"Poofy... things... Missus Thunderhawk?"

"Y'know, flowers and shit. Keep it simple."

Mayhem said, "Understated yet elegant."

"Yeah, that. At the ceremony, impress the guests with your design, then slice it up. We're not doin' the cutting the cake crap. Save us the top, though."

"Understood, madam."

"Then we're done here." Before I rose, I slid his trench coat over his bloody leg, hiding my bloodstained palm behind his back.

"Thank you for your time, Chef Franklin." Again, they shook hands. "Should questions arise, June knows how to get ahold of us."

"Understood, sir." Slight bow. "Madam."

Not sure what that was about, but whatever.

In the lobby, I kept my voice low. "Why're you bleeding?"

"May we discuss this upstairs, darlin'? Running Bear is waiting for us."

"He's in our suite?"

"He is."

In silence, we hustled up to the third floor, my mind whirling with one dire scenario after another. Inside the Presidential Suite, Kuruk wore an identical trench coat.

"What the hell?" I tore open Mayhem's jacket. Blood coated one thigh, more blood soaking through the knee of his jeans.

When I ripped open Running Bear's, blood saturated his charcoal tee from the pecs down.

Eyes bulging, I gnashed my teeth. "Strip."

Slight head shake from Mayhem. "Pardon?"

"You heard me. Strip. Both of you. Now."

"But, Kitty Cat—"

I wagged my finger at him. "Don't try to sweet-talk your way outta this. Strip, dammit."

They exchanged an urgent look. Within a few seconds, they both peeled off their trench coats, shirts, and pants. Two sorrowful faces stood before me in boxer briefs, blood dripping from deep slash marks.

My tongue ran my lower gumline. "One of you better start talkin'."

Fright exchanged between them.

Finally, Mayhem said, "We had a minor hiccup with a grizzly."

Nice and slow, I crossed my arms.

"It's true, Ghost Dog. We didn't realize he was there when we crested the hill."

"Excuse me? No way, not on my watch." My head would not stop wagging. "Do you really expect me to believe two Apache warriors, who are more attuned to their environment than half the people on the planet, missed the telltale signs of a grizzly bear?"

"Kitty Cat—" He stepped closer.

"Don't." A stiff finger stopped him cold. "Luther cuts you downstairs, and now this?" Eyes slitted, I got right in his face. "Doesn't make sense for a man who moves like the wind."

"To be fair, the grizzly was an impressive individual in size and stature."

"Don't give me that crap." I shook a fist in the air. "Something's thrown you off your game." Again, I narrowed my eyes. "What aren't you tellin' me?"

This time, their shared glance held hints of panic. Without a doubt, they were hiding something. But I had to play it cool. Neither responded well to screaming.

So, I dragged them toward the bathroom by the hands. "C'mon. Gotta clean you up before infection starts."

At the vanity, I positioned them on either side of the sink. Normally, I'd take a moment to enjoy the view as I lowered to the stool—both chiseled to perfection—but my adrenaline would not stop thrashing.

Once I washed debris out of the claw marks on my lover's thigh, I pressed a washcloth to the deepest wound. "Keep applying pressure while I work on Running Bear."

"Yes, dear."

"Not funny."

"Not even a little?"

"No." I rolled in front of Running Bear. "Whoa, he got you good." Soapy water cleared the claw marks. "Do I need to call Carolyne? I bet she knows what you're hiding from me."

"Please don't, Ghost Dog."

"Then I suggest you start talkin', bro."

A pleading gaze shot to Mayhem. "Shadow Wolf—"

For a split second, he winced. "Not here, Kitty Cat." Desperation edged his tone. "Please."

"Why can't we talk—?" My heart stalled. "It's not about the mission."

"No."

Whatever he had to tell me couldn't be good if he needed *Shicheii* close by.

# Chapter 41

> *"They are scared of women like you. Women with hearts big enough to house suitcases full of pain. Women with laughs so therapeutic, they can heal wounds. Women with passion fierce enough to start wildfires. They are scared of what they can't tame..."*
> —Billy Chapata

**9:03 p.m.**

Shawnee appeared numb during their appointment with the wedding concierge, nodding as the bubbly blonde named

Tory described the layout of the grounds and where she envisioned the trellis of white roses, under which they'd stand.

After the appointment, Mayhem suggested they return to the homestead for some well-needed R&R. Jacy Lee spent most of the day tending to their wounds, during which Cat stayed quiet, her intuition functioning at a remarkable new high.

If he had any hope of salvaging their relationship, he needed to confess to the part he played on that fateful night long ago. But if Cat couldn't forgive him, he might lose her forever.

While admiring the sunset as a family, she sat at the opposite end of the blanket to separate herself from him. Every time he leaned back behind the others, she refused to acknowledge him, secretly showing him what life would be like without her.

He missed her laugh. He missed her smile. He missed gazing into her deep emerald pools—those eyes held the most beautiful soul.

Jacy Lee brought up the mission and its importance to all Native People. "Did Cheveyo tell you the Buffalo weren't the only victims of the senseless slaughter?"

"No." She leaned forward to shoot him a fiery glare. "Add that to the running tally of subjects he avoids."

*Ouch. That woman wasn't shooting to wound.*

"Easy, Ghost Dog. Even I felt that."

Jacy Lee leaned around Running Bear, as though he expected a response from Mayhem. But he had nothing to say. Cat's retort held merit.

A few silent moments passed before Jacy Lee returned to the lesson. "The white man also killed Prairie Dogs by the millions. These adorable critters dig for miles and miles. This behavior churns and plows the Earth, bringing vital nutrients to the surface. Above ground, Prairie Dogs prune and crop vegetation. The Buffalo also help by donating dung and urine to enrich the soil. It's an unusual marriage, but an effective one. Their symbiotic relationship is also one of the cutest unions on the prairie."

Jacy Lee glimpsed Mayhem again, and that old familiar pit widened inside him.

"As a totem," he continued, "the Prairie Dog gives us the medicine of retreat. This rest message tells us our bodies are running low on fuel and it's time to stop to refill our energy wells. Quieting the mind gives us strength and inspiration to replenish our life force. Only then can we access dreams or visions because we are not encumbered by the chaos of the world."

To let his teachings sink in, he paused. "After the retreat, we're able to re-enter daily life with a calmness that produces progress. Just as the Prairie Dog runs into a tunnel when they sense a predator, we must sometimes retreat to our silent burrow to regain energy, so we may reach our full potential."

*Precisely. Thank you, my friend.*

"Mm-hmm, I get what you're sayin', *Shicheii*. But what if we're running away from our problems? Like—oh, I dunno—avoiding the truth. Our energy wells would stay empty, right?"

Another glance at Mayhem—Jacy Lee visibly uncomfortable. "They would, yes."

A deafening silence continued for several more minutes, consuming Mayhem more and more till he finally rose. In front of her, he extended his hand. "May we talk in private?"

Defiant, her arms crossed. "I'm good right here."

Tears burred his vision. "Please, Kitty Cat."

Holding his watery gaze, she accepted his hand. He led her to the firepit, each step closer breaking his heart more and more.

Seated in front of the Sacred Fire, he stared into the flames in search of the kindest words, and to pray she wouldn't demand to return home to Massachusetts.

"The night you lost your parents"—he paused for air, but his lungs refused the offer—"I'd been tracking Red Buffalo for hours."

The mere mention of that painful period brought her to tears.

Oh, how he longed to spare her this memory. "I trailed him to your home four separate times. Even after your parents left, he stayed a while longer, as though deciding whether to enter."

Weeping, a soft squeal escaped her lips. "To ambush them when they got home?"

"Perhaps. Had he gained entry, however, he would have found you and killed you." A hard breath heaved his chest. "When Red Buffalo left, I followed for several miles."

"Did you warn Mom and Dad?"

Staring into the flames for strength, he uttered a soft, "No."

She jolted to her feet. "Why the hell not?"

"Your mother would have insisted on heading home to protect you." He rose with her. "So, I backtracked to your house. Hours later, when your parents still hadn't returned, I drove around the vicinity of where I last spotted their vehicle. Unfortunately, I arrived too late."

"No." Her head shook. "No. This can't be right."

"It's true. I wish things turned out differently but..."

A wave of anger washed over her. "You coulda saved them—and didn't!"

He pleaded with her to understand. "I chose you, Kitty Cat."

"You sentenced me to hell!" Hatred dripped off every word.

"I was young, inexperienced. I didn't know what to do. I made a split-second decision under impossible circumstances."

"Are you even sorry?"

"About choosing to protect you? Your mom would've wanted me to."

"I don't care!" She cried so hard, she gasped for air, chest rising and falling in choppy bursts. "You chose wrong! I died that night too!"

"I know you did." More tears slipped down his wet cheeks when he reached for her, but she recoiled. "How could I have known what he'd do?"

"You suspected enough to follow him." She turned icy cold. "All those years, all those foster homes, all those fuckin' animals touching me, raping me... it's all because of you."

"No." Her words daggered his heart. "Please don't say that. I chose you, Kitty Cat. I've always chosen you. For years, I missed birthdays, school plays, celebrations... out roaming the streets of Boston searching for you. I couldn't rest, knowing you were out there. I couldn't live with the—"

In milliseconds, she shortened the gap between them, her aura soaked in detestation. "I wouldn't've been on those streets if it weren't for you."

"*Please...*" Soul shredded, he couldn't take much more. "I didn't kill your parents."

"You didn't save them, either." Hatred raged in her eyes. "I can't even look at you." She stormed toward the house, tossed over her shoulder, "Don't you dare follow me!"

Awash in devastation, he fell to his knees, a hollowness widening inside him, swallowing him whole. He lost her. Forever.

Time stopped.

Pleading for mercy, he stared into the Sacred Flames, the heart carved from his chest. No amount of prayer could repair the past. How could he live without her?

Restless, he paced around the circle of white stones.

Why would Ferron betray him? He didn't understand. Through the decades, she was his confidant. She helped him through Kimi's illness, her death, and all the years he protected Cat on the street. Once he found happiness again, why'd she force him to destroy it? Why? Nothing made sense.

After endless amounts of time, he glimpsed the log home.

Perhaps Jacy Lee reasoned with her by now. Should he go after her? She said not to follow. How could he fix this?

He scrubbed a hand over his face.

On the porch, he chanced a peek through the glass wall. Jacy Lee and Running Bear stood alone in the great room.

Careful not to let the hinges squeak, he inched open the screen door, his voice low and whisperous. "Is Cat upstairs?"

"No, Cheveyo. She left."

"Left?" He barely comprehended the word. "To go where?"

Dried tears streaked Running Bear's face. "She refused to talk to us, Shadow Wolf. I didn't know what to do, so I called Mama Hen. Ghost Dog grabbed my phone and took off."

Blinking, it took a minute for the explanation to penetrate. "What happened to catching her if she falls?"

"We tried. But she only wanted Mama Hen."

"Might I remind you, Ferron is the reason we are in this predicament."

"Cheveyo, that's unfair."

"Is that so?" He sneered. "Did *you* confess to the part you played that night?"

Running Bear's jaw dropped.

Jacy Lee threw up his hands. "I refuse to speak to you when you're heated, Cheveyo."

"Cat is out there," his voice boomed, "alone in the darkness, with predators and Klansmen in the area. And neither of you"—his stiff finger stabbed the air in front of them—"bothered to notify me?"

"Klansmen?" Jacy Lee clutched his heart. "The Ku Klux—?"

With time slipping away, he kicked open the screen door. Halfway to the wood line, he called Ferron.

She answered right away. "She's safe, Cheveyo."

That told him nothing. "Safe, where?"

"You know where."

"I don't!"

"Follow your heart, Cheveyo. It soars with hers."

"I am out of patience for your riddles tonight, Ferron. Tell me where Cat is!"

No response.

"Ferron?"

No response.

"Ferron!"

He checked the face of a blank screen. She'd hung up.

"Ooh, that woman will be the death of me."

*Follow your heart. It soars with hers. Soars... soars...*

Somewhere high? The plateau. He sprinted through the forest, zigged and zagged up the hiking trail, then slowed when he reached the summit to avoid startling her.

The plateau sat empty.

*Where are you, Kitty Cat? Follow my heart. Follow my heart. It soars with hers.*

The answer slapped him across the face, and he raced down the mountain and through the forest, slapping branches out of his way. When he reached the treehouse, he closed his eyes, flattened a hand on the trunk to sense her.

*There she is.*

On the deck, he poked his head through the doorway. Inside, Cat lay on the futon, softly weeping, her face buried in the back cushion.

Without a word, he curled his body around hers, two chests heaving as one. *Oh, how he loved this woman.*

Cat refused to acknowledge him.

Being near her was enough.

Several more minutes past before he worked up enough courage to slip his arm around her. Her delicate fingers threaded through his. Hope soared like a rainbow parting the clouds, but he didn't dare make assumptions. She still refused to face him.

Her quiet, emotional tone broke the silence. "When you found my parents, were they dead?"

"Only your father." Another hard breath hitched his chest. "Your mom died in my arms."

A soft squeal escaped her lips.

More silence engulfed him, its maw devouring him whole.

"Your wife died in mine."

"She did, yes."

Several more moments slogged by before she spoke again.

"That's gotta mean something."

He'd never made the connection before, but she's right. It must. "What do you think it means, Kitty Cat?"

"I dunno." When her head reclined on his shoulder, he rested his cheek against hers. "Maybe destiny connected us long ago because we were always meant to wind up together."

"Certainly feels like outside forces at work."

She flipped to face him. "Your eyes, they're bloodshot." After kissing each eyelid, her tenderness swept down his cheek. "I'm sorry I blamed you. Mama Hen filled me in on the parts you skipped. She said that night almost destroyed you, that protecting me on the streets damn near wrecked your life, and that for decades you couldn't let me go."

Tears blurred her image, the pain as raw today as then.

"*Shicheii* should've never pushed you to watch over me. You were too young to juggle a family, work, and keeping me safe. She also said something inside you—inside us—kept drawing you back to me."

Another painful wave hit, and he broke down again. Through the tears, all he managed was, "It's true."

Thank you, Ferron, for saying everything he couldn't.

"I should have told you sooner, Kitty Cat." His chest rose and fell. "I wanted to tell you so many times, but I feared—"

"*Shh...*" A gentle finger pressed his lips. "You're allowed to make mistakes."

No one had ever uttered those words to him. Not once.

"Just promise me one thing." She swept away his tears. "From this moment forward, no more secrets between us."

"No. Never. You have my word."

Her arms tightened around his neck. For several moments, she didn't speak. And then, her soft whisper penetrated his ear. "Make love to me."

His heart leapt.

The first taste of her sweet lips healed the haunting, lingering ache that only she could cure, the long-buried secret no longer able to crush him.

Kissing her, he rolled her to her back, and her legs curled around his waist. He ripped off his shirt. Kissed her longer, deeper. Her essence drove him wild. Crisp and fresh, hints of citrus and earthy tones enveloped his senses, repairing his broken spirit from the inside out.

Helpless to end the kiss, he held her tighter when he rose, unlatched the locks of the futon, then dragged it open, his tongue unable to stop swirling with hers.

Onto the mattress he crawled with her pressed to his chest. When he lowered her, their lips parted long enough for him to hold her gaze. Nothing but love showed in her eyes.

If Ferron hadn't pushed him to reveal the painful details from their decades-long history, they'd have never reached this level of intimacy—every emotion stripped raw—the strongest foundation from which to build.

His hand froze on the bottom hem of her "broken-in" tee. "May I?"

"You have full consent tonight, sugar bear. I already told you what I want."

"If that changes, you'll let me know?"

"Hundred percent."

That's all he needed to hear. He tore her t-shirt in half, lavishing kisses down her neck.

"God, I love that."

So did he. After caressing her ample breasts with his tongue, he kissed and licked across her sculptured abdomen and down below her belly button. Her hips lifted for him to drag off her sweatpants.

While kissing his way up her toned leg, light knocking at the door froze his lips on her inner knee.

Only one other person knew the location of Heaven. "Go away, Running Bear."

"Is Ghost Dog alright?"

"I'm fine," she called out. "Go away."

Anticipation building, he dragged his tongue up her inner thigh.

"Oh, yeah," she whispered. "Don't stop."

He didn't intend to.

"Believe me," Running Bear called back, "I would love to get the hell out of here, but I can't without answers for Jacy Lee."

"Tell *Shicheii* I'm fine. We'll be home in an hour."

"An hour?" he whispered. "We need more time, Kitty Cat."

That drew her full attention. "We do? How much more?"

"Three?" He lowered her thong. "Four?"

"Hours?" She bit her lower lip. "Go away, Running Bear!"

Incessant tapping shot his gaze to the window. In the glass, Poe stood with his head cocked, bill parted in disbelief.

*Oh, for goodness sake.* He snapped up Cat's sweatpants, trying to cover her nakedness long enough for him to locate his shirt.

As she slipped into her panties, she held the sweats over her breasts. "We need a long weekend. Alone."

He adjusted his aching member. "We do."

Once Cat buttoned into his shirt, he answered the door. "Why, pray tell, would you bring Poe here?"

"Poe's here?" Running Bear strode past him. "What makes you think he followed me?"

"Oh, by all means, come in." The sardonic tone was intentional. "Cocktail, Kitty Cat?"

"Abso-friggin'-lutely." In his collared shirt and no pants, she crossed her arms for Running Bear. "And you cock-blocked me, why?"

As he shook the shaker, filled with her favorite ingredients, her sharp wit amused him to no end.

"Not my intention at all, Ghost Dog." He strode to the window to let Poe in.

He flew straight to Dad's shoulder, nuzzling his feathery crown against his neck. Mayhem kissed his cheek. "Hello, handsome."

*Rattle, rattle. Rattle, rattle.*

"Did you follow me, bud?"

Poe's bill hit his chest feathers.

"In the future, please refrain." He poured the cocktail over two tumblers of ice. "It's not safe for you to traverse a darkened land-scape alone." On his way into the living room, he hushed to Poe, "Behave yourself, young man."

Running Bear's arms swung wide. "You didn't make me one?"

"Correct. You are not staying."

"I'm afraid, I am. You dropped a bomb and walked out, leaving me to pick up the pieces."

Cat shot a thumb over her shoulder. "What's he talkin' about?"

"I haven't the foggiest idea."

"Shadow Wolf told Jacy Lee about the Klan."

"I did no such—" His heated speech spiraled through his mind. "Oh, boy." A headache bloomed behind his eyes, and he massaged his forehead. "I did, didn't I?"

"You sure did. I danced around it the best I could, but I can't return till we figure out what to tell him."

Any chance for a wild night of passion vanished in an instant. Cat guzzled half her drink, ice clattering against the glass. Evidently, she just came to the same conclusion.

"I'll take that cocktail now, please." Arms out, Running Bear fell back on the mattress. "Why isn't the skylight open?"

Mayhem's abdominal muscles clenched. This would undoubtedly be a long night.

"Before we figure out what to tell *Shicheii*, I need to show you somethin'." She rooted in the pocket of her moccasin. "I pieced together Elliot's paperwork." On her phone, she scrolled through Photos. "Here we go." The first page of a children's book filled the screen. "What does A is for apples mean?"

"May I?" Once she passed her cell, he scrolled through multiple pages. "Cat, you found the cipher."

"I did?"

Running Bear said, "Someone want to fill me in?"

Rather than explain the mountain goat incident, he kept it brief. "In Elliot's ledger, we found an alphanumeric code next to the names of Killzme board members. We've been searching for the cipher ever since."

"And Ghost Dog found it?"

"After much labor-intensive work, she did, yes." He showed him the photos. "Elliot worked as an accountant. Makes sense he'd attach a numeric value to each letter. How many apples do you see, Kitty Cat?"

"Three."

"Then three equals A." A puzzled looked crossed her beautiful face, so he scrolled to the next image. "How many bananas?"

"Two."

"Thus?"

"B equals two. I get that, but how do numbers tell us anything?"

"Reverse it. The numbers give us letters."

"Then what about the letters after the names?"

"They remain as written."

"So, it's really a code within a code."

"Precisely. Did you photograph the ledger as well?"

"Shit. No."

"Not to worry. We'll decode it at the suite." He backed her into his chest, kissed the top of her head, his arms holding her tight. "Brilliant work, Kitty Cat."

"Thanks."

Poe's foot pushed her away.

"Fine." She tsked. "He's all yours... for now."

Oh, boy. Would the animosity between them ever end? After what Poe witnessed tonight, the odds were not in her favor.

# Chapter 42



There had been no way around it. With the hunt scheduled for tomorrow, we had no choice but to tell *Shicheii* the truth last night. He took the news of the Klan meeting better than expected, but that didn't stop him from insisting we spend the morning in prayer. Not that I minded. We needed all the spiritual help we could get.

A thunderstorm rolled in after breakfast, so we lounged in the living room till it passed. My lover and I sprawled on the couch, sardine-style to remain respectful, with my bare feet crossed on his shoulder, his ankles propped on the back cushions.

Poe glared at us from the armrest of *Shicheii's* chair, Spirit Crow and Odin nestled together on the loveseat with Running Bear.

"What's on the agenda for today, Cheveyo?"

"Target practice. We need to improve Cat's aim."

As if he hadn't said a word, *Shicheii* rose. "Would anyone like tea?"

We all raised our hands.

Dimples deepened with my grandfather's smile. "What an enjoyable morning."

Didn't take a genius to figure out someone preferred the warm waters of denial. Must run in the family, because it'd always worked well for me, too.

Once *Shicheii* strolled into the kitchen, I waved my foot. "Do you do foot rubs?"

Running Bear chuckled. Why, I had no clue. Maybe Odin was showing off for Spirit Crow.

"I do, in fact." His gray eyes sparkled. "Would you like a foot massage?"

"Yes, please."

"Oh, boy." Running Bear laughed harder.

When he lifted my foot, I twisted to peer over the armrest. "What's so funny?" His fingers hit a spot in my heel, and a sensual spark shot through me. "Whoa. What was that?"

"*Shh*, lay back and relax, Kitty Cat."

Warmth and tingles shot to all the right spots, and my eyes rolled closed on their own. "Oh, my God."

Running Bear slapped his thighs. "Well, that's my cue to leave."

My foot massager said, "Take Poe with you, please."

"C'mon, bud."

Footfalls trailed into the kitchen.

"Oh, my God." More sparks added to the inferno inside me. "Oh, my God, yeah." I slapped the cushion. "Oh... my God."

The tremor curled my toes while he worked an area in my heel and two places in the arch. "I think I'm gonna..." My hands clawed into the sofa, the sensation of a climax building and building. "How is this even possible? Oh... my... God." I jolted upright. "Stop."

His fingers froze. "Stop?"

"Yes. No. I dunno."

"Yes, I should stop? Please be clear."

I glimpsed the kitchen. "Continue, but can you get me there quick?"

"I can." He winked. "And will."

Sure enough, an orgasmic wave engulfed me, my body jerking in response.

*Ca-caw, caw, caw!* Poe landed on my chest—hard, like he added extra oomph—glaring down at me, his beady eyes full of judgment.

I slid my foot out of his father's magical hands. "This time you got me, fair and square."

The eyes slitted.

"Okay, alright. What's it gonna cost to buy your silence? Fruit cup?"

One slow nod.

"Mashed potatoes and gravy?"

Another nod.

"Crispy bacon?"

A third nod.

"Then we'll be cool?"

He whipped around, borrowed tail feathers swishing behind him as he swaggered to his father.

I leaned around the little diva. "You are an evil, evil man."

"*Moi?*" Splayed fingers spanned his chest. "You asked for a foot massage. I merely obliged."

"Payback's a bitch."

He winked. "That is my understanding, as well."

To block us from speaking, Poe caped his wings around his dad's face.

"What can I do for you, handsome?"

*Rattle, rattle. Rattle, rattle.*

*Pah-lease.* When I crawled off the couch, Odin and Spirit Crow weren't on the loveseat anymore. Shit. Did they leave because of us? Heart sinking, I whirled around.

"What's wrong, darlin'?"

"I, err…" How could I tell him? "Gotta go change."

"We're training after tea, so please dress accordingly."

"Got it." I boogied up the stairs, banged a left into my bedroom, but stopped short. In the middle of the bed, Odin was mounting Spirit Crow. Before they noticed me, I backed out the door.

Guess we weren't the only ones in this house with a raging sex drive.

In the hall, I waited, my crotch drenched from his voodoo magic, or whatever the hell was in that foot massage. When Running Bear told me about his mastery of women's pleasure zones, I never once considered areas below the ankles.

*Gronk, kuk, kuk, kuk.*

*Coo… Coo… rattle, whisper.*

Unlike most birds in the Animal Kingdom, corvids had sex for fun, intimacy, and love, outside of mating season.

*Awkward.* To muffle their cries of passion, I covered my ears. But I still needed clean clothes.

"Mourning Dove," *Shicheii* called up the stairs, and I poked my head around the corner. "Tea's ready."

"Did you do laundry by any chance?"

"I did, but I haven't put the clothes away. What do you need, my love?"

"Buckskins?"

"Laundry room."

"Underwear?"

"There as well."

"Perfect. Thanks." At the bottom of the stairs, I kissed his cheek. "Love you, *Shicheii*."

The skies cleared by the time we all filed out to the porch. Except Running Bear. Not sure where he went. A bow and quiver leaned against the railing below Poe, who wouldn't stop glowering at me for not keeping my end of the bargain yet.

"I told you I'd do it, and I will, but I gotta train first. Geez, can't you cut me a break for once in your life?"

*Shicheii* said, "What did you promise him, Mourning Dove?"

"Fruit cup, mashed potatoes with gravy, and bacon."

"Is this a peace offering of some sort?"

"You could say that, yeah."

"Come, child." He cradled Poe in his arms, and the brat's beady-eyed gaze strayed back to me, as though he'd just won *Shicheii's* affection. "There's cubed melon in the refrigerator."

*Rattle, rattle, rattle.*

Before the screen door closed, I called out, "He's my grandfather, so it counts."

In the yard, Mayhem helped me with my archery stance. "Do you feel more comfortable using the chin as your anchor point, or the labiodental groove like I do?"

Aligning the vane of the arrow with the same place on my face was supposed to improve my aim, but I hadn't had much luck in that department.

"Haven't tried the *blah, blah* groove yet."

He chuckled. "Labiodental." When he demonstrated with the bow, the feather vane cradled the space between his lower lip and chin. "You may have better control if you anchor here."

"Can't hurt, right?" I copied his stance with the bow. "What's my target?"

"Me." Running Bear hustled down the porch steps with the antique war shield from the kitchen wall. And he did not look pleased. "I still say we could've rigged up a pulley system."

"Noted." Grinning, he winked at me. "Head straight back ten yards."

"Copy that."

I whispered, "Why do I get the feeling this is punishment for barging in on us last night?"

"He won't make that mistake again, will he?" He chuckled. "Let's see how you do with a stationary target and go from there." He waved his arms for Running Bear to stop. "Stand still for the first few shots."

Once Kuruk complied, Mayhem thanked him. "Whenever you're ready, Cat, please proceed." He whirled toward the porch, where *Shicheii* sat at the table with Spirit Crow, Odin, and Poe, all three more interested in their fruit cups than watching me. "Please ensure no one takes flight."

"Will do, Cheveyo."

"Thank you."

"Do I exhale with the release of the bowstring?"

"Excellent question, Cat. When coming to a full draw—bow-string taut but before anchoring—slowly and naturally release thirty to fifty percent of your breath. Then hold from that point forward, including the follow-through."

*How the hell do I measure the amount of air in my lungs? Meh. I'm sure I'll figure it out.*

With complete confidence, I said, "Got it."

The eyebrows arched.

"I do."

"All right, then. Please proceed."

The first arrow sailed high, the second low, but the third struck center mass. Applauding erupted behind me from the porch.

"Brava, Cat. Take a few more shots."

"But I know what I'm doing now."

"Regardless, let's raise your accuracy ratio a bit."

*Whatever that means.*

"As it stands now, your accuracy ratio is thirty-three-point-three percent. Ideally, I'd like to see it around eighty before you try your hand at a moving target."

Once I retook my position, I checked my stance. Anchored in the groove. The fourth arrow sailed straight, nailing Running Bear in the shield in front of his chest. The fifth and sixth also hit the mark.

"Nicely done, Cat." He gave me a congratulatory headlock squeeze. "What changed?"

"I focused on my breathing."

Behind us, Odin and Spirit Crow joined the cheering section on the porch. "Wonderful job, honey." *Gronk, gronk. Caw, caw, caw.* As usual, Poe stayed silent, probably praying to the crow gods that I'd shoot myself in the face.

"Way to go, Ghost Dog!" As Running Bear jogged back to the porch, he punched the air. "I knew you could do it!"

*Gotta admit, this might be one of my favorite training moments ever.*

"Time is a factor. We lost half the morning." He patted down the excitement till everyone quieted. "There are three components to striking a moving target. The speed of the target. The velocity of the arrow. And the distance of the shooter from the target. For practical purposes, let's combine the second and third into the general term of distance by considering the velocity of the arrow, a constant factor."

I scratched my cheek. "Were you speaking English just then?"

Two fingers pinched the bridge of his nose.

"Cheveyo, she learns faster through demonstration."

"Thank you, my friend." He lowered his voice. "Cat?"

"He's right." I passed the bow. "I do."

"Fair enough. Running Bear, we'll start with the cross shot."

"Wait—" He rubbed the back of his neck. "You're shooting?"

"I am."

"Under any other circumstances," he whispered, "I would've never intruded last night."

"For the cross shot, we'll do twenty yards."

"Shadow Wolf—" His whole body pleaded for forgiveness. "It will never happen again."

"Correct."

With desperation in his tone, he turned toward me. "Ghost Dog?"

"You'll be fine," I said. "Just go."

"Promise me, sis."

"I promise." I elbowed Mayhem. "Right?"

"We're wasting daylight, Running Bear. Take your mark, please."

"You promised, Ghost Dog." After jogging straight twenty yards, he ran right and left in a line.

"Don't shoot him," I whispered. "I gave my word."

"I never intended to, Cat." While raising the bow, he chuckled under his breath. "To compensate for the speed of a moving target on a cross shot, bring the bowstring to a full draw." At the usual spot, he anchored. "Then swing in a horizontal arc. Stand behind me to watch how I match his speed."

And so, I did.

The bow stayed right with Running Bear. "Got it."

"That takes care of the first component. To compensate for the remaining factors, which we combined into distant factors, increase the rate of movement." The bow swung faster. "Stay across and in front of the moving target. Because the velocity of the arrow remains constant, allow for distance during release. Of primary importance, keep the bow in motion after release as well—the follow through, if you will—or you'll nullify your previous efforts and miss the target."

While the bow never stopped swinging, the arrow whizzed through the air, nailing the shield dead-center.

"Wow." The way he shot resonated with me, and I stood taller, straighter. "Got it."

He passed the bow. "It may feel awkward at first. Don't get discouraged if your initial attempts miss the mark. As long as you keep the bow in motion, you may be surprised by how quickly you'll get the hang of it."

A zing of excitement spiraled up my spine when I drew back the bowstring. The first arrow missed, but not by much. My second shot hit the shield. And so did my third, fourth, and fifth shots.

The cheering section erupted behind me. *Coo... coo... coo... Gronk, gronk.* "Proud of you, honey."

"Nicely done, Cat. You shoot better at moving targets than stationary ones."

"I know, right?"

"Then let's make sure your prey runs." The wink cracked me up. "You'll also want to keep the target horizontally to you."

"How?"

"Go wide until he crosses at the proper angle. Then stop and line up your shot to measure distance, velocity, and speed."

"I can do that."

"I know." His warm smile lingered on me for a moment. "There is one other matter we need to discuss, though not in present company."

Uh-oh. Not good.

# Chapter 43

*"If you, too, can come to love
this land as our ancestors did,
all the problems of the world
will fall away like autumn
leaves in the wind."* —Tony
Ten Fingers, Oglala Lakota

**12:15 p.m.**

Because of the boat rental policy, he and Cat stopped by the front desk to speak with June. If anyone could make them relax their rules, she could.

"How are you, Mister and Missus Thunderhawk? Did you choose a cake?"

"We did, thank you." Crowds of people, all vying for attention, surrounded them. "May we have a quick word in private, June?"

"Certainly." She darted out from behind the desk. "Is there a problem?"

"Minor hiccup. My wife has her heart set on wedding photos of us on the lake under the moonlight." He stroked Cat's hair. "Don't you, sweetheart?"

To act disappointed, she rested her cheek on his chest.

"Because the ceremony takes place tomorrow night after the boat rental closes, I'm at a loss for how to fulfill her wish."

The clerk's expression showed how deeply Shawnee's performance plucked her heartstrings. "Who did you speak with at the boat rental?"

"Alexander. Nice young man."

"Alex is my nephew." She rubbed Cat's arm. "Not to worry, Missus Thunderhawk. I'll take care of everything."

"Really?" She perked up. "You're just the best. *Gaagii*, I told you we could count on her."

June blushed. "Where and when would you like the boat delivered?"

"Closest dock to the hotel, please." Mayhem withdrew his money clip. "Please ask your nephew to fill the tank. The card on file should more than cover the cost of fuel." He peeled off three crisp hundreds. "We appreciate you, June."

"I couldn't, Mister Thunderhawk. It's my fault the ceremony had to be rescheduled."

"Nonsense." He folded the gratuity into her palm. "You've gone above and beyond for us, and we could not be more grateful."

"Thank you both." Praying hands cupped her mouth. "I just adore you two."

"We're fond of you as well, June. One more thing, if I may. Is it possible to have the boat delivered today, for the rehearsal?"

"Let me call Alex. Did you want to wait, or should I phone your suite?"

He glanced at Cat. "Sweetheart?"

"Let's wait. It's important to me, *Gaagii*."

What a superb performance. "The lady has spoken." He pointed to an empty loveseat by the window. "We'll wait over there, June."

Incognito, Running Bear sat in the upholstered chair across from the loveseat.

When they lowered to the cushions on the other side of the coffee table, Mayhem slung his arm around Cat. Focused on her, he curled a strand of hair around her ear. "Is that my fedora?"

Running Bear flipped a page in the local paper. "It was in the Benz, and I needed a disguise."

With his full attention on Cat, he kissed her cheek. "Is there some reason you couldn't wait in the car?"

Playing her role, she tossed her head back and laughed. "You're awfully frisky this morning, honey bun."

"Something is about to go down out back."

He nuzzled her nose with his. "Could you be more specific?"

"Too much?" she whispered. "I adlibbed."

"Not you, darlin'."

Running Bear leaned forward. On the coffee table, he exchanged the newspaper for a magazine. "Not sure yet. Slip me the keycard and I'll monitor them."

Her soft lips pecked his. "My specialty." Years on the cold streets of Boston taught her all sorts of survival skills. On the sly, she withdrew the keycard from Mayhem's jacket pocket. "Follow my lead."

When she rose, she twirled, tripped, and fell against the upholstered chair, the keycard sliding down the arm to Running Bear's leg. "Oopsie. Sorry, sir." Swaying in place, she acted tipsy. "Dance with me, *Gaagii.*"

"Not here, sweetheart." Across the walkway, two ladies swooned when he rose. "We'll dance in the suite."

She fell against his chest. "Just one little spin?"

Running Bear headed for the elevator.

"For you, my love? Anything." He spun her twice, then dipped her. When he raised her up, June was heading their way.

"Aren't they the most adorable couple?" she said to the two ladies, awing over their quick dance. "They're renewing their vows tomorrow night."

Again, they swooned.

The whiter-haired lady patted her heart. "Mable and I love weddings."

"You should come," Cat said. "The more the merrier."

"I'll get you the details, Gladys." June passed Mayhem a printout. "You're all set, Mister Thunderhawk. Alex is scrubbing the boat as we speak. The keys should arrive at the front desk no later than two o'clock. I can call you, so you'll know when they're here."

"Perfect, June. Thank you."

"My pleasure. Is there anything else I can do for you?"

Cat said, "Can you send champagne and strawberries up to the suite?"

"I'd be happy to."

"Thanks, June." She cradled his arm. "Ready, snookums?"

The term of endearment made him chuckle. Only she could get away with that. "Let's not tempt fate with the elevators."

After climbing the stairs to the third floor, Mayhem used the spare keycard to enter the suite. Out on the balcony, Running Bear squatted, hawkeyed on the grounds below.

Mayhem slipped through the sliders but stayed low and out of sight. "What have you learned?"

"They're leaving."

"With luggage?"

"No."

Leaning on the railing, Mayhem lit a Dunhill International Red. Below, camouflage-clad hunters headed away from the cabins. He raised the cigarette to speak behind his hand. "Makes sense to get the lay of the land prior to the hunt."

Cat slipped through the opened sliders with three flutes filled with fresh strawberries and champagne. Keeping one for herself, she distributed the other two then backed against the railing beside him. "What'd I miss?"

"It appears our prey is headed to the hunting grounds."

"Why?"

"Perhaps to familiarize themselves with the landscape."

"All of them?"

"I believe so."

"Then their cabins should be empty awhile."

"Brilliant." The sweetness of strawberries tickled his tongue. "Can you get in and out without a trace?"

Her hand sifted through the back of her hair. "Did you forget who I am?"

"Humility is much nicer look. Wouldn't you agree?"

"Hey, don't hate the player. Hate the game."

With a slight head shake, he said, "Again, that expression has nothing to do with these circumstances."

"I know, but it fits." To examine the job, her elbows rested on the railing. "Old windows make it easier." Her gaze swung to the balconies on their left and right. "Lookie Loos may be a problem."

"You let us worry about that." To Running Bear, he said, "Do you recall the ruse we used in upstate New York?"

"Oh, no." The head wagged in defiance. "No way. Never again."

"What choice do we have? Cat needs to be free to enter the cabins."

He shot back his drink. "Then we'll think of another way."

"Do you or do you not agree time is of the essence?"

"I do, but—"

"Do you not also agree protecting Cat rises above any uncomfortable feelings we may have?"

"I'm not doing it, Shadow Wolf."

"Oh, yes, you will."

He stormed into the suite, muttering, "I should've *never* left Alaska."

"Wanna clue me in? He doesn't say no to you. Ever."

"To be fair, it's a tough pill for any man to swallow."

Laughing, Mayhem headed into the suite, where Running Bear pouted on the sofa. To give him time to come to terms with the upcoming ruse, he sat at the table, jotting down the numeric value of each letter.

When Shawnee strolled into the living room, she passed Running Bear a fresh cocktail. "Thought you might need this."

Focused on the numeric values, Mayhem said, "Cat, could you please read me the codes?"

"Yep." She leafed through the ledger. "Ready?"

"I am."

"Rupert Russell. G, eight, nine, three, G, twenty-two, fourteen."

"G-Dragon." Mayhem's gaze shot to hers. "Elliot not only discovered their ties to the Klan but their ranks, as well."

"Whoa. Think he planned to tell the iceman?"

"If he suspected trouble, he might. Or perhaps, he kept the intel for job security. Fire him and he'll expose the board members."

"So, maybe *Shicheii's* visit didn't matter."

"Unless they feared what Elliot told him. Either way, it's valuable to us." He shot back the last of his drink. "Not helpful for this mission, but valuable nonetheless." He towered over Running Bear, who refused eye contact. "Time to get ready."

"This is the last time I'm ever doing this, Shadow Wolf."

"We appreciate your sacrifice. Don't we, Cat?"

She tossed her hands in the air. "I don't even know what we're talkin' about."

A chuckle busted loose from Mayhem as Running Bear stormed into the bedroom, slamming the door behind him. Emasculating him was the last thing he wanted to do, but innocent lives were at stake.

# Chapter 44



After I changed into a black spandex catsuit and heelless knee-high boots, I shot back a second flute while Mayhem answered the hotel phone.

"Thank you, June. We'll be along shortly." When he hung up, he said, "Boat keys."

"Figured as much. Need the putty knife."

"Duffle bag."

"Where?"

"Under the table by the door."

While I rummaged through the duffle, his shadow darkened the sunlight on the carpet. "We need to hide your natural hair in the fedora. Thank you for wearing the colored contacts. I know you're not fond of them."

"Don't want to confuse June. Got an elastic?"

He slid one off his braids.

I gathered all my hair into a high ponytail. "He's been in there forever. What's taking him so long?"

"Go easy on him, Cat. Pride is a feral beast."

"Whatever that means."

Still had no clue what they'd planned, but it didn't matter. I had to focus on my job, which wouldn't be easy in broad daylight with a busy hotel filled with guests, any of whom could stroll out to their balcony and bag me.

While we waited, I scrolled through the hotel registry. "I'll start with five-oh-five, Luther's cabin."

"Good idea." He peeled back the cuff of his trench coat. "If he delays much longer, we may miss our window."

I'd just tipped back flute number three when Running Bear emerged, champagne spraying from my mouth.

There he stood in a miniskirt and blouse, his feet flattening the backs of my heels. The brown eye shadow and red lipstick enhanced the warm chestnut of his complexion, long, silky hair and my extensions framing his high cheekbones.

"The fake lashes kill me." In tears with laughter, I pressed a hand to my abs, the other raised for air. "Stop. I can't even..."

Mayhem's lips jiggled with amusement. "You look beautiful, Running Bear."

He really did.

"However, you're too tall. Those we've met will know you're not Cat."

"He's supposed to be me?" I laughed harder, unable to catch my breath.

"Glad my humiliation amuses you, Ghost Dog."

*Yikes. He's pissed.* "Sorry. The getup caught me off-guard." I wrangled my mirth under control. "His legs are too muscular."

"At least he shaved."

That explained what took so long. Not that Native men were hairy. Far from it. "Why can't he wear moccasins with the skirt? I do. Plus, it'll help hide those shins."

Immediately, Running Bear kicked off the heels. "Just so we're clear"—he slipped his feet into his regular footwear—"I will *never* do this again. I mean it, Shadow Wolf. We've reached my line in the sand."

"Noted."

"You're lopsided." When I peeked into his blouse, I snarled. "Did you have to wear my favorite bra? You're stretching the shit outta it."

"Cat, please. I'll buy you a new one." He offered Running Bear his arm. "Shall we, darling?"

And I almost died laughing. "Stop. I can't take much more."

"We'll stay right behind you," he said with a smirk. "Take the stairs, please."

I pulled the fedora low on my head. "I'm on it." Once I checked both ends of the hall, I hustled into the stairwell. Down the stairs I clamored. Three flights later, I poked my head out the back exit. "Clear," I tossed over my shoulder before heading straight for the cabins.

Finding 505 took longer than expected. In search of the easiest entry point, I circled the unit. Metal tabs held the screens of old windows. I whistled for the happy couple, jabbed my head at the target. Scooted around the side till they moved into position. And by position, I mean, Running Bear stood in front of the entry point while Mayhem faced him with his hand on the wall, like he was leaning in for a kiss.

With two guys taking up so much room, I slinked up behind my body double to remove the screen. Running Bear kicked his leg back for me to push off, and I slithered inside the cabin.

"Hurry, Ghost Dog. Please, sis."

"Don't get your panties in a bunch." Cheap shot. "Sorry, couldn't resist. You're just so pretty."

"Eyes on the prize, Cautious Cat. His breath is atrocious."

"I purposefully didn't brush to keep you away."

"Care for a mint, darling?"

"No, Shadow Wolf, I wouldn't. But I have had enough of the darling shit."

"If you drape your arms on my shoulders like Cat does, I'll back up a bit."

Not sure how that went because I was doing my thing.

"Fine. But don't you dare kiss me."

"Why on earth would I?"

"This sucks, Shadow Wolf. The bra strap digs into my back in this position."

"Running Bear," aggravation filled his tone, "you are testing my patience."

The bickering continued as I ventured farther into the dark cabin. About forty empty beer cans—Hey Bear and Old Faithful Ale—littered the coffee table. No personal belongings in the main room, kitchenette, or bathroom. I twisted the doorknob of the bedroom, and the door flew open.

Frozen in place, my gaze crawled up a flounder white beer belly to a blockhead with a buzz-cut.

"Who the fuck are you?" he said.

I slapped on a fake smile. "Housekeeping."

"Housekeeping? Dressed like that?" He visually raped me from head to toe.

"Slow your role, pal." Even from this distance his rank body odor sickened me. "Just messing with ya."

"Did Luther send you?"

Luther? This guy must've arrived late. "Yeah. He wants you to meet him at the site. All the guys are there."

"And who are you?"

"Mister Russell's assistant, Molly." I jutted out my hand. "Nice to meetcha."

"Jennifer is his assistant."

"Yep. I'm from the temp agency, filling in while she's on vacation." My boots shuffled backward. "Well, my job is done here. Better not keep 'em waiting." When I spun to get the hell out of there, a meaty hand clamped around the nape of my neck.

Inches from my face, stale booze breath twitched my nose. "The boss would never send a temp."

I kneed him in the balls. When he buckled over, I booked it through the living room. But he tackled me from behind. I flipped, kicked, and swung. "Help!"

Running Bear dove through the window. With the mini skirt half-hiked to one hip, he withdrew a knife from his moccasin. "Get off her."

Mayhem kicked in the door. In milliseconds, he wrenched back the dude's head to free me, the hunting blade pressed to his throat. "Darling, please slide out from underneath him." Into the guy's ear, he said, "Your first mistake was laying your filthy hands on my wife. Don't make another."

Frightened baby blues bulged from the sockets. With a breathy exhale, he uttered a soft, "Redskin." The eyes shifted to me. "Then you must be…"

Mayhem grimaced. "If you value your life, do not finish that sentence." His harsh tone softened for me. "Did he hurt you, sweetheart?"

"I didn't enjoy eating the carpet. Other than that, no."

With the poacher still pinned to his chest, he turned to Running Bear. "Do you recall the Holiday Inn we visited in Tampa?"

"Copy that." He hustled into the bathroom. Moments later, the whoosh of rushing water coursed through the paper-thin walls, but why remained a mystery.

"Have you gone through his belongings, Cat?"

"Not yet. He jumped me before I could."

"Now might be a good time." He smiled like this was an ordinary day, and he wasn't about to murder this scumbag.

"I'm on it." Though I hustled into the bedroom, there wasn't a chance in hell I wouldn't watch his back, so I dragged the military duffle into the living room.

"If you answer my questions, Mister…?"

"Jameson."

"Thank you. If you answer my questions, Mister Jameson—truthfully, and without malice or suspicious intent—you may survive this encounter. If you refuse, your life ends today. Do you have a preference? I will say, I'm leaning toward the latter."

"Please, Redskin. I have a wife, too."

"Then I suggest you stop using Killzme's racist codeword for me. You will address me as sir. Am I clear?"

"Yessir."

"Now you've taken a step in the right direction, Mister Jameson. What do your associates know about us?"

"Not a lot. Just that you're either animal activists or conservationists. Maybe both. And for us to keep an eye out for you."

"Do they know where we are?"

"Rupert said you were in the area. That's all."

"Not at a specific hotel?"

"No."

"How do you know which individuals in the herd possess the ancient bloodline?"

All the coloring from the dude's chubby cheeks drained in an instant. "You know about that?"

"We do."

"Did you steal the Bison from the barn?"

"We freed him, yes."

Should he be telling him this stuff? What if Jameson uses it against us? "Um, hon? What if he talks?"

"Mister Jameson and I are building rapport."

"It's true, ma'am. You can trust me."

"See?" Quick smile for me. "Nothing to worry about."

Uh-huh.

"Do you need me to repeat the question, Mister Jameson?"

"They marked the herd's leader."

Mayhem and I exchanged a look of disbelief. "Marked how?"

"Red paint on his horns."

"Oh, my God." Tears rose in my chest. "Resi."

"Who?"

The blade bit into Jameson's neck, trickles of blood snaking down his throat. "No one questions my wife. Understood?"

"Yessir."

"Did you see Mister Abbott last night?"

*That'd be kinda tough, considering he's dead.*

"No. My flight got delayed. Didn't get here till two a.m. Why?"

"Hey"—I stalked closer—"he asks the questions, not you."

"Adorable," he mouthed, with a little nose crinkle. "Considering you and Luther Abbott share a one-bedroom cabin, is it fair to say you two are close? Secret lovers, perhaps?"

Inside, I snickered. The Klan would never allow gay men to join their ranks. Too racist, too simple-minded, too filled with hate. But that didn't stop Mayhem from insinuating otherwise. Such a great sense of humor.

"Hell, no. We're like brothers."

From the bathroom, Running Bear called out, "Ready when you are, Shadow Wolf."

Mayhem put the dude in a headlock. His forearm squeezed until Jameson lost consciousness, a pasty white body melting before me. "Please grab his ankles, Cat."

"Isn't this more a job for Running Bear?"

"If you do not possess enough physical strength, I'd be happy to ask him to assist."

"Nope." He'd never let me live down that speech on the stairs. "I got it."

Quick wink. "Thank you."

With me on the ankles, my faux hubster suspending him by the armpits, we carried the big lug into the bathroom, where Running Bear waited next to a full bathtub.

"I got him, Ghost Dog." He and Mayhem lowered the unconscious poacher into the water.

Not sure why, though. "Are you drowning him?"

With a wrist in each of their hands—held beneath the surface—they splayed open the veins. The water crimsoned in seconds flat.

"Questions, Cat?"

I'd have to be an idiot to not figure out this scene. "Nope."

He dried his hands on a towel, which he pocketed. "Did you find anything useful in Luther Abbott's belongings?"

"No. Just clothes and stuff."

In the living room, he rummaged through the duffel, tossed clean camouflage pants and a black tee to Kuruk. "Cat, please slip Running Bear's outfit over yours and give him the fedora. You and I need to head to the front desk before June comes looking for us."

Stripped to his boxer briefs, Running Bear passed me the mini skirt, blouse, and hair extensions. "Want the bra?"

"After you stretched the shit outta it? Hard pass. But I will take my lashes." When he leaned forward, I peeled them off. "Hope there's enough adhesive left."

"There should be, Ghost Dog. I usually add too much."

"Usually?" The curl to his upper lip made me backpedal. "Sorry."

I slipped the outfit over my catsuit while Running Bear washed off his makeup. Since I didn't feel like re-witnessing the literal bloodbath, my faux hubby covered my cherry-red tresses with the hair extensions.

Killzme must've rented all the cabins. Without poachers here, ghost towns had more activity.

Our team leader peeked out the door. "Let's move out." Footfalls padded down the front steps.

With one more scan of the cabin—all signs of us erased—Running Bear and I boogied out to the porch. On the ground below, Mayhem pressed the last tab on the window frame to secure the screen in place. From the outside, no one could tell there'd been a violent struggle indoors. The door sat a little cockeyed from him kicking it in. Other than that, everything appeared copacetic.

Running Bear continued straight to the parking lot while we hustled up the back stairwell to the lobby. I didn't love the looseness of my fitted mini skirt, but I rolled with it.

As we approached the front desk, crowds of vacationers spilled into the foyer. "This may take a while."

While we waited in line, he smiled at someone, but I couldn't see past the heads of other guests. Standing six-foot-two had its advantages, I guess.

"Mister Thunderhawk—" June's high pitch lasered through the muddled chitchat and crying toddlers. Seconds later, she bustled over with the floatable keyring. "Life jackets are in the boat, parked at slip four. Tank is full, per your request."

"Splendid, June. Thank you. When does the rental expire?"

"Eight o'clock Saturday morning. If you plan to sleep in, return the keys to me at the ceremony."

*She's attending our fake wedding?*

My pretend hubby must've had the same thought, because he said, "We didn't realize you'd be joining us, June."

"Of course. Wouldn't miss it." The smile faded. "Unless you don't want me there?"

"No, no. We'd love for you to attend." He slung his arm around my shoulders. "Wouldn't we, darling?"

"Absolutely. The night wouldn't feel the same without you."

"Yay." Her light clapping nauseated me. "Now, I've confirmed with Tory, Chef Franklin, DJ Dan, and the caterer. All I need is the name and phone number for the wedding officiant to confirm with him or her, as well."

Mayhem fake-patted his pockets. "His details must be in the suite. If he called you, would that work?"

"Sure. What about the photographer?"

"We're on our way to meet with him. In fact, he's the one who suggested a rehearsal boat ride."

"Wonderful. Then your special night should go off without a hitch. Oh, Mister Thunderhawk, you need to choose a song."

"A song?"

I patted his chest. "Don't you remember, hon? Tory asked us to pick a song for our first dance."

"I thought she meant you."

"These days, the bride and groom each pick one."

"My apologies, darling. I misunderstood." He refocused on June. "May I tell you the song to relay to Tory?"

"Certainly, but not in front of the bride."

"Pardon?"

"It should be a surprise."

He glanced down at me. "Did you choose a song?"

"Yep."

"All right, then." He smiled at June. "I'll call you after our appointment with the photographer."

Bouncing on her toes, her excitement bubbled over. "I can't wait to hear what you choose."

*That makes two of us.*

# Chapter 45

*"One's dignity may be assault-
ed, vandalized, and cruelly
mocked, but it can never be
taken away... Unless it is surrendered. Never surrender."*
—Native American Honor-
ing Our Ancestors, Culture &
Spirituality

*3:30 p.m.*

Sunbeams danced across the water as Mayhem lowered to the bench seat beside Cat. In front of them, Kuruk stood at the helm of the eighteen-foot boat with a fold-out canopy and open bow. Nothing fancy but it fit their needs.

A quizzical expression crossed her face. "Why do we need a boat?"

"Too many variables along the route from the hotel to the hunting grounds to nail down a consistent timeframe."

"Like what, grizzlies?"

*She caught on quick.* "Running Bear believes we can halve our arrival time by cutting across the lake."

"Do you agree?"

"We'll find out soon enough."

"What song are you gonna pick?"

"What did you choose?"

She swayed her shoulder. "Not tellin'."

"Nor am I." He winked.

Up ahead, the lodgepole pines framed a separation. "Head for that opening, Running Bear."

"Copy that."

Shawnee's hand slid across his upper thigh, her fingers lingering on the inner seam of his jeans, near the crotch. "What a gorgeous lake."

"Kitty Cat, we're working."

"I know." Refusing eye contact, she gazed out at the water. "You're the one who says we should take a moment to appreciate our surroundings. That's all I'm doing."

"My mistake."

Once her hand moved to his knee, she allowed him to focus on work. "Maybe you should get your mind outta the gutter."

*She's not wrong.* "Yes, dear."

"So, did you hire the actor yet?"

"I tasked Jacy Lee with the job."

"What? Why?"

"He wanted to help, Cat. What could I say, no? Besides, the interviews will keep him occupied."

Her torso jerked. "The what?"

"I called the local theatre group. They're sending a few candidates to the house."

"For *Shicheii* to interview? Alone? What does *he* know about hiring an actor?"

"You really should give him more credit. He is more than capable of handling a minor task."

When the boat neared the shoreline, the outboard motor shutdown.

At the stern, Mayhem lifted the propeller from the water. "Eleven minutes. Good job, Running Bear." He hooked an arm for his team to follow him to the bow. When only one arrived, he said, "Please join us, Cat."

"Sorry. Thought you meant him."

After lifting her onto dry land, he dragged the boat to shore. Running Bear carried Klee's camera in case anyone asked questions.

"Our only objective is to watch and learn. If Killzme plans to post sentinels, we need some idea of where they'll be. Also, this opportunity allows us to familiarize ourselves with the hunting grounds in the daylight. Questions?"

Her hand raised.

"Speak freely, Cat."

"Aren't all the poachers here?"

"They are."

"So, we...?"

"Need to steer clear of them. For now, we are outmanned and under-armed." He waited for a response, but she accepted the dangerous circumstances. "Okie doke. Let's proceed."

Sunlight poured through the conifers, illuminating a clear path through the trees. They must stay together in case someone questioned them. At that point, they'd simply look like a bride and groom searching for photo opportunities.

Movement hastened Mayhem's steps, and he backed into the shadows with Cat.

High on a limb, two men secured tree stands to the trunk of a tall lodgepole pine. A few yards away, more men engaged in a similar activity. Near the lake's perimeter, he detected more movement.

Running Bear aimed the camera.

"Do not photograph them," he whispered. "We can't risk a flash. Simply, zoom in and report."

For several moments, the camera skimmed from tree to tree.

"Update me, please."

"We need to leave, Shadow Wolf. Now. Before they spot us." He grabbed Cat's arm to walk her out. "C'mon, Ghost Dog. You shouldn't be here."

Mayhem winced. Bold move on his part, but not at all effective. She was not the type of woman who took kindly to being treated like a delicate little flower. He'd learned that lesson the hard way.

"How dare you." Jerking her arm from his grasp, she dug in her heels. "I am your equal, dammit. And you will treat me like one." She jabbed a chin at Mayhem. "Right?"

*So adorable when she's angry at someone else.* "Yes, indeed."

"See?" With tight fists on her hips, she stepped even farther into her power. "If you don't tell us the problem, we can't fix it." She glanced over her shoulder. "Right?"

Suppressing a smile, he rocked a yes. "Precisely."

Running Bear's hand wagged between them. "Is this some type of foreplay?" The creases between his eyebrows deepened. "If we don't leave now, we'll be surrounded within five minutes. Six, tops."

"Okie doke. Cat?" When he extended his hand, she latched on. "Thank you." On the trek back to the boat, he said, "How many men?"

Running Bear clawed back his hair. "At least twenty. Maybe twenty-five."

"What activity? Target practice?"

"No. Securing the perimeter. Best guess? They'll plant Knighthawks in tree stands to prevent us from reaching the hunting grounds."

With the cost of an all-weekend event—fees, bribe money, cash prizes—Killzme guarding the woodlands was the smart play. Earlier, in cabin 505, Mr. Jameson confessed to receiving an alert from Rupert Russell to stay on the lookout for him and Cat. Additional security protected their bottom line.

What the entitled white man failed to consider was the heart of a warrior.

No one could prevent his team from battling the enemies of the Natural World. The Innocent Ones counted on them to win this war. And that's precisely what he intended to do. Killzme might have numbers on their side, but they lacked three crucial components—passion, destiny, and rectitude.

What Mayhem and his team lacked in manpower, they more than made up for in determination, perseverance, and heart. Ruthlessness also helped even the score.

*See you soon, dear trophy hunters.*

# Chapter 46



*Friday, 4:30 a.m.*

The importance of this mission weighed on me, and I tossed and turned all night. So, I hit the head, then slogged across the hall to see if my love machine was awake in the loft.

Not only did his bed sit empty, but the one beside it for Running Bear did, too. Guess they couldn't sleep, either. The stakes had never been higher. If we failed, Killzme would drive the one true American Buffalo to extinction. Forever.

Native People might never recover from a hit like that.

Even after my first encounter with the mighty creatures, I couldn't deny the connection between us. If my honey bun and *Shicheii* hadn't educated me in our shared love and respect for the animals, I probably wouldn't've pinpointed why they intrigued me so much, but everything within me strived to protect them.

Moonlight cascaded through the full-length window at the end of the hall. I strolled closer to bask in its energy. Grandmother Moon hung low in the sky, a visible face of craters, the circumference ringed by hues of bluish lavender.

A moonbeam traveled down into the yard, spotlighting the sexiest man alive. He hung upside down from a tree limb, his jean-clad knees hooked around it.

Eyes widening, an overabundance of saliva pooled on my tongue.

Shirtless, his chiseled abs and pecs flexed with every repetition of sit-ups. Hands clasped behind his head, the left elbow touched the right knee, the right bumped the left, deep creases around his hip bones more prominent than ever before, his light chestnut skin glistening with sweat.

A chin hit my head. "Enjoying the show, Ghost Dog?"

I sighed. "Every millisecond of it. I wish he did this every day."

"He does."

"He does? Why have I never seen it before?"

"You're probably asleep."

"Does he have a set time?" *So I can set my alarm.*

"Around four, four-fifteen, somewhere in there. How do you think he stays so ripped?"

"Guess I never really thought about it before. Does *Shicheii* know?"

"He's out there now. So was I before I caught you drooling in the window."

I dragged the back of my wrist across my lips. "I am not."

"Uh-huh. Come out with us. Jacy Lee made tea."

"Think Shadow Wolf would mind? What if he doesn't want me there?"

"To admire his physique? Yeah, you're right. What man would want that?"

I backhanded his chest. "Very funny."

"So, are you coming?"

"Not yet, but I could probably get there if you stopped hovering over my shoulder."

The one-liner cracked him up. "I bet you could." Around my neck, he slung a loose arm. "C'mon, he won't bite... unless you want him to."

Again, I backhanded him. "Shut up."

When Running Bear and I stepped out to the porch, he announced my presence. "Look who I found."

"Mourning Dove." Cradling my face in soft palms, *Shicheii* kissed my forehead. "Did you sleep well, honey?"

"Not really, but I'm okay. Too wound up. There's a lot riding on tonight."

"It *is* an important night." His wide smile confused me. "Sit. I made tea."

I couldn't tear my gaze away from Mayhem. None of us could. In the zone, he crunched and crunched, rising and lowering, twisting left and right, his long braid dangling with him.

"Cheveyo is an impressive man, isn't he?"

"Mm-hmm..."

Running Bear kicked me under the table.

"I mean, yeah, he sure is." I raised the mug, my lips searching for the rim without missing a beat of the show. "What's the rope for?"

No sooner did the words leave my mouth, and he did one last upside down crunch, snagged the rope hanging from the branch above, and pulled himself upright. Now standing in the tree, he leaned against an upper limb, and stepped off into nothingness.

My breath tangled around my ribs. A fall from that height could crack open his skull.

Doing push-ups on a tree branch, legs suspended mid-air, he used only brute strength to rise then lower, rise then lower, biceps, triceps, and lats flexing.

Jaw slacked, I could barely trust my eyes. "Wow. Just... wow."

While he pumped up and down, I bit the lip of my mug. This might be the sexiest thing I have ever seen, though catching him in the yard, buck naked and hosing himself down, was a close second. Back in Alaska, Poe bagged me that night, too.

"Where *is* the little diva? Super surprised he's not standing guard."

"He's sleeping in the nest with Spirit Crow," *Shicheii* said, a somberness to his tone.

"What about Odin?"

"Banished to the rim. Poe missed nesting with his mother. He's been feeling excluded lately."

Shit. Never thought about that. First, Odin steals his mom. Then I steal his dad. "Poor little dude."

*Shicheii* patted the top of my hand. "In time, he'll adjust."

If I survived that long. In the meantime, he could stab me in my sleep. Hell, he's probably sharpening his bill right now.

**6:39 a.m.**

After morning prayer, my grandfather served cheesy eggs—another of my favorites—biscuits and gravy, and granola topped fruit parfaits with chia seeds blended into Greek yogurt. Everyone waited for me and Spirit Crow to dig in before indulging. Chivalry never got old.

Mayhem raised a sideways fist in front of his mouth. "Delicious, my friend."

"He's right, *Shicheii*. Everything's perfect."

With a packed mouthful, Running Bear shot a thumbs-up.

"Thank you. I'm pleased you're enjoying it so much." *Shicheii* folded his hands on the table. "So, Cheveyo and Mourning Dove, any last-minute nerves?"

My lover's fork stopped midway to his mouth. "Nerves?"

"For your nuptials."

"Jacy Lee, we discussed this. The ceremony is part of our cover story."

"I'm aware of that."

He returned the bite to his plate. "Did you find someone to act as officiant?"

"I did."

"Does he know when to arrive?"

"He does."

"And he's aware he cannot blow our cover?"

"He is."

"Did he ask why we hired an actor to officiate a fictional ceremony?"

"He did not." *Shicheii* sipped his tea. "I think my decision will please you."

Gray eyes in a squint, he fired off more questions. "Did you call June?"

"I did."

"What aren't you telling me, Jacy Lee?"

Good question. It's not normal for him to refuse eye contact.

*Shicheii* raised the ceramic boat. "Would anyone like more gravy?"

Hand in the air, Running Bear grunted through all the food in his mouth.

"Jacy Lee, I would appreciate a response."

"Don't interrogate me, Cheveyo."

"This is not an interrogation. I simply asked if there is anything I should know."

All three corvids stared at *Shicheii*, prompting him to do something. But what remained a mystery.

"Oh, all right. I suppose now is as good of a time as any." He rose with Poe in his arms. "We have a surprise for you and Mourning Dove." Into the cabin he bustled with Spirit Crow and Odin flying close behind.

I suddenly lost my appetite. "What's he up to?"

"God only knows, Cat."

Many silent moments scrolled by before *Shicheii* emerged with Odin. A white bowtie circled his neck, tiny white buttons trailing down his chest. *Gronk, gronk.*

My heart overflowed with love. "*Awww...*"

Even Mayhem cracked a smile.

When Odin strutted closer, I leaned in. "How'd you do the buttons?"

"They're glued to a black pipe cleaner attached to his bowtie." *Shicheii* darted back into the cabin. This time, he set Spirit Crow on the table. With a pink ruffled collar, a ring of flowers haloed her angelic crown feathers. Hips wiggling, tail feathers swishing, she sauntered straight to her husband.

"You look beautiful, sweetheart."

*Coo... coo... coo...*

"Maid of honor." *Shicheii* hustled into the cabin. Through the screen door, he announced, "And here is your best man."

Poe hit the table donning a white bowtie and buttons like Odin, only with a top hat strapped under his bill, gold bling shimmering on ebony chest feathers. He struck several poses for an imaginary crowd of raving fans.

His dad's smile enveloped his face. "You are dashingly handsome, bud."

*Rattle, rattle. Rattle, rattle.*

A furrowed brow replaced the smile when he turned to his lifelong friend. "Though I admire your creativity, I'm afraid I don't quite understand."

"Every couple needs a bridal party, Cheveyo."

Running Bear slapped his mouth, and I sucked in my lips, neither of us willing to touch that comment.

His head shook as if trying to unscramble the nonsense. "You are aware, they cannot attend the ceremony. Nor can you, for that matter."

"Don't be silly. Of course, we'll be there."

"No, you will not."

"Cheveyo, be reasonable. Surely, you wouldn't prevent us from attending my granddaughter's wedding?"

"Her *fake* wedding. And yes, I am."

With the chinstrap in his talons, Poe slapped down the top hat in front of his dad. Spirit Crow leaped to my shoulder and Odin dove for Running Bear.

"Why are you angry with *me*? Cat and I have work to do. This is not a celebration."

Poe kicked the top hat off the table.

"Come on, bud." His father returned it to his head. "You know I'd take you if I could."

This time, Poe whipped the hat at me, and I quailed back, hands raised in surrender.

"Don't blame, Cat, either. Jacy Lee should never have raised your hopes."

"Mourning Dove"—*Shicheii* reached for me—"would you like your family to attend your wedding?"

"Her *fake* wedding."

"Cheveyo, you know better than most that I never thought I'd see my granddaughter again, never mind witness her grow and flourish and marry a man I have loved since he was a little boy. Real or fictional, why can't you let me have this one night?"

*Aw, man. Shicheii hit below the belt with that one.*

Mayhem held his gaze for what felt like hours. When he finally broke the silence, his raspy tone lacked its hard edge. "You promise not to get carried away?"

"I do."

"And you'll let us work?"

"I will."

"And you realize this is a fictional wedding?"

"I do."

"Cat," he said, probably hoping I'd be the voice of reason, "would you like your grandfather to attend the ceremony?"

The sad puppy dog eyes from *Shicheii* melted my heart and left only one correct response. "Yes."

"All right, Jacy Lee. You win."

Our corvid family erupted in cheer. *Rattle, rattle. Coo... coo... coo... Gronk, kuk, kuk, kuk.*

"Don't make me regret this decision."

"We won't, Cheveyo." *Famous last words.* "We'll stay in the background. You'll never even know we're there."

Why'd I get the feeling this would backfire?

# Chapter 47

*"Our first teacher is our own
heart."* —Cheyenne


*3:30 p.m.*

After training all day, Mayhem drove his team for a late lunch. In the parking lot of the Old Faithful Inn, he instructed Running Bear through the rearview mirror. "Please give us a head start for appearance's sake."

The bride and groom didn't normally dine with their wedding photographer.

As they strolled toward the entrance, he and Cat's clasped hands swung between them. "Good work today."

When she peered up at him, her electric emerald eyes quickened his heartbeat. Earlier, she forewent the colored contacts but agreed to wear the hair extensions. Hence why he opted for a different hotel.

"Your aim has greatly improved, Cat. Stay consistent, and you'll complete your second trial."

To become a full-fledged warrior, she must excel at four trials composed of various tasks, including but not limited to, successful missions.

"Really?"

"Really."

"Wow. Thought it'd take me a year to get my second."

"You've worked hard, Cat."

"Hey," her voice lowered to a whisper, "you're not giving me a pass because of Heaven, right?"

Dead in his tracks, he stopped. "Why would I? Our personal life has nothing to do with your training. Are you finding it difficult to separate the two?"

"Nope. Easier that way."

No reluctance shown on her. "If or when that changes, you'll let me know?"

"Hundred percent."

He smirked. "Are you peckish?"

"Put it this way. I could eat the butt cheeks out of a charging bull."

Never did he tire of her comical phrases. "The bull may object to that."

"Ha ha. Everyone's a comedian."

At the entrance to the dining hall, he braced open the door for Cat while Kuruk headed into the Bear Pit Lounge next door.

Inside the restaurant, a black-painted walkway led to a stone hearth and chimney. A crackling fire enhanced the ambiance.

"Whoa." Cat admired the open beam scissor trusses beneath a log ceiling. Modest chandeliers hung from chains, shades capping each light. "This is amazing."

"Fun fact. The Old Faithful Inn is one of the oldest standing log structures in the country."

The hostess's sudden appearance diverted Mayhem's attention away from the architecture. Because she was dressed in all black, Kendra's brass nameplate stood out. "Do you have a reservation?"

"We do not. Is one required?"

"For dinner, yes."

"What about a late lunch?"

"We're changing to the dinner buffet now."

*Only self-serve dining here?* "Does the Bear Pit Lounge serve food?"

"Sure does."

"Thank you for your time, Kendra." He escorted Cat into the lounge. Casual but nice atmosphere, with its etched glass panels and vintage furniture. The lack of a hostess sparked an idea. "We need guests for the ceremony, correct?"

"Yeah. Why?"

"Let's use this opportunity to our advantage." He led her to two tables pushed together to seat ten, pulling out her chair before lowering into his. "With limited seating at the bar, diners must share table space."

The menus depicted Old Faithful erupting.

As she perused the lunch options, her voice cracked. "Almost everything has bison meat in it."

"Seems counter-productive, doesn't it?"

"I can't eat here."

"What about the chicken burger?"

She tossed the menu on the table. "Fine, but if someone sits at our table with cooked Buffalo, I'm gonna lose my shit."

"Care for a cocktail, darlin'?" Mayhem didn't wait for a response. Instead, he darted to the bar, where Running Bear bit into a juicy bison burger. "Please don't let her see you eat that. She's having a difficult time reconciling the hunter/gatherer lifestyle with the mission."

With packed cheeks, he said, "Her loss."

"Looks delicious." The beefy aroma watered his mouth. "Sauteed onions and mushrooms?"

"Mm-hmm. Want a bite?"

"No, thank you. I value my home life."

The bartender—a cheery fellow named Isaiah—slapped down a bar napkin. "What can I getcha?"

"Do you have any peppermint schnapps?"

"No, sorry."

"Kahlua?"

He wagged another no.

"All right, then. Two Huckleberry Cosmo Martinis, please. May I also place our lunch order with you, Isaiah?"

"Sure."

"Thank you. Two Red Bird natural chicken burgers."

Through a packed mouthful, Running Bear chuckled.

"And two Caesar salads, please."

Moments later, Isaiah set the martinis down in front of Mayhem. "I'll bring your meal to you."

"Thank you kindly."

Another couple had joined Shawnee at the far end of the table, both actively engaged in perusing the limited menu items.

Lowering to his chair, he slid the cocktail to Cat. "Try that on for size."

"What is it?"

"Huckleberry Cosmo Martini."

"That tells me nothing." She sniffed the drink. "What's in it?"

"Grand Teton Huckleberry Vodka, Triple Sec, lime juice, and orange zest. Try it. I think you'll enjoy it."

"You think, or you know?"

"Cat, please." He pinched the bridge of his nose. "I did not create the menu."

The stiffness of her shoulders eased. "I know. It just sucks to think of Resi's relatives confined like cattle, fattened in feedlots, and raised for slaughter so some scumbag can serve them on a bun."

He slung his arm around the back of her chair, whispered, "Please lower your voice."

"Why? Everyone should know what's happening. How can they admire majestic animals through the window while gnawing on their flesh?" She zeroed in on Running Bear. "What's he eating?"

"For lunch?" To buy time, he sipped the martini.

"Looks good."

"It does, doesn't it." Again, his mouth watered. "How's your cocktail, Kitty Cat?"

Two men in fatigues entered the lounge, one with a camouflage cap, one with a shaved head.

Mayhem swiveled toward her, his voice low and whisperous. "Do you recall how we photographed the gala?"

"Where are they?"

"Heading to the bar."

Right on cue, she jumped into his lap, her cell held out in front of them to take a selfie as a memento. Instead of the snapshot button, she thumbed video record, the phone waving to the right, left, up, and down, their heads bobbing into and out of the frame.

"Can you do it, *Gaagii*? I can't get the right background."

"Certainly, darling." As the poachers ventured farther into the lounge, he swiveled her with him. Cell held high and away, their foreheads stayed at the bottom of the screen. "How's that?"

"Perfect. Let's take a few shots." She held her lips on his cheek while he thumbed an imaginary button. "Funny face." She posed with her tongue lolled out the corner of her mouth. "Now, serious." She sucked in her cheeks. "And... kiss."

With his gaze hidden behind the smoky sunglasses, he focused on the trophy hunters while holding the kissing pose. Because the prey stood at the back of the line, the ruse worked remarkably well.

"Thanks, honey bun." She leaped out of his lap.

When Isaiah delivered their lunch, he smiled at her antics, but the woman at the end of their table diverted his attention.

"Can you take our order?" she said.

Isaiah set a Caesar salad in front of Mayhem. "Sure."

"Two Moose Drool Brown Ales and two bison burgers, medium."

*Oh, boy. Please don't lash out, Cat.*

Sure enough, she sneered at the couple.

"Before you go, Isaiah. Could we have takeout containers? My wife suddenly isn't feeling well."

"Sure."

"Thank you. Apologies for the inconvenience."

Under the table, he texted Running Bear.

> Cat can't stay here. We'll wait for you outside.

> Copy that.

While Mayhem packed their lunch to go, she guzzled her martini. Once she polished off every drop, she eyeballed his. "You gonna finish that?" Grimacing, her glare flicked at the couple. Before she lost her cool, he passed her his drink, and she shot it back in one gulp.

"Okie doke." He offered her his arm. "Shall we, darling?"

As they passed the couple, Cat leaned in between them. "Hope you choke on that bison burger, you fuckin' hypocrites."

"Excuse me?" The wife looked appalled, and rightfully so.

"Nervous bride on her wedding day." Mayhem slapped down two hundred dollars. "Let me pay for your meal."

As he pushed Shawnee toward the exit, her arms flung wide. "Why come to Yellowstone? To eat the animals?"

Unwilling to cause a scene, Mayhem tossed her over one shoulder.

She pounded his back. "Put me down, dammit."

"I will not let you destroy this mission," he said through gritted teeth. "Now, settle down, or you and I *will* have a problem."

Defeated, her stiff body limped on his shoulder.

In the parking lot, he lowered her feet to the pavement. "Well, there went the completion of your second trial."

"Really?" Nothing but confidence exuded from her. "What if I did it on purpose?"

"Did you?"

"Wait and see."

"Cat, please help me understand why you'd purposefully jeopardize the mission?"

*Did she roll her eyes?*

"Like I told you before, I know how white men think."

"In the future, I wish you'd run things by me."

Running Bear slid into the backseat. "Ghost Dog's performance rattled them."

"See?" Her smug smile held merit.

"I stand corrected. Good job, Cat." Into the rearview mirror, he said, "Rattled how?"

"Right after you left, both started texting like crazy."

"We need those phones."

"It'll be faster on foot."

Mayhem leaped out the driver's door.

"What about the crowds? The park's jam-packed." Cat jogged to keep up with their long strides, fearlessness evident in her gait. "What if we looped wide to cut 'em off?"

"Good idea, Cat."

When the trophy hunters hit the trailhead, they trekked behind a large group of hikers for a half-mile before Mayhem gestured for Running Bear to head East. He and Shawnee veered West into unbroken wilderness, the terrain thick with undergrowth. If they didn't make up time, the prey might escape.

Mayhem accelerated into a sprint, with Cat right on his heels. Through the forest they ran, slapping branches out of their way, until they'd circled an impromptu campsite. When he stopped, he pulled her to squat beside him.

The trophy hunters sat in folding chairs in front of a smoldering campfire. Strange objects dangled from the arms of skeletal branches, but Mayhem was too far away to distinguish any details. Beyond the site, Running Bear crouched in a tree, hand-signaling for them to approach.

That was not the smart play. Men put their guards up around other men. His gaze strayed to Cat.

"You want me to walk up to 'em, huh?"

"I do."

"And say what?"

"Get creative. You excel in that area."

"Flattery will get you everywhere."

As she headed for the camp, she dragged sticks and debris from her hair extensions. Once she emerged from the thick underbrush, she drew the attention of both men, who acted startled to see a gorgeous lone female.

"Sorry to bother you." Cat waved with her cell in her hand. "A grizzly chased my fiancé, and I've been trying to find him ever since. Do you guys have service? I got no bars."

The bald one said, "A grizzly, huh?"

"Yep. Can I log into your hotspot or borrow your phone?"

"Weren't you in the Bear Pit Lounge earlier?"

Crouched low, Mayhem darted closer. Running Bear lowered down the trunk.

*Choose wisely, dear trophy hunter, or your next move may be your last.*

# Chapter 48

*5:01 p.m.*

Playing stupid, I said, "Where?"

"Those eyes." The bald dude's buddy backhanded him. "Check the photo. I think we just found the golden goose."

*Aw, shit.*

In the Arctic, after that asshole, Witherspoon, tacked the million-dollar bounty to our heads, he faxed our photos to five thousand Killzme Corp members.

Now, even with the hair extensions, these two camp-dwelling dirtbags recognized me. In hindsight, I probably should've worn the colored contacts, but with little sleep and training all day, I didn't feel like it. Bad enough I had to keep them in all night.

"Look, pal." On the outside, I played it cool, nerves sizzling under my skin. "Can I use your phone or not?"

Multiple tree branches suspended tiny red discs.

"What are those?" I rose to tippy toes, my neck straining for clarity.

Once I made the connection, my heart dropped to somewhere near my ankles. Each disc depicted a white cross with a blood droplet in the center. Another symbol of Klan affiliation.

My frantic gaze searched for a safe place to land but couldn't find any. So, I spun to bolt, but the skinhead grabbed a fistful of hair, my extensions dislodging to free me.

The skinhead raised the ebony strands. "What the fuck is this shit?"

After I kneed him in the balls, I almost made a clean getaway till Running Bear caught me.

"Lean into it, Ghost Dog. We need intel." With a loose arm over my shoulders, he walked me straight back into danger. "Your ol' lady shouldn't run through the forest alone. About a half-mile from here, a grizzly tore apart some poor bastard."

"What?" Fake bawling, I broke away from him. "Charlie," I wailed. More fake tears accompanied my pacing. "Someone call the wardens!" I whirled toward Running Bear. "Can I borrow your phone? I can't get a signal out here."

"Thanks for bringing her back to camp." The skinhead dropped my hair extensions. "We'll take it from here."

"Are you sure? I'm happy to loan her my phone."

"All good. We've taken up enough of your time."

When the skinhead leaned forward to shake his hand, Running Bear head-butted him in the face. His buddy drew a pistol. But before he got a shot off, Mayhem rose behind him like the Grim Reaper, severing the Klansman's throat from ear to ear.

The skinhead flashed milky-pink palms. "Easy now. No one else gotta die today."

"Oh, really?" I got right in his face. "What about all the Buffalo you plan to slaughter tonight?"

"Valid question, darling." Piercing gray eyes focused on the skinhead. "Disrespect the lady, and I might lose my patience." A hard breath huffed out his nostrils like a bull ready to charge. "Phone, please."

A shaky hand withdrew the cell from the leg pocket of his camos. Once Running Bear passed it back to me, he muscled the skinhead into a chair.

After scanning the dude's ugly mug, I scrolled through the most recent texts, my heart fissuring from the names Redskin and Mutt.

I shoved the screen in his face. "Who'd you send this to?"

Ever so slightly, Mayhem's head rocked. "Does the message not list a recipient?"

"He blocked it."

"And you cannot unblock because...?"

"Already did. The contact has no name." I smoothed my lips. "May I do my job, please?"

His throat cleared. "Certainly."

Inches from the skinhead's face, I shook the screen. "Well?"

"Above my paygrade."

I stepped back. "Kill him."

Flat hands flew out in front of him. "Wait!"

*Works every time.*

"We had orders to text a location to that number if we spotted you."

My two protectors looked to me for a decision on whether to believe him.

"I call bullshit."

"It's true!"

"Then why block the number?"

"Err…"

"Good catch, darling." With the tip of the hunting knife pressed under the Klansman's chin, he raised the skinhead to his feet. "Full name, please?"

"Gary Hilton."

My chest tightened. "Horace Hilton's son?" CEO of Killzme Corp's shell company.

"Nephew."

"Interesting." An evil little grin crossed Mayhem's lips. "Will your uncle join the festivities tonight?"

"Can't. He's in Kenya for a few weeks."

*As in, Africa?* "Doing what, exactly?"

"He's got nothing to do with tonight's hunt."

"Fine." I swayed a disinterested shoulder. "Kill him."

My personal badass raised the knife.

"Wait!"

I got right in the skinhead's face. "What's he doing in Kenya?"

"Organizing a hunt."

"No shit, genius. What's he hunting?"

"Big game."

"Are you stupid or just ignorant? What. Animal?"

"I'd rather not say."

With the pistol aimed at the skinhead, Running Bear racked a bullet into the chamber. "I've had enough of this racist."

"Do not react in haste." Two gloved fingers pushed away his gun. "He was about to offer valuable intel. Weren't you, Mister Hilton? And this time, you best answer the lady's question. You are dangerously close to death."

Cowering, he squeaked out, "Elephants."

A numbness branched through my body. I couldn't speak, couldn't comprehend the cruelty. The species barely hung on, with poaching wiping out ninety-six elephants per day. Every. Single. Day. And the problem only worsened.

My anger got the better of me, and I drove my heel into his balls. Hands on his gonads, he keeled over. I lunged on top of him, scrambling to straddle his hips.

"Whaddaya think your buddies in Kenya would say about your Klan bullshit?" I slid my knife out of my moccasin—raised it over my head in two hands—and drove the blade into his cold, ruthless heart, my chest heaving from the adrenaline rush.

"Cat?" Once he lifted me off the skinhead, gentle touches swept sweaty hair off my face. "How are you, darlin'?"

I stared straight through him. "Not sure yet."

"Okie doke. Let's head back to the suite so you can rest." With my bloody fingers stitched with his, he led me away from the two dead Klansmen—good riddance. "Running Bear, would you mind handling things from here?"

"Sure, but you're my ride home."

"Valid point. How about this? Drag the corpses into the tent. With Klan affiliation evident in the trees, it should persuade authorities to look elsewhere if the wildlife doesn't devour them. Cat and I will wait for you on the ridge."

"Copy that."

After trekking through heavily wooded terrain, my spirit broken from Killzme's future plans, I leaned back on a tree, one raised moccasin flat on the bark. "We can't let 'em hunt elephants. We just can't."

"Cat, what do you propose we do, fly to Kenya?"

I flung up my hands. "Yes—"

"How would we transport our family?" He played with the ends of my hair. "International travel is tricky."

"They're killing elephants. Elephants! You know how much they mean to me. Can't you at least consider it?"

Instead of answering me, he withdrew his phone, his thumbs working the keypad. "We can't leave your extensions behind. You'll need them for tonight."

"What about the elephants?"

He massaged his forehead. "Cat, may we please concentrate on one mission at a time?"

"Does that mean you'll mull it over, see if it's doable?" I batted my lashes. "*Please...*"

When his head rocked, I knew I had him. "You wield your feminine weapons well."

"That a yes? You'll think it over, try to figure it out?"

Audible exhale. "Of course, I will."

Running Bear clomped through the underbrush, long bloody hair clasped in his fist. "Probably want to wash it first, Ghost Dog."

"Gee, ya think? How am I supposed to walk past the front desk now?"

Mayhem stripped off his shirt for me to wear over mine, so hikers wouldn't spot the blood on our return trip to the Benz. "We'll enter through the back."

"With all the trophy hunters there?"

Heading toward our path through the wilderness, he didn't respond. Not that I blamed him. What choice did we have? I looked exactly like Killzme's photos. Might as well paint a bullseye on my back.

**6:40 p.m.**

Parked in front of the Lake Hotel, I scrolled through the skinhead's phone while we waited for Running Bear to grab me some sort of disguise from the gift shop.

"Any luck matching a name to the recipient, Cat?"

"Not yet. Does the other phone list the same number?"

"It does."

"Blocked?"

"It is."

"Any texts?"

"Only one. Identical to the message you found."

"What if we baited the recipient?"

The eyebrows lifted. "With?"

"Dunno yet. Just throwin' it out there."

"Fair enough. Let's circle back once you have a solid plan in place."

Was this like a final exam for my second trial? I wouldn't rule it out.

Running Bear slipped into the backseat, tossing a shopping bag on the middle console.

I dragged out a tan bucket hat and hot-pink shades shaped like cat's eyes. "You can't be serious. Do you even know me?"

"There weren't many options, Ghost Dog."

The oversized tee—also tan—had a giant Buffalo head. Sparkly lettering beneath read *Yellowstone: More Valuable Than Gold*. "I like the slogan, at least. Why do I need this?"

"I doubt Shadow Wolf wants to enter the hotel shirtless."

Good point, but his taste in clothing sucked. "Clearly, he learned nothing from shopping with you."

He chuckled. "I can only do so much, Cat."

With the t-shirt on, I stuffed my hair into the ridiculous hat and slid on the equally stupid shades. "I look like an idiot."

"Agreed. It's perfect. Good job, Running Bear." He darted around to my door.

When I rose, I said, "Agreed?"

"Pardon?"

"I said, I look like an idiot. And you agreed."

His Adam's apple rose and fell. "Did I?" Over the roof, he said, "Meet us no later than eight-forty-five but do not—I repeat—*do not* let Jacy Lee run wild. And please try to talk him out of bringing the others. We have no way to keep an eye on them."

"He's my elder, Shadow Wolf."

"Mine, as well. He is also reasonable, level-headed, and fully aware of the stakes."

"I'll do my best."

"Thank you. If you don't spot us right away, please reassure Jacy Lee we are on our way, so he doesn't come looking for us."

"Copy that. See ya on the flop, Ghost Dog." He ducked into the driver's seat.

Moments later, the Benz cruised down the road while we moseyed around the side of the building. Activity beyond the cabins slowed my steps, but he squeezed my hand, urging me to "keep your eye on the prize" aka the back door.

In the distance, a work crew assembled a white canopy over rows of chairs.

"Is that for us?"

"It is."

"What're we gonna do about the guest list?"

He swung open the door. "Let me worry about that."

"Do you have a plan?"

"I usually do, Cat. Most of life's problems aren't that difficult to solve."

Up the staircase, I trekked, trying to unravel the deeper meaning to his words. Maybe he meant day-to-day struggles, like misplacing the phone charger or running out of batteries for the remote. Or even, rushing around after waking late for work. Minor things that tended to snowball into a day from hell.

Rather than continue to let minor inconveniences pile up, he taught me to stop. Inhale, mindful of every breath. Exhale, slow and long. This allowed the mind and spirit to regain its normal rhythm. All we needed to do was get out of its way. Easier said than done while entangled in chaos.

He never allowed outside forces to rattle him. A trait I hadn't mastered yet, but it wasn't easy while being hunted by a ruthless corporation who'd stop at nothing to protect their bottom line.

Chivalrous as ever, my faux hubby palmed open the suite door for me.

Once inside, excitement spiraled up my spine. "A coded message."

Blank stare. "Pardon?"

"The text." I ripped off my ridiculous disguise. "We send it in code. We've got the cipher. Why not use it to our advantage?"

"Correction. We have Elliot's cipher."

"So?"

"If Killzme used the same one, any of their top-tier could decode the dirt he uncovered."

"Right. Sorry." I massaged my forehead. "Sleepless nights are wearing me down."

"Once we complete the mission, what if we stole a few days alone?"

Body tingling all over, I bit my lower lip.

"Kitty Cat, I didn't mean now. We have work to do."

"I know." I let my gaze wander from head to foot. "Just enjoying the view."

He stepped closer—hesitated—then backed away. "That sensuous look makes it awfully difficult to flip off the switch."

"I want those days."

"As do I."

"Alright, deal." I glanced away. "Veering back into work-mode."

"Thank you."

When I headed for the living room, he followed. "I bet Luther or one of his cronies stashed the cipher on their phones. How else would they respond to texts?"

"Perhaps they memorized it."

"All of 'em? Even the skinhead?"

"It does seem unlikely."

"Right?" I nestled into the loveseat. "Let's word the text, so it requires a response."

Across from me, he lowered to the upholstered chair. "You are plum full of ideas tonight."

"Probably get even more creative with a little bubbly in me."

With a chuckle, he slapped his thighs and rose. "You *are* a character."

"Thanks. I think."

While he fetched the champagne, I lined up the devices on the coffee table. All three phones had the same mystery number in their contacts. Scrolling through the text messages, I found several with a numeric code, every digit separated by an underscore, some as high as one-hundred-one. None of the texts used one-hundred-two or higher.

Also, the second digit never rose above twelve. No consistency or commonalities for the remaining numbers, including the amount. Some messages had only six coded words, some strings much longer, which probably meant they were instructions of some sort. The incoming texts contained many more digits than the responses.

I rubbed my palms together. "Now we're getting somewhere."

In the foyer, my pretend hubby chatted on the landline. Curiosity piqued, I curled my hair around my ear. *Shicheii's* medicine, prayers, and attentive nurturing improved my hearing on the right side, but the eardrum still crackled and popped at times.

"Pleased to hear it, June. The reason for my call may seem anomalous at first. Believe me, I understand the magnitude of my request. Because of the scheduling change, many of our guests canceled due to the inability to find earlier flights."

Smart to remind the nosy bitch of her mistake. How could she say no?

"Of course not. No one blames you, June. These things happen. Pardon?" he said, like she'd talked over him. "Aren't you sweet. Thank you. The reason for my call is this. Every bride wants her special day to be perfect, though I'm afraid the cancellations have hit Kai rather hard. My wife is such a tender-hearted soul."

Silence filled the suite.

"I don't know what we'd do without you, June. Couples and single ladies only, please. Pardon?"

June must've interrupted him again.

"Same sex couples would fall into that category, as well. Mm-hmm, yes. Gay men included. Oh, I see what you're asking. Allow me to expound. Any couple, regardless of sexual orientation or gender, is more than welcome to attend. Neither I nor my wife judge individuals by who they love. What matters most is Kai's comfort level. I think you'd agree she is extremely easy on the eyes."

*Aww... so sweet.* Warmth flushed my cheeks. "Hence my reluctance to invite single straight men," he added, ensuring she didn't invite Killzme scum, "who may ogle her or misread nonverbal cues from other female guests."

The next pause lasted the longest.

"Tory?"

She must've rambled because a lot of "uh-huh's" followed.

"Oh, that sounds perfect. I cannot thank you enough, June. Kai will be so relieved." Quick pause this time. "See you then."

When he returned to the living room, he passed me a flute filled with fresh strawberries and champagne. "June agreed to handle the guest list."

Pretending I hadn't overheard the conversation, I said, "Cool. One less thing to worry about." I patted the cushion beside me. "Gotta show you somethin'."

"Did you identify the recipient?"

"Not yet. Still working on the cipher, but I noticed some consistencies." While I explained the cutoff number and how the second digit stayed below twelve, I shared the screen of Luther's phone. "Why would the first two numbers show commonalities across all four devices?"

"They must refer to the cipher itself, and the remaining digits carry the message."

"Then it can't be more than a hundred and one pages long."

"Agreed."

"Hmm... Must be a document of some sort, no?"

"Possibly."

While he scrolled through Luther's phone, I snatched Russell's laptop. Silence filled the room as we combed through documents, searching for anything with exactly one-hundred-one pages.

After an hour of hitting one dead end after another, he said, "If you plan to shower, Cat, you may want to stop searching. The ceremony begins in a little over an hour."

"You go. I'm too close."

"We may not find the cipher in time."

"Yes, we will."

"I admire your positivity. I really do. However, sometimes answers stay beyond our reach."

Focused on the screen, I shooed him away. "I'll jump in when you're done."

"All right, then."

When the water turned on, I reclined my head. If it's not a document, what else had that many pages?

# Chapter 49

*"If you are distressed by any-thing external, the pain is not due to the thing itself, but to your estimate of it. And this you have the power to revoke at any moment."* —Marcus Aurelius

*8:10 p.m.*

Mayhem was braiding his wet hair when Cat barreled into the bedroom. "Found it!" Jumping up and down, her excitement was infectious. "I found the cipher."

"Brava. Did you decode the message?"

"Not yet. I'm on it." She sprinted out of the room.

He darted after her. "Cat, you need to jump in the shower."

"What time is it?" She snatched a phone off the coffee table. "It's after eight?"

"Where's the cipher? I'll decode it while you get ready."

When she spun the laptop, he squinted at the screen.

"It's like their bible, I guess."

*Kloran: Knights of the Ku Klux Klan.* "How many pages?"

"Exactly one-oh-one. All four have a digital copy. Every member must get one when they join."

As he scrolled through the booklet, the sheer volume of vitriol and superiority astounded him. Their so-called "Kreed" on page two sickened him.

> *We recognize our relation to the government of the British Empire, the supremacy of its constitution, and the constitutional laws thereof, and we shall be ever devoted to the sublime principles of a pure patriotism and valiant in the defense of its ideals and institutions.*

The laws they held in such high regard viewed Native People as "backward" and dangerous. In their limited view, American Indians represented what English men and women thought they were not, and more importantly, what they must not become.

Leaders warned the colonists to strictly adhere to the laws and "moral guidelines" that defined their communities. Otherwise, they'd become "Indianized," meaning uncivilized and to serve the devil.

A fiery rage simmered inside him as he lowered to the loveseat.

In the age of Columbus, Europeans viewed themselves as Christians, the most "spiritually pure" people in creation. Yet this ideology excluded Muslims, against whom Christians waged holy wars for centuries, and Jews, who remained outsiders to European society.

Such strong beliefs in a unitary religion caused the white man to target nonbelievers for conversion to the "one true faith" or segregated them for enslavement and/or death.

Shawnee's soothing hand rested on his shoulder. "You alright?"

Gazing up at her, he forced a grin. "Be mindful of the time, Kitty Cat."

"I'm on it." She darted into the bedroom.

While she showered, Mayhem worked on the message that used Killzme's racist codewords. First digit was the page number, second showed paragraph. From there, he counted individual words to convert the hidden text.

*Nighthawks stationed in multiple tree-stands to shoot Redskin and Mutt on sight. Text coordinates if you spot the couple. Cash rewards for accurate sightings plus extra points added to your score.*

He texted Running Bear.

*Round up the locals.*

*All of them?*

*Yes, please.*

*That's different.*

Thumbs working the keypad, he chuckled.

*Bring Poe.*

*Couldn't talk Jacy Lee out of it, anyway.*

When Cat emerged from the bathroom, she wore a black leather boned-bodice with underwire cups. A black, feather-like train circled her hips and flowed to the floor, the tops of her thighs concealed underneath, silky material framing her sculptured legs. The Apache-Tear-and-bone choker he'd bought her ringed her neck.

"Did you pack my armband?"

"You're stunning, Kitty Cat." He couldn't tear his gaze away. Though he'd helped her choose this dress, he returned to the men's side of the boutique before she tried it on. "Absolutely breathtaking."

A blush swept across her high cheekbones. "Thanks." Compliments made her uncomfortable. "Armband?"

"Zippered compartment."

"Need to put the contacts in before we go. Did you decode the text?"

"I did." He explained Killzme's plan to ensure a successful hunt, and the best course of action to stop them. At this hour, sending a coded text would do little good, but he saved the info for future dealings. "Crossing the lake might be more challenging if they positioned Knighthawks around the perimeter."

"We'll be exposed out there."

"Not if we spot them first."

Wagging her head, she flashed her palm. "Don't even say it."

"Cat, please. Poe has binocular vision. We do not."

"You saw his reaction at Heaven. It's bad enough he's attending the wedding. How do you think he's gonna take it when he watches me exchange vows with his dad? He won't know it's fake. And he'll enact revenge the second we're alone in those woods."

"I will speak to him about it."

"Before or after he slices my throat?"

"Poe is a valued member of this team. You know as well as I do, he has never let personal grievances stand in the way of a successful mission."

Muttering to herself, she strolled into the bedroom, the train billowing behind her.

*Let's hope Poe doesn't forego his professionalism tonight.*

**8:50 p.m.**

As he and Cat neared the ceremony grounds, Tory bounded over. "The groom can't see the bride before the wedding." She shuttled her away. "It's bad luck."

Cat glanced back at him. "But we're already married."

Under the canopy, Jacy Lee sat in the front row, all the seats behind him full of happy strangers. Though nothing suspicious stood out, it'd not be out of the realm of possibilities for Killzme to plant an undercover operative.

"*Yá'át'ééh*, my friend." Mayhem patted his shoulder. "Where's the officiant?"

"Stefon is speaking to the DJ, I believe. Did Mourning Dove—?"

"Kai."

"Did Kai want a specific song to walk down the aisle?"

"Not that I'm aware of, no. Where is the rest of our family?"

He glimpsed Grandmother Moon, rising higher in the night sky. "Waiting for you to head down the aisle."

"Thank you for handling this so well, Jacy Lee. I apologize for any reservations I may have had."

When Mayhem stepped onto the carpet that led to an archway of roses, Odin and Poe landed in front of him. The audience oohed and ahhed. Poe seized the opportunity to lap up the attention, striking several poses with his top hat and bowtie.

Little rascal.

A man with a wild mane of blond hair stood at the altar. "You must be *Gaagii*."

"I am." He shook his hand. "Pleasure to make your acquaintance, Stefon."

When the instrumental music began, Mayhem turned. Spirit Crow sauntered down the aisle, hips wiggling, tail feathers swaying. A flowered halo cradled her feathery crown, pink ruffles ringed around her neck.

Behind her, Jacy Lee walked Cat down the aisle. Perhaps he'd stepped in to offer comfort. All the coloring of her face drained, like she'd blurred the lines between fact and fiction.

Though she would make a beautiful bride one day.

Once she reached the altar, Mayhem loaned her soothing energy through clasped hands. Behind them, Spirit Crow and Odin stood across from one another while Poe sought more praise from the audience.

Rather than take his seat, Jacy Lee squeezed in beside Stefon. If he performed the ceremony—Mayhem's frantic gaze shot to Cat, and her shoulders lifted.

"Thank you all for joining *Gaagii* and Kai on this special night," he said. "Because of Kai's mixed heritage, Stefon represents her European roots while I honor Native tradition. Let's pray."

Upper cheek twitching, Mayhem thinned his eyes. *What do you think you're doing, Jacy Lee?*

"Now, you will feel no rain, for each of you will be shelter for the other."

His cheery tone clenched Mayhem's abdominal muscles.

"Now, you will feel no cold, for each of you will be warmth for the other. Now, there is no more loneliness, for each of you will be a companion for the other. Now, you are two persons, but there is only one life before you. May beauty surround you both in the journey ahead and through all the years. May happiness be your constant companion and your days together be good and long upon the Earth."

Satisfaction gleamed in his smile. "Stefon?"

If the actor led the vows, they should be fine. Weight lifted off his shoulders.

"*Gaagii*," Stefon said, "please face Kai."

When Mayhem turned, he reassured her with a gentle squeeze of her hands.

"Repeat after me, please. I choose you, Kai, again and again."

But telepathically, Jacy Lee's voice drowned out the actor. *I choose you, Cat/Shawnee, again and again. At the start and finish of every single day, no matter the season, no matter the year.*

With panic thrashing at his ears, he glared his lifelong friend. *What are you doing, Jacy Lee?*

*Marrying my granddaughter. Neither I nor the Holy Ones will let you make a mockery out of marriage.*

The word *mockery* rocked him back. He of all people knew how Mayhem cherished the sanctity of marriage. Hence why he'd hired an actor to avoid offending the spiritual realm.

Speechless, Mayhem parted his lips.

After several moments of silence, Stefon hushed, "*Gaagii*, do you need me to repeat the vow?"

"Yes, please."

*Jacy Lee, you are stripping your granddaughter of her free will.*

His gaze returned to Shawnee. *Cat! Can you hear me?* But she didn't react—the warning cry blocked by her grandfather's dominance.

*Repeat the vow, Cheveyo. Now.*

*Jacy Lee, please don't do this to her. You are robbing her of the ability to consent. I'll marry her when the time is right, if—and only if—she wants to marry me.*

*The longer you delay, the more you risk losing her. Recite the vow, Cheveyo, or you will endanger the woman you love.*

With no alternative, Mayhem said, "I choose you, Kai, again and again." He stole a moment to catch his breath, his heart bleeding for Cat to at least have the option to walk away. "At the start and finish of every single day, no matter the season, no matter the year."

Stefon's tone barely registered in the background, Jacy Lee's unmatched prowess more powerful than ever.

*I choose you to struggle and succeed with, to fight and make up with, to love and grow old with. I choose you, Cat/Shawnee, knowing there are still trails we must travel, knowing there are mountains left to climb. I choose you to always be by my side, Cat/Shawnee.*

When Mayhem echoed the vows, tears glassed her chocolate brown contacts. "I choose you to always be by my side, Kai."

The routine continued, with Jacy Lee telepathically instructing his granddaughter to recite the vow. Even with Cheveyo in place of *Gaagii*, Mayhem couldn't tell if she understood what this meant.

*By the power invested in me, I now pronounce you husband and wife.*

Jacy Lee quieted for Stefon to say, "You may kiss the bride."

Applauding, the audience rose to their feet.

Her sweet lips soothed his frazzled mind. "Kitty Cat, if I'd known—"

"Known what?"

Oh, boy. This news may not land well. But with the possibility of Killzme here, he'd have to wait until they cleared the wedding grounds to tell her.

Before he and Cat left the altar, Jacy Lee slipped the marriage certificate into Mayhem's pocket.

*Be sure you both sign, Cheveyo. There is your consent.*

*If she feels trapped or cornered in any way, I will never forgive you for this.*

*Understood. Keep my granddaughter safe. Many obstacles await you tonight.*

# Chapter 50



My faux hubby acted strange after the vows. No idea why. Personally, I enjoyed having *Shicheii* with us. So what if he led the opening praying? The actor performed the ceremony. No harm done.

"Ladies and gentlemen," *Shicheii* addressed the guests, "it is my honor and privilege to introduce Mister and Missus Thunderhawk."

The audience went wild when we darted down the aisle. Running Bear snapped multiple photos before dragging us off to the side, where Poe kicked around his top hat, taking a total hissy fit.

*Guess someone forgot to tell him the ceremony wasn't real.*

Squatted in front of him, his dad said, "Hey, bud."

Talons pulled at his bowtie, like he couldn't stand to wear it another second.

"I understand you're upset, Poe. Jacy Lee didn't leave us much choice."

"What'd *Shicheii* do?"

After ripping the bowtie-and-buttons-combo over his head, Pissy Pants whipped it on the ground with his top hat.

"What would you have us do? You are fully aware of the stakes, are you not?"

Poe literally turned his back to his father. Bold move. Not sure what was happening here. At the altar, he acted fine in front of Stefon. Why would *Shicheii* upset him? Or maybe, his attitude had nothing to do with us.

Regardless, something royally pissed him off.

"Yoo-hoo, Mister and Missus Thunderhawk." June dashed over, a wide smile enveloping her face. "Tory asked if DJ Dan could play your first dance songs?"

When my pretend hubby rose, his legs blocked a spitting mad Poe. "Certainly." He pulled me to his side, his muscular arm locked around my waist. "Kai and I will be right there."

"Mable and Gladys swooned over the bridal party. Are they crows or ravens?"

"Both, actually."

"Just adorable. And so well-behaved."

Poe nipped at the back of my shins.

"Two are, anyway." Little bastard was lucky he didn't draw blood. Still, every bite ground my molars more and more.

"Pardon?" June's head cocked like a pup watching their human cry for the first time. "The best man was the cutest little thing ever. What a character."

"Kai's pride and joy." He jostled me. "Isn't he, darling?"

*Not even close.* "I thought Tory was expecting you."

"Ooh, thank you. I better run. Congratulations on the nuptials." She skipped away, like she'd gotten married tonight. Too bad I couldn't tell her the ceremony was all a cleverly plotted mirage.

Once she left, I whirled toward Poe. "What the fuck is your problem?"

"Cat, please. Not now."

*Was he flustered? Huh. Never seen that before.*

"Is the boat ready, Running Bear?"

"'Course. It's onshore beyond the trees, like we discussed."

Must've missed that plan, but whatever. At least now, we didn't need to trek all the way to the docks.

"And the locals?"

"Standing by."

"Perfect. Thank you, Running Bear. After Cat and I dance, urge us to head to the lake for wedding photos."

"Copy that."

Again, my fake hubby squatted in front of the little diva. "I need your cooperation tonight, bud. Would a peanut help raise your spirits?"

One slow nod.

He dropped the bribe at Poe's enormous feet.

While the brat picked at the shell, his dad redressed him in the bowtie and top hat. "Thank you, handsome."

*Rattle, rattle.* Pissy Pants glanced me up and down with disgust, like I'd intruded on their private conversation. Friggin' psycho needed an attitude adjustment.

The only reason I didn't wage a counterattack for biting me was for the mission. On any other night, I would've let him have it.

But the truth was, we did need his help, as much as it pained me to admit.

Arm-in-arm, my pretend hubby and I strode to the grassy area doubling as a dancefloor. Before the music blared, I whispered, "Let's dance our way."

"Our way?"

"Yeah, y'know, surrender like that night in the yard."

"As you wish." He peeled off his tuxedo jacket.

Whitney Houston sang "I Believe in You and Me," my choice for our first dance.

Gazes locked, he held me close, his thigh prodding me backward. The lyrics said everything I wanted to tell him but hadn't worked up the courage yet.

We glided across the grass, two bodies moving as one. The palpable love in the air warmed me deep inside. At the chorus, he backed away. I kicked off my heels, ran to him, leaping off his bent knee into a swan-dive above him. He rolled me face-up, and I reclined my head, still spinning mid-air—the most freeing sensation ever.

When he readjusted his grip to lower me, a light flashed in my peripheral.

"Problem," I said, rolling into his arms.

"Problem?"

After twirling me five times fast, I fell against his chest. "Lights on the lake."

As the song ended, he dipped me but stayed close. "Boat lights?"

"I think so. Can't be sure. Does your song have a part for another lift?"

Air sucked through his teeth. "I went in a different direction."

The DJ announced, "The groom dedicates this next song to his beautiful bride. Lionel Richie's 'Truly.'"

"You dedicated this to me?"

Slight nod. "Do you know it?"

"No. Never heard it before."

"Try not to lose sight of the mission, Kitty Cat."

*What an odd thing to say. I'm a warrior, dammit. A professional. Why would I—?*

At the first "truly" he lifted me to his sightline and spun. The I-love-yous in the lyrics melted my heart. He pulled me close, and more love showered over me.

With a tight hold, he arced backward, rolling me with him, our bodies perfectly mirrored like that night in the yard. His fingers slid over the top of my hand, interlocking as we reached right... left... his leg lifting mine into a slow pivot turn... powerful arms now locked around me.

The song illuminated one heartfelt truth—he needed me as much as I needed him.

Every beautiful word of those lyrics brought me to tears. He moved with such grace and fluidity, every sway aligned with the music, every step timed to perfection.

When Lionel Richie sang about the man always being there for the woman if she truly cared, I lost it, bawling like someone died.

With me emotionally crippled, he held me tighter, his body enveloping me in a spiral. When we stopped, he whispered, "Sweetheart?"

But I couldn't respond, my arms tightened around his neck, my bare feet dangling above the grass, I cried harder, my face buried in the crook of his neck.

Now, he danced for both of us. Everyone in the audience, including *Shicheii* and June, shielded their mouths, clearly touched by the song or my reaction to it.

When he dipped me for the final time, he stayed close.

"Did you mean that?" I asked.

He thumbed away my tears. "Every word."

"I... I..."

At the worst possible moment, Running Bear moved in with the camera, and prevented me from professing my love to the man who changed my life for the better, the man who never lost faith in me, the man who taught me about life, courage, compassion, and endless devotion by his tireless, perfect example.

Bright flashes almost blinded me while he snapped multiple photos in succession, my eyeliner probably halfway to my chin by now.

Quietly, Kuruk hushed, "You okay, Ghost Dog?"

But I couldn't respond, awash in the outpouring of love, tears flowing like hot lava.

"She will be. The lyrics affected her in unexpected ways." Holding me close, he stroked the back of my hair. "Please request something more dramatic. We need to ensure the lake isn't compromised, and another love song may push her beyond the point of no return."

*He's not wrong.* No man had ever romanced me like this. That said, if I didn't pull it together soon, dozens of Innocent Ones would die tonight.

So, I shook off the love spell. "Tell DJ Dan to play my song from the *Bodyguard* soundtrack."

They exchanged a befuddled glance, probably questioning my mental stability.

"Trust me. It's perfect."

"Copy that."

While we waited for the music, we held our usual pose, one arm draped over his shoulder, our fingers interwoven on the opposite side, our hands tucked close. Near the beginning of "I Have Nothing," I backed away, my shoulders and head striking two dramatic beats. His arms slipped around my waist.

At the chorus, we separated, and I charged for the swan-dive. When he lifted me above his head, the lights on the lake brightened, moving closer, but I couldn't be certain with only brief glimpses between spins. Still in the air, he flipped me on my back, and I reclined my head to inspect the approaching boat.

*Aw, shit.*

He rolled me into his arms. "Well?"

"Looks official, like a warden or ranger."

"Distance?"

"Undetermined." In line with the lyrics, I set a flat hand on his chest to walk him back a few steps. "Keep me up longer." I dragged him behind me by the tie.

When the chorus played again, I pushed off his thigh, and he twirled me above his head. First, on my stomach, then on my back. He repositioned me to kneel on his shoulder, my arms swaying to the melody to steal a clearer view of the lake.

Headlights raced straight at our boat, tucked onshore.

Before he lowered me, I signaled to Running Bear, who rushed over with the camera.

"Intercept the warden, please." He dipped me. "Explain the photoshoot."

"Copy that."

While we danced to the final beats of the song, Running Bear hauled ass for the lake. At the end, the audience rose, clapping and tinging glasses.

He planted one hell of a kiss on me. Not that I minded, just wasn't expecting it with my grandfather here.

*Shicheii* bustled over, his eyes welled with joy. "Are you happy, my loves?"

"We will not discuss this here, Jacy Lee."

Whoa. Why the attitude? It's a simple enough question.

"If you could please entertain June while we're gone, I'd appreciate it."

"Of course, Cheveyo. Happy to help."

"Thank you." He jerked my hand. "Time to go, darling."

Halfway to the tree line, I said, "What's up with you and *Shicheii*?"

"Let's focus on the mission, Cat."

"Something obviously happened between the two of you."

"The three of us," he corrected, his gait growing longer, his pace faster.

"Whaddaya mean?"

Apparently, I didn't jog quick enough because he swept me into his arms to increase speed. "Jacy Lee performed the ceremony."

"No, he didn't. The actor did." My legs dangled over his arm as we neared the row of conifers. "Look. He probably shoulda told us he was gonna do the opening prayer, but I don't see what the big deal is."

"No?" For a hot second, his gray eyes froze open. "What is your grandfather known as, Cat?"

"Walks Sacred. So?"

"Correct. He's a Medicine Man. A Holy man."

"So what? Stefon did the vows."

"Did you or did not hear Jacy Lee's voice in your mind?"

"Well, yeah, but I figured he was helping me in case my ear started crackling again."

"Whose name did he say in the vows?"

*Fuck. Cheveyo, not Gaagii.* He lowered my bare feet to the grass. And that's about when it hit me. "Wait, wait, wait." I dropped his hand, and he picked mine back up. "Are you saying he married us? Like... for real?"

"May we discuss this later, darlin'?"

"No, dammit." I stopped short. "I think I have a right to know now."

Once the warden's boat trailed into the darkness, he hustled to help Running Bear load our watercraft with an oversized duffel bag, bows, and the long-range rifle case—all previously stashed among the trees.

When he returned, he lifted me into the boat without a word.

The second my bare feet hit the cool floor, I stomped. "Are we married?"

Ignoring the question, he dragged off his shoes and socks, rolled up his pant legs to the knees. "Climb in, Running Bear."

Which only pissed me off more. "Are we fuckin' married or not?"

He heaved the boat into the water. "The colorful language is not helpful, Cat."

"Answer me, dammit!"

"No one can force you to sign the marriage certificate."

"What's a piece of paper matter?" I flung my hands in the air. "We recited vows before Creator."

Deeper into the lake, he pushed the boat. "We did, yes."

"So, we *are* married?"

Running Bear hollered back, "Yes, Ghost Dog. You guys are hitched, husband and wife. Congratulations. Now, can we focus on the mission?"

Mouth agape, I could not stop blinking. "Isn't it a little early for marriage? Our relationship started on Tuesday. It's Friday!"

He climbed into the boat. "Hence the turbulence with your grandfather."

When he hand-signaled to the tree line, Poe and Odin flew in, still donned in their wedding attire. After he dragged off their collars and top hat, he peeled off his silk vest, tuxedo shirt, and the loose bowtie I'd undone during the dance. Running Bear stripped down to his black khakis.

From the duffel, my new husband withdrew three sets of moccasins. Good thing, or I would've had to go barefoot.

Refocused on Poe and Odin, he said, "When you find prey in the treetops, flap your wings for Running Bear. No vocalizations, please. Tell the others to do the same."

They leaped into the air to take flight.

He clamped a hand on Kuruk's shoulder. "No collateral damage tonight."

"For the hundredth time, Poe flew into my shot."

"Had you'd been mindful of his position, it would never have happened."

"Copy that."

"Cat?" He joined me at the back of the boat, where I'd collapsed on the bench seat, still baffled by the whole marriage thing. "This is an important night for you."

The completion of my second trail. "In more ways than one, apparently."

A smirk lurked right below the surface. "We need to set that aside for now."

"I know. Alright." I rolled the bones in my neck, shook out my arms. "I'm ready."

"Might I make a small suggestion? The train adds unnecessary baggage. Wouldn't you agree?"

Skimming my dress, I admitted, "Yeah. Probably."

"Is it detachable?"

"I dunno." I peeked behind me. "Is it?"

He gestured for me to stand. "Let's find out."

Unbuttoning the train off the dress left me in a leather bustier body suit. And a risqué one at that. He must've had the same thought, because he reached into the duffel for his black button-down shirt that I wore in Heaven. Which he held open while I slipped my arms into the sleeves.

"Much better. Also"—his fingers slid through my hair, gathering the strands behind my ears—"the extensions might allow them to grab you."

Now behind me, he braided my hair, tucked the pigtail under my shirt. "Are you comfortable in this outfit?"

The shirt hit mid-thigh. *Kinda cute with my moccasins.* "Yep. I'm good."

"Mission-related questions?"

"Running Bear's gonna take care of the Knighthawks, right?"

"He will. You and I must focus on the trophy hunters. And more importantly, safeguard the herd."

"Got it."

"Regardless of what transpired earlier, we need to treat this mission like any other."

*Was that meant for him or me?* "Got it."

"Need a hug?"

"Nope. I'm good."

He pulled me into his chest, powerful arms wrapped around me, his lips pressed to my scalp. "Please be careful, Kitty Cat."

"You better be hugging Running Bear next."

Chuckling, he released me.

Taloned soldiers topped all the pine trees in the forest, like ballet dancers frozen behind a curtain before the show. Moonlight trickled down from the heavens, the lake bathed in a golden smolder, though not bright enough to pinpoint minute details. Tall conifers cast long shadows across the water like a looming presence of danger.

When the boat neared the shore, Running Bear killed the engine. Mayhem dragged the outboard motor from the water. From where I sat, no one would ever suspect dozens of killers stalked those woodlands.

Uninhabited.

Quiet.

Dangerous.

The men hopped out—Running Bear off the bow, Mayhem off the stern—then pushed/pulled the boat to shore, masking our only means of escape in a thicket of trees. Without a word, our team leader extended his arms to lift me out, after which he passed me a bow, quiver, and my favorite curved knife. Running Bear ventured into the shadows with his long-range rifle case.

My outfit left few places for the sheath, so I clipped it to the cuff of my moccasin boot. Rocking a no, he unwound a Velcro strap from around his shin that held one of his many backup knives, now tucked in his waistband.

He velcroed the band around my thigh.

Much better placement for the knife.

In a low and whisperous voice, he said, "Remember to align for the cross shot."

I nodded.

He slung the quiver on his back and checked the position of Grandmother Moon—Her coordinates showed the time. Together, we inhaled a deep cleansing breath through the nostrils, exhaled through our mouths. After four to reach a *hozho*, he led me into the wilderness.

Almost immediately, multiple wings flapped overhead.

A black-hooded Klansman crashed to the ground behind us.

If Running Bear wasn't an expert marksman, we could've easily died then and there. The gentle squeeze of my hand helped slow my thundering heartbeat.

More wings flapped.

A second Klansman fell from another tree stand.

Shit. Killzme had this place locked down, with security positioned everywhere, all vying for a shot at us. A silenced bullet whizzed past my shoulder. Poe released an angry alert, *ca-caw, caw, caw* coiling through the treetops. Running Bear must've missed his wing flap.

Another black-hooded Klansman dropped like dead weight. A silhouetted body crashed through the tree, snapping branches in half, each strike as loud as lightning.

Mayhem pointed out two trophy hunters up ahead.

*Here we go. Time to rock 'n roll.*

# Chapter 51

*"We can't choose what kind of
music life plays for us, but we
can choose who to dance with."*
—Anonymous

***10:05 p.m.***

If the game warden hadn't delayed their departure, they could
have beat Killzme's Knighthawks to the hunting grounds.
Alas, that was no longer an option.

Once Mayhem gestured for Cat to circle wide, they took off,
sprinting through the woods to set the prey at an optimal angle.
The trophy hunters traveled horizontal to them now.

She stopped.

The bow swung back and forth.

Flawless technique.

When she released the bowstring, she followed through like a pro. The arrow sailed straight, nailing the prey through the neck. Before the trajectory revealed their position, Mayhem also fired.

Both trophy hunters collapsed.

He galloped through the underbrush, with Cat right on his heels. The two poachers writhed on the ground. Mayhem yanked his arrow from the dying man's heart. A quick blast of warm blood splattered across his chest.

When Cat pulled her arrow, crimson bathed her bare legs. Hence the problem with neck shots. In her own time, she'd learn. For now, she fluctuated between being pleased with her performance and disgusted by the mess. A beautiful irony he never tired of.

Black-hooded Klansmen fell like dominos, the woodlands crackling with falling timber and dead weight.

American Buffalo rarely roamed through wooded terrain at night. Vastness offered safety and sustenance. Thus, until the trophy hunters breached the clearing, the herd remained un-harmed. Unless others ventured there earlier.

With money on the line, nothing would surprise him. How strictly Killzme guarded the start time remained a mystery. Would the judges care if a Buffalo fell before ten-thirty? Doubt-ful.

"Cat," he whispered, soft and low, "do you recall where we freed Resi?"

"Yeah, but I don't know my way from here."

"Fair enough. Under a mile in that direction." He motioned East. "If we're separated, I'll meet you there."

"Okay," she said, but uncertainty edged her tone. "Hey, if we don't make it outta here alive, I need you to know how I feel about—"

Negativity produced counter-productive results.

"Tell me later tonight." Leaning closer, he rested his hands on her shoulders. "You are powerful. Unstoppable. Invincible. Nothing can touch you." Positive reinforcement helped build confidence. "Say it, please."

With her gaze pinned to his, their souls danced. "I am powerful. Unstoppable. Invincible. Nothing can touch me."

"You are all of that and more, darlin'. Ready?"

"Abso-friggin'-lutely," she said with a renewed confidence. "Let's do this."

*There she is.*

The local ravens searched the treetops, stopping only when they found a Knighthawk.

Staying on ground-level hamstringed Mayhem, so he gestured for Cat to head for the clearing. When she sprinted toward the rendezvous point, he scaled the nearest tree for a bird's eye view.

In the distance, Buffalo herded together. It was safer for them to stay clustered at night so predators couldn't separate the young from their parents.

A Wolf pack lurked in the shadows. Patient. Persistent. Plotting their next move.

If Cat didn't stay vigilante, she might divert their attention away from the herd. Though not normally on their menu, a lone woman could be the difference between starvation and living to fight another day.

Five teams of two men flanked her sides—ten trophy hunters headed straight for her. Why, oh, why did he send her off on her own?

Mayhem jumped off the trunk, knees bending on impact. He careened through the wilderness.

Running Bear veered out of the shadows and caught up, the long-range rifle slung on his shoulder. "Ghost Dog shot through here alone."

"I'm aware." He ran faster, harder, hopped fallen logs and streams.

"What's the play here, Shadow Wolf?"

"Five teams of two moving in from the sides. Cover her from the West."

"Copy that."

Without losing momentum, Running Bear broke right. Mayhem stayed straight. Bullets struck the ground around him, like daggers thrown by an angry god. To avoid getting shot, he zigzagged around trees. Repositioning their only safety net meant the advantage shifted to the Knighthawks.

A blanket of ravens flew overhead. Ebony wings masked Mayhem's location as he sprinted beneath. Poe dropped low to fly in front of him.

He should have known this was his brilliant plan. Let's hope it worked long enough to find Cat.

# Chapter 52

*10:20 p.m.*

Bullets whizzed past me, and I ducked behind a tree. Running Bear must not be as far in as me yet. How many Knighthawks did Killzme post? Every twenty feet I got shot at. Mayhem taught me to zigzag but break it up so they couldn't predict my movements. So far, it worked.

Two trophy hunters crossed up ahead. Perfect angle for a shot, but if I left the safety of the tree, a Knighthawk could nail me in the back. When I was about to lose hope, Odin swooped low. *Gronk, gronk.*

"Hey, buddy. *Shh...* There's one in the tree behind me. Can you do the signal?"

He flew straight up to the canopy. Moments later, a black-hooded asshole crashed on the forest floor.

*Thank you, Running Bear.*

Arms pumping to increase momentum, my moccasins clomped over conifer needles and fallen timber, the sweetness of pine overpowering my senses.

When I finally caught up to the trophy hunters, I stopped.

Swung the bow to gauge distance, velocity, and speed. I fired. Reloaded. Fired again.

Nailed them both—one in the face, the vane protruded out his eye socket. Whoops. He wobbled like a drunk. The other one I hit in the chest, and he dropped.

With so many poachers here, I needed every arrow. So, I booked it through the trees. Up close, my shot looked even worse. Good thing my mentor wasn't here. This was a definite fail.

The dude stumbled around like he had no clue where he was or what happened to throw him balance. Maybe I could use his disorientation to my advantage. I slung the bow on my back. On the sly, I unsheathed my knife, its serrated edge itching for a taste of poacher meat.

With the blade hidden behind my back, I approached. "Hey, you alright? Looks like you could use some help."

"Did I bag a Bison?"

"Yep. A big bull."

"I want the head." A sloppy smile stretched his thick lips, and my fingers tightened around the knife handle. "Are you one of the judges?"

"You could say that." *You'd be wrong, but...* I stepped closer to end this fucker.

In an instant, his demeanor changed, and he latched onto my upper arm like the staggering was all an act to lure me in. "Hello,

Mutt." Hatred dripped off his words. "Losing an eye just made me a millionaire."

Hand like a vice, he squeezed my turquoise armband into my skin. I elbowed him the Adam's apple—spun—and slashed open his throat. Blood smacked me in the face, fake lashes fluttering to clear my vision.

The dirtbag collapsed.

With my foot on his forehead, I tugged the arrow, but it wouldn't budge. Tried again. Still couldn't remove it.

Soon, I sensed Mayhem behind me.

Into my ear, he whispered, "Need help, darlin'?"

I planted a fist on my hip. "It's Cat or Ghost Dog while we're working."

"You're right. My mistake." A smirk lurked right below the surface. "Interesting placement." He meant the arrow. "Ineffective, but interesting nonetheless."

"You gonna help me or not?"

"Certainly, if you do not possess enough physical strength."

*Why'd I ever deliver that speech?* "For the record, I do. Just might be quicker if you pulled it out."

"Cat, our differences do not debase you. We're meant to complement one another."

"Oh." Never thought about it like that before.

"Asking for help shows we're intelligent enough to recognize our strengths and weaknesses." The arrow slipped out of the eye socket like a knife through warm bread. "When I defer a job to you, it's an area where you excel." He wiggled out the second arrow. "Heart shot. Perfect."

My confidence soared. "Thanks."

Poe swooped low to draw our attention. Flapping away, he kept glancing back over his wing. And so, we followed, my head in a continual scan—on the lookout for trophy hunters.

Moonlight brightened a path to the clearing, Mother Earth spotlighting where She'd hidden her precious Innocent Ones. As we neared, my heart detached from its valves.

Around the perimeter, among the trees, poachers knelt to one knee, rifles raised, silencers aimed at the herd, with Resi front and center.

I gasped for air. "Whattawe do?"

"Spook the herd." He hand-signaled for Poe.

"Won't that cause a stampede?"

"Potentially, yes."

"But won't the adults trample the calves?"

"I don't like it any more than you do, Cat. What's the lesser of two evils? If we do nothing, the entire herd perishes. Including Resi."

An invisible fist gut-punched me.

Poe buzzed my head—probably on purpose—landing on his father's forearm.

When Running Bear emerged, Odin perched on his shoulder. "Can't get a shot with the herd between us. What's the play here, Shadow Wolf?"

"Spook them. Once the Innocent Ones are out of danger, we'll take out the poachers." He fluffed Poe's chest feathers. "Counting on you, bud."

I swear that crow winked at me. Didn't take much to translate, either. *Who's his favorite now, bitch?*

"Wait for my signal, please."

With one dip of the bill, Poe took flight.

Mayhem grabbed my hand and took off, almost dislocating my shoulder in the process.

Where we were heading or why, I had no clue, but I gave it all I had to keep up with his long strides. We circled the perimeter. Now, with a beeline to the trophy hunters, still waiting for the order to shoot, he signaled to Poe.

Dozens of corvids scolded with harsh, throaty caws. Multiple ravens and one big-mouthed crow all hollered at once, Mother Earth rumbling beneath my feet. Resi galloped ahead, the entire herd stampeding behind him.

Mayhem released the bowstring. The arrow sailed straight, nailing a trophy hunter in the heart. Another poacher's head exploded from Running Bear's bullet, chunks of skull and brain matter splattering the trees.

Another arrow, another perfect shot.

Trophy hunters dropped one by one.

The corvids reverberating scolds, the herd stampeding, the Earth rumbling, projectiles flying, the worst of society dying, and the blood—all that blood—amounted to a savage mayhem like I'd never witnessed before.

Only we weren't the savages. Our motives stayed pure. Our motives, steeped in love. Our motives protected the Natural World and didn't rape Mother Earth of Her Innocent Ones.

If we didn't do this job, who would? The law didn't deter a damn thing. A poacher faced a year in jail, at most, for multiple murders and dismemberment.

Mayhem snuck up behind one of the last few trophy hunters, wrenched back his head, and dragged his blade across the scumbag's throat. And I reveled in every second of it. A life for a life seemed fair.

In the clearing, a calf rolled out from the back of the stampede. I charged to save him before some dirtbag shot him.

"Cat, no—"

A bullet whizzed under my arm when I brought it forward. But I didn't care. I kept running, my sole focus on the baby left behind. A man's body struck my back, and I fell forward. Mayhem blanketed me as more bullets sailed above us.

After several more heart-stopping minutes, the entire world silenced. No scolds from the treetops, no projectiles pierced the air, no thundering hooves. I peered out from under his arm at the calf, who struggled to stand but kept falling.

"Get off me!" I squirmed beneath him. "He can't die!"

He rolled me onto my back, pinning my arms above my head. "Hysteria will not benefit him. Or you." With a quick glance at the herd, he jerked me to my feet. "Time to go, Cat." He tossed me over his shoulder.

My fists pounded his back. "Put. Me. Down!"

But he ignored me, which only pissed me off more.

He sprinted for the wood line. "Lower the volume, please."

Through gritted teeth, I said, "Put. Me. Down. Right fuckin' now."

"Cat, please, you don't understand."

I twisted, struggled, punched, and kicked. Nothing worked. He kept running, with me bouncing on his shoulder, heat excoriating my insides.

The instant my moccasins touched soil, rage enveloped me, and I stomped my foot. "I want a divorce!"

And he laughed—in my face. The balls on this guy.

Without a word, he spun me toward the clearing. A big bull with red-painted horns escorted the Buffalo mother to her calf.

*Aww... Resi's a dad.*

Gentle nudges from Mom coaxed the little one to his wobbly legs. Mayhem's muscular arms snaked around my waist, his chin rested on my head. The attentive mother patiently waited for her calf to gain his bearings. Then together, they lumbered to Resi, who escorted them back to their family.

Celebratory grunts welcomed them home.

With gratitude, I exhaled a deep breath. If he hadn't rescued me, the protective mother would've perceived me as a threat to her young. Best case scenario at that point? She broke every bone in my body. Worst case? I'd endure a long, tortuous death.

A raspy voice whispered, "Still want a divorce, Kitty Cat?"

"No." My gaze stayed with the herd. "Do you?"

He squeezed me tighter. "No."

Admiring the Innocent Ones, I basked in the warmth of his love. "I never wanna forget this moment."

"Nor do I, Kitty Cat." He kissed my scalp. "Nor do I."

"Hey, what's my last name?"

"Daniels."

When I spun to face him, I backed up. "I meant my new name."

"Would you like to take mine?"

I swayed one shoulder. "Depends on what it is."

"You already know it, darlin'. Didn't Ferron tell you?"

"Tell me what?"

"Klee is my brother."

"You two look nothing alike. Wait. Mama Hen is my sister-in-law?"

"She is. In fact, it wouldn't surprise me if she nudged Jacy Lee to marry us."

"You're blowing my mind." Something still didn't make sense, though. "Why borrow Klee's credit card? If you share the same surname, why not use your own?"

"Good for you for catching that detail." He winked. "If Killzme were to research the hotel registry like we did, they'd discover Klee Thunderhawk is a world-renowned wildlife photographer. A trip to Yellowstone makes perfect sense for him, thus quashes any and all curiosities or suspicions for us."

Dragging his arms around my waist again, I spun back to the herd. "Shawnee Thunderhawk. Has a nice ring to it."

He squeezed me tighter. "Yes, it does, Kitty Cat."

"You know what would make this moment even better?"

"Tell me."

"A piece of that wedding cake."

He laughed. "Oh, boy. The grocery bill alone will break me."

"Stop." Facing him, I slapped his chest. "We skipped supper. Aren't you hungry?"

With a sensual sigh, he smirked. "Starving."

Blushing all over, I leaped onto his waist, my arms draped over his shoulders, his hands clasped behind my back. "You are not suffering from starvation. You are hungry."

"Sweetheart, I passed hunger days ago."

"Me too." As he carried me across the clearing, I spot-cleaned his face with the cuff of my sleeve. "How're we gonna return to our wedding?"

"Are you familiar with the phrase 'blood in the water'?"

*He expects us to wash in the lake with a game warden on patrol?*

# Chapter 53

*"My destination is no longer a*
*place but a new way of seeing."*
—Kira Wolf Moonfae

**11:05 p.m.**

Surprisingly, the game warden never returned. Odd. Unless Killzme planted him as a lookout. What a shame he and Cat hadn't unearthed the names of those who accepted bribe money in exchange for innocent lives.

Once his team buried the duffel and weapons in thickets of trees near the shore and had changed into their wedding attire, Mayhem unbraided Cat's hair.

"Running Bear, please return the boat key to June. We'll gather our belongings later."

"Copy that. Or I can return for our stash later tonight."

"Above and beyond. Truly." The kind gesture filled Mayhem with warmth. "Thank you. I appreciate your dedication."

"I just don't want to leave my rifle here."

He laughed. "Fair enough."

When they reached the wedding grounds, the reception was still in full swing—music blaring, happy couples on the dancefloor, including Jacy Lee and June, who, by all outward appearances, quite enjoyed each other's company.

"*Shicheii* can dance?"

"Of course. Dance is part of our culture."

"No, I know, but he's twirling her and stuff."

A delicious idea flitted through his mind. "Why don't you cut in? I'm sure he'd love to dance with you." He kissed her cheek. "I'll meet you there."

Moments later, she separated her grandfather from June. Mayhem headed for the DJ booth to request a song. Not only for his bride but to test how well Jacy Lee thought through his plan to marry them.

A wide smile split DJ Dan's full mustache and beard. "Brave choice, Mister Thunderhawk."

"Why, thank you, sir." He stuffed a crisp fifty in his tip jar. "Could you please dedicate the song to my wife?"

"Is her family here?"

"Yes."

"And you still want to dedicate it to her?"

He dropped another bill in the tip jar. "I do."

"Bold move, Mister Thunderhawk. You're my new hero."

Chuckling, he strolled to the outskirts of the dancefloor, where Running Bear watched Cat dance with her grandfather. When they waltzed past, Jacy Lee smiled at Mayhem.

"I've never seen him so happy." Running Bear sidled closer, lowering his voice. "Do you think he planned to marry you all along?"

"Oh, yes. Yes, he did."

"Meh." He shrugged it off. "It all worked out in the end."

"Regardless, he needs to learn not to meddle. Or one day, his recklessness will kill us all."

Running Bear stepped back to study his demeanor. "What are you up to, Shadow Wolf?"

"*Moi?*"

"You're up to something. What is it?"

A chuckle busted loose. "Oh, I would hate to ruin the surprise."

"This next song," DJ Dan announced, "is a special dedication from the groom to his beautiful bride. You may want to give them some room." A chortle echoed through the speakers before he cut the mic.

When Mayhem strolled out to the dancefloor, Cat switched partners, draping her arms over his shoulders. The introduction of "I'll Make Love to You" by Boyz II Men began innocent enough. Neither she nor Jacy Lee made the connection right away.

Anticipation built in his chest as they glided across the grass. He twirled her, catching her in his arms.

At the chorus, he swung her low. Rising, her eyes widened at the lyrics, gaze straying to her grandfather, whose jaw slacked. Running Bear buckled over in laughter. So much so, he had to step away before he got himself into trouble.

As the lyrics specified details of a passionate night, he dipped her in front of Jacy Lee. Lavished tender kisses down the curve of her neck and across her shoulder. When Cat's head fell back, Mayhem winked at his lifelong friend, frozen stiff just a few feet away.

A vast difference existed between accepting their marriage would eventually be consummated and gaining intimate knowledge of when.

Beside Jacy Lee, Poe's bill parted. Not so with Odin and Spirit Crow, the song enhancing their amorous sides, feathery heads nuzzling together.

Mayhem hiked up Cat's knee, her body melting into his tight embrace, the black train billowing behind her. The lyrics grew more and more descriptive, sensual, and sexy. For a moment, he reveled in Jacy Lee's reaction.

Soon, his elder was the last thing on his mind—now fully focused on his new bride. With one arm around her slim waist, the other draped across her back, their bodies rolled with waves, reigniting the unquenchable fire between them.

With a spring in his step, he bounced back. Rocked her forward, backward, forward, backward. By the waist, he lifted her, and her sculptured legs curled around him, his fingers sliding up through the back of her silky hair. When she leaned in, he kissed her with more fervor than ever before.

Breathlessly, she whispered, "Can't wait."

Neither could he. "Shall we head to the suite?"

"Oh, yeah, absolutely."

Fingers interlocked, he first led her to Jacy Lee. "My *wife* and I will not be home tonight."

Silent, she squeezed his hand.

"May I have a word, Cheveyo? Alone."

"Speak freely in front of *my wife*. A strong marriage is not built on secrets."

His frantic gaze shot to his granddaughter, a pleading to his tone. "Mourning Dove?"

"I love you, *Shicheii*, but it is our wedding night."

His whole body pleaded with her to reconsider. "But, honey—"

Mayhem swept her off her feet, cradling her in his arms, her arms hooked around his neck. "See you tomorrow, Jacy Lee." He strolled a few feet away, stopped, then turned back. "On second thought, we'll see you Monday."

Victory never tasted so sweet.

As they headed for the hotel, Cat wagged her head, her eyes sparkling through the contacts. "You are an evil, evil man."

"You didn't enjoy that?" He crinkled his nose. "Even a little?"

"Alright, maybe a little." Her giggled warmed his heart. "If you're gonna carry me, do it our way."

He swung her in front of him, hands clasped around her back.

"Are we really staying all weekend?"

He kissed her nose. "Only if you want to, Kitty Cat."

"I do."

"Then we shall."

"Regarding our marriage, you know I'm the boss at home, right?"

*Adorable.* "I do."

They rounded the side of the hotel.

"Also," she said, "I need to call you something else."

"How about Cheveyo? It is my name."

"Yeah, but then it wouldn't be special. Only you call me Cat."

His heart swelled. "Then rename me." *Such a beautiful spirit.* "In the meantime, I've mulled over your proffer from the campsite. Yes."

"Yes?"

"We'll fly to Kenya to save elephants."

She showered his face with tiny kisses. "Really?"

"Sweetheart, I find it difficult to deny you, well, anything."

"You are so gonna get lucky tonight, Mister Thunderhawk."

A boisterous guffaw burst from deep inside him. "Have I mentioned my fondness for elephants? They're my new favorite animal."

# BOOKS BY SUE COLETTA

**THE MAYHEM SERIES**

**WINGS OF MAYHEM, #1**

Released: March 2023

ISBN: 9798987998014

**When the cat burglar and the serial killer collide, HE looks forward to breaking her will, but SHE never gives up. Not ever. And especially not for him.**

Shawnee Daniels — cybercrimes specialist by day, cat burglar by night — ignites the hellfire fury of a serial killer when she unknowingly steals his trophy box.

**BLESSED MAYHEM, #2**

Released: March 2023

ISBN: 9798987998038

**A cat burglar stumbles across a serial killer at work. SHE piques his curiosity, but HE doesn't allow witnesses. Or is it serendipity by design?**

When Shawnee Daniels, a seasoned cat burglar, breaks into a seemingly affluent home in the middle of the night, she expects to find jewelry, cash, and other valuables. But what she discovers instead is a grisly scene of torture and murder. A serial killer is at work, and Shawnee is now his latest target. With nowhere to turn and no way out, she must rely on her wits and street smarts to survive. Will Shawnee ever escape the terror that lurks in the shadows?

**SILENT MAYHEM, #3**

Released: March 2023

ISBN: 9798987998052

**HE has left a trail of beheadings. SHE is working for the cops but when he warns her she will be next, how can Shawnee Daniels believe — or trust — a vicious serial killer?**

When a familiar crow drops a cryptic scroll at Shawnee's feet, she's compelled to open it, even though everything in her power warns her not to. Mr. Mayhem — the most prolific serial killer the North Shore has ever known — claims her life is in danger. He "claims" he wants to help her, but just last year he threatened to murder everyone she loves.

While Mayhem taunts her with oddly-placed feathers, like The Creator left at his crime scenes, an interstate killing spree rocks Massachusetts and New Hampshire. A madman is decapitating men and women, dumping their headless corpses on two area beaches. But what Shawnee soon uncovers shatters all she's ever known, her memories shredded, the whispers of the past in shambles on the ground.

Can she find the strength to move forward, or will the truth destroy her?

**I AM MAYHEM, #4**

Released: March 2023


ISBN: 9798987998076


**As severed body parts show up on her doorstep, Shawnee Daniels must stop the serial killer who wants her dead before she becomes the next victim. But can she solve his cryptic clues before it's too late? Or will she be the next to die a slow, agonizing death?**

With crows stalking her every move, Shawnee can barely function. Things worsen when body parts show up on her doorstep. An unstoppable serial killer wants her dead. Mr. Mayhem threatens to murder everyone she loves, sending Shawnee a piece at a time. As Mr. Mayhem sits in judgement, his cryptic clues must be solved before the final gavel drops.

The game rules are simple — win the unwinnable or submit to a slow, agonizing death. When Shawnee tries to fight back, she discovers her very existence is based on lies. But will the full impact of the truth become the headstone on her grave?


**UNNATURAL MAYHEM, #5**


Released: March 2023


ISBN: 9798987998090

**Polar opposites unite to save animals from trophy hunters by any means necessary. Even murder.**

Explosive news of a crow hunt rings out in the White Mountain Region of New Hampshire, and 100 crows are in the crosshairs. The only way to protect the innocent is for Shawnee to team up with the man who tried to kill her more than once in the past.

Can she trust him?

**RESTLESS MAYHEM, #6**

Released: April 2023

ISBN: 9798988163817

**Amidst a rising tide of poachers, three unlikely eco-warriors take a stand to save endangered Eastern Gray Wolves — even if it means the slow slaughter of their captors.**

Deep in the woods of Jackson, New Hampshire, an ancient evil lurks. Armed poachers patrol a secret enclosure, holding captive a pack of majestic Eastern Gray Wolves. But three unlikely eco-warriors are determined to free the wolves, embarking on a dangerous mission to end their torture. With courage and conviction, Shawnee, Mayhem, and Jacy Lee march onward, even if it means risking their own lives to take down the poachers and restore freedom to the wolves. It's a battle between justice and injustice, and the eco-warriors are determined to win—no matter the cost. But what if something even more evil lurks in those woods? What if Shawnee's not ready to answer the cry for help?

**TRACKING MAYHEM, #7**

Released: June 2023

ISBN: 9798988163848

**Three eco-warriors are on a mission to save the lives of polar bears from the nation's largest animal trafficking organization — one dead poacher at a time.**

When three eco-warriors race across the country in a desperate fight to save polar bears, they expect to end up in the crosshairs of the notorious Killzme Corporation, but what they soon discover raises the stakes even higher. Shawnee, Mayhem, and Jacy Lee march onward to stop the killing of

Innocent Ones, the voiceless who can't fight for themselves. They must stay one step ahead of the traffickers while trying to expose their sinister plot. But Shawnee, Mayhem, and Jacy Lee have something Killzme never will — Native spirituality and an innate connection to Mother Earth. Can they evade Killzme's relentless pursuit in time to make a difference?

The war to save polar bears begins now.

## MERCILESS MAYHEM, #8

Released: October 2023

ISBN: 9798988163862

Shawnee and Mayhem continue to wreak havoc on the Killzme Corporation — the largest animal trafficking ring in the country — by killing one poacher at a time. The stakes grow increasingly higher when the nefarious group retaliates by putting a bounty on their heads.
Meanwhile, the traffickers set their sights on capturing Orca for profit and pleasure.
With a ticking clock and no place left to hide, Shawnee and Mayhem alternate between undercover surveillance and clandestine battles to save their family and the Innocent Ones from Killzme's evil plans. Skills are tested. Tenuous alliances are formed. Not everyone will make it out alive.
Set in a world of cultural wonder, environmental threats, and looming danger, this heart-stopping eco-thriller will have you glued to the page from the first sentence to the last.

## SAVAGE MAYHEM, #9

Released: April 2024

ISBN: 9798988163886

**Amidst the wild and unforgiving landscapes of Yellowstone Park, join Mayhem, a fearless Apache warrior and champion of the Natural World, and his partner and protégé, Shawnee, as they race against the clock to protect an American Buffalo herd from the ruthless Killzme Corporation.**

With a massive bounty on their heads and an army of killers on their trail, Mayhem and Shawnee must use all their cunning and survival skills to outsmart their enemies. They will risk it all to preserve the sacred lineage of the Innocent Ones.

There is no line Shawnee and Mayhem won't cross.

Even murder.

As the danger intensifies and the clock winds down, will they be able to save the herd? Or will this be the mission that finally breaks them?

## **GRAFTON COUNTY SERIES**

**MARRED, # 1**

Released: November 2015

ISBN: 9781311566508

When Sage Quintano barely escapes from a brutal serial killer, husband Niko, a homicide detective, insists they move to rural New Hampshire, where he accepts a position as sheriff. Sage buries secrets from that night — secrets she swears to take to her deathbed. Three years pass and Sage's twin sister goes missing. Is the killer trying to lure Sage into a deadly trap to end his reign of terror?

## CLEAVED, # 2

Released: May 2017

ISBN: 9781370387946

Sage Quintano writes about crime. Her husband Niko investigates it. Together they make an unstoppable team. But no one counted on a twisted serial killer, who stalks their sleepy community. Women impaled by deer antlers, bodies encased in oil drums, nursery rhymes, and the Suicide King. What connects these cryptic clues? For Sage and Niko, the truth may be more terrifying than they imagined.

## SCATHED, # 3

Released: July 2018


ISBN: 9780463607176


When a brutal murder rocks Alexandria, Sheriff Niko Quintano receives a letter: Paradox vows to kill again if his riddle isn't solved within 24 hours. Niko turns to his crime writer wife, Sage, for help.

But she's dealing with her own private nightmare. A phone call from the past threatens her future. Can Niko and Sage solve the riddle in time, or will the killer win this deadly game of survival?


**RACKED, #4**


Released: August 2019


ISBN: 9780463275467


Five missing boys and an adult corpse found in the town's water shed was only the beginning for Sage and Niko. After a hooded stranger gives their son, Noah, a stuffed toy—the exact Christmas moose given to all the missing boys days before their abductions—their lives spiral downward into uncertainty.

Will Noah be the next boy to go missing? The truth of what they discover blows everyone's mind.

**HALOED, #5**

Released: October 2022

ISBN: 9781005734039

A string of gruesome murders rocks the small town of Alexandria, New Hampshire, with all the victims staged to resemble dead angels. All the clues point to the Romeo Killer's return.
Except one: He died eight years ago.
Dead serial killers don't rise from the grave. With only hours left to live, how can Sage convince her Sheriff husband before the sand in her hourglass runs out?

## <u>TRUE CRIME/NARRATIVE NONFICTION</u>

**PRETTY EVIL NEW ENGLAND: True Stories
of Violent Vixens and Murderous Matriarchs**

Released: February 2020

ISBN: 9781493052332

Female killers are often portrayed as caricatures, however, the real
stories are much more insidious.

Nineteenth-century New England was the hunting ground of five
notorious female serial killers: Jane Toppan, Lydia Sherman, Nellie
Webb, Harriet E. Nason, and Sarah Jane Robinson. In *Pretty Evil
New England*, author Sue Coletta tells the complicated stories of
these five women. From broken childhoods to first brushes with
death, she examines the overwhelming urges that propelled these
women to take the lives of a combined total of more than one
hundred innocent victims.

The murders, investigations, trials, and ultimate verdicts will stun
and surprise readers.

www.ingramcontent.com/pod-product-compliance
Lightning Source LLC
Chambersburg PA
CBHW060512160726
47991CB00001B/6